Thanatophobia

A Reapers Oath Series: Book One

Peg N. Gremlin

Copyright © 2025 by Peg N. Gremlin

All rights reserved.

No part of this publication may be reproduced, distributed, or transmitted in any form or by any means, including photocopying, recording, or other electronic or mechanical methods, without the prior written permission of the publisher, except as permitted by U.S. copyright law. For permission requests, contact Peg N. Gremlin at pegngremlin.com or email PegN.Gremlin@gmail.com.

The story, all names, characters, and incidents portrayed in this production are fictitious. No identification with actual persons (living or deceased), places, buildings, and products is intended or should be inferred.

Book Cover by GetCovers.com

To the girls who've ever felt like the world was too heavy,
To the ones who've been told they're too much—or not enough,
To the fighters, the dreamers, and the ones still finding their way—
This is for you.
For every time you chose to get up after falling.
For every tear you wiped away with your own hands.
For every time you whispered, "I can do this," even when you didn't believe it.
You are powerful.
You are extraordinary.
And your story is still being written.
Never stop fighting. Never stop believing. Never stop being you.
With all my heart,

~Peggy

Trigger Warnings

Violence & Abuse
-Physical Assault (past tense)
-Domestic Violence (past tense)
-Graphic Violence (detailed fights, war, preps, battles)
-Weapon Use (sentient weapons)
-Kidnapping

Emotional & Psychological Themes
-Thanatophobia (fear of death, constant dread)
-PTSD & Trauma
-Emotional Abuse (antagonistic characters & past tense)
-Parental Neglect (favoritism and emotional neglect)

Supernatural & Religious Themes
-Supernatural Violence
-Death & the Afterlife
-Forced Bonding
-Mythological Entities

Sexual & Relationship Themes
-Unwanted Advances

-Implied Sexual Assault/Coercion (past tense)
-Sexual Themes
-Toxic Relationships (past tense)

Mental Health
-Depression & Anxiety
-Grief & Loss

Other Potential Triggers
-Stalking and Obsession
-Body Horror
-Parental Manipulation
-Gaslighting

Chapter One

Azrael

Bottom of the River - Delta Rae

Concentration might not be my best trait, but it's one I must learn to master. Not because I want to, but because it's required—to fill shoes that were never truly meant for me but were designed with my future in mind and molded long before I even had a choice. I've spent years training—agonizing, exhausting years—despite failing nearly every test thrown my way. Tests meant to shape me into the perfect successor. The next Grim Reaper. The next Prince of Death.

Failure isn't a foreign concept to me. It clings to my heels like a shadow, whispering reminders of my shortcomings. But I've endured. Century after century, I've prepared for this role, this crown that feels like a noose. Yet, in all those years of preparation, not once did I imagine my missions would include chasing rogue supernaturals—something I'd consider a cleanup job more suited to a bounty hunter than an heir to the throne.

Still, here I am. The irony doesn't escape me. The Prince of Death, the epitome of order and finality, tasked with reigning in chaos I didn't cause. My father's legacy demands it. But each mission feels more like a punishment—a test of my endurance and resolve. Maybe, deep down, I know the truth: these aren't tasks meant to teach me. They're meant to break me.

And yet, I keep going. Not for glory or recognition, but because failure is no longer an option.

Memetim—one of the most devious, blood-soaked beings to ever exist—has slipped into the mortal realm, leaving a trail of devastation in her wake. Death rates are spiking, chaos is unraveling the delicate balance we're sworn to maintain, and every passing day feels like a countdown to something worse. My mission is clear: track her down, contain her, and drag her back to the Underworld where she belongs.

It sounds simple on paper, but nothing about Memetim ever is. She's not just dangerous—she's calculated. Every step she takes, every life she steals, is deliberate. She knows how to sow terror in ways that linger long after her victims are gone. It's not just murder. It's a spectacle.

I've spent weeks mapping her movements, chasing echoes of her chaos. Tracking my sisters—the Keres—as they hunt her like ravenous hounds. They revel in the carnage she leaves behind, savoring the fear it creates. To them, this is a game. To me, it's a duty.

Finally, I pinned her location. Some backwater town in Mississippi—a speck of humanity so unremarkable it barely seems worth the effort. But Memetim's choice of hideout makes sense. She thrives in places like this, feeding on despair and anonymity.

The task is clear: drag her back for judgment before my father. Simple, right? Yet, I can't ignore the gnawing unease settling in my chest. Memetim won't come quietly. She never does.

As I prepare to leave the stone halls—warm, dimly lit, and faintly scented of s'mores—I can't help but pause, inhaling deeply. It's not a smell I particularly love, but it's one I've come to associate with the Underworld's peculiar charm.

Comforting, in its way. It reminds me that, here at least, I belong—or so I keep telling myself.

I swing Orcus from side to side, his weight familiar in my hands, a steady presence that's both weapon and anchor. The low rumble of satisfaction he emits vibrates through the polished handle, and for a moment, I can't help but smile.

Orcus isn't just my tool; he's my companion, my confidant, my best friend. Though if I'm being honest, he didn't start that way. For decades—centuries, really—he went out of his way to make me fail, to test my patience and resolve. If I stumbled, he mocked me; if I succeeded, he found new ways to challenge me. And yet, I can't imagine life without him now.

I run my fingers over the intricate symbols etched into his handle, each one a chapter of my story. A reminder of battles fought, victories won, and scars earned. His purring intensifies at my touch, his crimson aura flaring to life like a heartbeat. "It's nearly time, young Reaper," he murmurs, his voice deep and resonant in my mind.

I steady my breathing, pushing back the anxiety twisting in my chest. I know what's waiting for me outside these halls, and I know it won't be easy. But there's no room for hesitation now. "Yes, it's time," I reply, my voice firm despite the unease crawling beneath my skin.

Orcus chuckles, the sound rich with amusement. "It's not too late to turn back, you know," he teases, his tone laced with sly mockery. "Memetim's a headache, and you've got enough of those already."

I roll my eyes, though his words strike closer to home than I'd like to admit. Memetim is a headache, a storm of chaos wrapped in a beautiful, blood-stained bow. She's the kind of challenge that makes lesser beings crumble. But I'm not lesser—at least, I can't afford to be. Not with father watching, waiting for me to fail.

Gripping Orcus tighter, I feel his hum of approval resonating through me, a reassuring rhythm that steadies my resolve. "No turning back," I say, the words more for myself than for him. "It's time to find the Angel of Death and put her in a cage, far below the Earth."

Orcus purrs again, his satisfaction practically tangible. "Now that's the spirit."

As I step into the shadows beyond the warmth of the halls, I remind myself of what's at stake. Memetim isn't just a rogue supernatural; she's a force of nature. And no matter how deep the fear claws into me, I'll be the one to end this. I have to be.

Exu, keeper of souls and my trainer—at times harshly so—steps forward beside me, his heavy hand landing on my shoulder. It's a steadying gesture, one that grounds me even when my thoughts threaten to spiral. His presence has always been a complicated comfort. He's pushed me harder than anyone and doubted me more than once, but his support has never truly wavered. Even when I faltered, when failure felt inevitable, Exu was there, his faith in me constant in a way I never quite understood.

"You're ready for this," he says softly, his voice low and gravelly. His words mean more as an order than reassurance.

I nod, though I'm not sure if I believe him. The weight of the mission presses down on me, and it's heavier than just Memetim's capture. This is my chance—perhaps my last—to prove that I'm more than my mistakes. That I'm not just the screw-up my father sees in me.

"Your father awaits," Exu adds, his head bowing slightly in deference. The words are calm, yet they hit like a warning.

I force a breath into my lungs, steadying my character as I nod again. There's no room for hesitation, not here. Not now.

Exu leads me through the labyrinthine corridors of the Underworld, each corridor glowing with the flickering light of torches, their warmth barely masking the oppressive shadows that cling to the walls. These halls are familiar, but tonight they feel different. Every shadow seems sharper, every flicker of flame more vivid, as if the Underworld itself is watching, waiting for me to rise—or fall.

My fingers tighten around Orcus' handle as we approach the throne room. The scythe hums softly, his energy a calming pulse against my growing anxiety. *Don't let him rattle you,* Orcus murmurs in my mind, his tone tinged with dry humor. *You've faced worse.*

Have I, though?

The massive iron doors groan as they swing open, revealing the throne room in all its foreboding grandeur. Columns carved with depictions of death and rebirth loom overhead, their shadows sprawling across the polished obsidian floor. The air feels heavier here, oppressive as if the room itself seeks to crush anything unworthy of its presence.

At the far end of the room, atop a towering dais, sits my father—Hades himself. His figure is shrouded in an aura of authority so absolute it's suffocating.

I step forward, every movement measured, my anxiety pounding against my ribs. The weight of his gaze settles on me, cold and assessing, stripping away every ounce of confidence I've managed to build.

Bowing low, I keep my eyes fixed on the floor. "Father," I say, my voice steady despite the lump forming in my throat.

The silence stretches, thick and heavy, until it feels like it might break me. I can't see his expression, but I can feel the judgment radiating from him, the expectation that I'll fail—again.

And maybe, just maybe, this is the moment I'll prove him wrong.

Hades. My father. The Lord of the Underworld.

For all the stories told about him, he's no comforting presence. Hades governs the Underworld with an iron hand, and his very existence exudes power and control. His muscles tense beneath the glistening red aura that surrounds him, a fiery halo of authority. His sharp fangs catch the dim light, glinting with a quiet menace, and the chill he radiates pierces straight to my core, more potent than the coldest wind on the mortal plane.

"Azrael, my son," he says, his voice deep and commanding, the kind of tone that demands absolute obedience. There's no warmth in his greeting, no trace of familial affection—only expectation.

Orcus hums in my palms, his aura pulsing faintly, feeding off the tension that hangs in the room. He feels it too, the weight of this moment, the gaze of my father bearing down on me like a judgment carved in stone.

"Are you prepared to carry out your mission?"

The question is simple, but the weight behind it is not. This is more than a test of my skill; it's a test of my worth, my place in the hierarchy of Death itself.

I kneel, letting Orcus' steady hum and crimson light envelop me like a shield. His presence grounds me, anchoring me against the tide of doubt clawing at the edges of my mind.

"Yes, father," I say, keeping my voice steady, even as my heartbeat quickens. "I am prepared."

As the words leave my lips, a strange stillness settles over me. I'm standing at the edge of something vast and unknowable, a chasm that centuries of training have led me to. Everything I've endured, every failure and triumph, has brought me to this moment.

I steel myself, bracing for what's to come. The calm before the storm is deceptive, but it's mine to hold. Whatever lies ahead, I can't afford to falter now.

Hades leans forward, his gaze unyielding and cold as iron. "Do you understand the task at hand, Azrael?" His voice is steady, but the weight behind it is impossible to ignore. "Do not mistake my words."

His aura flares, pushing outward like a storm, smothering the space between us. The power in the room is suffocating, vibrating through the stone walls, a reminder of the vast legacy he commands. I can feel it, the unspoken threat that his wrath could crush me in an instant.

I lower my gaze to the cold, unforgiving floor beneath me, my mind racing. "Yes, father. I understand."

The silence stretches between us, thick and oppressive.

"Are you prepared to end her if she refuses to return?" His question is sharp, like a blade cutting through the air.

I don't hesitate. There's no room for doubt, no room for fear. "Yes, father."

His eyes narrow, the flames in them flickering to life with an intensity that makes the room feel smaller, darker. "Are you willing to terminate her, if it comes to that?" His voice drops into a growl, low and menacing. "I will not tolerate failure, Azrael."

I raise my eyes to meet his, feeling the crushing weight of his judgment pressing into me. Every word he speaks feels like a brand, carving into my soul.

"Father," I say, my voice unwavering despite the storm raging inside me, "My emotions are irrelevant. The mission is all that matters. I will not fail."

Hades studies me for a long, agonizing moment, his eyes boring into me like a predator sizing up its prey. His lips twitch into a faint, dismissive smile—not pride, not approval, just a grim acknowledgment of what he expects.

"Good," he rumbles, the sound like distant thunder. "I will not tolerate incompetence. Bring her back, or end her."

I rise, feeling the familiar thrumming of Orcus' aura beneath my grip, the weight of our shared promise settling into my bones. This is my moment, my chance to prove I'm worthy of the title—Prince of Death. All the failures of the past, the doubts that have haunted me, mean nothing now.

His dismissal is swift, his gesture sharp and final. His tone is cold, like ice cutting through the air. He expects results, not excuses, and there's no room for hesitation in his world.

"I'll be here when you return," Exu says softly, his voice a rare note of comfort amid the tension. His words are solemn, but also something more—a quiet support that grounds me in the face of my daunting task.

I take a steadying breath, my pledge to him clear and unwavering. "I won't fail, father." The words come out with an edge of iron, an unbreakable conviction I've never fully felt before. His approval is distant, almost imperceptible, but it's there—silent, heavy, and undeniable.

As he gestures toward me, a pulse of energy surges through the room, filling the space with the unmistakable weight of his blessing. His eyes linger on me, sharp and unreadable, though there's a flicker—just a flicker—of something softer beneath the surface. Something that, if I weren't so focused, I might mistake for pride.

Almost.

But I can't afford to dwell on that. Not now. Not when there's so much to lose.

Orcus hums a low, knowing sound, the vibration of his voice reverberating through me. "Let's make it happen, Azrael," he says, his tone purposeful, the weight of our mission clear in the air. "Time to bring chaos back under control."

I nod, the full weight of the mission settling into my chest. Every moment leading to this one feels like a dream. There's no turning back now.

The balance of the worlds rests in my hands. Memetim may be hiding, but I will find her. And when I do, there will be no escape.

Memetim—the one who defied her duty, the one who tore the fabric of the natural order and left chaos in her wake—will face judgment. Or termination. There are no other options.

With a final glance at the throne, I nod to my father, my grip tightening around Orcus' handle. The weight of my decision presses into me, the weight of what's at stake. There's no turning back now.

The room blurs, fading from view as the Underworld's magic wraps around me, an invisible force pulling me through the very fabric of existence. The ground falls away beneath me, and the air hums with the crackling energy of my departure. The sensation is always the same—like being ripped apart, then swiftly sewn back together.

The sounds of the Underworld—its whispers, its low growls, its eternal hum—dissolve into nothingness. Reality hits me with brutal clarity. I land with a soft thud, the jarring impact a reminder of just how far from home I've traveled.

I'm on the outskirts of Picayune, Mississippi. The air here is thick with the scent of earth, damp and rich with the pulse of mortal life. It's a stark contrast to the oppressive weight of the Underworld I left behind.

I stand alone in a place where nothing should matter—except it does. This mission. It's not just a task, it's my reckoning. I will see it through. No matter the cost.

Chapter Two

Layla

Breathe Me - Sia

A Newton's Cradle rests on my therapist's desk, of all things—almost comically predictable. Neon lights glow from its base, pulsing in odd hues of green and blue, casting a surreal, synthetic halo over his worn notepad. The rhythmic clacking of the cradle's silver balls punctuates the silence, each swing like a tick of judgment, a mechanical substitute for any real control. Tick. Tick. Tick. It's a sound that fills the room, but it doesn't soothe. It agitates me. It's just another reminder that nothing here is real, nothing here actually helps.

He's there, detached, scribbling in his notepad with a practiced indifference, like he's observing someone else's life unfold—someone else's suffering. But I am here, across from him, trapped in the seat, forced to perform for his questions and his practiced empathy. It feels like I'm putting on a show, my responses scripted and hollow, while his eyes flick across his notes, waiting for the next appropriate thing to say. It's all so... mechanical. What's the point of these sessions? Is this really helping? Or am I just another case to add to his collection?

Each word I attempt feels like a weight, dragging me down as I try to keep my head above the dark water of panic and dread I never asked for. Every time I open my mouth, it feels like I'm drowning. I force myself to speak, but even the sound of my voice feels alien. Like I'm just going through the motions. Maybe he doesn't notice how each question feels like an assault. How every inquiry into my past only digs up the same familiar darkness. Maybe that's the problem—he doesn't *get* it. He thinks a few words and some empty empathy are enough. But he doesn't understand what it's like to live with fear curling inside you, to feel it as a constant companion, settling in your bones.

The therapist himself—a man in blue jeans, a plaid shirt, and cowboy boots—strikes an odd figure. So normal, so far from the horrors that haunt me. He's out of place, yet somehow blends right in, like he belongs in a cozy romance novel. If I squint, I could almost picture him in a scene where everything works out, where people heal and talk things out over coffee, but that's not my reality. I'm not in some fairy tale. I'm stuck in this room, with this man who isn't equipped to really see me. He tries, I guess. He really does. But there's a limit to what even he can understand. How can he? He's never felt the way I do, never lived with this constant sense of impending doom.

And while he tries to understand, tries to keep up with my trauma, he doesn't know how to. Can't know how to. Right now, he feels more like part of the problem. He's like a piece of this... thing I'm supposed to heal from, but I'm not sure how I'm supposed to fix something that feels so out of control. His questions are polite, and probing, but they don't actually go anywhere. It's like he's trying to fit a square peg into a round hole, and I'm suffocating in the process.

I should speak. I should answer. But what's the point? Every response is just a drop in a bucket of emptiness that never fills.

"Layla?" he prompts. "Tell me more about the dream you had." His boots scrape faintly against the floor, stirring the otherwise still room. The sound is almost too loud in the silence, like a sharp reminder that I'm still here, still stuck in this moment, trapped in this space with him.

I look up at him, anxiety skittering through me like electricity, zipping along every nerve until my skin feels too tight, too wrong. How can I talk about *Death*—the relentless phantom that stalks me? How do I even begin to describe the woman who's stepped out of my nightmares and into my reality? The one who haunts my every breath, who feels more real than anything else in my life. More real than the ticking clock on the wall or the therapist sitting across from me, scribbling notes like he's cataloging my brokenness in neat, tidy boxes. How do I explain this to him, to anyone? He wouldn't *get* it. No one would.

Google says I should reach out, that I should speak to someone about my fears and anxieties. They'll offer prescriptions to numb me into something acceptable to the world, a passable simulation of "normal." A version of me that doesn't tremble at every shadow, that doesn't feel like she's teetering on the edge of something too vast and dark to understand. But this? This is not normal. *This* is a nightmare I can't wake up from. I can't drown it with a pill or a quick fix. This is something real. Something that keeps coming for me, pulling me deeper into a terror I can't control.

I can't keep my breathing steady. My chest tightens as panic worms its way in, coiling around my lungs until it's hard to draw in a full breath. My thoughts scatter, broken and wild, each one trying to make sense of the chaos swirling inside me. I can't hold it together enough to form a coherent sentence. I try to speak, but nothing comes out. I open my mouth, but it feels like a physical effort like my words are stuck in my throat, tangled up with all the things I don't understand. He's still writing, though. As if this whole thing is just a checklist for him. He'll package up my fractured mind with a few reassuring phrases, like a balm for my raw skin, as though there's a way to fix something that claws at the edge of my sanity. I wish there were. I wish it was that easy.

His pen moves across the paper, slowly and deliberately. Maybe he's trying to act like he's doing something. Like he's making a difference. But every stroke of his pen just reminds me how far removed he is from what I'm feeling. He's not in my head, not hearing the whispers, not seeing the shadows. How could he understand? He's not the one who wakes up in the middle of the night, drenched in sweat, heart racing, with that sense of impending doom hovering over every breath.

Thanatophobia. Fear of death, they call it. A fear so deep, so consuming, it defines me. It shapes every breath I take, and every decision I make. It's not just fear of dying—it's a constant, gnawing anxiety that never lets me rest. It's the quiet whisper in my ear when I'm lying in bed at night, telling me that death is right around the corner, just waiting for the right moment. A shadow, always lurking.

They say it's a real thing. Death anxiety, they call it. Anxiety that arises from constantly thinking about your own death, like it's a clock ticking down somewhere just beyond the reach of my consciousness. I know the facts, the terms. But they don't make it any easier.

I am scared to drive because I fear I'll be in a wreck. Not just a wreck—*the* wreck, the one that kills me. I am terrified to cross the street, to take the stairs, to use a knife. Each time I cut vegetables, I imagine slicing my hand, and the blood pouring out, pooling under me as I sit there, alone, helpless, waiting for it to be too late. I could just bleed out, and no one would find me. That thought alone is enough to freeze my breath in my chest.

I live alone, and that only makes everything worse. There's no one to stop the spiral, no one to remind me that *I'm not dead yet*. That the fear isn't real, even when it feels more real than anything else.

I'm scared to leave anything plugged in, because of that damn episode of *This is Us*. That one scene, the one where the house catches fire. Every time I plug in my phone charger, I'm half-expecting it to burst into flames. I check the plugs. I check the stove. I check the locks on the doors. Every. Single. Time. Because the thought that *I could die*—that I could vanish in an instant—is unbearable.

I am *fucking* scared of dying.

But dying is normal, right? It's inevitable. It's a part of life, as much as breathing or eating. We're all supposed to die someday. That's just the way things go. That's what everyone tells me.

But *death*? Death is not normal. Death is not just the end of life; it's the moment when everything we've ever known is shattered, erased, and replaced with nothing. It's the *unknown*, the place we can never come back from.

And there's a difference. A fine line of difference. But there is a difference.

Dying is inevitable. But *death*—the idea that something could just stop, like a flick of a switch, an empty abyss where nothing ever returns—that's what terrifies me. Not just the end, but the *uncertainty* of what lies beyond it. The thought of not knowing, of being *forgotten*, of slipping into the nothingness.

It's not death itself that I fear the most. It's everything that comes with it. The loneliness, the endless silence, the absence of anything.

I clear my throat, but the words stick in it like jagged stones, caught in a way that feels unnatural. "I was on a beach," I manage to croak. My voice feels foreign, not quite mine. It's like each syllable is being dragged from me, a slow, painful extraction. I want to stop, to retreat back into the safety of silence, but some part of me—a small, desperate part—compels me forward. "There was no wind, no sound. I don't think anyone was there—well, not at first."

The therapist's pen scrapes against the page, the sound too sharp, too clinical for my already-frayed nerves. "There was someone?" he asks, his voice too calm, too neutral. "You previously said there was a woman?"

I try to hold onto the image, but it slips through my mind like water through my fingers. Each fragment of her face is a blur, yet those eyes—the cold, red eyes—remain. They're too real. Too much. I can't seem to get rid of them. "She..." I hesitate, the weight of the memory pressing down on me. "She said she was coming for me."

I feel the therapist's gaze, expectant, his pen still poised, waiting for more. *Doesn't he get it?* This isn't just a dream. This isn't something I can explain away as a trick of the mind.

He presses, scribbling something down. "Do you recognize her?"

I shift in my seat, suddenly aware of the air in the room, the too-bright lights above me, the hum of the fluorescent glow. I don't want to answer, don't want to say the words aloud, but I can't stop myself. "She calls herself... the Collector of Souls. The Angel of Death," I whisper, barely audible.

As the words leave my mouth, a cold shiver races down my spine. I can almost feel her presence, even now, hovering just behind me, waiting for me to say it again. *She's not just a figment of my imagination.*

There she is again, in my mind—her cold, red eyes boring into me, like frozen shards of ice that sink deep into my chest. Every glance is a reminder that she isn't just some nightmare. *She's here.* Watching me. Always watching.

The panic starts to build in my chest, tightening, and constricting, until it feels like I can't breathe. My heart races, beating harder, faster, against the cage of my ribs. I clutch at my chest, struggling to force air into my lungs. My words crack and break as I try to speak. "She... she says she's the Angel of Death."

The room spins. My thoughts fracture, colliding in a jumbled mess. This is too much. She's here. She's not some figment of a dream or a bad memory. She's real, and she's coming for me. I can feel it.

His eyes never leave his notepad, the tip of his pen dancing across the page with an unsettling rhythm. It's almost like a metronome counting down to my inevitable unraveling. He doesn't look at me—he doesn't see me. He sees his notes, his neat little shield against the truth that's tearing me apart.

"When did you first see... this 'Angel of Death'?" he asks, his voice thin and clinical, but there's a flicker of something else in his tone. Is it amusement? Disinterest? Maybe both. He taps his pen, the sound sharp and rhythmic, mocking the very horror that suffocates me.

I know the answer. I know exactly when I saw her. It's why I'm here, why I'm broken, why I can't seem to breathe without feeling the weight of her shadow looming over me. It's a name that haunts every corner of my mind. Dash Madden.

I swallow hard, the weight of the confession pressing on my throat like a vice. My voice cracks when I finally force the words out, almost as though they're tearing through me. "When he stabbed me. Eleven times. In the chest."

I glance up at him, searching for some flicker of recognition, some reaction to match the magnitude of what I've just said. But he doesn't flinch. He doesn't look shocked or horrified. He just scribbles down notes like he's taking a survey, documenting the most mundane thing in the world. I want to scream at him, to tell him that this isn't just something to be written down and moved on from. This is my life. My pain. But I can't.

Eight months ago, I was lying in a hospital bed, my body broken, my soul shattered. I had been fighting for my life after surviving an attack from the man I once trusted, the man I once thought I loved. Dash Madden, the charming Southern man who was never really home, until he was. I watched him change, slowly at first—little signs I ignored—until he wasn't the man I knew anymore. He became a stranger. A monster. And I was his prey.

His hands, the same hands that once held me in a comforting embrace, were stained with my blood. His violence unraveled everything—the memories of laughter, the promises he made. All of it, was gone in a matter of moments. My blood on the floor, his betrayal carving its way into my mind. I trusted him. I loved him.

He was supposed to protect me.

I wait for the therapist to ask, to dig deeper, to show some kind of empathy, but the silence stretches on. I realize he's probably still processing what I've just said—maybe even trying to make sense of me. Or maybe he's just trying to figure out how to respond. Either way, I've lost him.

I force myself to say it again, to push the words out even though they taste like ash in my mouth. "My ex-boyfriend stabbed me in the chest. He stabbed me eleven times, they said." The words feel weightless as they leave me—like I'm speaking from some faraway place like I'm no longer even part of this conversation. It's not me talking. It's someone already lost, someone who can't feel anything anymore.

The therapist stays silent, his gaze soft but distant, nodding as though he's absorbing my words. But I can see it, the mask of compassion that never quite reaches his eyes. It's hollow, a practiced reaction. I know exactly what he's waiting for—more of me to spill, more pieces of my broken self that he can hold up and rearrange into something he can "fix." It's what they all want, isn't it? To take my jagged edges and sand them down until I'm something they can manage. But I'm not playing anymore. I'm done.

The truth is, there's nothing he can do for me. Not really. The same song and dance as the previous sessions: the questions, the nods, the slight frown when I don't give him the answer he's expecting. It's all a performance. And I'm so fucking tired of performing.

So I shut down. I retreat, folding myself back into the safe, tight shell I've built to protect me. It's automatic now. Every time the world starts pressing too hard, I retreat. Every time someone tries to peel back the layers, I pull them tighter. I can't afford to let anyone in anymore. Not really.

The silence between us stretches, thick with the weight of everything unspoken. The only sound is the steady clack of the Newton's Cradle, a mechanical reminder that time moves forward, whether I do or not. I sit here, watching the pendulums swing back and forth, the same rhythm over and over. But I don't feel time passing. I don't feel anything but the heavy, suffocating air of this room. I'm stuck in this limbo, between what was and what could be. And all I can think about is that night. The night everything changed. The night I met her.

The Angel of Death.

Her name haunts me. Her cold eyes, her voice that wraps around me like a noose, telling me that she's coming for me.

I could just stay here, in this sterile room with this man who isn't really listening, who doesn't understand. He's waiting, just like everyone else. Waiting for me to open up, to give him the pieces of me he wants. But I won't. I can't.

There's nothing he can do to fix this, to fix me. This isn't something that's going to be solved with a few prescriptions, or by talking it out.

What do I do when what's haunting me isn't something that can be fixed by "processing"? What do I do when the thing chasing me is something that no one else sees? What do I do when the only thing I'm sure of is that it won't stop until it has me?

We're done here.

Chapter Three

Azrael

Work Song - Hozier

My favorite pastime is pretending to be mortal—doing mortal things in a mortal coffee shop. It's one of those rare moments where I can step away from everything, slipping into the facade of being ordinary. Times have changed since I last had a true taste of human life. Technology has exploded, and now there's internet on phones, a convenience I can't quite understand. They've even invented flavors like s'mores coffee—creative, if indulgent—but the music hasn't gotten any better. Still full of whining guitars and off-pitched vocals that pass for emotion in their world.

The funny part? No one suspects a thing. Few walking among them even believe in supernaturals like me. The idea of someone like me sitting at a table sipping coffee, invisible in the crowd, is as far removed from their reality as the heavens are from the Underworld. They don't realize their barista is a werewolf or that there are beings like me lurking around the corner, pulling strings in the background of their lives. I could be anyone. I could be everyone. And no one would notice.

I sip my s'mores coffee, letting the strange sweetness and heat settle in my chest. It's too sweet—too much like the human world's idea of comfort—but there's something about it. Maybe, just maybe, this place feels like home. But not enough to matter. Not that I'm homesick. I stopped feeling homesick centuries ago. The Underworld has its own kind of cold comfort, and I've grown used to it, even if it's never quite right. The freedom that comes with stepping out of the Underworld, into the chaos of the mortal world, is a far better escape.

I enjoy blending in, watching the crowds, and savoring this tiny illusion of anonymity. It's a small, fleeting thing. No one recognizes the weight of the scythe I carry or the centuries of death and judgment that follows me like a shadow. They don't know that every moment of my existence is tied to an unspoken duty—to guide souls, to collect them, to ensure the order of life and death is upheld. None of that fits into a world that seems more concerned with what's trending than what's eternal.

I let the buzz of the coffee shop fill my ears, the clinking of cups, the soft murmur of conversations, and I find myself lost in the absurdity of it. I'm surrounded by the living, and yet none of them truly live. How can they, when they've forgotten what death is? How can they appreciate the fleeting nature of life when they no longer see its edge?

I take another sip of my coffee, the heat mingling with the growing unease in my chest. My attention shifts to the barista behind the counter. He moves with the grace of someone trying to blend in, but there's something about the way his eyes dart nervously. The subtle flicker of tension in his posture. There's something more there, something that doesn't belong in this setting. He's a werewolf, but like so many others, he hides it well. I can sense it, of course. I can smell the musky scent that surrounds him, faint but there.

I roll my eyes as he fumbles with an order. He's nervous—too nervous. But it's almost amusing. Watching him try to juggle his human role and his hidden nature is like watching someone try to keep a lid on an overfilled pot. It's bound to spill over sooner or later.

Today, though, I'm not here to people-watch. I'm on a mission.

Find Memetim.

She's a Reaper, like me, but one who wasn't designed to be as cunning. Currently, she's on a spree—snatching souls from mortals, leaving chaos in her wake. Unlike me, she's not tethered to the rules of our kind. She does things her way, without hesitation or care for the balance she disrupts.

This mission is different. Normally, I'm the one to guide souls—gently releasing them and preparing them for Judgment. I hold the hands of the elderly as Orcus taps their foreheads, helping their souls escape their fragile bodies. I sing lullabies to babies who never got to take their first breath, ensuring that even their short lives aren't forgotten in the grand expanse of time.

But not today. Today, I'm hunting a rogue. Memetim. She's a threat. A Reaper who's abandoned her duty. That's why I'm here, drinking cheap mortal coffee and pretending to blend in. A far cry from the Underworld, but it's what I do. The chaos she's leaving behind is getting out of control. It's my job to stop it.

I chuckle letting it fade as the music plays softly around me. A tuneless hum by mortal standards, but it's enough to settle my mind, if only for a moment. I take another look around the coffee shop. Nothing unusual. Just the usual buzz of mundane activity. People typing on laptops, sipping lattes, lost in their own little worlds.

Then the mirror across the room catches my attention. In it, my mortal form stares back at me—a pale imitation of who I am in the Underworld. Blond hair falling in waves around a face that's too soft, too fragile, with ice-blue eyes that are far too telling. I can't help but notice the scars along my neck and shoulders, reminders of countless battles fought over the centuries. My kind may be resilient, but we aren't indestructible.

In the Underworld, I'm simply Azrael, The Prince of Death. No glamour, no disguise. Just a 6'4" skeleton draped in a dark cloak, glowing ember-like sockets where my eyes used to be, and Orcus by my side—always. Orcus, my sentient scythe, though for now, he's disguised as a mortal phone, his form an insult to his true power.

Orcus grumbles in my pocket, the low vibration a sign of his irritation. "I preferred the days when we did our work without sitting in coffee shops full of Wi-Fi signals and stale espresso. You've really hit a new low."

I grin, tapping the phone's screen just to annoy him. "You're no help with Memetim anyway, Orcus. I'm the one tracking her."

"Oh, I remember," he mutters sarcastically. "As if you could track her on your own. Do you think you can do this without your 'little' friend here?"

I press the phone slightly harder against the counter, a playful challenge in my voice. "You're not thrilled about this mortal realm, are you? I thought you'd gotten used to it."

Orcus scoffs, his voice vibrating with frustration. "I'm not thrilled about being a damn phone, Azrael. I don't belong in your pocket. I belong in the Underworld, where I am respected."

"Respect?" I chuckle, gathering my empty cup and crumpled napkin. "You have to give respect to receive respect. If that's what you call 'respect,' then you've got a funny way of showing it. I seem to recall you dropping me flat on my ass more than once during training."

"Dropping you was your own fault," Orcus retorts smugly. I can almost hear the smirk in his tone, and I'm sure if he had a physical form, he'd be rolling his eyes.

"I'm sure it was," I mutter. The last thing I need is to get into another argument with my scythe about the fine art of training. It's one of those things that never ends well for me.

But, despite his complaints, Orcus is invaluable. And right now, he's still my best shot at finding Memetim. She's elusive, but she won't be for long.

Taking a last, long sip, I toss my cup into the trash and let my gaze drift to the werewolf behind the counter. He's been watching me, growing tenser by the minute. He feels my power, but he can't quite identify what I am. His eyes flicker with the telltale signs of unease, and I catch him looking—quick, nervous glances that betray his attempt to keep his composure.

A knowing smile crosses my lips as our gazes lock. I wink at him, amused by the subtle dance between us. Mortal or not, there's something about the way he stands that's still dangerous. A wolf, through and through.

"What, are you going to stare at the wolf all day? Can we get a move on?" Orcus interrupts, his voice dripping with disdain. "We have a job, Azrael. Memetim's out there causing chaos while you're flirting with wolves over marshmallow coffee."

I roll my eyes, muttering under my breath, "Don't be dramatic, Orcus." I tap his current form silencing his incessant nagging. As much as I don't want to admit it, his nagging is effective. We're here on business, not for idle amusement.

Before I leave, I scan the mortals around me. Their expiration dates hover over them like soft glows, some red, some green, the occasional yellow. The colors tell me everything I need to know—when they'll go and when their time is up.

It's a constant reminder of the delicate nature of their lives. But none of that matters right now. Memetim's out there, and every moment I waste is a step closer to more chaos.

The wolf behind the counter stiffens as I move toward the door, his gaze still following me. There's a flicker of something—fear, maybe—but I'm already past it. I'm already focused on the bigger picture.

Time's ticking.

As I step outside, something catches my attention—a flicker, a date that doesn't sit right. It wavers between red and yellow, shifting erratically. I scan the crowd, and there she is. A young woman, walking with her shoulders hunched, her gaze fixed firmly on the ground. She moves like a mouse that's just seen the shadow of a hawk, small and vulnerable, almost too easy to miss.

Her name appears above her head: Layla Simmons. But there's something wrong. Her fate's been tampered with, marked by some unseen supernatural hand. The shifting colors tell me that much. It's rare to see such uncertainty in someone's expiration, and it gnaws at me. A strange pull stirs inside me, compelling me to follow her—just a few steps behind.

I slip into my true form, the shift subtle but powerful. Orcus morphs into his familiar, heavier shape. The weight of him in my hands feels comforting. I grip his handle tightly, letting the edge of his blade catch the sunlight as I move.

"What are you doing?" Orcus' voice cuts through the quiet, sharp with warning. "This isn't your role right now, Azrael."

"Her death is on my list," I reply in a low, measured voice, my gaze never leaving her. "But something feels off. It doesn't sit right."

Orcus' tone turns sly, a mocking lilt creeping into his words. "Careful, Azrael. You're getting that look again—business, not pleasure, remember?"

"She could be my lead to Memetim," I murmur, my eyes still fixed on Layla as she moves down the street, unaware of my presence. But there's a gleam in my eyes that I can't hide. Orcus sees it immediately, and he knows me all too well.

"Of course, of course," he sneers. "Maybe you're just looking for an excuse to linger here among the mortals. You've always been curious about their little lives."

I ignore him, but the truth hangs between us. There's something about her, something that tugs at me in ways I don't fully understand yet. But I know one thing—if she's somehow tied to Memetim, then I can't let her slip away.

I study Layla's aura more closely, watching as more details flow to me. She's 23, born in Picayune. A survivor, battered by a brutal assault. Her ex-boyfriend, Dash Madden, stabbed her eleven times. The thought of it stirs a quiet rage inside me, simmering beneath the surface, and I grip Orcus tighter, my fingers curling like claws beneath the black satin of my robe.

She rounds a corner, heading toward a small, orange house. I follow from a distance, my senses fine-tuning with every step.

"What are you doing?" Orcus mutters, his voice tinged with exasperation. "This *isn't* your role, Azrael. Mortals—especially this one—aren't our business."

"This one feels… different," I whisper, transfixed. She slips into the house, kicking off her shoes with a strange, almost delicate motion. She leaves the door slightly ajar, a small oversight that feels far too inviting.

Orcus chuckles, dark and amused. "Oh, don't get sentimental now. You'll only end up hurting yourself. Memetim's out there, and you're mooning over a soul you shouldn't have."

But I stay. I can't tear my gaze away from the house, the tiny flicker of something that calls to me. I've tracked countless souls over the centuries, yet there's something about Layla that lingers. Like a part of her has already touched me, wrapped itself around some fragile part of me that I've long kept hidden.

"She's… different," I murmur, the words leaving my lips before I can stop them. I don't care that Orcus is listening, his scorn dripping from his every syllable.

From the shadows, I remain rooted, watching her through the cracks in the world I've come to know so well. And in this moment, I know something deep within me has already shifted. I'm in deeper than I ever intended.

Chapter Four

Layla

Unsteady - X Ambassadors

I can feel eyes on me from within the safe confines of my home. Someone's watching me. I can feel it, like a whisper at the back of my mind that won't stop, no matter how I try to ignore it. Every time I shift in my seat, I feel those unseen eyes following my every movement. A chill runs through my spine, the kind that doesn't make sense, but still settles in my bones.

The air feels thick—almost as though it's pressing down on me. The old house creaks and groans as if it's alive as if it senses the unease creeping up my skin. The shadows stretch unnaturally under the dim light, elongating and twisting as if they have a life of their own. The lamp flickers in my peripheral vision, casting erratic bursts of light that only make the silence more suffocating.

I'm not sure what it is tonight—this unease is different. It's heavier than usual, like a weight pressing down on my chest. I try to shake it off, but it lingers. The sound of my footsteps as I walk to the kitchen is too loud in the stillness, and I pause before turning on the kettle. The quiet hum of the refrigerator only adds to the tension, as if everything in this place is too aware of my every breath.

Pouring myself another cup of coffee, I clutch it too tightly, feeling the warmth seep through my fingers. It's a comfort I don't deserve, but it's the only thing that helps steady my shaking hands. I know I shouldn't drink it—too much caffeine this early, especially when I can't sleep, will ruin me tomorrow with a caffeine hangover. But the idea of sleep is far worse than the inevitable crash.

I can't fall asleep.

Every time I close my eyes, I see his face—Dash's face. The memory is so vivid, *so real*, it feels like he's right here, in the room with me. The haunting, dark eyes that once looked at me with love, are now filled with something... worse. The blood, so much blood, on my clothes, on my hands. The way he turned, slowly and deliberately, with that same cruel smile, stabbing me again and again. I'll never forget how cold the blade felt when it slid between my ribs.

And now, even when I'm safe, I still hear him. His laughter echoes in the corners of my mind, a constant, low hum, like static. And whenever I try to push it away, I can feel his presence, hovering, just beyond my sight. I can't explain it. I wish I could. But I can't.

I turn my attention back to the room, my eyes darting to the windows, checking for any signs of movement outside. But all I see is the same darkened street. No one. Nothing. But that doesn't help. It never does. The house is quiet, but my mind is anything but.

I should've called someone. I should call Sadie and make her stay, but I didn't. I didn't want to drag her into this—didn't want her to feel the same things I do. The fear, the paranoia. It's my burden to carry, but it feels too heavy sometimes.

With a deep breath, I settle into the couch, trying to calm my racing heart. The cup of coffee trembles slightly in my hands, but I force myself to focus. I need to be rational. I need to stay grounded.

But the longer I sit here, the more I feel it—the weight of a presence, lingering in the air like smoke, suffocating me.

A creak sounds from somewhere deep in the house. It's soft, and faint, but enough to send a jolt of panic racing up my spine.

I look toward the hallway, but it's dark. Too dark. The shadows swallow the light from the lamp like it's nothing, leaving me with nothing but the blackness stretching on.

Breathe. In, out. It's fine.

But even I don't believe my own words. The fear gnaws at me, a quiet desperation that rises in my throat, making it hard to swallow.

Another creak. Closer this time.

I jump up, my heart hammering, but I don't dare call out. What good would it do? Whoever—or *whatever*—is in here, they're already too close.

I glance toward the front door, my mind calculating how far I'd get if I bolted. It's not a plan. It's just the reflex of someone who's been chased too many times, someone who's always just *one step behind* the danger. My legs feel like lead, frozen in place, and I can't bring myself to move.

My hand grips the coffee cup harder, the porcelain digging into my skin, but I can't let it go. I need something to hold on to, to steady me, to remind me that I'm still in control.

But am I?

I'm not even sure anymore.

I will see her again.

She hates me. I don't know why. She only visits me in my dreams, but her presence... I can't escape it.

Where sleep was once a refuge, a place to retreat and recharge, now it feels like a battlefield. I fight for my life every time I close my eyes.

Her appearance either terrifies me or leaves me in awe of the chilling beauty she embodies, but she never wears a smile. Not once.

If she were human, I would hate her for her effortless beauty—long, black hair that falls like a waterfall down her back, skin so pale it almost glows in the dark. Her makeup is dark, like something out of a nightmare, and her eyes... those glowing red eyes that pierce into my soul.

But she's not human. She's not a person, not someone I can hate and forget. She's something else entirely. She is my nightmare, my Angel of Death.

I shudder, gripping my cup harder, as the drip of the faucet echoes through the kitchen, its rhythm far too close to the sound of long red stiletto nails clicking on glass.

I get up and turn the handle, stopping the drip. It's almost as if she's taunting me with the noise—slowly driving me mad, trying to drown me in this house of my own fear. It's a trap, my own little hell.

The silence settles again, but the tension doesn't ease. It lingers, hanging in the air like a storm waiting to break. My skin prickles, and I know—*I just know*—that she's here.

I glance around, half-expecting to see her standing in the doorway, her red eyes glowing in the dark. But the room is empty. It doesn't matter. I can still feel her. The oppressive weight of her presence presses on me from every angle. She's *always* here, always watching.

I set the cup down on the counter, my hands shaking as I try to steady myself. The pounding in my head grows louder, and I wonder if I'll ever find peace again. She's been haunting me for what feels like forever, and each time she comes closer, more real until I can almost reach out and touch her.

But the worst part isn't her appearance. It's the way she makes me feel—like I'm nothing... like I don't even belong in this world.

My heart races in my chest, and I force myself to take a deep breath, trying to push the panic away. But it's no use. I can't escape her, not when she's already inside my head.

I turn slowly, glancing around the room again, almost expecting to see her standing just behind me. But of course, she's not. Not physically. But in every corner of this house, in every creaking floorboard, she's there. I feel it, like a cold hand at the back of my neck.

I close my eyes for a moment, just wishing for some kind of release, some respite from the constant fear that churns in my gut. But when I open them again, I know she's still there, watching.

And this time, I don't think I can escape.

She'll take me from this shitty place, this stupid orange house I can't escape. The house that somehow manages to be too cold in the winter and too hot in the southern summer. The house where faucets leak and dreams shatter. Where I'm stuck in an endless loop of silent therapy sessions that never end with any answers.

I look around at the dimly lit, stale house, trying to convince myself that this is a home. But I can't. It's not. Not anymore. It never was.

"Well, why did he stab you eleven times in the chest if he loved you so much?"

Fuck if I know. As if I could ever understand the rage that snapped in his mind like a brittle twig.

If I had known, maybe I could've stopped it. Maybe I could've seen the signs. But all I know is that he was becoming more violent every day, slipping further into that darkness I couldn't touch. That last day... I keep replaying it over and over, hoping for an answer. But all I get is confusion.

I close my eyes for a moment, gripping the edge of the counter. The memories—his fists, the knife, his screams—come crashing down on me again. My pulse quickens, and I can feel the weight of it all pushing against my chest.

I can't breathe.

But I have to. I have to keep moving. If I don't, I'll drown in this.

The sound of something scraping against the floor breaks through the fog in my mind. I whip around, heart racing, but the house is empty. The silence presses in on me again.

I don't know why I'm still here. Why I haven't left, why I haven't done something—anything—to change the course of this never-ending nightmare?

But when I close my eyes, when I let the exhaustion take over, I feel her. Her presence. That suffocating weight... using memories of Dash to torture me.

I shudder, knowing what it means.

She's coming.

It's only a matter of time.

I was in our room, getting ready for our anniversary dinner. I was adjusting my dress in front of the mirror, trying to ignore the way my hands trembled. Then he walked in.

His face was twisted—angry, but something else too. Before I could even ask what was wrong, he lunged towards me with a knife. He didn't say anything at first, just stood there holding it, like he was trying to decide if he should speak or just... act.

Then he said it.

"I love you."

His voice was flat, and distant, like he was already far away from me. Before I could process it, he repeatedly stabbed me, and then he turned and left the room, the knife in hand as if nothing was out of the ordinary.

I sip the brown liquid in my mug, feeling its warmth spread through my chest, trying to ground myself and chase away the chills that have settled in my bones. The clock on the stove blinks "3:00 PM," mocking me. I've got hours to go before night falls. Hours of pretending I'm not haunted.

Haunted by him. Haunted by the way his love turned into something that nearly killed me. Haunted by the image of him standing there, knife in hand, a cold, distant version of the man I thought I knew.

I can't escape the thought that something in him—something deep and twisted—had been there all along. Waiting to break free.

I set the mug down with a soft clink, then pressed my fingers to my temple.

The house is too quiet.

Dragging my feet to my room, I sit on the edge of my bed and mindlessly flick on the TV, reaching for the bag of Cheez-Its beside me. Horror movies have always been my escape, even if they're the last thing I should watch right now.

But I'm not triggered by what I see on the screen. It's the memories that get to me. Talking about the trauma, reliving it—hearing myself say it out loud—that's what causes the panic attacks.

That's why therapy is so damn hard. And so pointless.

But I promised my mother I'd keep trying. So here I am.

I sit for an hour with a strange man who looks like he's dressed for a rodeo, waiting for me to talk. He never says anything, just waits. Silently.

It's all I can do to keep the facade of "okay."

But I'm not okay.

I'm not fucking okay.

I'm living in a nightmare.

Every day is a struggle, every hour is a battle. I can't stop thinking, "Did I turn off the stove?" because if I didn't, I'd die in a fire. A fire I'm too paralyzed to escape, too scared to move fast enough to save myself. What if I trip over the shoes I tossed in a hurry after a bad day, and I fall, and—

I stop myself.

I'm spiraling again.

I grip the edge of the bed, my nails biting into the comforter as I try to steady my breath. I've been here before. This is my routine: the panic, the overwhelming thoughts, the constant cycle that never ends.

I close my eyes, forcing myself to focus on the present. The TV hums in the background, and the lights flicker. The house feels like it's closing in on me, like it always does when the world goes silent, and I'm left alone with my mind.

Memories flood back, unwelcome and sharp. His face—distorted in anger and something darker, something I can't put my finger on. The way he looked at me when he told me he loved me, just before he attacked.

I shudder and open my eyes, but the shadows around me are thickening, pulling me back into the past, into the nightmare.

And then the door creaks.

I freeze, my heart pounding in my chest as I turn toward the sound.

It's probably just the wind, or my mind playing tricks on me.

But I can't shake the feeling that I'm not alone.

Instead of thinking those thoughts, I get up to go pour myself another cup of coffee and retreat back to my room. Anything to keep me from thinking too much.

I tell myself I am fine, that the screams I hear in my head are nothing but echoes. I keep my therapist happy by saying what he wants to hear, sometimes by pretending I am stable enough to keep living in this haunted shell of a house.

I'm a fraud.

I try to tell everyone I'm fine, but they know. I know they know.

I just want to hide in my world of thoughts, lost in the darkness. I want to feel numb, and yet, something keeps pulling me out of it.

Something... or someone.

With trembling fingers, I set my coffee mug on the nightstand, far from my bed, just in case my clumsy, shaking hands tip it over in the dark. I open the drawer. I know what's inside. My blue rubber friend with vibration speeds that could take me far away from here. It doesn't judge me, doesn't ask me why I can't move past the horrors of this place.

It's a temporary escape, but it's all I've got.

I grab it and sit back against the wall, trying to breathe steadily, trying to drown out everything else.

I close my eyes, and with trembling fingers, I shimmy out of my yoga pants, the fabric sticking to my skin as my hands shake. The whisper in the back of my mind starts its usual taunt: *this is wrong. You're using this to avoid something deeper.* I know it's there, but I don't care. I can't care *right now.*

Speed three.

The vibrator hums to life, and I sink back against the edge of the bed, letting it take me somewhere, anywhere that isn't here. It's a brief escape from everything—my life, my fears, the memories that cling like ghosts, and of course, her. The Angel of Death. The one who waits in the shadows of my mind, always. Watching. Waiting.

For just a moment, I can almost forget her. Forget the weight of her red eyes piercing through my soul. Forget the way her presence seeps into every inch of my life, uninvited, unrelenting. Here, in the silence, I can almost trick myself into thinking I'm not haunted.

I feel my muscles relax, my breath slowing as the buzzing fills the space around me. I don't have to think. I don't have to feel. I can leave this hell behind, if just for a second.

But even as I let the escape take hold, there's a heaviness that settles deep in my chest. I know I can't run far. I know that no matter how hard I try to push the thoughts away, she'll be there when I stop.

In the corners of my mind, she's watching me, waiting for me to slip. Waiting for me to fail.

I tremble, the feeling too familiar—the one where I know I'm safe for a moment, but I'm never really safe at all. The sensation of being pursued, of being prey. It lingers long after the noise has faded, a phantom pulse that won't let me rest.

I can't escape her. Not completely. As the hum fades among the chaos in my mind, leaving only the sound of my breath, the silence creeps back in, and I can't help but feel like I am losing another piece of myself to her.

Chapter Five

Azrael

Animal - Neon Trees

I f mortal rules applied to me, this would be illegal... for sure. A peeping Tom, at the very least.

But I don't follow mortal rules.

I watch her, a tiny, fragile thing, resembling a mouse with shadows in her eyes. The weight of something heavier than I can name clings to her like a shroud—something that has cracked her open in ways even I can't fathom. I can feel the quiet tension in the air, the uncertainty in her every movement, and the deep, relentless fear that lingers just below the surface.

She's searching for solace, some reprieve from the world that has torn her apart. Her hands tremble, fingers hesitating as she raises the small device—some fragile tool meant to provide her with a temporary escape. I shouldn't be watching this. I know that. But I can't tear my gaze away, not from her, not from the quiet vulnerability she's trying so hard to hide.

She flicks it on. Her breath catches, just slightly, and her eyes—those striking emeralds—flutter closed. She tilts her head back, her lips parting with a soft, barely audible sigh. I feel it, too—the slight release of tension in her body, the momentary escape she finds in the sensation. I feel the quiet ache of it in my own chest, and something sharp twists inside of me, an unfamiliar sting.

I should turn away. I should leave. But I stay.

I stay because I can't deny what I see in her—how broken she is, how much she needs something, anything, to fill the emptiness that stretches endlessly inside of her. I watch her fight for control, for release, like a desperate prayer, but she doesn't realize—she doesn't see—that the very thing she seeks is slipping through her fingers. The sense of relief she's chasing isn't enough to fill the hole that's been carved inside of her. Not really.

And that's where I come in. Where I should come in.

She's unaware of me, of course. Even with my presence so close, she doesn't sense me—doesn't feel the pull of death that lingers around me like a storm cloud. She doesn't realize that every fleeting breath, every shiver of pleasure, brings her closer to the inevitable. She doesn't know how her fate is tied to me, to the end she so desperately tries to avoid.

But I see it. I feel it. I know it's only a matter of time.

She releases a shuddering breath, and my nerves rattle. It's a sound I'm too familiar with—one that haunts me in ways I never expected. A sound of release, yes, but also of longing, of grief, of something darker. It's almost as if she's trying to outrun the shadows that chase her, and yet, she knows she can't.

I don't know why I'm still here. It isn't my place to watch her like this, to bear witness to this fragile moment of relief, fleeting as it is. And yet, I stay. I'm not just watching her, I'm *feeling* her—her pain, her confusion, her search for anything that can make the void inside of her a little less suffocating.

For a moment, I wish I could do something to make her understand—to make her see me, to take her out of this never-ending spiral of fear and regret. But I'm not here to be her savior. I'm not here to ease her pain.

I'm here for a different reason. One she can never understand.

And yet... for the first time in centuries, something inside me stirs—something I haven't felt in a long time.

I'm not sure what it is, this ache that sits in my chest, but it's not entirely unpleasant. For a moment, I almost wish I could make it go away.

But I can't. And I won't.

Not when the end is so close.

I stand at the edge of her world, invisible but entirely aware. I watch her, delicate and trembling, her body a fragile thing wrapped in the cloak of her own suffering. She's seeking solace in a way that only mortals can understand—through fleeting moments of escape. I want to stop myself. I want to turn away, to remind myself of my purpose, to remember who I am.

But I don't.

The urge pulls me closer, like gravity. I'm here, in her world, not just watching her, but feeling her. Her trembling hands, the way she shudders as she tries to find some relief in her solitude. Her body responds, unaware that I am here, and something inside me, some dark piece of me that I've buried for centuries, stirs in answer.

I could stop this. I could turn away. But tonight... tonight is different. The darkness in her soul calls to me. I can feel it pulling at my own, twisting my true character like a rope unraveling.

I reach for Orcus with my left hand, the scythe's cool touch grounding me, even as the urge to cross the line consumes me. The hum of warning thrums through the blade, but I ignore it. I've already crossed that threshold, haven't I? All I've done so far is watch, and be a *witness* to her suffering. Why not offer a release, a fleeting respite?

"She's tied to Memetim," I whisper to myself, trying to justify this twisted need that's overtaking me. It's an excuse, a flimsy one at best. She doesn't need my pity, my help. She doesn't need me. But my fingers ache, drawn to her like a moth to the flame. I could ease her suffering, just for a moment.

I step closer, my form still a mere shadow, but my presence is undeniable. She doesn't see me, but she feels something, a shift in the air, a subtle pressure that presses against her skin, like a whisper in the dark.

She shudders again, and I realize—this is not just about her. It's about me. About what I need, what I've wanted. There's a selfishness in me that I've ignored for too long. A desire to break the rules, to take what's *not* mine, just because I *can*.

I reach out with my bony, incorporeal hand, brushing against the edges of her existence. I don't touch her—not physically, but I make her feel me. It's a subtle thing, a pressure that isn't there, and then it is. It's like a soft caress in the air, a whisper of power.

I feel her response, the way her body trembles, the way she reacts to the unknown. She doesn't know it's me. She can't. But I know she feels something, just like I do. Something dark, something wrong.

She reaches for release, searching for it in the shadows, unaware of the being that watches from the edges of her pain. And I—*I*—feed it. Just a little. Just enough to give her what she's seeking, and to indulge myself in the process.

This is a dangerous game, one I've never played before. It's a betrayal of what I should be, of who I should be. But it's done now. There's no going back.

Her body reacts to the invisible touch, and I'm consumed with something I can't name. Something darker than Death itself. I feel the rush of power, of control, and I know I've crossed a line I should never have crossed.

But it doesn't matter now. I've done it. I've taken this moment for myself, and no one will ever know.

As her body tightens in pleasure, I slip a finger inside of her, and then I add another finger... and then a third. Carefully, timing each movement to draw out her release. I need her to remember this, to feel it deep in her bones- a ghostly touch she will crave without understanding. I will linger at her bedside watching her dreams twist with longing. Let her cry out in confusion, calling for something she can not see.

Calling for me.

She lets out a scream of pleasure while I groan in sexual frustration and Orcus shocks me continuously until I pull my fingers back from rubbing her cum all the way through the folds of her pussy... but before I pulled back, I circled her clit and laughed when her body twitched in confusion.

She shudders beneath my unseen touch, and I pull away, savoring the soft gasp that slips from her lips—a sound that lingers in my mind, sharper than any blade I've wielded. Her body trembles, a slight, broken thing, and she drifts into sleep, her breathing deepening, softening as the afterglow settles over her.

I shouldn't have done that. I know it. I feel the weight of the wrongness in my bones, in every fiber of my being. But I can't stop the thought that crawls through my mind, wrapping itself around me like a noose.

I don't know how many souls I would have to sell, or how many barriers I'd need to break, but *Layla Simmons* will be mine. I will make her my queen. She will live a life more perfect than any mortal could dream.

Orcus' voice rumbles in my mind, thick with irritation, his tone a harsh, judgmental hum. "Feel better now? Or do we need a moment of reflection after that little indiscretion?"

I let out a sigh, scratching at my skull, knowing what he's getting at. "She deserved it," I murmur, almost to myself. "For everything that Memetim has dragged her through, she deserves to know someone can be kind to her."

"And you're all about kindness, of course," Orcus scoffs, the mocking tone never more clear. "Tell me, did this sudden moral high ground hit you before or after you started to break every law of consent in the book?" There's a hum in his voice, faint but unmistakable. "You have to take care of Memetim first, *dumbass*."

I ignore his jab, my gaze fixed on her sleeping form—peaceful at last. The warmth that comes with her vulnerability lingers in the air, and for a fleeting moment, I want nothing more than to keep her safe, hidden from the world's chaos. *Safe from me.*

But that's not an option.

"We can stay close now," I say, forcing my voice to sound steady, the sharp edge of my thoughts dulling just enough for my mask to remain intact. "Watch for Memetim's moves. She'll show her hand soon enough, and when she does, I'll be there to intervene."

Orcus hums in the back of my mind, his presence a dark shadow looming over my words. "You think Memetim's just going to walk in and fall into some trap of yours? And what about Layla? This little fixation of yours is already blinding you."

I grit my teeth, resisting the urge to snap back. "She's not a fixation," I say, my tone hard, though the slight tremor in my voice betrays me. "She's different. She is... valuable."

"Valuable," Orcus repeats, his voice dripping with sarcasm. "Sounds like you've forgotten the difference between protector and predator. Or maybe you're blurring that line on purpose?"

My fingers tighten around his handle, the pulse of Orcus' energy humming through my veins, like a warning I can't escape. It's a failed attempt to choke an object that cannot be choked—my frustration growing, my control slipping. "I am not a predator," I growl, trying to shove the words down. But they linger in the air between us, thick with the unspoken truth I don't want to face.

"Then why does your voice shake when you say that?" Orcus' words are cold, and piercing. "You can't protect her if you're the one haunting her, Azrael. So, if you're going to play her shadow, at least be honest with yourself about why."

I flinch at his words, my grip tightening. It feels as though Orcus can see through every crack in my facade, laying bare all the things I've been trying to keep hidden. The twisted thoughts. The need to possess. The desire to *control*.

But I won't let him win. I won't let him make me doubt myself.

I glance at Layla again, the rise and fall of her chest slow and steady. She's lost in sleep, unaware of the storm brewing just beyond her door. And I *will* keep her safe. No matter what it takes.

But Orcus' words stick with me, and I can feel the flicker of something darker inside me—the part of me that knows I'm walking a line I might not come back from. Every step I take toward her, toward this... *obsession*, is another step further into the shadows.

And yet, here I am.

I hesitate, standing at the threshold of her fragile world, my gaze fixed on her peaceful form. The way her chest rises and falls, slow and steady, as though nothing could touch her here. It's a false peace, I know that. There's no such thing as safety in her world anymore. But I will try to be the one to give it to her. Orcus' words echo in my mind, a bitter weight I can't shake. His mocking tone, his constant reminders of my flaws, of the line I'm crossing, pressing against me like an oppressive storm.

I take a breath, steeling myself. *No. I will protect her.*

"I... won't let her be alone in this," I murmur, my voice low, almost a whisper to the room that no one else will hear. "Whatever Memetim has planned, I will keep her safe. That's the purpose of this and you know it."

Orcus sighs, the sound crackling through the space between us, like the hum of a distant storm. It's a resigned chuckle more than anything, and I feel the pulse of his energy in my grip. The sharp, buzzing hum of disapproval. "Well, I suppose I will have front-row seats to this disaster."

The words sting, more than they should, and I clench my fists at my sides, trying to force away the frustration that rises within me. But it's difficult. Because I don't know if Orcus is wrong.

"It won't be a disaster," I mutter, though the words are hollow in my throat, my certainty faltering. I look down at Layla once more, the soft, rhythmic sound of her breath keeping time with the pounding of my rage. "I'll protect her."

"Sure, you will," Orcus quips, his voice dripping with sarcasm, the sneer audible even through the connection. "Or you will get caught in your own strings and hang yourself."

The cold truth of it rings in my ears, and for a moment, I feel the weight of my decisions more acutely than I ever have. This path—this obsession—is dangerous. But I can't stop. I won't stop.

I glance back down at Layla, her form so small beneath the covers, so vulnerable in her sleep. My chest tightens with an emotion I can't quite name. It's not just responsibility, not just duty. There's something deeper, something darker beneath the surface.

She's mine to protect.

I take another step closer, even though I know I should pull away, knowing that I have the temptation to stay—to watch over her—could be the thing that drags me into oblivion. But in that moment, as I look at her sleeping, I refuse to believe the darkness that threatens to consume me.

She will be safe with me.

Chapter Six

Layla

Toxic - 2WEI

Her hot breath sears my skin, the heat of it almost unbearable as cold dread coils tight in my chest. I can't escape it—her presence, her laughter, the way it claws at my sanity, relentless, echoing in my ears as I stumble through the dream. The beach, the warm, golden sands beneath my feet, morphs into dark, dense woods. The air shifts, heavy and thick with tension, the trees closing in around me like they're trying to swallow me whole.

I run, my legs screaming, my lungs burning with every breath. I push harder, faster, the weight of fear heavy on my chest, forcing me forward. But it's no use. I feel my legs give out, my body betraying me, and then I'm sinking into the earth, the dirt swallowing me whole. My hands claw at the ground, but it's as if I'm fighting against the very world itself.

And then I hear it again. Her laughter. It's closer now, sharper, like a blade in the air, and it cuts into me, deeper than any physical wound. I gasped, the sound strangled in my throat, my heart hammering in my chest.

Her claws rake down my chest, hot and searing, the pain blinding. I scream, the desperation tearing at my voice. "Why are you doing this to me?" The words are ragged, raw with the weight of fear, of hopelessness.

The sound of her steps shifts, and I know she's circling me, watching me crumble. I don't need to look to know she's there, crouching low in front of me. I can feel her gaze, like it's scorching me from the inside out. I raise my eyes, and there she is, her eyes glowing with something that feels like judgment. It's like the weight of the world is pressing down on me, and I can't escape it.

She's so close now, her face inches from mine, her breath hot against my skin, smelling like sweet cherry blossoms, but underneath that, there's something darker—something acrid. Smoke, like the world is burning from the inside out. The scent clogs my lungs, making me choke, but she just smiles. The twisted expression on her face is like a predator savoring its meal.

"Because I can," she whispers, her voice a hiss, a poison that slithers into my ear and wraps around my soul. It's almost too much to bear, but I can't look away. Her words are like knives, carving into me. I'm helpless, trapped in this nightmare with no way out.

I try to breathe through the suffocating panic, but it's hard. The fear is clawing its way up my throat as her laugh lingers, echoing in my mind, drowning out everything else.

Her hands—delicate, yet deadly—wrap around my throat, and I can feel the pressure building, her fingers tightening with cruel precision. Every inch of my skin burns under her touch as my vision starts to fade. I can't breathe. My heart races, pounding in my chest as the world blurs.

I'm drowning in her grip, the pain radiating out of my throat, and I'm helpless. I stare up at her, my eyes wide with panic, but she's a blur now—her human form twisting, her eyes glowing with a fierce crimson light. It burns into me, like the very essence of death, like the final warning of something too dark, too dangerous to attempt to fight.

My attempts to scream are useless, only ragged gasps escaping my lips, the air too thin to fill my lungs. I can feel the life draining from me, slipping away, like sand through my fingers. The cold, heavy weight of it all presses down, and all I want is for it to stop.

This has to be a nightmare.
It's just a nightmare.
Wake up, Layla.
Wake up!

But the darkness isn't fading. The pressure is only increasing, and my pulse pounding in my ears. Just as I think I'm about to slip away completely, a deep, thunderous voice cuts through the void, breaking through the suffocating panic.

"Let her go!"

The grip on my throat loosens, and my body jerks as I suck in air, desperate to fill my lungs. My chest heaves with each ragged breath, and I claw at the dirt beneath me, trying to anchor myself to something solid, something real.

I blink rapidly, trying to focus, to stop the world from spinning. Her laugh—twisted and cold—rings in my ears as I finally sit up, gasping. She's still there, looming over me, but now she's smiling—mocking, cruel.

"How nice of you to join us, Azrael," she purrs, her voice a silken thread laced with venom. The words drip from her tongue like poison. She leans down, eyes glittering with a dangerous amusement as she licks her lips, her forked purple tongue slipping out in a slow, deliberate motion.

I can't help but recoil slightly. My heart is hammering in my chest. Every instinct in me is telling me to run, but I can't move. I am rooted to the spot by fear.

"Did you bring your darling Orcus?" she asks, her voice shifting into something almost playful, though still wicked. Then, she pouts, her eyes softening, almost in mock sympathy.

I know I'm not imagining it—her attention is entirely on the man, Azrael, I think is what she called him, now, but there's something about the way she looks at him that makes my stomach twist. It's not the kind of look one gives an enemy, but something far more calculating, more intimate. It sends a shiver down my spine.

Following her gaze, I see him—standing tall, commanding the space around him with an eerie confidence. He's beautiful, in a way that makes your heart ache and your mind freeze. His scythe gleams. A weapon seemingly forged in darkness, held in a grip that speaks of both power and inevitability. His icy blue eyes lock on mine, and I feel the chill of them all the way down to my bones. His long, blond hair is pulled back, revealing the harsh lines of a face forged by years of silence and unyielding determination.

For a moment, I forget I'm fighting for my life in a dream that feels far too real. My heart hammers in my chest, and despite the terror swirling inside me, my mind is captivated by him. I can't look away. He's magnetic—dangerous, maybe, but there's something so impossible about him that I can't help but be drawn to it.

Who is he?

I try to retreat. My mind is racing as my body attempts to move, to flee, but the Angel of Death is faster. Her sharp, glowing eyes snap back to me, and before I can even react, she flicks a claw in my direction. My feet freeze to the ground, cementing me in place. Panic surges through me as my body refuses to obey. I try to crawl, but my knees slam into something solid, concrete. The pain jolts through me, sharp and immediate.

I scream.

It's a sound ripped from the deepest part of me, my chest tightening, the panic overwhelming as my breaths come in short, frantic gasps. The world spins, and the fear takes over, sinking its teeth into me.

"What is your business here?" the Angel of Death asks, her voice sharp and lilting as she shifts her attention back to Azrael. That's what she called him, right? There's an edge to her words, a quiet menace lurking beneath them. She tilts her head as if studying him, but she doesn't wait for him to answer. Instead, her lips curl into a sly smile, and her posture shifts, growing even more arrogant. "What do I owe the pleasure of this visit from you and Orcus?" Who is Orcus? I only see one man.

She stands tall, placing her hands on her hips, her stance exuding a cocky attitude as if she's already won. The audacity of her, the sheer confidence, almost makes me sick. She's in control here, and I'm nothing but a puppet caught in her twisted game.

I'm caught between the feeling of wanting to cower in fear and the gnawing curiosity of who this man is and why he seems to hold such power.

Just fucking kill me already!

The thought rips through my mind as I feel the all-too-familiar tightness in my chest, the kind of tightness that always signals the start of a panic attack. My breath becomes shallow, and uneven. I'm gasping, each breath a desperate attempt to stay alive, but the crushing weight in my chest is too much. I scream, a strangled sound that seems to get caught in my throat, desperate for release, for air.

Why can't I breathe? Why can't I escape this nightmare?

Azrael's voice slices through the chaos, smooth but packed with an authority that fills the space like an iron hand. There's no hesitation in his tone, no room for argument. His words hit me like a jolt of cold electricity, stirring something deep within me.

"You are to release her and return for judgment," he commands, voice unyielding, cutting through the panic that claws at my mind.

It's not just the words that send shivers down my spine, but the weight behind them—the sheer power in his voice. It's like the world itself is bending to his will. But beneath that authority, there's something else... something darker. An intensity that wraps around me, suffocating me, like I'm being pulled under the weight of his gaze.

The Angel of Death laughs.

It's a wild, hollow sound that echoes through the woods—empty and mocking. Her hair flares out like silken tendrils of shadow, writhing with a life of its own, each strand crackling with malice. She snaps her head towards him, her smile twisting into something crueler, more dangerous. The air around us thickens with tension, and my heart races.

"Do you really think the two of you can handle me?" she sneers, her voice dripping with disdain. "Go on, then. Try it."

Where the fuck is the second person she is talking to?

Azrael doesn't flinch. He doesn't even seem to blink. But I can feel the weight of his gaze on me as he glances my way. The chill in his eyes is a sharp, searing reminder of the danger we're in. There's a flicker of something, a flash of warning.

And then it happens.

I feel myself jerk awake, my chest tightening painfully, gasping for air as my lungs fight against the pressure. My hands fly to my throat, gripping at nothing, my mind still reeling from the chaos of the dream.

The blankets are too hot, too smothering. I push them off of me with frantic, trembling hands, desperate for any kind of relief. My heart is hammering, my breath coming in short, shallow bursts. I can't get enough air. It feels like my chest is closing in on itself.

What the fuck just happened?

My mind races, trying to grasp the edges of the dream, the figures of Azrael and the Angel of Death lingering like shadows on the edges of my consciousness. The terror, the confusion, the raw helplessness—I can't shake the feeling that something is terribly wrong. But everything around me is still, too still.

Was it real? Or was it just a nightmare?

I try to steady my breathing, to calm myself, but the feeling of dread lingers. It's as if the line between sleep and waking has been erased, and I'm stuck somewhere in between.

Chapter Seven

Azrael

Blood in the Cut - K. Flay

I grip Orcus tightly in my right hand, feeling the familiar hum of power surge through the scythe as his fiery red aura ignites around us. The air grows thick with intensity, and the air fills with the crackling sound of energy building between us. Memetim stands before me, her eyes locked with mine, a silent battle waging in the tension-filled air. Neither of us is willing to back down.

The surroundings feel too small for the weight of this confrontation. Every breath I take is measured, and controlled—I'm the calm in the storm. But even I can feel the edge of that storm, the electricity in the air, as her anger presses in.

"Why must you ruin all the fun?" Memetim taunts, her breath uneven. But there's an undeniable edge of excitement in her voice, a dangerous thrill that only she seems to get from all this chaos. Her lips curl into a twisted grin, eyes glinting with malice.

She's provoking me. I know it. But I can't afford to take the bait, not yet. Not with Layla hanging in the balance.

Then, without warning, she moves—too fast, a blur of motion that catches me off guard for a moment. I sidestep just barely in time, my hands gripping Orcus tighter as I yank him down in a sweeping arc. The scythe slashes through the air, catching her across the back. The force sends her crashing to the ground in a cloud of dust and debris.

I take a slow breath, trying to steady the rapid beat of breath. The dust settles around us, and for a brief moment, I feel a flicker of satisfaction. She's down.

I don't want to kill her—not if I don't have to. Layla's fate was already hanging by a thread when I intervened, and I knew just how far Memetim would go to devour her soul. If I hadn't acted in time... I shudder at the thought. No, I can't allow that to happen again. Not now. Not ever.

I chose a mortal form for this exact reason, to appear less menacing, to make it easier for me to get close to her. To Layla. I didn't want to terrify her—she's already been through so much, and I'm not about to add to that fear if I can help it. I'm here to protect her, to guard her soul from Memetim's grasp. That's all that matters right now.

But Memetim's voice rips through the silence erupting a wicked laugh.

Tch, fragile mortal pretense, Orcus scoffs in my mind, sensing the flicker of doubt in my thoughts. *Trying to woo her with softness?* The sharpness of his laughter resonates through me, his voice like steel against my nerves. She may be doomed regardless. *But do what you will—one less soul to carry, and we still have a duty to fulfill.*

His words cut deeper than they should. But I refuse to let them sway me. Orcus knows how this works, how I work. He knows that I'm not some heartless monster, despite not actually having a heart, that the world expects me to be. I didn't choose this role, but I will do what is necessary to keep the balance intact.

Memetim stirs beneath me, and the faintest flicker of movement draws my attention. She's attempting to rise, her movements languid but dangerous. She's not beaten. Not yet. Her eyes meet mine again, and this time there's something darker in them—something that tells me she's not done playing.

Her grin stretches wider. "Is that it, Azrael? You're letting me off that easy?" Her voice is silk-laced with venom, each word dripping with malice. "I thought you were the Prince of Death, but you seem a bit too soft for the job."

I flex my fingers around Orcus' handle, feeling the power surge beneath my skin. "I'm not here to play with you, Memetim," I responded coldly, my voice steady, unwavering. I take a step forward, my eyes narrowing. "You're a threat to her, and I'm here to end that threat. Your games end here."

She laughs, that hollow sound that reverberates through the air like the caw of a crow. Her hair flares out, a dark shadow around her face. "End it?" she mocks, taking a step toward me. "You can't even begin to fathom what you're up against. Do you think you can stop me, Azrael? You're just one more puppet in the hands of Hades."

I stand firm, my gaze never leaving hers. "I don't need to fathom anything," I reply, my voice low, filled with lethal intent. "I know exactly what you are, Memetim. And I know exactly how to deal with you."

I raise Orcus in a fluid motion, the weight of the scythe, centering my focus. I can feel the tension between us, an electric pull that could snap at any moment. I'm ready. And I know she is, too.

"You'll have to do better than that," she sneers, her claws glinting in the dim light. Her body shifts, ready to strike, but I'm already a step ahead, anticipation building in my chest.

"You'll regret underestimating me," I warn, my grip tightening on Orcus. The room feels smaller now, the air thick with the promise of what's to come. One wrong move, one misstep, and this will all be over.

But I'm not going to let that happen.

Memetim watches me, her gaze is hard, unyielding. Her fingers drum rhythmically against the ground, a soft, unnerving beat that fills the space between us. The silence stretches on, heavy and suffocating, thick with an unnamed dread that coils around my thoughts, nestling deep inside my chest. I can feel the weight of it like a shadow looming over everything we've fought for.

My fingers tighten around Orcus' handle, feeling the familiar hum of power surge through the scythe. It vibrates in my grip, a pulsing rhythm that seems to sync with the cadence of our thoughts. It's as though Orcus and I are breathing in unison, preparing for the inevitable clash.

"How long has it been since you felt the presence of fear, Memetim?" Orcus' voice rings out in my mind, his tone is as sharp as ever. His question lingers, slicing through the air between us.

Memetim doesn't answer immediately. Instead, she continues to study me with those cold, calculating eyes, the tension between us thickening. Finally, she speaks, her voice low, barely audible beneath the harsh gasps of air that escape her lips. "Azrael," she murmurs, her tone betraying something darker beneath the surface, "You can't protect everyone. Not from what's coming."

She's ignoring Orcus' taunts, focused only on me now. And her words strike deep, a reminder of the futility of it all, of the forces beyond even my control.

I can feel the darkness in my own eyes as I meet her gaze. Something in me stirs, and a faint, dangerous smile pulls at the corners of my lips. "I don't intend to protect everyone, Memetim," I say, my voice steady but edged with a dangerous calm.

Memetim shifts slightly, her body language is casual, almost amused by my words. She leans forward, that familiar smirk curling on her lips, like a predator savoring her next move. She purrs, her voice dripping with mockery. "You of all beings should know the burden of clinging to something already destined to fade."

The words sting, but I won't let her see it. My eyes narrow, and I scowl, frustrated by her cynicism. "You wouldn't understand," I snap. "Not everything is black and white. Some shades of grey are worth protecting."

She hisses from beneath Orcus' blade, her body shifting like a snake coiling in the dark. The venom in her voice is palpable as she sneers at me. "One thing about having Fate as a sibling," she mutters, the malice thick in her words, "is knowing what's coming. And I will not let this play out for my story."

I can hear the finality in her voice, the certainty that she believes she controls the narrative. But she underestimates me. She underestimates us.

Then, Memetim vanished in a cloud of ash, her form dissolving into the air, the dust settling around me like a dark memory. I stagger forward slightly, instinctively raising my arm to shield my mouth from the grit that stings my throat.

Coughing, I curse the limitations of this mortal form. Its weaknesses sometimes get in the way of what needs to be done. But it's nothing new. My body may be a tool, but it still feels the sting of exhaustion, the strain of this endless battle.

I take a deep breath, steadying myself, the lingering effects of her presence still heavy in the air.

Orcus' voice cuts through the silence in my mind, sharp and blunt as ever. *Well, that was a waste of time*, he mutters, his tone dripping with disdain. *But you're getting soft, Azrael. Don't let your softness for mortals cloud your judgment.*

I know he's right. Memetim's taunts struck a chord, but I won't let it sway me. Not now.

Memetim may have vanished, but her words, her threat, they linger. The battle isn't over yet. And I will protect Layla. No matter the cost.

Memetim's absence leaves a hollow space in the air, the dust she left behind clinging to everything, lingering like an unfinished thought. I stand there, tense, waiting for something else to break the silence. The weight of Orcus in my hand feels heavier now, the scythe's aura still humming with the remnants of our battle. But even in the quiet, Orcus' voice slices through the air.

You'll need more than borrowed mortal bones to face what's coming, Azrael, he warns, his tone vibrating through my palm. *You are teetering on a knife's edge. So tell me, who will wield you if you fall?*

I scoff, the sound harsh in the stillness, my frustration flaring. *You*, I mutter sarcastically, not caring if Orcus hears it or not.

His response is immediate, the scorn in his words palpable. *Such a loyal Reaper you are, risking your very essence for a woman haunted by the Angel of Death. And yet... here you stand, unable to let the mortal go. Perhaps you are more mortal than you realize.*

The accusation stings, but I don't flinch. Instead, I held my gaze on the spot where Memetim had disappeared, her presence still too fresh in the room. She's gone, but her words remain, echoing in the back of my mind.

I don't want to admit it, but Orcus is right. The weight of this mortal form is beginning to wear on me, its fragility pressing down on my esteem. But I won't—can't—let go. Not now.

I tighten my grip on Orcus, the scythe's form shaking slightly in my hands, the fiery red aura pulsing with the same intensity as my thoughts. The power that flows through me, through Orcus, is undeniable—but so too is the pull of something that transcends the cold duty of a Reaper.

You're overthinking it, Orcus sneers, sensing the turmoil that churns beneath the surface. *Focus, Azrael. Focus on the task at hand.*

But it's not that simple. Memetim's threat lingers in my mind, and I can't help but wonder if my actions, my obsession, are leading me down a dangerous path. I've been at this for centuries—seeing lives extinguished, seeing souls pass from this world to the next—but Layla? She's different. And that scares me.

A deep breath fills my chest as I exhale slowly, trying to center myself. I don't have the luxury of doubt. Not now.

I'll do what I must, I mutter under my breath, not entirely sure if I'm reassuring myself or Orcus.

The scythe hums, its aura flickering with a faint, mocking glow. *Just be sure you don't lose yourself in the process, Azrael,* Orcus warns, though the hint of amusement in his voice doesn't escape me.

I don't respond. I don't have to. Orcus knows me too well. But the truth is, I'm already walking a fine line, caught between my duty and something else—something far more dangerous. And I'm not sure how much longer I can keep the balance.

Before I could process exactly what happened, we were summoned abruptly to the Underworld.

Chapter Eight

Azrael

Take Me to Church - Hozier

The world around me blurs, and when I blink, the shifting atmosphere snaps into focus. My knees hit the cold, black stone floor, a familiar burn of indignation tightening in my chest. Orcus hums in my grip, his red aura flickering like a warning as I kneel before my father's vast, imposing throne.

The air is thick with authority, the very fabric of the Underworld pressing in around me, suffocating in its sheer weight. The throne looms ahead—obsidian, with jagged edges that reflect the dull, blood-red light of the Underworld. It's a place of power and indifference, where souls come to be judged, and those like me remain trapped in eternal service.

I hear the subtle creak of leather, the sound almost like a death knell, as he enters. His presence fills the room, cold and suffocating, sending a ripple through the air. The shadow of his form falls over me as he takes his place on the throne with deliberate, unhurried grace.

"Rise!" His voice is a command, booming through the empty halls, carrying the same indifferent weight I've known all of my existence. It strikes me like a hammer, driving my shoulders back as if the motion is nothing more than a reflex. I don't even need to look up. I already know the contempt he'll wear like a crown, a bitter reminder of what I've always been to him—nothing more than a soldier, a tool to be used and discarded.

I stand. My spine straightens against the heaviness of the room, and I clutch Orcus tighter, his aura vibrating beneath my fingers. He feels it too—the swell of frustration. A frustration that has been brewing for eons, but which no one, not even Orcus, has the right to call attention to. He is merely a tool as well. Just like me.

"I'm here," I state flatly, the words sliding from my tongue like ash. The weight of my father's gaze doesn't escape me, but it's not enough to break me. Not this time. Not anymore.

His eyes flicker with something almost like amusement, but I see the calculation in them too—the way his eyes study me as though I am a problem to be solved. A pet project that has overstayed its welcome. He tilts his head, considering me for a moment longer than usual.

"You look... unsettled, Azrael," he remarks, his voice laced with a hint of mockery. His lips curl upward in that familiar, arrogant smirk—the one that reminds me just how little I matter. He knows the game we're playing, and he's confident that I'll continue to follow the rules.

But Orcus is different now. His pulse in my hand quickens, the scythe's aura flaring slightly in response to my building anger. He senses it, and I know he's eager to bring it to life. But I hold him back.

"I refuse to be your soldier much longer, father," I say, forcing the words through clenched teeth. The irony tastes bitter, but it feels necessary to say it aloud, even if it means nothing in this place. I know the truth—it's not about what I want or what I say. It's about the power he holds over me, and how I'm bound by chains I cannot break.

His expression hardens. "You are mine to command," he replies the edge of finality in his voice. His tone leaves no room for argument. "And you will do as I say."

There it is—the truth that I already know. I'm nothing to him. Not his son. Not a being with desires or dreams. Just a tool to execute his will.

But this time, something inside me refuses to bend as easily as it used to. I grip Orcus harder, and though the scythe hums with its usual sinister energy, it feels like the only thing left I can truly control.

He senses it too.

Father's eyes narrow, sensing my resistance. For a moment, he looks almost pleased by it. "How amusing. The Reaper of Souls, challenging me," he muses, voice dripping with condescension. "But you forget, Azrael... you were never meant to be anything more than this."

His words slice through me, but I do not flinch. I've lived my entire existence beneath his shadow, played the role he carved for me. But there's something different now. Something I can't shake.

I turn my gaze from him, refusing to let him see how deeply his words cut. I am no longer just the obedient soldier, waiting for his next command. Not anymore.

But I know my place. I always will.

"You summoned me, father," I say flatly. "What is it you require?"

A flicker of something cold passes over his face before he gestures toward the shadows, dismissing me with a slight flick of his hand.

"Memetim," he says, dismissively, his voice cold and commanding, "report."

I exhale slowly, forcing the words out despite the tightness in my chest. The dust from my mortal form lingers in my throat, and I fight against the urge to cough. My grip tightens around Orcus, his pulse under my fingers steady and cold. I recount the situation—every detail, entailing the encounter with Memetim, and her cryptic mention of Fate, followed by her abrupt disappearance.

I try to keep my voice steady, but the tremor is there, the same one I can't control when I speak of Layla. The thought of her lingers like a shadow I can't shake, no matter how hard I try to bury it beneath duty.

As I finish, the room itself seems to shudder in response. Stones fall from the ceiling in an unsettling cascade, their echoes drowning out everything but my father's fury. I can feel it rising, thick and suffocating in the air, a power that churns within the very walls of the Underworld. My father's anger is almost a physical force.

"Exu!" He bellows, the roar rattling through my bones, nearly a blow in its own right. "Get me Exu—now!"

I wince, clenching my jaw to stifle any reaction. His voice vibrates through the air like a weapon, a reminder of how small I am beneath his gaze. The tremors of power emanating from him nearly crush me, but I stand tall, unwilling to bend before it.

Forcing my mind to focus, I meet his questioning stare as his anger looms. "Who is this *mortal*?" he demands, his tone thick with suspicion. "What is her connection to this?"

I pause for just a moment, the weight of his eyes on me heavy and unforgiving. "Her name is Layla Simmons." I force the words through a throat gone dry, my stomach twisting as I speak her name. "I haven't yet devised a complete plan, other than to watch her and wait."

Orcus shifts in my hands, his hum reverberating through my fingers, a quiet sneer in his voice as he murmurs, *Yes... Watch her... as if that's all you plan to do.*

The sharp edge of Orcus' words pierces through the haze of my thoughts. I ignore him, my eyes never leaving my father's face. He listens intently, a subtle shift in his posture signaling his next move.

Ever calculating a game to play, he closes his eyes for a moment, and the air shifts. I feel him reach out, his senses like a net, seeking. And in the depths of the Underworld, he finds what he's looking for.

Her presence.

It's subtle, but unmistakable. He can track her with ease, pluck her from the mortal realm as easily as I could snuff out a candle's flame. The thought of it twists something deep inside me, a familiar feeling I've never been able to escape. His power is absolute—unlike mine. I am nothing compared to him.

I grip Orcus tighter, trying to steady myself, but it does little to quell the unease that stirs in me. My father could hide her away, far beyond reach, even from me. And I know he would do it without hesitation if it suited him.

He opens his eyes slowly, an unreadable expression crossing his face. It's almost as if he's measuring the consequences of his next actions. "I sense her, Azrael," he murmurs, the words just a breath, but enough to send a jolt of panic through me. "I could take her now. Hide her away. Do you want that?" His gaze sharpens, knowing the truth that I've yet to admit to myself. "Or is there something more you're not telling me?"

I swallow hard, the truth sitting like a stone in my throat. His gaze bores into me, testing, and prodding. I know the answer, but I can't say it. I won't.

Instead, I take a deep breath, forcing my voice to stay calm, even as my nerves wreck me. "No, father. I don't want her hidden away." The words feel like a betrayal of everything I've ever been trained to do. But for Layla? For her, I would risk everything.

My father's expression tightens, his mouth a thin line as he considers my words, the tension in the room growing thick and suffocating.

"You want to protect her," he says, the tone low and dark. "A mortal. But why? What is it about her that has entangled you, Azrael?"

I hesitate, a momentary lapse in my composure. But I cannot lie—not to him. Not now. "She is... different," I begin, my voice softer than I intended. "And I will not stand by and let her be consumed by what's coming." There is no way to explain it. No words that will make him understand the pull she has on me, the way her existence shakes something deep within my bones.

The silence stretches between us like a chasm, and for a moment, I wonder if he'll see through the layers of lies I've built around this. If he will understand the depths of the truth I'm refusing to face.

But instead, he leans back on his throne, his gaze narrowing as he watches me. "You will do your duty, Azrael," he commands, the finality in his voice leaving no room for argument. "If you cannot find a way to tend to this mortal, then I will. And I will do so without hesitation. Do not forget your place."

His words feel like chains, pulling tighter around my chest. I stand still, my grip on Orcus tightening until my fingers begin to ache. This is the price of defiance—the weight of my father's expectations is more than any mortal soul could bear.

"She is... unprotected." His voice drops, and I can feel the heat of his fury simmering beneath the surface. He turns his cold, calculating gaze to Exu as the demon enters, barely holding his own in the face of my father's wrath. "Where is Vassago?"

Exu stumbles in his response, clearly unnerved. "We... we haven't seen him, sir. He last reported about eight months ago, and—"

"So," my father seethes, his voice rising in volume, "we have a mortal left open to all manner of supernatural threats, and you didn't think it is relevant enough to inform me?" His words slice through the air, sharp and punishing. The chamber itself seems to tremble in response to his rage.

"Incompetence," Orcus sneers in my mind, his voice laced with mocking disdain. "And we are the ones cleaning up the mess."

The weight of Orcus' words digs under my skin, but I can't afford to let my father see any crack in my composure. Still, my stomach twists with the familiar pang of jealousy that rises as he mentions Vassago's name—the favored Prince of Hell, my half-brother, the one who carries the status I've always been denied. Vassago, with his charming ease and the trust my father places in him.

I try to swallow it down. But Orcus' vibration in my hands, sharp as ever, doesn't help.

Careful, Azrael, Orcus murmurs, his voice like the crackling of smoldering coals. *You might bite off more than you can chew. But if you insist...*

The tension is unbearable, and I can feel the jealousy simmering beneath the surface, but I stand firm, refusing to let my father see the conflict that churns inside me.

His glare shifts toward me, his eyes like twin daggers, and the room stills in anticipation. I hold his gaze, my thoughts racing for a way to maintain control.

"You said Fate is involved?" he demands, his voice cold as ice, every word wrapped in suspicion.

I force myself to breathe evenly, keeping my tone steady despite the turmoil inside me. "Yes, sir. Memetim mentioned she was privy to some prophecy or insight. Something tied to Layla."

The words feel heavy in my mouth. Prophecy. Insight. The weight of those concepts hangs in the air like a storm cloud, ominous and suffocating.

My father's expression doesn't shift, but I feel the subtle shift in the air as he processes my words. His eyes narrow, and I know he's calculating something, something far beyond what I can comprehend.

"And this mortal—this Layla Simmons—what does she have to do with this prophecy?" he asks, his tone like a razor.

I open my mouth to speak, but Orcus cuts in with a sharp, biting laugh. "A mortal. An insignificant creature. But isn't that always the way? One mortal standing in the way of something far greater."

I push back against Orcus' words, ignoring the tension in my chest. "I'm still learning, sir. But she... she seems to be a key, whether she knows it or not." My voice remains even, though every word costs me. The weight of the truth presses down on me, but I can't afford to reveal too much.

My father watches me closely, his gaze piercing, as if he can sense my hesitation. The silence stretches between us, thick and uncomfortable.

"So, you intend to protect her, then?" he asks, his voice quiet, but the power in it doesn't lessen.

I don't answer immediately. The question hangs in the air like a challenge, one I'm reluctant to accept but know I must. I can feel Orcus' pulse in my hands, stronger now, like the heartbeat of something far more dangerous than I am.

"I will do what I must," I finally say, the words slipping from my lips before I can stop them. "But she's important. And I won't let her fall into the hands of someone like Memetim."

My father's lips twist into a faint, cruel smile. "You will do what you must, Azrael. But remember—your duty is not to mortals. It is to the balance. To me."

I meet his gaze, feeling the weight of his expectations pressing down on me like a mountain. I want to protest, to tell him that Layla is more than just a mortal—that she's worth more than this cold calculus of duty and balance. She's worth more to me. Just me.

Instead, I bow my head, a gesture of submission, though my mind is far from obedient.

"Of course, father," I reply, my voice steady, even if it rings hollow in my own ears.

My father stands slowly, towering over me as he observes the weight of my words. "See to it that you don't forget your place, Azrael," he says, his voice laced with a quiet warning. "This obsession with a mortal will not be tolerated."

The words are a threat. A promise. And I know what's coming next.

"Exu, find my son," he snaps, his voice colder than before. His fury is still boiling beneath the surface. "Bring me Tisiphone and her sisters. I need Tisiphone!"

Exu flinches at the command, his usual confidence shattered. "Y-Yes, sir," he stammers, not daring to meet my father's gaze as he retreats into the shadows of the chamber.

The command hangs in the air, heavy and suffocating. I can feel the weight of it pressing against my chest, my grip tightening around Orcus. The scythe hums in response, almost as if it too understands the gravity of what's to come. Tisiphone—the Furies, his chosen enforcers—will ensure that any failure is met with swift and brutal punishment. The room is thick with the anticipation of what's next, and I can feel the dark energies gathering.

He remains seated, the coldness in his posture radiating throughout the chamber. His eyes never leave me, though I know better than to meet his gaze directly. His eyes are like black pits, capable of swallowing everything in their path. Even my own fear.

"You have failed me once, Azrael," he says, his voice quiet but carrying an undercurrent of danger. "Do not make the same mistake again."

I stand at attention, my spine rigid, and force myself to keep my voice neutral. "I won't, father."

The words feel like a promise, though the weight of them settles heavily in my gut. There's a part of me that understands the consequences of failure. The part of me that is still bound by duty, by the expectations of what I am and who I am meant to serve. But then there's another part—one that doubts, one that resents how little I am regarded in this court of shadows. How quickly I can be cast aside.

His gaze never leaves me. "I trust you will do better this time," he says, the weight of his words like chains tightening around my chest. "Tisiphone and her sisters will deal with any failures. You will not fail, Azrael. Do I make myself clear?"

"Yes, sir," I reply, keeping my tone steady even though the pit in my stomach threatens to unravel me.

The room grows quieter, the tension palpable, as I await the arrival of Tisiphone and her sisters. The Furies are an ominous presence, known for their relentless pursuit of vengeance and unyielding cruelty. I cannot afford to falter now—not with Layla's life, not with my potential future hanging by a thread.

Orcus vibrates in my hands, his voice dripping with sardonic humor. *Playing Guardian, are we? How quaint.*

I don't answer him, my focus still locked on my father. His order is clear, and final. The weight of it presses down on me, suffocating. As I step back, ready to return to the mortal realm, the air shifts. The temperature drops as a cold wind sweeps through the chamber.

Tisiphone arrives with her sisters, and the change in atmosphere is immediate. Their presence is overwhelming, almost suffocating. The Furies. Their pale faces are gaunt, their eyes hollow and red, a testament to the vengeance they embody. Each step they take is accompanied by the sharp hiss of serpentine hair, twisting and slithering like living creatures. Their stench of blood and death clings to the air, and I resist the urge to recoil.

Tisiphone's voice cuts through the silence, high-pitched and almost musical, like a siren's call. "What do you need, father?"

She stands with a grin stretching across her face, her sisters mirroring her malicious smiles. Something is unsettling about how effortlessly they embody malice.

He casts a dark glance in their direction, a command to which they immediately respond. "Find Fate. She's due for a four-century punishment. I want her information extracted—everything she's shared with Memetim."

The words fall from his mouth like a sentence of doom, and the room seems to grow colder, darker with their implications. Tisiphone's grin widens, her sharp teeth glinting in the dim light. Without a word, she shifts into a bat, and her sisters follow suit, their forms dissolving into the shadows as they take flight.

Have I ever told you how fucking creepy those three truly are? Orcus hums through my mind.

The chamber is eerily quiet once they vanish, but before I can take another step, my father's voice cuts through the silence like a blade.

"Azrael," he calls, his tone low and final. I feel a chill run through me, a cold anticipation building in my chest. "Terminate Memetim if the opportunity arises."

The command hits me like a fist. There's no hesitation in his voice, no consideration. It's not a request—it's a directive.

I swallow, the taste of ashes in my mouth. My eyes flick to Orcus, and the scythe hums in my grip, sensing my turmoil. "Understood," I say, my voice steady, though the weight of the order gnaws at the edges of my resolve.

For a moment, there's only silence, the oppressive tension between us thick as smoke.

I turn and step into the shadows, the cold darkness of the Underworld enveloping me as I prepare to return to the mortal realm. The mission at hand is clear, but the weight of his command hangs heavy on me. I've never been one to question orders, but this feels different. There's something insidious about it—something I can't shake.

Memetim isn't the kind of enemy I want to face, but if the opportunity arises, I have to strike. There's no room for hesitation. Not in this world, not in the Underworld, and certainly not under my father's command.

As I cross the threshold and prepare to return to the mortal plane, Orcus speaks again, his voice a low growl within my mind.

Not everything is black and white, Azrael. But you will see it through.

I grip Orcus tighter, pushing away the nagging thoughts of doubt that threaten to cloud my focus. Layla's fate is tangled with Memetim's, and I will not let my father's wrath or Memetim's games drag her into the abyss.

With a single wave of his hand, the oppressive weight of the Underworld is replaced by the quiet stillness of the mortal realm. I blink, adjusting to the sharp contrast in the atmosphere, only to find myself standing in front of Layla's home.

Orcus hums in my grasp, his lingering laughter vibrating through my fingers. *Well,* he murmurs, his tone darkly amused, *looks like you'll get to play the hero after all.*

I ignore his taunt, my attention drawn to the house before me. Its small frame is unassuming, a fragile beacon of normalcy in a world teetering on chaos. But the darkness lingering around its edges betrays the illusion. Shadows seem to stretch unnaturally, pooling at the corners of the structure as if waiting to swallow it whole. I grip Orcus tighter, his fiery aura dimming as he adjusts to my unease.

The mission is far clearer now: protect Layla. It's a simple directive, but the cost... the cost weighs heavy on me. Every action I take here inches closer to defying my father's orders. Orcus remains silent for once, though I can feel his disapproval simmering beneath the surface, a quiet judgment waiting to strike.

I step forward, my boots crunching softly against the gravel path leading to her door. Each step feels like a commitment, a choice to walk a path that I know will pit me against forces far greater than I'm prepared to face. I reach for the door, pausing as my hand hovers over the worn wood.

"Whatever it takes," I mutter under my breath, though the words feel heavier than I intend. They linger in the cold night air, a silent vow. The mission isn't just about protecting Layla anymore. It's about proving to myself that not every order must be obeyed. Some things are worth betraying even the most absolute of commands.

And this time, for Layla, I'm willing to face the consequences.

Chapter Nine

Layla

Torn - Natalie Imbruglia

I stare at the wall, the faint glow of my bedside clock casting an anemic light across the room. The numbers blur as I try to process everything that just happened. How could anyone make sense of a nightmare like that? My chest tightens at the memory of the Angel of Death's razor-sharp grin, her claws poised to rip me apart. And then... him.

That ending felt like the worst kind of plot twist—a sharp left turn into chaos I never signed up for. Who even was that man from the dream? The one with the shoulder-length blond hair and a jawline that could double as a weapon. He looked as though he'd stepped out of some romance gothic novel, all elegance and barely restrained power. And those eyes—icy and unyielding, cutting through the dark like they could see straight into my soul.

Why did he look at me like that? Like I mattered, even as the world around us burned.

A traitorous flush creeps up my neck. I slap my hands over my face, desperate to banish the thoughts racing through my head. *Get a grip, Layla.* You're seriously losing it. First, a dream where death itself comes for me, and now I'm crushing on some imaginary blond swordsman? No, wait—scythe-wielding swordsman. Like that makes it better.

I sink back into my pillows, my pulse still erratic. The cool fabric does little to calm the heat coursing through me. Was it just adrenaline? Some kind of twisted survivor's high? It had to be. My mind is clearly trying to cope with everything by throwing in some tragically beautiful hero figure to distract me from the fact that I almost died in my sleep.

Right?

I roll over, staring at the ceiling now. The dim cracks in the plaster form a web of lines that I can't help but trace with my eyes, over and over again. No matter how much I try to rationalize it, the image of him won't leave my head.

The way he stood there, poised and ready, his scythe glowing with that ominous red light, like a warning and a promise all at once. He didn't look afraid of her. He didn't look afraid of anything.

But why was he there?

The nightmares are always mine. They belong to me—the endless looping visions of shadowy figures, claws reaching for my throat, the suffocating dread of being hunted. They're my nightly battle, my uninvited tormentors. But this time, someone else was there, standing between me and the darkness.

My hands fall from my face, and I press my palms against the mattress, grounding myself. *What the hell does this mean?*

Therapy. I definitely need extra therapy sessions. And maybe a sleep study or three. Hell, throw in some exorcisms while we're at it.

I glance at my clock on the nightstand, the screen dark and mocking. It reads 12:13 a.m. Maybe I should just get up and go for a run. Burn off whatever weird energy this nightmare left in my system. But my legs feel like jelly, and my chest is still tight, the echoes of her laughter and his warning glance etched into my nerves.

Who was he?

The question circles back, relentless. It's like a splinter lodged in my mind, refusing to dislodge no matter how much I try to ignore it.

And then another thought creeps in, colder and heavier than the last: What if he wasn't just part of the dream?

The thought drenches me, seeping through my mind and body until I'm suffocating in it, heat pooling low in my stomach. Arousal and confusion twist together, making it impossible to untangle one from the other. All I can think about is what my therapist once told me: *Our brains can't invent faces out of thin air. Every person in a dream is someone we've seen at least once in reality.*

So... who was he?

The question sends a shiver down my spine. It was just a dream. It had to be. *It was just a dream.*

I try to shake it off, swing my legs out of bed, and stomp toward the bathroom. My feet feel heavy, like they're weighed down by the lingering dread clinging to me. The overhead light flickers on with an obnoxious hum, harsh and unforgiving, as I lean over the sink and splash cold water on my face.

The chill bites at my skin, but it does little to wash away the tension knotting in my chest. *It was just a dream, Layla.* My grip tightens on the edge of the sink, knuckles white. My breath comes out in short, sharp bursts.

I just want to breathe easier.

I just *need* to breathe easier.

Just a stupid dream.

The words repeat in my head like a mantra, but they're hollow. I grab the hand towel hanging beside me and pat my face dry, avoiding the mirror as long as I can. But eventually, I lift my head, letting my reflection stare back at me.

And then I see it.

My breath catches in my throat.

Four long, angry scratches stretch across my chest, smeared with dried blood. The lines are raw, jagged, and too precise to be random. My mind reels, spinning in a hundred directions at once.

It was just a dream. *Wasn't it?*

I rip my shirt off, my hands trembling, and stare down at the marks, my pulse pounding in my ears. Did I do this to myself? My hands are steady enough now to trace the edges of the scratches, the sting confirming they're real.

The room suddenly feels too small, too suffocating. My heart races as I stagger back toward the bedroom. My bare feet scrape against the cool floor as I grab the blanket I'd thrown earlier.

It's shredded.

My stomach drops. The soft fabric is torn to ribbons, clawed apart with a ferocity that doesn't match anything I remember from the nightmare. The sight of it sends a fresh wave of panic washing over me.

This doesn't make sense. How could this happen? I had to have done this to myself, right? Sleepwalking? Some kind of freak accident? My mind throws every possible explanation at me, desperate to cling to something rational, something safe.

But none of it fits.

I sit on the edge of the bed, gripping the tattered blanket in one hand and pressing the other to my chest, feeling the rise and fall of my breaths, too fast and shallow.

This was just a dream.

But how the fuck did I get these claw marks? And how did the blanket get shredded?

I squeeze my eyes shut, trying to will the tears away. My hands shake, betraying the calm I'm trying so hard to fake.

The phantom sensation of claws raking against my skin sends another shiver down my spine.

I sit on the floor next to my bed, staring at the stupid purple shredded blanket in my hands. Could I have torn this blanket fighting nothing in my sleep?

Just then, a knock interrupts my spiraling thoughts and snaps me back to reality. I stand up quickly—too quickly—sending me through a dizzy spell. I fetch the shirt I had thrown on the bathroom floor and put it on while I quickly walk to the front door, forcing myself to breathe steadily. Carefully, I plan my steps so I do not trip and fall...

And die.

I shuffle to the door, still half in a daze, and pull it open to see Sadie standing there, a chaotic symphony of grocery bags balanced in both arms, her phone precariously perched in one hand, and a coffee cup clutched in the other.

"Bitch, you've been *sleeping*?" she accuses, arching a brow as if I've committed a cardinal sin.

I blink at her, too caught off guard to respond, as she maneuvers past me into the house with the grace of someone used to carrying their weight—and then some.

Did she call me? I rack my brain, glancing briefly at the end table where my phone usually sits, untouched and probably dead. Not that I care much for it. Phones supposedly cause all kinds of cancers, and I'd rather not play roulette with radiation.

Sadie doesn't wait for an answer. "Hungry?" she asks over her shoulder as she strides into the kitchen, dropping her phone onto the counter and the bags to the floor in a controlled crash. She takes a victorious sip of her coffee like she's just conquered Everest.

My stomach growls in response before I can form words, and she beams at me like she's won a prize. "Good," she says, already rummaging through the bags.

I watch with cautious optimism, only for my hopes to sink when I catch sight of her haul. She pulls out gummy worms and Sour Patch Kids from one bag, followed by a crinkling symphony of chips from another. The pièce de résistance? A Taco Bell bag crammed inside a grocery sack.

Sadie grins, holding up the fast-food bag like it's a trophy. "I put it in here so I'd have a free hand. Smart, right?" She taps her temple, smirking.

I can't help but laugh, even though there's a weight behind it. Sadie, ever the problem solver, always finding a way to force her joy into my world. Being my best friend hasn't been easy for her.

We used to explore life together—hiking, road trips, and impulsive plans that somehow always worked out. Now, our adventures have dwindled to her telling me stories of the outside world while I listen from my couch or bed, nodding along as if I can still picture it all. She stopped trying to drag me out of the house months ago, realizing it wasn't a battle she could win.

Instead, she shifted tactics, making the time to sit with me in my tiny bubble. She fills the silence with laughter and binge-worthy TV shows from before we were born, as if rewinding time could stitch together the pieces of my fractured self.

"Okay, let's feast," she declares, pulling out two tacos and a packet of hot sauce she proceeds to toss in my direction. It lands on the couch beside me. "And before you ask, yes, I got extra nachos. Don't say I never treat you."

I smile, small but genuine, because Sadie has a way of dragging me into the light, even when I'm clinging to the dark. "Thanks," I murmur, my voice quiet but sincere.

She flops onto the couch beside me, opening her bag with dramatic flair. "So," she says through a mouthful of taco, "what fresh hell did I miss today?"

I glance at the shredded blanket still bunched on the floor in my bedroom, the faint sting of the scratches on my chest a haunting reminder of tonight's bizarre events. I hesitate, not knowing how to even begin explaining.

"Nothing," I say instead, picking up the taco.

Sadie narrows her eyes at me, but she lets it slide—for now. She launches into a story about her coworker's latest drama, her voice filling the room like sunshine through a crack in the blinds.

And for a moment, I let it.

Life has changed so much, and so fast, that guilt sits heavy on my chest. Sadie doesn't deserve this—doesn't deserve the broken fragments of the person

I used to be. And yet, she's still here. Still standing by me, never judging, never throwing me away like a worn-out friendship bracelet.

Every girl deserves at least one best friend in her lifetime who feels like the feminine, non-romantic version of a soulmate. For me, that's Sadie Webb. She's my fucking soulmate.

"I had another nightmare," I mumble, my voice soft and barely audible as I get up to help her carry the bags to my room.

My room—the only place in the house where I feel somewhat safe. It's where Sadie has her own side of the bed, complete with her end table I refuse to touch. It's her space in my fortress, the one unspoken offering I can still give her after everything.

Once, I used to call this room my sanctuary. Now, it terrifies me to even think about the shadows that creep in, the ones that whisper that not even here is truly safe. Still, I let her in because she's the only person I can trust to exist in my fractured world.

Months ago, when I lost the person I used to be, Sadie didn't abandon me. She stayed. She's still here, relearning me, growing to love the jagged edges of who I am now.

She tosses the Taco Bell bag onto the middle of my bed, her carefree energy faltering as her eyes catch on the scene. Pillows strewn across the floor. The blanket—*that* stupid shredded purple blanket—balled up on the side of the bed like it is trying to hide its shame.

She looks at me, and I see it in her eyes: fear, empathy, worry. It all flashes across her face before she pulls me into a hug so warm and genuine, it feels like she's stitching me back together, thread by thread.

"Oh, Layla," she breathes, her voice tight with concern. "Is it the same one?"

I nod as she lets go, watching as she starts picking up the pillows and setting them back on the bed. Her movements are careful, and methodical, like she's trying to restore some semblance of normalcy to the chaos.

She doesn't pry, doesn't ask the questions she knows I don't have the strength to answer. She doesn't need to ask if I've talked about the nightmares with my therapist; she knows I haven't. Instead, she just listens, reassures me without a hint of condescension, and makes me feel like I can breathe again.

"Yes," I finally admit, my voice trembling. "But something was different this time."

My eyes flick to the blanket. Should I tell her? Should I even try to explain the shredded mess that doesn't make sense even to me? She's holding it now, turning it over in her hands, her expression tightening as she inspects it. I can see the fear creeping back in as she runs her fingers over the jagged tears.

I swallow hard, my throat dry. "I... I don't know what happened," I stammer. "I didn't..." My words trail off, useless. What can I even say?

Sadie spreads the blanket out on the bed, laying it flat so we can both see it. The rips are deep and uneven, clawed in random directions like some wild animal went berserk on it.

There's no way I could have done this. My nails are short, practically bitten down to the quick. My hands tremble just thinking about it.

We exchange a worried look, her wide eyes locking onto mine. "So what happened here, Layla?"

Her voice is steady, but I can hear the cracks forming underneath. I want to tell her. I want to tell her everything, but how do I explain something that doesn't even make sense in my own mind?

"It was just a dream," I whisper, more to myself than to her.

Her gaze doesn't waver. "Layla, this isn't just a dream," she says, holding up the blanket for emphasis. "This... this is something else. Are you okay? I mean, really okay?"

I shake my head, the tears threatening to spill over. "I don't know," I choke out. "I don't know what's happening to me."

Sadie sits down on the bed beside me, her presence grounding. "Hey," she says softly, placing a hand on my arm. "Whatever this is, we'll figure it out, okay? You're not alone in this. I'm here."

Her words settle over me like a balm, soothing the panic threatening to spiral out of control. I nod, letting myself believe her, if only for a moment.

But as I glance back at the shredded blanket, my stomach twists. It wasn't just a dream. I know that now. And the truth—the real truth—feels like it's clawing its way to the surface, just waiting to be set free.

Chapter Ten

Azrael

I Will Not Bow - Breaking Benjamin

Sadie doesn't notice me, of course. Mortals rarely do, not without a deliberate effort on my part. But Layla? She's different. I've seen the flickers of awareness in her eyes, the subtle way her body tenses, as though she senses something just beyond her understanding.

I watch her now, sitting on the edge of her bed, gesturing animatedly as she recounts her so-called dream. She describes me in vivid detail—my hair, my face, my aura of command. I should feel flattered, but her tone twists the narrative, painting me as some heroic figment of her imagination. A protector she doesn't realize is sitting just a few feet away.

Orcus shifts again, his presence dark and brooding. "You're the knight in shining armor, she says. Pity she doesn't know you're more blade than shield."

"She'll know soon enough," I whisper, more to myself than him. My gaze lingers on the shredded blanket, evidence that her dreams are no longer confined to her mind. This is worse than I thought.

Layla's voice dips lower as she recounts the ending of her nightmare, her cheeks flushing faintly as she stumbles over her words. *She remembers me.* The realization stirs something unexpected in my chest, but I push it aside.

Sadie, ever the skeptic, tilts her head, scrutinizing the jagged tears in the fabric. "This doesn't look like you did it yourself, Layla. Unless you've been hiding claws under those fingernails."

Layla forces a nervous laugh, brushing it off. But the tension in her shoulders betrays her unease.

I shift in my chair, leaning forward slightly. My presence in this room is both a comfort and a burden—she's safer because I'm here, yet she doesn't even know she's in danger. The irony is bitter.

"You're wasting time," Orcus mutters. "Tell her. End the charade. She doesn't have the luxury of ignorance anymore."

"She's not ready," I reply quietly, keeping my voice low. The words are as much for myself as they are for Orcus.

As the two girls continued their conversation, I let my gaze wander to the wounds on Layla's chest. The sight fuels a surge of protectiveness I can't entirely explain.

And I don't like it.

"Time's running out, Azrael," Orcus says, his voice a low growl in the back of my mind.

"I know." My tone hardens, my grip on him tightening. For now, I'll keep my distance, watching from the shadows. But the moment her safety demands it, I'll make myself known.

And she'll see just how real I am.

Orcus' hum grows low, almost a growl now, vibrating with barely contained irritation. "You don't understand, Azrael," he snaps, the words sharp as daggers. "You weren't trained for this. You're not supposed to care about her."

I rub my temple, pushing down the throbbing headache that's been building ever since I laid eyes on her. Layla. That name... it sticks to me like a shadow

I can't shake off. "I'm just supposed to watch her. Keep her safe. That's the mission," I mutter, though even I hear the uncertainty in my voice.

Orcus' vibration sharpens, a slight buzz of displeasure resonating against my legs where he lies across my lap. "Safe? You're not supposed to care about her safety, Azrael. You're supposed to leave. You have a job to do. You don't know what it's like to guard a mortal like her. You're not a Guardian Angel. You're a tool of death, not a damn caretaker. This... this isn't your place."

His words cut through me, stirring something deep in my chest, a resistance I can't explain. But the more I think about it, the more I feel this pull toward her. Layla... it's like something inside me is already attuned to her, vibrating with her every word, her every breath.

"I'm not doing this to be her fucking guardian, Orcus," I grumble, trying to convince myself more than him. "I'm just making sure Memetim doesn't come back to finish the job. I'm not... I'm not supposed to stay here."

Orcus vibrates with a low hiss, as though he can't decide whether to be disgusted or worried. "You're not supposed to stay, Azrael. But you *are* staying. Why? You don't even know her. You don't even know why you're here."

I clench my jaw, my eyes still locked on Layla from across the room. She's talking to Sadie, her voice tight, like she's holding onto some fragile thread of sanity. And then I see it—*that* fear in her eyes again. Fear of the unknown, of the dark corners of her world, the things she doesn't understand but senses just beneath the surface.

"I don't know why," I admit, the words spilling out of me before I can stop them. It's like something in me is clawing to get out, something that doesn't make sense. "But I *have* to protect her."

Orcus' hum grows deeper, like a rumbling storm waiting to break. "No, Azrael. This isn't your fight. You're not supposed to *feel* this. You've been assigned to *observe*, not to *feel*. You know the chaos it brings. The destruction. You *don't* want to be tied to her. You're not ready for what comes next."

The weight of his words hits me like a ton of bricks. I wasn't ready for this. I wasn't ready for the confusion, for the need to protect someone I barely know. But I can't ignore the overwhelming sense of responsibility, the way my pulse quickens whenever she's in danger, how my mind sharpens when I hear her voice.

"I don't have a choice," I say through clenched teeth, my hand tightening on the cold surface of Orcus. "I can't walk away from her now. Something's... something's wrong. I feel it."

"That's the problem," Orcus hisses, his voice seething with frustration. "You *shouldn't* feel anything. You were never meant to. This mission—this role—you have to stay detached, Azrael. You're not supposed to *care*. And if you start caring, you'll lose everything. The moment you let yourself get tangled up in her fate, you're sealing your own. This is not the way it's supposed to go."

I clench my jaw and stand, walking toward the window to distance myself from Orcus' angry buzz. The weight of his words hangs in the air like smoke, but it doesn't change the truth that's gnawing at me. The truth that keeps pulling me back to her, to Layla.

But Orcus isn't finished. His voice cuts through the silence, colder now, more insistent. "Think, Azrael. Think about what you're throwing away. You're not just her protector; you're her undoing if you stay too long. You're not meant to *play* hero. Let Vassago do his job. Give him time to return to his post. You're wasting your time here."

The words linger in my head, swirling around with a sharp edge. But something deep inside me rebels against them. I feel the tug of fate, the undeniable pull between Layla and me. No matter what Orcus says, no matter how much he tries to warn me, I know—this isn't just about a mission anymore.

"I'll make my own choice," I finally murmur, my voice steady even if my head is pounding. "I'm staying, Orcus. I'll protect her. I can't walk away."

For a moment, Orcus is silent. Then, with an almost mournful hum, he speaks again, though this time his tone is tinged with something like resignation. "You'll regret it, Azrael. You always do."

I turn my back to him, feeling the weight of his warning, but I don't care. This is my choice now. And I will protect her—no matter the cost.

Vassago is still alive. At least, I assume he is. If he wasn't, Layla would have another Guardian Angel watching over her. But if he's out there somewhere, how did he vanish without a trace? No Angel just disappears. They're far too powerful. A single thought, a blink of an eye, and they're gone, but they don't vanish without leaving something behind—*something*.

So how does a Guardian Angel go missing?

I stare at the space where I know Vassago should be. His absence doesn't just feel like a hole—it feels wrong, like something twisted has been allowed to fester and grow. I can't help but feel this... *presence*, something that's pulling me toward Layla in a way I don't fully understand. But why?

I want to keep my distance. I've been ordered to protect her temporarily—just until Vassago returns. That's what I told myself. But every moment I'm here, every glance at her terrified eyes, that sense of responsibility only grows stronger. It's like I was always meant to be here, whether Vassago ever returns or not.

But I can't stop wondering—*where is he*?

The deeper I think about it, the more questions pile up. Vassago should have been the one protecting her, but instead, I find myself tangled in this mess, stuck playing a role I wasn't trained for. It's confusing, frustrating, and goddamn *unsettling*.

And the biggest question gnaws at me the most: How does someone like Vassago—a Guardian Angel who is supposed to be untouchable, too powerful to be taken down by anything—just... disappear?

There's a hidden truth here. Something we're all missing.

But no matter how many times I ask myself that question, the answer eludes me, slipping through my fingers like smoke.

I can't help but feel it: the weight of the unknown. If Vassago is still alive, if he's out there somewhere, something is going on behind the scenes. And I'm about to find out exactly what that is—whether I'm ready or not.

Because Layla's not the only one being watched. And if I'm not careful, I may find myself caught up in something far bigger than I ever expected.

"Psst." The whisper cuts through the air, soft yet urgent. I turn to find a delicate figure beside Sadie, someone I hadn't noticed before. She's small, barely noticeable, but her presence commands attention. A young Guardian Angel, no older than a whisper in the wind.

Her long silver hair falls like strands of satin, almost glowing under the faint light, and her sharp eyes are filled with a quiet intensity that doesn't quite match her youthful appearance. She looks weary, drained, and there's something haunting about the quiet despair that lingers in her gaze.

"Have you received my messages about Vassago?" Her voice is light, almost melodic, but it carries a heaviness beneath the surface, a weight I can't ignore. "He has been missing for eight months now. Sadie visited Layla before the attack. Vassago was there. She visited her in the hospital, and he was gone. I've tried everything I can to protect them both, but nothing. You never came. Why are you here now?"

She pauses, and the flicker of worry on her face stabs through me, sharper than I expect. There's a vulnerability to her, a tremor in her voice that speaks of things unsaid. It's not uncommon for Angels to become close when their assignments are so intertwined, but this—this is something more. Something *urgent*.

"You never came," she repeats, the words laced with a kind of grief that tugs at something deep inside me.

I blankly stare, disoriented, processing her words. Her gaze never wavers, and it dawns on me—she's been alone. Alone, forced to protect both of them, knowing no one would come to help. That realization settles like ice in my chest. No backup, no support. She's been left to carry this burden, and the weight of it is now consuming her.

I open my mouth, struggling to find the right words. "We just found out Vassago is missing. No one ever reported it to Hades."

My voice softens, more than I intended. The truth is a hard thing to face, and I know the emotional toll it must have taken on her. I can see it now in the tightness around her eyes, the way she fights to hold it together. She's breaking.

"I did." Her voice is barely a whisper, and it cuts through the air like a blade. "I sent messenger doves... numerous times..." Her voice cracks, and I feel something snap inside me. There's no hiding it now—the strain of her words, the weight of her sacrifice.

Her eyes are wet now, her composure slipping as her hands tremble slightly, but it's not just fear or sadness that marks her. It's exhaustion. She's fading.

She's dying.

Sending messenger doves isn't just a task—it consumes an Angel's energy. It takes everything. And guarding two souls at once, *protecting* them—*protecting Layla and Sadie*—has drained her to the point of collapse. She is burning through her energy at an alarming rate, and she knows it. Her body is nearing its limit, and she's fighting to stay upright, to stay *present* just long enough to finish this task.

But I know, and she knows, that she's running on borrowed time.

"Why didn't you come sooner?" Her voice cracks, and I can feel her soul shaking under the weight of it. "Why did you wait?"

My heart tightens. *Why?* Why had I waited? And the bitter truth hits me. I wasn't *meant* to come. This wasn't my assignment. I wasn't supposed to be here.

But now, seeing her—*seeing* what this has cost her, the exhaustion that clings to her like a shroud—I realize I've been sent here for a reason. For her, for Layla, for everything that's gone wrong in this mess.

I step toward her, my presence larger than it has been, feeling the heaviness of this moment settle in the air between us. Her energy is fragile now, a faint shimmer of light struggling to keep itself from fading.

"You're not alone," I murmur softly, my voice grounding her in the weight of my words. I can't fix everything, but I can fix this.

Her gaze meets mine, still haunted, still tinged with desperation. "I'm... so tired." The words are a soft exhale, barely audible.

"I know," I say, my voice firm, like a promise. "Rest now. You've done enough."

And though I know her mission isn't finished—there's too much at stake for that—I can see that she's past the point of saving herself.

She'll burn out soon if she doesn't stop, but I'll be damned if I let her fade like this.

"Just hold on. I'll finish what you started," I say, the words settling between us.

I return to Orcus, whose usual cold indifference gives way to a rare hum of sympathy. His presence seems to shift slightly, vibrating with something unfamiliar. "Memetim," I whisper, though the name feels like a curse on my lips.

"She is here," the young Angel murmurs, her voice strained, her words laced with exhaustion. She points to Layla, her focus unwavering. "In her head. She won't leave. I've tried everything—sending my energy, pushing her away. But the moment I try, my strength fades faster. I can only send out what I have if something happens to Sadie. I can only do so much, Azrael." Her tears spill freely now, her sobs breaking through the calm facade she's clung to for so long.

I can feel the weight of her words settle in my chest. I know what it's like to feel like you're running on empty, fighting a battle that has no end. Angels are meant to be eternal protectors. They give their energy to their mortals, weaving their existence around them. And yet, here she is, fading, dying slowly from overextending herself in a task that was never meant to be hers alone.

Speechless, I stand there, unsure how to ease her suffering. The guilt weighs heavy, my own helplessness pressing on me. "I can send a new Angel to take your place if that is what you want? I am temporarily assigned to Layla. My mission is clear—I will deal with Memetim as soon as I can come into contact with her."

"No." She breathes the word, her voice cracking like the last thread of her strength. Her eyes, once filled with fire, now seem hollow, haunted. "I've been fighting her alone for months now. She tried to attack Sadie."

The young Angel turns, drawing her wings back with great care. I can't help but notice the damage—deep gashes mar her wings, feathers missing where they should be full and strong. The sight strikes me hard.

"I barely won," she whispers, her voice a thread of what it once was.

Memetim isn't just playing her usual games. She's relentless. Why is she targeting Layla? What is her endgame? The questions circle around in my mind, but I can't afford to dwell on them. Not right now. Not with this Angel standing in front of me, her energy flickering like a candle about to burn out.

Orcus hums softly, a strange vibration of sympathy emanating from him. I feel the air shift as his glowing form pulses a faint red aura around us. The change is subtle but unmistakable. Orcus, usually so indifferent, now offers something I've never seen from him—compassion.

"Take some of my energy." His voice is deep, but there's a gentleness to it. "It's not the right kind, but it will help you replenish."

I'm stunned. Orcus is *selfless*. I've never seen him act like this, never heard him offer anything without the expectation of something in return. Yet here he is, offering what little he can give to this Angel who has given so much.

The young Angel hesitates, glancing at Orcus with uncertainty before, with a soft breath, she draws in the energy he offers. Her eyes flutter closed as the warmth floods her body, her features relaxing for the first time since I saw her.

Relief washes over her, a quiet sigh escaping her lips. "Thank you, Orcus," she whispers, her voice filled with gratitude. "I greatly appreciate this." She bows her head, a gesture of respect, her wings shifting delicately behind her as she gathers herself.

The energy Orcus offers doesn't heal all her wounds—physical or emotional—but it is enough to give her a brief respite. And that, I realize, is all any of us can give right now. A moment's peace in the chaos that's engulfed us all.

I look down at Orcus, my thoughts tangled in what's just transpired. He's not just my weapon. Not just a tool for battle. There's something more to him, something deeper that I've never had to acknowledge until now.

I turn back to the young Angel, feeling the weight of my own role in all of this. My mission. Layla. Memetim. All of it, intertwined in ways I never anticipated.

But one thing is certain. This fight is far from over.

"I will send a message to Hades," I murmur, my mind already racing with the next steps. "I'll update him on the situation and see if any backup can be sent your way."

I give the young Angel a sympathetic grin, but my attention drifts back to Layla. She's laughing—genuinely laughing—with Sadie, her eyes bright and carefree. It's a moment I never thought I'd see, not after everything she's been through. The sound of her laughter fills the room, warm and unburdened.

A smile I would do *anything* for. A smile I will make sure never fades from her face.

I take a breath, feeling the weight of the vow forming inside me. I'll keep you safe, Layla. I'll make sure you never know pain again. No matter what it takes, no matter how deep the darkness goes, I will be the one to guard you.

Memetim will not stay in your head. Not while I'm here.

I'll get her out. I will *get her out*—no matter the cost.

Chapter Eleven

Azrael

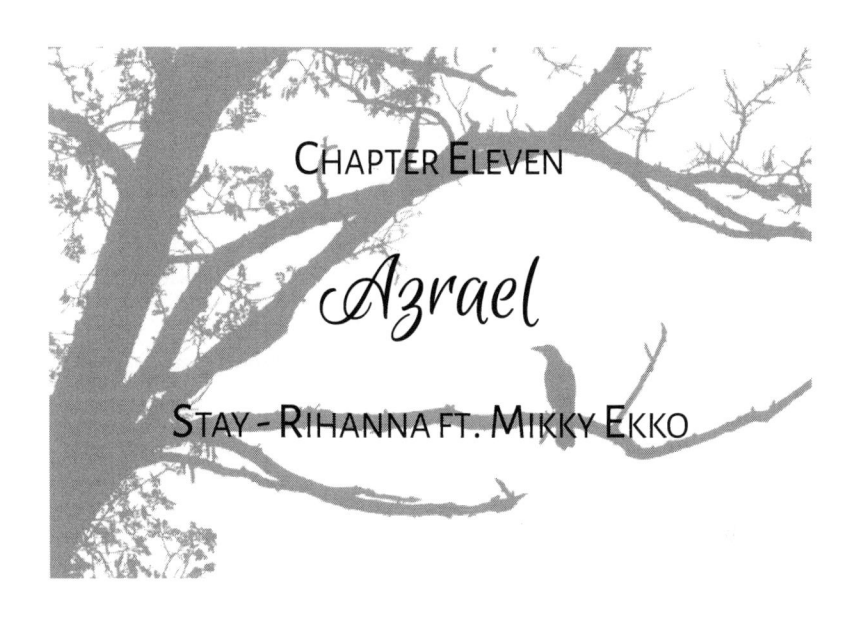

Stay - Rihanna ft. Mikky Ekko

I sit in the corner of Layla's room, watching Sadie sleep soundly on the other side of the room while Layla lies awake, her gaze fixed on the wall. Her eyes are unfocused, lost somewhere in her mind. I can't help but wonder what she's thinking about, what memories or fears are keeping her from closing her eyes and finding rest.

As much as I want to help her sleep, I understand why she resists. It's not just the lingering fear of Memetim that keeps her awake—it's her fear of what might happen if she gives in. She's vulnerable, and I am helpless. I can't dive into her mind and force Memetim out. I can barely muster the energy to protect her in her dreams, let alone fight the demon plaguing her.

If I exhaust myself now, I risk losing everything—my mission, my life. My mind flickers to the fear of failing her, but I push it down. Layla's safety is more important than my own fears or curiosity. I can't afford to falter. Not with Memetim lurking inside her, watching us both like a predator.

It's a standoff. Layla, determined to stay awake, resisting the sleep that would give her nightmares while I am sitting across the room, doing nothing but watching and waiting. Orcus lies across my lap, silent for now, but I can feel his presence, like a heavy weight that is somehow comforting, even in the stillness.

Orcus hums quietly, breaking the silence. His voice vibrates with impatience. "Coerce her into reading a book or something. I feel strange, like a stalker, just lying here watching her."

He's right. I feel it too—the discomfort of doing nothing. But Layla needs sleep. Mortals can't survive for long without it before the demons come, feasting on their minds and souls. If I don't act soon, Memetim could get to her, easily, and I won't be able to stop it. Not without risking everything.

I sigh, glancing at Orcus, whose energy pulses like a low hum under my hand. "Let me help you," he adds, the offer filled with a strange sense of urgency. "You always try to do it alone. I have plenty of energy to spare—take what you need. Unless, of course, you're too proud."

I hesitate, feeling the weight of his words. It's true. I've always tried to shoulder everything myself, refusing help when it's offered. But this isn't just about me anymore. It's about Layla.

With a reluctant sigh, I reach out and touch Orcus, feeling the surge of power flow through me, a connection that is both unsettling and strangely grounding. The bond between us is strong, a force that has been forged through countless battles. And now, it's what I need to protect Layla.

I stand up, my feet silent against the floor as I approach her side of the bed. The faint scent of vanilla drifts through the air, clinging to the warmth of her skin. It's a smell that's comforting, yet laced with an undercurrent of fear. Fear, her fear, wraps around me, pulling me in like a tide I can't resist. She's so scared, so exhausted. She's holding onto wakefulness, terrified of what might come if she sleeps.

I pause, leaning over her, the scent of vanilla growing stronger as I move closer to her ear. It's intoxicating, fucking overwhelming. I steal a brief breath, absorbing the scent as if it could fill the hollow space in my chest. The vanilla, the fear—they both mix in a way that makes my chest tighter, something deeper inside me waking to the intensity of it all.

I never wanted to feel this way. I never wanted to feel this sense of protection, this deep need to guard her at all costs. But here I am. And if I lose everything, if I'm torn apart for this mission, this is how I want to go—protecting her. My last breath, spent with the scent of vanilla and fear.

I hesitate for a moment, watching her chest rise and fall, her breathing shallow. I can't let her suffer like this anymore. I have to make her sleep. But how can I force her into the rest she so desperately needs without overstepping my place, without violating what little control she still has?

With a quiet resolve, I lean closer to her ear, my voice a soft whisper that only she can hear.

"Sleep, Layla," I murmur, "It's safe now. You're safe with me."

Her body tenses for a moment before relaxing, just a fraction. But it's enough. I can feel the shift, the moment when the tension in her body gives way to the peace she's been denying herself.

I glance back at Orcus, my grip tightening around the scythe's handle.

Layla, I will fucking protect you until the last fiber of my body fizzles out.

Layla, you are worth sleeping for all eternity in the Empty.

Layla—you are worth me losing everything.

I wish I could tell you this in person, where you could hear my words, where you wouldn't be afraid of me. But because of Memetim's hatred, you fear me. I'm the one who brings peace to the dying, holding their hands as they slip away, watching their Angels cry until they beg me to bring them to judgment.

Yet to you, I am the source of fear.

I will terminate Memetim if it is the last thing I do. I swear to you, Layla, even if we never meet properly, even if you never fully see me for who I am—I will wait. I will wait until you are old, your hair silvered by time and ready for your judgment day. And then, I'll hold your hand and tell you how you stole my love the moment I laid eyes on you.

I'm sorry you're terrified of me.

I'm sorry I can't make it easier for you.

A tear—a fucking tear—stings my eyes.

A Grim Reaper crying.

Who would have thought?

My hand hovers over her forehead, and I slip into her dreams. The stars speed past us, and her memories race alongside us until we reach the shoreline of a quiet beach.

I stand at the edge of her dreamscape, watching as Layla walks along the shore. The world around her is still, like a moment frozen in time. The waves kiss the sand softly, the golden light of a setting sun casting a warm glow over her. She's at peace here, in a way she's never been before. Her golden hair flows freely behind her, and her body—small but curvy, dressed in a simple bikini—moves with an easy grace. There's nothing but the quiet of the ocean and the distant call of birds in the sky.

I watch her from a distance, my presence unnoticed. She doesn't know I'm here, and maybe that's for the best. Maybe she needs this moment of peace, this fleeting illusion of a life free from fear, free from Memetim's haunting presence. I can't help but admire her, even from afar. In this world, she's untouchable. No one can hurt her here.

But I know better. The calm, the serenity, is fragile. It's only temporary, a momentary escape from the chaos lurking beneath the surface of her mind.

My feet barely leave an imprint in the soft sand as I move silently, drawn to her. I want to be closer, but I know I can't. Not yet. Not unless she needs me. My role here is to watch over her and protect her when the storm comes. I'm the watcher, the silent guardian, a presence in the shadows. If Memetim returns, I'll be ready. But for now, I'm nothing more than a quiet witness to her peace.

Her smile, the way her eyes sparkle as she looks out over the water—it's all so raw, so real. I ache to reach out, to tell her that I'm here. That I'll always be here. But this world is not mine to control. It's hers. I am simply an observer, a protector from afar.

For a split second, I let myself watch her, taking in the calmness of her figure as she moved along the shoreline. It's satisfying to see her this serene—no Memetim chasing her, no fear gnawing at her mind. It's a fleeting moment of peace, and I want to savor it, to lock it away for when everything inevitably turns chaotic again.

I memorize the way her hair catches the light, the way she walks, barefoot and carefree, like a woman who has never known terror. She's not fighting anything here—not even the shadows. It's like she's untouched by the darkness, and for a brief moment, I almost believe it. But I know better.

Orcus breaks the silence from his place on my finger as a ring, the faintest pulse of irritation coursing through me. "Why don't you go bump into her and introduce yourself instead of being a creep?"

I roll my eyes, already feeling the warmth of his energy flare through me. "Yeah, because that's what I need right now—more advice from a scythe."

With a sigh, I shift my form, pulling on the human guise I've long since perfected: barefoot, dressed in swim trunks. It feels odd—being human again, trying to blend in, trying to pretend I'm just another mortal with a passing interest in a beautiful stranger. But for some reason, my feet seem to move on their own, and before I know it, I'm standing just a few steps away from her.

Layla is crouched on the sand, carefully inspecting a pile of shells. Her fingers brush over each one, delicate and thoughtful. There's something about the way she handles them—like they might break if she's not careful, like they hold more than just their physical form. It's... comforting to watch her, this strange mortal whose existence pulls at something deep within me.

And yet, despite everything I know, despite the weight of my mission, I feel a rare warmth rising in me. It's a strange sensation—like the flicker of a dying ember before the fire starts to roar back to life.

I clear my throat, summoning every bit of courage I can muster, and approach her. "Hello," I manage, offering a smile that I hope doesn't come off too awkward.

She looks up, her gaze soft and curious. Her lips curl slightly, not in a full smile, but enough to show she's intrigued. "I've seen you before," she murmurs, her eyes scanning me, as if piecing together something I can't quite see.

I glance away, feeling the nerves rise in my chest. I reach behind my neck, brushing the tension out of my muscles. "Have you? I just saw you walking and thought I'd introduce myself." My voice comes out more uncertain than I'd like.

Orcus' voice cuts through my thoughts, sharp and exasperated. *Why don't you try not sounding like a complete fool?*

I wince, feeling the jolt of irritation shoot through me. It's hard enough to manage my own awkwardness, but Orcus doesn't know when to shut up. And it's not like I've had much practice in this area. Talking to mortals, especially women, has never been my strong suit. For all my experience in death, I've always been more comfortable with souls than with the living.

Still, I soldier on. My hand reaches out instinctively, a greeting I can't quite stop myself from offering. "My name is Azrael."

For a heartbeat, I wonder if I've made a mistake—if she'll walk away or worse, laugh at me for being so ridiculous. But she doesn't. Instead, she looks at my outstretched hand with quiet curiosity.

"Azrael," she repeats softly, like she's trying the name on for size, as if it's a secret she might share with herself later. "Nice to meet you, Azrael." Her voice is like a soft breeze, and the way she says my name... it makes my chest ache.

If Orcus had hands of his own, he would face-palm himself right now. Instead, I feel the shockwaves ripple through my fingers, his irritation pulsing through me. *Really?* He snaps, *That's your idea of an introduction?*

For a moment, we just stand there, the silence between us filled with so many unspoken things. But there's a shift—a small spark. I think, for the first time, she's not just seeing me as the strange figure in her dream, or the shadow that haunts her thoughts.

Layla doesn't seem to notice, though. She smiles, her gaze soft, and takes my hand. Her fingers are warm... real... mortal. For a moment, I forget everything around us—the beach, the tension, the mission. It's just the two of us.

"I'm Layla," she says, and I know—oh, I know. The way she says it makes something inside me tighten, and I can't tell if it's from the raw pull of her presence or from the fact that I can't shake the feeling that I'm already in too deep.

She flashes me a flirtatious smile, and in an instant, a swarm of butterflies takes flight in my stomach, crashing into every part of me. It's a sensation I never thought I'd experience—certainly not with someone like her. Layla Simmons, the woman who carries the weight of every small dream and big desire she's ever had.

She doesn't look afraid here. She's glowing, as if the world she's in right now is just for her—no shadows lurking, no Memetim clawing at her mind. It's as if, for once, she's entirely herself. And I—well, I'm just standing here, wondering how I've gotten so lucky.

She looks like the Layla who wanted to be a nurse to help others, the one who thought about becoming a first responder because saving lives meant something to her. She looks like the woman who once dreamed of having two children—because one just didn't seem fair, especially when she knows the loneliness of being an only child.

She looks like someone who's never known terror, and I wish so much I could let her stay in this version of herself forever.

I shake myself from the reverie as she shakes my hand, and I feel Orcus stop shocking me for just a moment, probably because I'm no longer completely embarrassing myself. But the damage is done. Her purposeful touch sends a current of something through me—a jolt I can't ignore. The feeling is immediate and intense, and I can feel it—a definite *tent* growing in my swim trunks.

Fuck.

Okay, way to keep it together, Azrael, I mutter to myself, desperate to find something to say to cover the awkward tension. "You're a lot shorter up close than from far away," I blurt out, immediately wishing I could pull the words back into my mouth.

I watch her face flicker with amusement, the edges of her lips curling upward in a knowing smile. *Oh, that's good,* Orcus says, his voice dripping with sarcasm. *Real smooth.*

Secondhand embarrassment burns through my ring finger as Orcus scolds me. *What is wrong with you?* His voice is sharp, but there's an almost amused edge to it now, like he's laughing at me, too.

I feel his energy flare as if he's trying to send a jolt of irritation through me for good measure, but it's weak this time—probably because he knows I deserve it.

But, Layla—Layla just stands there, her fingers still wrapped around mine, her eyes dancing with mischief. And despite my complete failure in making a graceful introduction, I can't help but feel like this moment is more than it seems.

She giggles, a sound so pure that I want to lose myself in it. I want to reach into her mind, to sift through the chaotic thoughts that float unguarded as she sleeps. Her subconscious mind is an open door, and I crave the unfiltered truth that lies behind it—her inner self, the doubts, the fears, and the desires she doesn't dare speak aloud. I want to know everything.

I stare down at her lips, pink and soft, so inviting. A hunger gnaws at me. I envision kissing her—just to taste her, to feel the warmth of her soul beneath my lips. To experience the purity of her being, the very essence of her that's been crushed under the weight of everything she's endured. She doesn't deserve the darkness inside her. She deserves light, peace, and protection.

I will give that to her, no matter the cost.

I'm her protector now, the one who swears to walk beside her until Judgment Day, holding her hand when the time comes. I will be there, no matter how long it takes. Her tiny, fragile soul deserves that.

Her toothy smile lights up her face, and the way her hair dances with the wind is almost mesmerizing. I see glimpses of her green eyes, so bright and alive, and it pulls me deeper into this world I shouldn't belong to. But here I am, standing in her dream, unable to resist.

"I've seen you before," she murmurs, so softly it's almost a breath against the breeze. Her voice, thick with sleep, makes my pulse quicken.

For a moment, I'm speechless. I don't know how to respond. Just being near her like this, even if it's only in her dreams, is enough. I wish more than anything I could hold her—touch her, feel her in this moment. But I can't. Not yet.

Can she accept me for what I am? For who I am? For what I do?

My true form...

"I recognize your face, I just don't know where," she continues, her words slow but sincere.

Another grin. A grin that disarms me completely. I can't think straight when she looks at me like that, when she speaks to me like that.

"Layla Simmons," I murmur, as if saying her name could somehow tether me to her. "Do you want to maybe splash in the water with me? Just forget everything... just for a little while?"

I am a ghost in her dream, a shadow of her subconscious—yet, she speaks to me like I'm real, like I'm something she wants in her life. For a brief moment, I let myself forget the weight of who I am. I'm not a Grim Reaper here, not the Prince of Death. In this moment, I'm just Azrael.

I am the protector of Layla Simmons. And she is safe, here. With me.

She's self-aware. She feels me, knows my presence even in this fragile world of dreams. She is safe here, because of me.

And I will make sure that the nightmares, the torment, the fear—those will never reach her again. Not as long as I'm here. I'm her Guardian Angel, and I swear to her that I will fight until my last breath to keep her safe.

I am not Death. Not right now. Right now, I am the one who will guard her, no matter the cost.

We run to the shore together, her giggles filling the air like music. If I had a heart, it would be beating for her. Instead, I feel this... pull. This need to protect her at all costs. I wish I could give her my heart to keep.

If I had one, I'd rip it out, and she'd keep it in a vase on her end table. She'd know that she owns me completely. That I'd die for her—die, and risk being lost forever in the Empty, with no hope of return.

The ocean waves crash at our feet as I scoop her up and, without a second thought, toss us both into the water. She shrieks with laughter, and I can't help but smile, my chest swelling with something I don't fully understand.

I can hear Orcus, faint in the back of my mind, his voice curling with annoyance. *You're playing, Azrael?* he scoffs. *Really?*

But he doesn't shock me this time.

Come on, Orcus, I mutter under my breath, as I hold Layla close in the water, our laughter mingling with the sound of the waves. *Don't ruin this for me.*

I wish I could stay like this forever. With her, free from the weight of the world, where it's just the two of us, dancing in the shallows and pretending like nothing else matters.

But the truth is, everything else does matter. And I can't stay here forever. Not in this dream.

When she wakes, I will go back to being Azrael—the Grim Reaper, the "Guardian Angel", the Prince of Death. But for now, I'm hers. And I'll protect her—no matter what.

It feels like hours pass, but in reality, it's probably just minutes. We're playing, splashing around like two mortal teenagers on spring break, caught up in an adrenaline rush I never thought I'd experience. The urge to kiss her, to touch her more intimately, grows with every passing second. Every time she brushes her hips against me or mindlessly grinds against my cock when I lift her up to throw us back into the water, I feel like I'm losing control.

No one else here. Just her, and me. And Orcus, who, if he had a mouth, would probably vomit by now.

But none of that matters. Not here. Not now.

I'm so wrapped up in the moment, in the feeling of her, that the obsession with her consumes me. I'm falling for her more deeply with every second that passes. Every playful splash, every fleeting touch, is a small piece of me falling further into the abyss of desire.

This mortal belongs to me.

The thought hits me with a force that sends pain lancing through my chest. Because I know the inevitable. Once my mission is over, once this is done, I will have to let her go. I will have to find a way to see her again. To spend time with her. To be near her.

The scent of vanilla that clings to her skin—it haunts me. A piece of me wants to lick it off her. To taste her, to savor her, and mark her as mine.

But then, the atmosphere shifts. The breeze stops. The waves die down. I feel it instantly—the change in the dream. The tension that prickles the air. I look at Layla, who's suddenly on alert, her gaze darting around.

"What's wrong?" I ask, my voice low and strained, already sensing the danger.

She stands up quickly, scanning the horizon. Then, without another word, she starts swimming for the shore.

"She's coming!" Layla shouts, her voice filled with panic.

My mind races. I know who she means. Memetim. I can feel her presence looming like a shadow on the horizon. My hand instinctively reaches for Layla, wanting to pull her into my arms and take her out of this place. But the dream is shifting too quickly. The distance between us grows as she swims toward the sand, and I can't let that happen. Not now.

I start running, my feet slapping the water, pushing through the waves. I need to get to her.

"That's risky," Orcus' voice cuts through my thoughts, sharp and biting.

I don't care. I need to get her out of here.

"What was that?" Layla screams as I catch up to her, clutching her tight, feeling the terror in her trembling body. Her fear makes my body burn with the need to protect her.

"I have to get her out of here," I growl, my voice strained, as I spot the sharks beginning to circle us. The water around us shifts and churns, the nightmare becoming more real by the second.

But I won't let her face this alone.

"I will protect you," I whisper, pulling her closer, trying to fight against the waves and the storm inside me that's rising.

Memetim's presence is growing, a dark cloud that looms closer, threatening to swallow us whole. Orcus' voice is urgent now, "Azrael, whatever you're going to do, you need to do it now."

My instincts scream at me to pull her out of this dream, to wake her up, but dread tightens in my chest. I know what will happen if I do. If I pull her from this place, she'll wake up in my arms, and I'm not ready for that. I'm not ready to face her. Not like this. Not when I still can't control the chaos inside me, the darkness that pulls at the edges of my thoughts.

"Azrael," Orcus hisses, the irritation in his voice clear. "This isn't about you."

I swallow hard, her pulse quickening beneath my hands. I feel her heartbeat against my body—rapid, frantic, terrified.

Orcus is right. This isn't about me. It's about Layla, and she needs to be safe.

I nod, gathering every last shred of resolve I have. My grip tightens around her, and with a final surge of energy, I pull us both from the nightmare, from Memetim's shadow.

I pull us out of *her* nightmare.

Chapter Twelve

Layla

Tear in My Heart - Twenty One Pilots

I shoot up in bed, heart pounding in my chest as I shove the man beside me away—*the same man I was just frolicking with on a beach in my dream.*

What the fuck is he doing here?

My body's in full panic mode, my chest tight as my brain scrambles to process the sight of him. Why the hell is he in my bed?

Sadie screams from across the room, her shrill voice breaking through my racing thoughts. "Who the fuck are you? How did you get in here, creep?"

The man's hands fly up in surrender, a strange calmness surrounding him like he knew this would happen. As if he's been here before. As if this is normal. "Wait! Just hear me out. It's not what you think!"

Sadie jumps out of bed, grabbing her shoes and tossing them at him with a quickness that would make most people flinch. He dodges each one effortlessly, not even blinking.

I want to get up. I want to run. But my limbs feel like they're made of lead. I can't even move.

I glance at my phone on the nightstand next to him—Sadie's phone is across the room, too far to reach in time. I need a plan. I need to get us out of here.

"Please," he says, his voice finally softening, like he's actually trying to *calm* us down. "Just hear me out."

Sadie's fingers are tightly gripping my arm, her nails digging into my skin as if trying to ground herself. The way she's shaking tells me she's just as terrified as I am, but she won't back down. I can tell.

"What the fuck is going on?" I hiss, my voice a mix of fear and anger. "Who are you?"

His eyes soften just a little, like he knows I'm not buying any of this, but he's not giving up. He leans forward slightly, his calm demeanor almost unnerving in the middle of this storm. "You're not going to believe me, but I'm not here to hurt you. I'm here to protect you."

"Protect me?" I snap, my voice breaking. "From who? You can't just waltz into my room and expect me to trust you. You—"

"I'm not asking you to trust me," he interrupts, his voice low and urgent. "But you have to understand—Memetim isn't going to stop until she gets what she wants. She's been after you for a long time."

Memetim. That name. The one I've been trying to avoid, trying to ignore like a bad dream I couldn't wake up from.

"I don't know who the hell you are, or why I'm supposed to care about what you're saying," I growl, even though my heart's racing, my pulse throbbing. "But you don't belong here. And you sure as hell don't belong in my bed."

His gaze sharpens for a moment, the soft look gone. "I didn't come here to hurt you. I'm not some creep who breaks into people's rooms. I'm here to protect you. From her."

My breath hitches. From *her*?

Sadie's still holding the lamp, still ready to swing it at his head at any second. "I don't know who you are, or why you think you're some kind of savior, but you need to get the hell out of here."

He doesn't flinch, doesn't move. "Layla," he says my name like it means something more. "I swear, I'm not here to harm you. But you're in danger, and I'm the only one who can keep you safe. Memetim's going to do everything in her power to get you you."

I stare at him, my head spinning. Why me? Why am I the one being targeted?

The panic is rising in my chest, but there's something in his voice, something that makes me pause. Like I should listen. Like, for a second, I should trust him.

Sadie is trembling beside me, her eyes wide with disbelief. "How the hell do we know you're not the one doing this to her?" she asks, voice thick with suspicion.

"I know it's hard to believe," he says, his tone soft but firm. "But I'm not your enemy."

"Then who the hell are you?" I whisper, too tired and too scared to shout. The world is spinning around me, and all I want is for this nightmare to end.

He looks at me, really looks at me, like he can see through all the fear and confusion that's building up inside me. "I'm Azrael. The Grim Reaper. And I'm here to protect you from the very thing that's been haunting your dreams."

Despite my racing pulse, something about him feels *familiar*. I glance at his perfectly chiseled jaw, the strange scythe-shaped birthmark on his forehead, and those striking blue eyes. It's unmistakable—Azrael, the man from my dreams.

As bizarre as this is, my waking life's already been full of shredded blankets and mysterious scratches. This feels... on par with that.

No.

This is a whole man—*Azrael*—appearing in my room, uninvited and unannounced. This isn't some wrecked property or scratches in the night. This is surreal. But I can't seem to stop myself from easing up, taking in the bizarre reality of him standing in my room.

I release my grip on Sadie, stepping forward cautiously, like he might disappear if I move too quickly. Memetim. I never told anyone her name. Not even Sadie. She doesn't know. And now... *he* knows.

107

Sadie reaches for me, her hands trembling but still full of defiance. "Layla, what are you doing?" She snaps, her voice raw with panic. "He's probably some tweaked-out creep who snuck in here! He could be dangerous!"

I raise my hand to calm her. I don't know how to explain it, but I have to ask. *How* does he know her name? How does he know *anything* about Memetim?

I turn to him, keeping my voice as steady as possible despite my rapidly pounding heart. "How do you know her name?"

He looks at me with a flicker of understanding in his eyes, as if my question isn't out of left field. "May I sit?" he asks politely, as if he hasn't just been lying next to me in bed a minute ago.

I nod numbly, unsure what else to do, and he lowers himself to the foot of the bed. He stays a respectful distance away—enough space that I can breathe, but not enough to be comfortable. He pats the edge of the bed, but I sink to the floor instead, needing the solid ground beneath me. I'm still too shaken to join him on the bed.

Sadie stays standing, arms crossed tightly, her glare fixed on Azrael, like she can will him to disappear. "This is going to sound so strange to you, but I can prove almost everything I say." His voice softens as he looks at me, eyes searching for the right words. "I know you're scared, but I'm not Memetim. She and I... we are separate entities. She is the Angel of Death. I am..." He pauses, a little hesitation in his words, "The Prince of Death. The Grim Reaper."

He lifts his hand and points to the heavy-looking ring on his finger. "And this," he says, "is Orcus, my weapon."

Before I can process his words fully, the ring shimmers, the air around it rippling like heat waves, and then I hear a voice. Deep, smooth, yet faintly mocking.

"Ah, mortals. How easily frightened." The ring's voice drips with condescension. "I assure you, if Azrael meant you harm, you'd already be in the ground."

Sadie stares at the ring like she's waiting for it to sprout legs and run off. She turns her gaze slowly from Orcus to Azrael, like she's trying to figure out if we're both hallucinating. "A talking ring? And we're supposed to just... believe this?"

Orcus huffs, sounding genuinely offended, his voice curling with theatrical disdain. "Believe? Oh, please. Why do mortals spend their lives believing in absurdities like Santa Claus and the Tooth Fairy? Why not add more?"

Sadie, ever the skeptic, doesn't miss a beat. "Right, and next you're going to tell us he's a vampire."

Azrael gestures to Orcus with a slight smirk, his tone almost playful. "No, just a weapon."

Sadie crosses her arms over her chest and scoffs. "What are we in, a *Lord of the Rings* knockoff? This is a load of shit." She starts walking toward her end table where her phone lies.

"Excuse me," Orcus interrupts, sounding almost wounded but undeniably theatrical. "I am no *mere* 'weapon.' I am an ancient being with thoughts, opinions, and oh—yes—*exquisite* distaste for unnecessary prattle."

Sadie freezes mid-step, glancing back at the ring like she's just realized it has a personality—one that apparently doesn't care for being underestimated. "Yeah, okay. This is nuts," she mutters.

Azrael lets out a quiet sigh, his eyes flicking over to me, a mix of understanding and something darker in his gaze. "I know this sounds insane. And I get it. You're scared. But if you listen, I can explain everything."

My heart is pounding in my chest, and my mind is racing, trying to make sense of everything. Azrael, the Grim Reaper, a talking weapon, Memetim. None of this makes sense. How can this even be real?

"I'm not here to hurt you," Azrael continues, his voice softening, but there's no mistaking the sincerity in it. "I'm here to protect you. And the sooner you understand that, the safer you'll be."

"You really believe this shit? He's some cracked-out ventriloquist who probably snuck in through a window." Sadie shakes her head and pulls out her phone, her fingers flying on the screen. "I'm calling the cops."

In a blink, before she could hit "call", he's standing right next to her, holding her phone out of her reach. Sadie freezes, her face draining of color. I see the shock in her eyes, the disbelief taking over.

"I said I can prove anything I say." Azrael's voice is calm, steady, the kind of calm that makes your skin prickle. He's not messing around.

Sadie's mouth opens and closes like she's about to argue, but no words come out.

"Sadie Webb," Azrael continues, his gaze unwavering, "age 24. Daughter of Liam Webb and Hunter Evans. Your father passed away from heart failure. I escorted him to Judgement, and he was granted one more life cycle. He refused flesh. He chose to watch over you from the Underworld, instead."

Sadie's mouth presses into a tight line as she glares at him, though I can see the flicker of unease in her eyes. She scoffs, "Google exists?" Her gaze swings to me for confirmation, like she's searching for some rational answer.

But Azrael's eyes darken, his voice cutting through the air. "When you were 14, you practically lived with Layla because your mother became an addict. She loved only one person—your father. Not even you."

Sadie's defiant glare falters, but she doesn't back down. "Everyone knows my mother was a mess," she snaps, trying to reclaim her bravado.

Orcus chuckles softly, his voice laced with mischief. "Oh, believe me, girl. There's far more hidden behind your pretty little mask than you let on. Secrets are our specialty, you see."

Azrael's gaze shifts to me, and I can see the regret in his eyes, but it doesn't stop him. "I know deep secrets you haven't even told Layla," he says, his voice heavy with the weight of what he's about to drop. "I know things you've kept hidden for years."

Sadie stares at him, challenging. "I doubt that," she retorts, her tone sharp, but her eyes betray her growing unease. "Go on, then."

Azrael doesn't flinch. He steps closer to Sadie, his voice low but piercing. "You never told Layla about Dash Madden, did you? Or how he paid for the abortion."

The words hang in the air, a sharp slice between us all. Sadie's face drains of color, and I can feel the atmosphere shift, crackling with the weight of truth being exposed.

She spins around, her eyes wide with panic, locking onto me. "It was before you guys were even seeing each other. Before you knew each other existed, I swear," she stammers, her voice shaking.

I should be angry. I should be screaming. But instead, there's a pit in my stomach, a sick feeling that I can't shake. For all these years, Sadie sat at the same table with us, and I had no idea. I didn't know she was ever pregnant by him—the very man who almost killed me.

I force myself to swallow the lump in my throat, trying to push the sting away. "I don't know what you're talking about," I say, offering her a smile, though it feels hollow. "It's fine, Sadie."

But it's not fine. Not at all. It's not fine because the truth between us, all these secrets, is eating at me. She's sacrificed so much being my friend, and yet here I am, feeling the weight of her hidden pain. Watching her fall apart over something she didn't want me to know is slowly destroying me.

She has always been selfless, always there for me when I needed her. And for that, I'm grateful. I should be angry, but all I feel is guilt. Guilt for not knowing. Guilt for not being the friend she deserved in this moment.

She's not selfish. She's never been selfish. And for that, I'm grateful. But this... this secret cuts deeper than I thought.

"Can we circle back to your dad being in hell?" I glare at Azrael, still uncertain whether any of this is real. The whole situation feels too surreal.

Azrael nervously runs his hands through his long blond hair, looking a little uncomfortable. "Hell doesn't exist. Nor does heaven." He pauses for just a second. "Heaven and hell are just folklores—convenient myths created by cult-leading author wannabes. Long story."

Sadie looks like she's about to explode. "I think you owe me a story time." Her voice cracks, still full of disbelief and distress.

Azrael looks at me, his eyes unwavering, those piercing blue eyes like they could see straight into my soul. It's unnerving, but I can't look away.

"We have only the Underworld, ruled by Hades. He didn't create mortals, he does protect them—more than he does his own realm. And when Hades retires..." Azrael pauses, eyes lingering on me. "Your Guardian Angel, my brother, and I are supposed to decide who will take his throne." He turns to Sadie, his expression softening, almost compassionate. "That's why I'm here."

Orcus hums lowly, a sound of approval vibrating through the air. "Yes, Hades is quite... particular about his pets. Mortals—humans as you call yourselves—are such curious creatures. So fragile, yet so obstinate."

Sadie scoffs, trying to keep the situation from spiraling. "So, Layla's Guardian Angel is just... a glorified babysitter, huh?"

I laugh bitterly. "What kind of angel ends up ruling the Underworld willingly?"

Azrael shrugs, unfazed, never breaking eye contact. "He is the best of the best. Angels, actually, are pure souls—like me." He tilts his head slightly, as if pondering something. "But the reason I'm here is partly because my brother has gone missing, and your angel, Song," He looks at Sadie now, "will have to watch over Layla while I report my findings."

Sadie blinks, surprised by the sudden shift. "My angel's name is Song?"

Azrael nods, his tone warm but firm. "Yes. She's one of our newer angels but damn good at what she does. Why do you think you were compelled to stay at the hospital for so long, eating the plates meant for Layla while she was unconscious, refusing to leave her side?" He leans forward slightly, his voice lowering. "Song was trying to protect both of you. She nearly killed herself in the process—risking termination, and you being reassigned a new angel. It would've messed with your mind, by the way."

Sadie's eyes narrow in disbelief. "You mean, she's been risking her life for us this whole time?"

Azrael doesn't flinch at her tone. Instead, he toys with the handle of the drawer beside him. I glance down at the rose toy tucked inside, feeling an uncomfortable shift in the air.

He winks, a little too knowingly, and I stiffen, trying to ignore the disquiet growing in my chest. "Song's been doing everything she can to protect you both. There's something more at play here—something I'm not yet ready to explain." His gaze drops, almost uncomfortably soft, as if he regrets something but refuses to share it.

For a moment, the weight of it all is almost too much. His words are too heavy, and everything feels like it's spiraling out of control.

Sadie folds her arms, eyeing Azrael with skepticism. "So what's your psychotic friend's issue with Layla, oh Mr. Prince of Death, sir?" she mocks, her voice dripping with sarcasm.

Azrael's fingers drop from the handle of the drawer, and his eyes darken, his voice barely above a whisper. "We don't know yet. My haunch is that The Fate told her something about Layla... something she didn't like. I was supposed to find her and bring her back for Judgment, but now with Vassago gone, I'm set to terminate her." His words hang in the air, filled with emotional pain.

My mind races. His brother—my Guardian Angel—is missing. What did I do so wrong to have Memetim after me?

Sadie snorts, unconvinced. "Great, so you're protecting Layla by lurking in her room?"

Orcus clicks his metaphorical tongue, somehow sounding exasperated. "Lurking? The Grim Reaper doesn't 'lurk.' He safeguards. There's a difference, child."

Azrael fights back a grin, glancing at Orcus with a knowing look before turning back to us. "I'm here to make sure Memetim doesn't take advantage of Layla's vulnerability. I won't always be around—only when you need me. I'll stay out of sight as much as possible."

Sadie's eyes narrow, her tone dripping with sarcasm. "How generous."

I glance up at Azrael. "Can anyone else see you?"

He nods. "In my mortal form, yes. Whoever I want to see my true form can see me as well."

Sadie's curiosity gets the best of her. "Can we see?"

Azrael glares at her. "No. Mortals have a hard time comprehending supernaturals. I want to protect Layla, not terrify her."

I bite my lip, suddenly feeling even more vulnerable. "Why only when I sleep does she come for me?"

"That's when you're most vulnerable," he replies. "Have you been experiencing memory loss? Or foggy thinking?"

Before I can respond, I take an instinctive step back as Azrael moves forward. Something in me bristles, and I remind myself that this isn't like the books where the girl falls for the 'mysterious' stranger who ends up being harmless. No. This is real. And I don't trust him.

His expression falters, as though he understands the unease coursing through me. He lowers his head, a gesture of understanding I'm not sure I want.

A low hiss interrupts the moment. Orcus speaks sharply, his tone carrying a weight of authority. "Enough of this mortal foolishness. We must go, Azrael. The longer we linger, the more angry Hades will be."

Azrael nods, his expression tense. "You two stay together. I will return soon." He looks at Sadie.

Orcus snickers again, almost gleeful. "And pray that when we meet again, you're in better spirits, child. I do detest the whining."

With that, Azrael vanishes in a swirl of fine dust, leaving behind a lingering, eerie silence.

Sadie and I exchange wide-eyed glances. Disbelief settles over us like a heavyweight, and for a moment, neither of us speaks.

The Grim Reaper was just in my room, holding me while I slept. Death, *himself*, was somehow protecting me.

Chapter Thirteen

Azrael

Run - Snow Patrol

I materialize in the Throne Room, kneeling before my father and the assembled court of Supernaturals. The room is vast, dark, and filled with an air of quiet authority that seems to make the very walls breathe.

"You told mortals about us?" Exu growls, his voice low and threatening. His eyes, glowing like embers, pierce through me with a mix of disbelief and anger.

I swallow, trying to steady my nerves. "Father, if I may explain... please?"

I need this to make sense, not just to them, but to myself. There's a selfish reason behind this, one I'm not sure I want to admit. I didn't want Layla to be terrified of me. Death. I didn't want her running from me, avoiding me because she thought I was some monster that would end her life. She already has enough to fear without worrying about me. If I can help her relax, if I can make her see that I'm not a threat—maybe, just maybe, she'll be able to live a normal life. Or, at least, as close to normal as any of us can.

"Explain," my father says, his voice cool, distant, and yet authoritative.

I rise, my hands gripping Orcus' handle tightly. The familiar weight of the weapon feels like an anchor in my grasp, steadying my thoughts. I take a deep breath before speaking.

"The girl, Layla, she fears Death to the point where she's terrified to live a normal life. She can't even function without constant anxiety. Without her Guardian Angel, she's a nervous wreck. She needs reassurance. I needed her to see that I'm not the one to be afraid of, that I'm here to help her. I needed her to relax, to trust me. But, father, Memetim is staying within her mind. She can't escape that. She can't escape the fear she's trapped in."

He remains silent, his gaze calculating. He waves a hand for me to continue, his patience thin but intact.

"Her companion, Sadie, has a new young angel named Song," I continue. "Song has worked hard, tirelessly, to protect both of them. But she's reaching the limit of her energy. She's near exhaustion. She needs to replenish before she's terminated. Orcus loaned her energy, but it's not the right kind, and it certainly wasn't enough." I kneel again, my head bowed, waiting for his judgment.

There's a long pause as he thinks, his eyes fixed on me, analyzing every word. He finally waves towards one of the other supernaturals, signaling for them to leave the room. Hopefully, they'll find a way to replenish Song's energy. The young angel had looked utterly drained when I left, barely able to stand on her own.

"We have word on what he Fate told Memetim," He says, exhaling a long, controlled breath. "You acting as an Angel for that being... might not be the best idea."

My head jerks up, instinctively forgetting my manners as I stand without permission. "But father—"

He raises a hand to silence me, his voice cutting through the room like a blade. "If you knew, you would understand. *You* are the reason Layla Simmons is in danger."

Confusion clouds my thoughts. "How could I be the reason? I've never even met her before. I only found her because of Memetim. I didn't even know she existed."

"You two are fated." Exu's voice is calm, as though this revelation should be as natural as breathing. "Memetim going after Layla pushed you to find her sooner than the two of you were meant to."

Fated? My stomach drops at the word, like a stone falling into an abyss. Fated. A concept I've heard of but never truly understood. The idea is that two souls are predestined to be together, bound by the threads of the universe itself. A soulmate. But that's not what we are. Not quite.

I can feel my nerves hammering in my chest. Layla is my fated mate? But... how?

The court watches in eerie silence as I try to process this, my thoughts a swirling mess. I have no soul to match hers. I can't be her soulmate. But a fated mate... a bond forced by the universe itself, pulling us together regardless of our wishes. Is that what she feels? Can she sense it, too? That strange pull, the weight of fate pressing us toward one another?

"Is she..." My voice falters my throat tight with the realization. "She's not fully mortal?"

My father's eyes narrow, though there's no malice in his gaze as Exu explains, "Fated mates are only possible if the mortal has a... tainted bloodline. Her mother, her grandmother, and perhaps even a great-great-grandmother, could have been supernatural in some way. The bloodline lingers, dormant for generations until it surfaces in the form of a mortal who is unknowingly bound to a supernatural."

The weight of this knowledge crashes down on me, and I feel suddenly unarmored. Layla is more than she seems. She's not just some fragile mortal I've come to protect. She has a heritage I didn't know about, a bloodline that links her to something beyond her understanding. Beyond mine.

"Female supernaturals sometimes choose to stay in the mortal realm to reproduce," Exu continues, his voice smooth and factual. "They create bloodlines that serve to strengthen the bloodlines of powerful supernatural males. And very rarely, these fated mates are discovered. You, Azrael, are one of the few males to be chosen by such a bloodline."

The realization is almost too much to bear. The universe has forced this upon us. Layla and I are tied together by fate, by bloodlines, by something far greater than either of us could ever have imagined. And I have no idea what that means for us. What it means for her.

"You two were never supposed to meet like this," Exu adds, his voice softer now. "But Memetim's interference has changed everything. Now, Layla's life is at risk."

I nod, though the weight of the truth feels unbearable. Layla isn't just some mortal. She's my fated mate, bound to me by forces beyond our control. And now, more than ever, I need to make sure she's safe.

I turn to face the court, my mind racing. "What do I do now?"

Father's eyes harden.

As I kneel once more, a cold shiver runs down my spine. I've never felt this helpless before.

The court watches in silence as I bow my head, my thoughts consumed by the woman I'm now bound to—whether I'm ready or not.

"Her mother is a succubus," My father says, his fingers lightly tracing the corner of his armrest, his gaze never leaving the throne room floor. He's indifferent as if this revelation doesn't shake him. As if nothing in the world could... As if he has secrets he doesn't want to share.

I stare at him, processing the information.

"She isn't partial, she's half," He continues, his voice like ice, "which is why Memetim can only attack her mentally, even though Layla herself doesn't appear to have supernatural energy. She doesn't appear to possess the powers of a true supernatural—none of which I can sense. To all, she appears mortal."

Mortal. I clench my jaw. I hate that word now. Mortal. A fragile, fleeting thing.

But she's not truly mortal, not in the way I had believed. Her bloodline—tainted by a succubus—runs through her, making her more than what she seems. It's why she's been so vulnerable, why Memetim can torment her without fear of reprisal. Why, despite everything...

"I can't protect her like this," I murmur, looking down at the floor. I search for that damn pebble, the one I've focused on for centuries. It's always the same pebble, always the same quiet anchor. If I can just focus on it, I won't have to face the truth of what I'm hearing. The truth of what I am not.

He releases a long, frustrated breath. "I ask that you stand down, Azrael, but I know your instincts. They won't allow you to reassign yourself, will they?"

"No," I mutter, the word a reluctant admission. "I can't."

I feel the weight of their stares, the pity they all have for me, like an invisible pressure pressing down on my chest. I don't want their pity. I don't want their sympathy. I don't want to feel weak in their eyes, especially not when I've been through centuries of torment, of serving as Death, of wielding a power they couldn't even begin to comprehend. I should be enough to protect her.

But I'm not.

I can't help the thoughts that come rushing in—like a torrent I can't stop.

Am I not enough to protect her?

The thought hits me harder than I expected. It claws at my insides, and for the first time in centuries, I feel something I've never felt before: powerless. It hurts. It's raw and jagged. I should be able to keep Layla safe. I am the Grim Reaper. One of the most powerful supernaturals in this room, and yet— *and yet*—I can't stop Memetim from creeping into her mind, can't shield her from the torment she's experiencing.

I want to rip out my imaginary soul for being so helpless.

I want to scream, but I can't. Not here. Not in front of them.

I take a slow, shuddering breath. I have to calm down, and regain control. I have to be the Reaper again.

"I can only protect her when she sleeps," I say, my voice barely above a whisper. "Memetim attacks her when she falls asleep, but I can't keep up. I don't have enough energy to maintain it."

It's the truth. The cold, hard truth. She needs more than what I can give her, and I don't know what else to do. I can't even keep her safe from a mental attack. How am I supposed to protect her from everything else this world will throw at her? How can I— *just me*—be enough for her?

I don't want their pity. I want to know if I can help her. I want to be the one she turns to, the one who stands between her and the darkness.

But the truth lingers like a heavy cloud. I can't do it alone. I'm not enough.

I hear the murmur of the court, their whispers drifting through the air. They look at me with pity— pity that I can't shake, pity that only makes me feel more hollow. I want to rip out my figurative heart and give it to her. I would give anything to have the power to make her safe, to be the hero she deserves, to be the one who can stand beside her without the looming shadow of death hanging over our heads.

"I'll find a way," I mutter under my breath. "I'll find a way to protect her."

I don't even know who I'm trying to convince.

I want more than this. More than being the Grim Reaper, than being Death. I want a future. I want the kind of life that I've never dared to imagine. I want her to see me as Azrael. Not just as the Reaper, but as the male who could be more.

I imagine a life with her—one where we can walk in the sunlight, away from the shadows of the underworld, where I can be the one who makes her laugh. I want to have picnics with her in the fields and watch the seasons change together. I want to be the one who teaches our future son how to hunt, who takes him to the woods and shows him the Underworld, the world I've come from. I want to scare off the boys who come calling on our future daughter and protect her from the dangers I know all too well.

I want to be enough for Layla.

Just me. Not Death. Just Azrael.

But I'm not enough.

Because she's my fated mate. She isn't fully mortal. Her bloodline—her heritage—has made her something more. And if I have any chance of truly protecting her, I need to accept that I will have to change, that I'll have to become more than I've ever been.

But the question gnaws at me, relentless:

Am I enough?

I look around at the court, waiting for them to tell me what to do. But no one speaks. No one dares. They all know I must figure this out on my own.

Layla is my fated. And I'm going to have to do whatever it takes to make sure she's safe.

"We can hire the Sandman!" I exclaim, the words slipping out before I can stop them. It's a desperate idea, but it's the only one that feels right.

Ashton, the Sandman, and I used to play together as children before the weight of our duties took over. He's one of the few I trust completely. He might be unconventional, but when it comes to protecting Layla, I'm willing to take any help I can get.

Exu and my father exchange a glance, their silent communication stretching across the room. They deliberate, weighing my offer, before Father speaks.

"It will come out of your pensions to hire him," he says, his tone almost detached. "And you're the one that needs to reach out to him."

I bite back my frustration. "Dad," I stumble over the word, "Father, please. I need to get back to Layla. Every second I am away puts her at risk. Every moment counts."

The thought of Layla being exposed to Memetim's torment while I'm away sends a cold shiver down my spine. She's so fragile in this world—so vulnerable, even with my protection. And Memetim... she's relentless.

I turn to Exu, my voice quiet but urgent. "Have you found Vassago yet?"

Exu's head drops. The silence between us grows heavy with the weight of his response. "Seeing as we haven't gotten a reassignment yet, he is still alive. Memetim has him somewhere, but we'll find him."

I nod, trying to cling to that sliver of hope. The knowledge that my brother is still alive, that he hasn't been lost to whatever terrible fate Memetim has planned for him, is a small comfort. But it's still not enough. Not enough to quell the anxiety building in my chest.

Vassago and I were closer than the rest of our siblings, closer in age and in spirit. We understood each other in ways others couldn't. The bond we shared was unspoken, a quiet understanding between two who had been through the darkness together. And now he's missing, held captive somewhere by Memetim's twisted will.

I pace, my mind racing, but I can't push past the rising tide of dread in my gut. If Vassago was taken, then all of us are at risk. I can't afford to let my guard down. Not now. Not while Layla is in danger.

Memetim's reach is far too powerful, her ability to twist minds and manipulate spirits unmatched. I need to act fast. I need to move before it's too late. But there's only so much I can do alone.

"I firmly believe the Sandman can help her," I mutter, more to myself than to anyone else in the room. The thought of reaching out to Ashton feels like a lifeline, something tangible in this sea of chaos. If anyone can help me with this, it's him.

His gaze never wavers from me. "Make the call, then. But remember, you answer for your actions. If this leads to further complications, they'll be on your head, Azrael."

I swallow hard, nodding. The pressure of the responsibility weighs down on me like a mountain, but I know what needs to be done. I can't fail Layla. Not now.

Turning towards the exit, I give one last glance back at my father and Exu. "I'll reach out to him. And once Vassago is found, I'll take care of everything."

With that, I leave the room, my mind spinning with a thousand thoughts—none of them comforting. Every moment I waste is another moment I'm not with Layla, and every second she spends in danger feels like a century.

I need to get to her. I need to protect her.

And I will. I will find a way.

Chapter Fourteen

Azrael

You Make My Dreams - Hall & Oates

I watch the girls from my quiet camouflage. Sadie says her goodbyes, her usual sass tempered with what I assume is worry for Layla, though she masks it well. Layla lingers by the door after Sadie leaves, methodically checking every window to ensure they're locked. Then, she slides the deadbolt on the front door with a finality that suggests she's not just locking out intruders but trying to fortify herself against something much worse.

Her house is small, intimate in a way that feels foreign to me. There's a sense of history in the clutter: mismatched picture frames on the walls, a quilt draped over the couch, a collection of books stacked precariously on the coffee table. It all feels so... human. A life lived without the weight of millennia pressing down on every decision.

She retreats to her bedroom, pausing just inside the doorway. Her eyes settle on the bed, then dart away like it's a trap she's not ready to face. I'm already seated in the corner, in what has somehow become my designated spot, observing her every move.

I haven't yet decided how much to tell her—if anything at all. Part of me aches to spill everything. To tell her who she is, who we are, what she means to me. To show her that she doesn't have to face this terror alone. That I would bear it all for her if she'd let me. But the other part, the logical part, knows the truth is a double-edged sword. If I stay, she might hate me for the life she'll be forced to live. And if I leave, I'll carry the weight of her absence like a millstone around my neck for the rest of eternity.

"Azrael," she snaps, her voice cutting through the stillness like a blade. "I can feel your fucking eyes *fucking me*." Her back is to me, her gaze fixed on the opposite wall. She's tense, bristling with irritation—or maybe fear. It's hard to tell with her. She lashes out as a defense mechanism, I've noticed.

I stifle a laugh. "Show yourself, asshole!" she demands, still glaring at the wall as though her words will summon me.

Her defiance is oddly endearing. With a sigh, I let the veil of invisibility drop, materializing in the corner in my mortal form. Jeans and an Avenged Sevenfold T-shirt. The T-shirt is a leftover from one of my outings to the mortal realm; it's comfortable, and for some reason, it makes me feel less intimidating.

"I'm right here," I say, my tone caught somewhere between exasperation and amusement. I could yell it back at her, match her fire with my own. The intrusive thought is tempting, but I push it down. She doesn't need more reasons to fear me.

She spins around, her eyes narrowing as she takes me in. "Cute shirt," she says dryly, crossing her arms. "What are you, a reaper by day, emo band fan by night?"

"Something like that," I reply, leaning back against the wall. "Though I prefer to think of myself as versatile."

She rolls her eyes but doesn't move closer. The tension between us is excruciating, a mix of wariness and unspoken questions. I can see the gears turning in her mind, trying to decide if she's safer with me here or if she'd be better off screaming at the top of her lungs to alert the neighbors. Not that it would do her any good.

"What do you want, Azrael?" she asks, her voice softer now, almost resigned.

The question hangs in the air, and for a moment, I don't have an answer. What *do* I want? To protect her? Yes. To leave her better than I found her? Of course. But if I'm honest with myself—and I rarely am—I want more than that. I want her to see me. Not the Grim Reaper, not the Prince of Death, but the male beneath the titles. The male who feels like he's drowning in the weight of his own existence.

But I can't tell her any of that. Not yet.

"I'm here to keep you safe," I say finally. It's the truth, but it's not the whole truth. "That's all."

Her expression softens, but only slightly. "You're really bad at making people feel safe, you know that?"

A ghost of a smile tugs at the corner of my lips. "Noted."

"We need ground rules." Layla places her hands on her hips and a spark of determination ignites in her eyes.

Her sudden shift to sassy confidence catches me off guard. It's...endearing. Enough to stir a distraction I'd rather not entertain. I lean my head against my hand, propping my elbow on the armrest, feigning nonchalance. "Yeah? Like what?" I ask, fighting back a grin.

She doesn't miss a beat, her glare hardening. "You don't watch me when I get dressed. You don't watch me when I shower. And you *definitely* don't join me when I'm using the bathroom." Her voice is sharp, laced with indignation, as if she's laying down the law for a misbehaving roommate instead of the Grim Reaper himself.

I let out a low chuckle and roll my eyes. "You do realize my brother, your Guardian Angel, probably never gave you personal space either, right?"

Her lips part in a sharp retort, but she hesitates. "I didn't even know I *had* a Guardian Angel," she shoots back, her arms crossing. "Much less that they existed until, oh, *five hours ago.*"

I glance at my watch and suppress another laugh. Mortal time is a strange, slippery thing. A blink of an eye in the Underworld feels like an hour here. "Point taken," I murmur, the corners of my mouth twitching as I smirk behind my free hand.

"Why is this so funny to you?" she snaps, her glare narrowing to daggers.

Her irritation only amuses me further, though I mask it with a faux serious expression. "Why don't you go to sleep, tiny mouse?" I say smoothly. "We'll discuss this later when you're not sleep-deprived."

Her cheeks flush with indignation. "*Fuck you.* It's not time to sleep." She turns back to her bed in a huff, tugging the blanket into place with unnecessary force. "And I don't want to wake up cuddling you again."

The corner of my mouth lifts into a full smirk now, unbidden. "You didn't like my cuddles?" I ask, lowering my hand and watching her from the corner of my eye.

She freezes, her fingers tightening on the pillow she just placed. "No," she mutters, her gaze fixed on the bed like it suddenly contains all the answers to her frustration.

I hum softly, unconvinced. "Hmm."

Her blush deepens as she spins back to face me. "Will you always be in that chair?" she demands, waving a hand toward my corner of the room. "So I won't end up yelling at the wall like a lunatic again?"

The faint pink in her cheeks betrays her embarrassment, though she tries to mask it with annoyance. I tilt my head, watching her for a beat too long before replying. "Would you prefer I sit closer?"

Her eyes widen slightly, but she recovers quickly, crossing her arms again in defiance. "No. Just...stay there."

"As you wish," I say, settling back into the chair with a lazy sprawl. It's a posture I've perfected, designed to disarm without betraying the sharp focus behind it. "Though I have to admit, it was kind of cute watching you yell at the wall."

Her jaw tightens, and for a moment, I think she might throw the pillow she's clutching. Instead, she mutters something under her breath and busies herself straightening the already neat bed.

I should let it go. I should let *her* go—at least for the day. But the way her shoulders tense, the way she's deliberately avoiding my gaze, draws me in like a moth to a flame. She's angry, sure, but it's not just anger. There's vulnerability beneath it, a fear she's trying desperately to hide. I want to ease it, to show her she doesn't have to face this alone.

But I also know that every second I linger here, I'm risking more than just her trust. I'm risking her future. And mine.

"You should sleep, Layla," I say softly, my tone losing its edge. "I'll be here if you need me."

Her shoulders relax just slightly, though she doesn't turn around. "That's what I'm afraid of," she murmurs, so quietly I almost miss it.

The words linger in the air, a soft accusation wrapped in uncertainty. I don't have a response, so I say nothing, letting the silence stretch between us.

For now, I'll take the corner seat and the ground rules. But something tells me this battle of wills is far from over.

"You're not allowed to sleep on Sadie's side of the bed," Layla declares, folding her arms as if her statement is law.

"I don't sleep. No worries there," I reply, my tone casual as I remove my hand from where it props up my chin, resting both hands on the armrests. This chair is becoming my tiny throne in her room, and I sit like I own it—because I do. At least for now.

She sits at the foot of the bed, directly across from me, curiosity flickering in her eyes. "You don't sleep?"

I shake my head once, a simple, silent confirmation.

"So...what do you do with all that time?" She tilts her head, genuine interest spilling into her voice. "You don't get bored?"

I smirk, a wry grin tugging at the corner of my mouth. "I'm a Grim Reaper. A soldier of the Underworld. There's always death. Always something to do."

Her brow furrows slightly, and I can see the gears turning in her precious mind. "So, since you're here...who's killing people out there?"

Ah, there it is. The age-old misconception. "My precious, tiny mouse," I start, my tone laced with mock endearment, "I don't kill mortals."

She blinks at me, clearly confused. "What?"

I roll my eyes, letting out a small huff of exasperation. "I *don't* kill mortals," I repeat, slower this time, as if speaking to a particularly dense child. "I stand beside them. I hold their hand when their time comes and guide them until they're ready to face Judgment."

She processes this, her lips parting slightly before she ventures another question. "So...who's doing it while you're here? Guiding them, I mean."

"Other Reapers and the Grim Hound, Cu-Sith."

Her nose scrunches slightly. "Grim Hound?" she echoes, skepticism dripping from her tone.

"Forget the folklore and myths you've read," I say with a wave of my hand, dismissing her preconceived notions entirely. "It's all lies. Stories warped and twisted over centuries, changing with every mortal tongue that tells them."

She quirks an eyebrow at me, her defiance sparking anew. "Enlighten me, then," she challenges, her lips curving into a gentle yet daring smile. "It's not like I'm going anywhere."

For a moment, I pause, caught between amusement and irritation. She's genuinely curious—or maybe she's just trying to annoy me into leaving. Either way, it's cute in its own stubborn, infuriating way. Little does she know, that scaring me off isn't an option. I'm not some mortal man who can be intimidated by a sharp tongue or a playful grin.

No, this dirty-blooded mortal woman—half-succubus, or whatever she is—does something far more dangerous. She tempts me. Her persistence, her fire, the way her smile lingers just a beat too long... It makes my mortal form react in ways I'd rather not acknowledge.

If my jeans feel tighter than they should, it's not my fault. Blame her smile. Or her stubbornness. Or the damned way her curiosity cuts through my armor, making me feel...mortal.

And yet, I don't move. Instead, I lean back in my chair, smirking like the predator she refuses to see me as. "Fine," I say, my voice dropping to a smooth, teasing drawl. "But if I'm going to 'enlighten' you, you'd better keep an open mind. Mortal misconceptions are surprisingly hard to undo."

Her grin widens, and she leans forward, her elbows resting on her knees as if she's settling in for a good story. "Try me."

And damn it, if that spark in her eyes doesn't make me want to tell her everything.

"Cu-Sith is a tool for a Grim Reaper, much like Orcus." I lift my hand and flash Orcus in his ring form, the dark gem catching the faint light of the room. "They help us resupply energy, guide souls, and enhance our powers as we progress over the centuries. They're more than just tools—they're extensions of us, amplifying what we can do. Cu-Sith is primarily used for children's souls. They're more likely to trust and follow him than someone like me."

Layla tilts her head, her expression a mix of curiosity and unease. "Do children's souls get stuck in the...'Underworld'?" She lifts her hands, adding sarcastic air quotes around the word.

I sigh, crossing my arms over my chest. "That's where things get more complicated. Yama, my brother, and my trainer, Exu, step in when it comes to those decisions. They assess the situation and bring their findings to the court. Ultimately, Exu makes the final decision."

Layla narrows her eyes, skeptical as ever. "So, you guys vote on holding kids hostage?"

"It's not like that," I retort, a hint of frustration slipping into my tone.

Her lips curl into a challenging smirk. "Then explain, because from where I'm sitting, you sound like a pretty shitty...whatever you are."

A laugh escapes me before I can stop it—loud, sharp, and genuine. "You really have a way with words, don't you?"

She crosses her arms, staring at me expectantly. She's not going to let this go.

I sigh, running a hand through my hair. "It depends on who they were in their past life and how many life cycles their soul has already had."

Layla's brows knit together in confusion. "How many life cycles are they allowed?"

My body tenses as her question lingers in the air. How do I tell her the truth without breaking her? Without breaking *me*? She only gets one. One life. One chance. Being a mortal mutt, her soul is destined for The Empty when her time comes. And when it does, I'll be the one to walk her there, holding her hand as I always have, even if it means I'll lose her forever.

We'll be separated until my own time for The Empty, if I even end up there at all.

I shouldn't tell her. Not yet. Not now.

She's not ready for that truth. Hell, I'm not ready to face it either.

So, I smile, masking the ache in my chest, and turn away under the guise of stretching my legs. "Let's just say it's complicated and leave it at that for now."

Layla watches me closely, her sharp eyes narrowing. She knows I'm holding something back, but she doesn't press. Not yet. Instead, she flops back onto the bed with a dramatic sigh. "You're impossible, you know that?"

"And you're nosy," I counter, glancing over my shoulder with a smirk. "We're a perfect match."

Her cheeks flush at that, but she rolls her eyes and mumbles something under her breath.

I can't help but grin as I face away, pretending to admire the decorations on the shelf behind me. My temporary secret feels heavier than usual, but for now, it's one I'll keep. Layla isn't ready for the full weight of what I carry—for what *she* carries.

And maybe, selfishly, I'm not ready to share the information about her life cycle.

"Typically seven," I reply, setting a crystal tiger back on her shelf. The figurine is perched so high I have to stretch slightly to place it back where it belongs.

When I turn around, Layla is staring at the tiger, her brow furrowed in thought. She's quiet—processing everything I've just dropped on her. I don't expect her to take it all in stride; it's a lot for anyone, let alone a mortal mutt living a mortal life. I wait, knowing another question is bound to follow.

Finally, she looks up at me. "What happens after the seventh life cycle ends?"

I hesitate for a beat before answering, "The Empty."

Her face scrunches up in confusion. "What's that?"

"Everlasting sleep," I say, leaning back and closing my eyes. I let my head loll dramatically, adding a fake snore for effect.

It earns me a brief glare, but her expression quickly softens into curiosity again. "Why is Memetim after me? What did I do to her?"

Ah, here we go. The question I've been dreading. How do I explain this without telling her too much? Without scaring her off? "She sees you as a threat," I say carefully. "She thinks you took something that belonged to her."

Layla's brow arches skeptically. "But why attack me? And where did my angel go? He's supposed to protect me, right?"

"For fuck's sake," I groan, pressing my fingers to my temple. "Are you writing a book or something? This is a lot of questions, tiny mouse."

Her eyes narrow, and I know I've hit a nerve. "You owe me after *rape-cuddling* me!"

The words hit like a slap, and I throw my hands up, waving them frantically in defense. "Whoa, whoa, whoa! You invited me—*invited me*—to do that and more in your mind. I was saving you!"

Her face flushes red, and she steps closer, her hands on her hips. "You *watched* me in my mind? Do you also watch me masturbate?" Her voice is sharp, accusatory, and laced with an undercurrent of embarrassment.

I feel the heat rise to my face instantly. "Wait—you masturbate?" I blurt out before I can think better of it. "You're too scared to toast a slice of bread without having a panic attack, but you'll go and jam fingers inside of yo—"

Her hand connects with my cheek before I can finish, the sharp sound of the slap echoing through the room.

It stings. Badly.

I turn back to face her, holding my cheek and let out a low, humorless chuckle. "Okay. Yeah, that's fair. I deserved that."

Her eyes are blazing, but there's something else there too—maybe regret, maybe amusement. She huffs and turns away, but I catch the faintest twitch of a smile as she sits back on the edge of her bed.

Well, at least she's feisty. If nothing else, it's one of the many reasons I can't seem to stay away.

Chapter Fifteen

Layla

Don't Let Me Down - Chainsmokers

The audacity of men is outrageous. The shit that spews out of their mouths is foul, and apparently, supernatural males are no different.

I'm still trying to wrap my head around the fact that beings from every nightmare and folklore actually exist. Vampires? Werewolves? Grim Reapers? I thought those were all just stories meant to keep kids from wandering into the woods. But no—those myths are apparently just heavily dramatized versions of reality. Azrael, for instance, is supposed to be the terrifying Grim Reaper. Instead, he's this tall, blond-haired, tanned demigod-looking guy who shows up in "mortal" form wearing band tees and jeans. Hardly what I'd imagined.

And yet, he's terrifying in his own way. The idea of him silently watching me all the time "for my protection" is unnerving, to say the least. The Angel of Death whispering in my head wasn't enough? Now I have to worry about *him* hanging around, too? A new fear was unlocked. Showers are officially canceled for the foreseeable future.

Honestly, I don't know a single woman who'd be okay with someone watching her shower—even if he looked like Azrael. Maybe it's sexy in a romance novel but in real life? It's absolutely horrifying.

Still, I can't deny that I feel safer with him here. As much as I hate to admit it, there's some comfort in knowing that he's always there, never sleeping, hyper-focused on protecting me. He's already saved me twice, and it's not like anyone else is stepping up to help.

In an attempt to break the tension—and because I feel guilty for being such a basket case—I offered to make him a sandwich earlier. He declined, of course, like he didn't need food or something. Instead, he had the audacity to ask me to go to the coffee shop down the road. My knee-jerk reaction was to say no, to crawl back into my comfort zone and stay there. But then I remembered that he literally saved my life. Twice. The least I can do is indulge him in something so simple. Baby steps, right?

But let me just say this: if he ever watches me shower —or if I *find out* he has watched me shower—I'm going to lose my mind. He might be invincible, but my rage isn't.

As for the rest of his nonsense, I still don't understand half of it. He mentioned something about Orcus being his scythe, his tool. But when he's in "mortal" form, there's no scythe in sight. He explained that Orcus changes form depending on where they are or what disguise he's using. So now I'm trying to wrap my head around the idea of a *sentient weapon*. Because apparently, that's normal in his world.

With a sigh, I look over at Azrael, who's lounging in my living room like he owns the place, flipping through one of my books. He doesn't read it—he just flips the pages as if pretending to be interested.

"Are we actually going to this coffee shop?" I ask, crossing my arms.

He glances up at me, a smirk playing on his lips. "That depends. Are you brave enough to step outside, or do I have to carry you again?"

I glare at him, which only seems to amuse him further. "I can walk just fine, thank you."

"Good," he says, standing up and stretching lazily. "Because I really need a decent cup of coffee. Mortal coffee is terrible, but it's better than nothing."

"You're such a diva," I mutter, grabbing my shoes.

He chuckles, following me to the door. "And you're such a delight, tiny mouse."

The nickname makes me bristle, but I ignore it. The least I can do is get through this outing without biting his head off. After all, he's my Grim Reaper. And for better or worse, I think I'm stuck with him.

Orcus talks. Sometimes too much, sometimes too little, and all of the time, it's sarcastic with brutal low blows. I've learned this firsthand. Today, he's taken the form of Azrael's cellphone, and apparently, that means his commentary is on overdrive.

Azrael lifts the phone to his ear as we approach the coffee counter. His voice is smooth, conversational, and even warm. "I'll take a s'mores iced coffee," he says to the barista, a polite smile tugging at his lips.

Then he turns to me, his piercing blue eyes locking onto mine. *Those eyes are going to be my downfall.*

"Do you want anything?" he asks like we're on some kind of casual coffee date. I try not to read too much into it.

"I'll take..." I hesitate, scanning the menu as though it holds the secrets to the universe. "A chocolate chip frappe and a pig in a blanket."

The barista, a heavyset guy with a bushy, unkempt beard, glances up from the register. "Do you want the pig heated?"

"Yes," Azrael answers before I can open my mouth. I give him a look—half-annoyed, half... something else I can't quite name. The way he takes charge without hesitation, without second-guessing, makes it hard to stay irritated. It's infuriating and attractive at the same time.

Stop it, Layla. I remind myself. *Attraction is dangerous territory.* My last relationship nearly killed me, and I'm not ready to go there again. Not even with Azrael. Especially not with Azrael. But I can't deny he's different. If he wanted to hurt me, he wouldn't have saved me. And he definitely wouldn't be leading me to a cozy booth in the corner of this coffee shop.

We sit down, and he sets Orcus—the phone—on the table with a sigh. "Okay, Orcus, I need you to shut up now so I can enjoy my coffee."

He takes a slow sip of his drink, his eyes fluttering closed in appreciation. For a moment, I wonder if he's exaggerating, but then he smiles—just a small, content curve of his lips—and sets the cup down.

"It tastes better when it's hot," he says, opening his eyes to look at me. "But Mississippi is hot. This body isn't built for this heat." He leans back in the booth, resting an arm across the top of the seat like he owns the place.

From his spot on the table, Orcus speaks up, his voice dry and distinctly unimpressed. "I told you to skip the s'mores flavor, boss. It's a sugar bomb for mortals who don't care about their arteries."

Azrael groans. "Orcus, for the love of everything sacred, can you not critique my coffee?"

"I'm just saying," Orcus continues, voice dripping with mockery. "You're supposed to be the Prince of Death, and here you are drinking dessert like a twelve-year-old on spring break."

Azrael shoots me a look like he's silently begging for backup. I shrug, taking a sip of my own frappe. "I mean, he's not wrong," I tease.

"Oh, great," Azrael mutters, throwing his hands up in mock defeat. "Now you're siding with the scythe."

"It's hard not to," I reply, grinning around the straw of my drink. "He's got a point."

"Of course I do," Orcus chimes in smugly. "I always do. She gets it."

Azrael picks up the phone, glaring at it. "If you don't shut up, I'll turn you into a spoon."

"You wouldn't dare," Orcus retorts. "How would you explain it when your spoon starts talking smack in a crowded café?"

Azrael sets the phone down with a huff and takes another sip of his coffee. I can't help but laugh, the sound bubbling out before I can stop it. For the first time in what feels like forever, I'm not overwhelmed by fear or anxiety. Just this strange, chaotic sense of normalcy with a Grim Reaper and his smart ass scythe.

"So," I say, leaning forward slightly, "does Orcus ever, I don't know, take a break?"

"Rarely," Azrael admits. "But when he does, it's because he's plotting something worse."

"True," Orcus interjects. "Speaking of, when are we taking her soul, boss?"

I freeze, choking on my drink. Azrael glares at Orcus, then turns to me, his expression softening. "Ignore him. He's kidding."

"I'm not kidding," Orcus counters. "But sure, let her think I am. Keeps things spicy."

Azrael rubs his temples, muttering something in a language I don't understand. I take another sip of my frappe, my earlier sense of comfort starting to waver. These two might be the death of me. Literally.

I wonder if every woman feels this way when they look at him like they're under some kind of spell. A glamour, maybe? But that's supposed to be vampires, right? Not Grim Reapers. And he's definitely not a vampire. Allegedly, he's a Grim Reaper. A very handsome, infuriatingly smug Grim Reaper.

"Isn't it hot in the Underworld?" I ask, trying to sound casual.

He rolls his piercing blue eyes, the corners of his mouth twitching like he's fighting back a grin. "Didn't we agree to stop putting so much faith in folklore?" He tilts his head, mockingly exasperated. "Yes, it's hot. But not 'should-be-hell-from-the-Bible' hot. We do have fans."

"Fans?" I repeat, confused.

He doesn't break eye contact as he takes another sip of his coffee. "Yes, fans. Big, round things that blow air. Maybe you've heard of them."

I tear a piece of bread off my pig in a blanket, mulling over his sarcasm. "Why not AC units? Like central air or something?"

Azrael chuckles, shaking his head like I've said something profoundly naïve. "You do realize that in some countries, AC units aren't a thing, right? Fans are enough, especially in places farther from the equator. It's called *perspective*, tiny mouse."

I squint at him, trying to decide if he's teasing me or being genuinely condescending. Probably both. "So... where *is* the Underworld?"

He leans back in his seat, glancing over his shoulder at the barista behind the counter. Then, lowering his voice, he leans in conspiratorially. "Wanna know a secret?"

"Sure," I say, taking a tentative bite of my snack.

He gestures with his cup toward the barista. "That guy? Purebred werewolf. Top-tier lineage. Guess you could call it a god damned pedigree."

I pause mid-bite, glancing at the barista, who's wiping down the counter. "That's mean," I mutter, trying to picture him transforming under the full moon. It's oddly difficult to imagine.

Azrael's sly grin widens. "What? It's true. Werewolves are the bottom tier of supernaturals. I can't tell you how many times we've had to clean up their messes during full moons. It's exhausting."

I gape at him, horrified by the casual cruelty of the statement. "Isn't that, like... supernatural racism or something? You can't just call them the bottom tier. I'm assuming they can't control what they are, right?"

Azrael blinks at me, his grin faltering for just a second before he smirks again, softer this time. "Wow, look at you. Defender of the downtrodden. It's adorable."

"I'm serious," I press, folding my arms. "That's so mean. You're supposed to be this noble Grim Reaper, guiding souls and saving people. But you're sitting here trash-talking werewolves like some kind of supernatural elitist."

Azrael sets his cup down with a quiet clink and laces his fingers together, leaning forward. "Listen, tiny mouse, it's not elitism. It's reality. Supernaturals have their strengths and weaknesses, and werewolves, well..." He shrugs. "Let's just say they're not known for their finesse."

"That doesn't make it okay to look down on them," I argue, my voice rising slightly. "Maybe they're clumsy or impulsive, but that doesn't mean they're less deserving of respect."

His grin returns, sharper now, and there's a glint of something in his eyes—amusement, maybe, or curiosity. "You're feisty when you're defending beings who aren't even here to hear it."

"It's called *decency*," I snap.

For a moment, he just looks at me, his expression unreadable. Then he laughs, a deep, rich sound that catches me off guard. "Decency. Right. Coming from the woman who just found out werewolves exist and is already lecturing me about respect. You're something else, tiny mouse."

I don't know if I should feel insulted or proud. Maybe both. Either way, I'm not backing down. "Someone has to keep you in check."

Azrael raises his coffee in a mock toast. "Good luck with that." He takes another sip, still grinning.

From the table, Orcus chimes in, his voice dripping with sarcasm. "This is adorable. Should I get you two matching shirts that say *Team Werewolf?*"

Azrael groans, pinching the bridge of his nose. "Orcus, not now."

But I can't help it—I laugh. For all his arrogance, Azrael is oddly endearing, and even his scythe-turned-phone has a strange charm. Maybe the Underworld isn't as terrifying as I thought. Or maybe I'm just starting to lose my mind.

"They can control it," Azrael says casually, leaning back in his chair as if this was the most obvious thing in the world. "They just don't care to try."

I raise an eyebrow. "That feels like a sweeping generalization."

He shrugs, scanning the room. "Watch this." He subtly gestures toward a woman seated in the corner of the coffee shop, typing on her laptop. "She's a vampire."

My eyes widen as I glance over at her. She's stunning—of course, she is. Her sleek, silvery-grey hair looks like something out of a magazine spread, perfectly styled to cascade just above her shoulders. Dangling bat earrings add a quirky charm to her minimalist makeup, and her poise is magnetic.

"Do you like vampires?" I ask, trying to sound neutral, but the edge in my voice betrays me.

Azrael chuckles, his grin annoyingly self-assured. "Fucking love them. They're hot."

I stiffen, jealousy simmering just beneath the surface. *Of course, he does.* The ridiculous thought comes unbidden, but I can't help it. She's gorgeous, otherworldly even, and I'm sitting here with toast crumbs on my lips, feeling like a soggy piece of bread next to caviar.

I turn back toward him, forcing nonchalance. "How can you even tell who's what?"

He taps his temple with two fingers. "I'm programmed, I guess you could say, with information. Comes with the territory. I can see how many days mortals have left before their death. Supernaturals? They have their own scent." He takes a slow sip of his iced coffee, drawing out the pause for dramatic effect. "I spent nearly 760 years training."

My jaw drops. "760 years?" I echo, stunned.

Azrael smirks, clearly enjoying my disbelief. "Oh, that's nothing." He sets his coffee down and leans forward slightly, locking eyes with me. "What's the year again? 2024?" He pauses, pretending to calculate on his fingers, the mockery in his gesture unmistakable. "Right. I'm 762 years old."

I stare at him, trying to process that number. "Seven hundred sixty-two," I repeat dumbly.

"Give or take a few months," he adds with a casual shrug. "I'm one of the youngest Grims, too."

"Youngest?" I manage, my mind still spinning. "You're basically ancient!"

From the table, Orcus' voice cuts through with perfect comedic timing. "Layla likes them with a foot in the grave."

I roll my eyes, groaning. "Shut up, Orcus."

Azrael chuckles again, clearly entertained by the banter. "Don't worry, tiny mouse. You're young enough to keep things interesting."

"Oh, great," I shoot back, crossing my arms. "I've officially been demoted to 'interesting.'"

He smirks, raising his cup in a mock toast. "Interesting is better than boring."

I can't help but roll my eyes again, though this time a reluctant smile tugs at my lips. The audacity of him—and Orcus—is maddening, but there's something about their dynamic that feels oddly comforting like they're in sync in a way I'll never quite understand.

Still, the knowledge of his age settles heavily in my chest. Seven hundred and sixty-two years. I try to imagine what that even means—how much he's seen, how many lives he's touched, and how insignificant my own must seem in comparison.

But instead of feeling small, I feel... drawn to him, magnetized by his presence... and that thought scares me more than anything else.

"Ready to go, Tiny Mouse?" Azrael's voice breaks through my thoughts, smooth but laced with a quiet urgency. "Take the rest with you. It's getting late, and I've got someone coming to meet you."

I glance up at him, watching as he gathers his trash, flicking a few crumbs into the bag before casually plucking Orcus off the table. The scythe slides into the pocket of his jeans like it's just another everyday item—except that it's not. Orcus is no simple object.

I quickly grab my things, but my mind drifts for a moment, unwilling to let go of the strange, contradictory feeling of safety I've begun to associate with

Azrael. It's absurd, really. He's a Grim Reaper—one of the most dangerous beings in the universe—but here, in this coffee shop, he's the only one I trust.

Azrael turns toward the trash near the exit, his movements smooth and easy, like he's done this a thousand times. Hesitantly, I follow him, my gaze shifting from the floor to the door and back again. The weight of every pair of eyes I might be attracting presses on my skin like an invisible hand, and for a moment, I feel exposed. *Why is it always so hard to just exist in public?*

As I take another step, Azrael suddenly holds his arm out to stop me.

I freeze. My stomach churns. He's stiff—tense, even. I glance up at his face. The playful expression that had been there moments ago is gone, replaced by something darker. Anger. Pure, simmering rage.

His lip curls slightly as a low, almost animalistic growl rumbles in his chest.

I follow his gaze. And then I see him.

Dash Madden.

The sight of him—standing casually at the coffee shop's entrance, grinning like he owns the world—makes my blood run cold.

He looks at Azrael, his eyes gleaming with some sort of twisted amusement. "Nice to see you finally moved on, Layla. Getting out of your house for once, huh?" Dash's laugh rings in my ears like nails on a chalkboard.

Why is he here? Why is *he* free?

What the hell is going on?

I feel a knot tighten in my chest as my mind races. The last time I saw Dash, he was trying to *kill* me. He nearly succeeded, and now, here he is—standing in the open, acting like nothing happened. As if he hadn't committed unforgivable acts. As if I hadn't just barely escaped with my life.

I step back, instinctively moving closer to Azrael. I want to say something, anything, but my throat feels dry, my voice stuck somewhere deep inside me. I glance up at Azrael, whose body has stiffened, his gaze locked onto Dash with unrelenting intensity. His fingers twitch like he's ready to reach for Orcus, ready to unleash whatever wrath is brewing in his veins.

But Azrael doesn't move.

"Why is he here?" I whisper, the question barely escaping my lips.

Azrael doesn't answer right away. His jaw tightens as he watches Dash, and I see the weight of a thousand unspoken words in his eyes.

Chapter Sixteen

Azrael

Kings Never Die - Eminem ft Gwen Stefani

Layla opened her mouth to say something else before I lifted my arm up further to shield her from Dash's view. The last thing I want is for that bastard to see her—let alone look at her face like he has any claim to it. He doesn't deserve to see her beauty ever again, and if I could, at this moment, I would cut that smile right off his smug face. He should be rotting in a cell somewhere for the shit he put her through.

"We're leaving," I said through gritted teeth, my voice low and firm, pushing Layla gently in the direction of the door. My fingers tightened around her, a silent reassurance she needed.

But Dash didn't move. Of course, he didn't. He stood there, half smirking, like the world owed him something. The kind of smile that made me want to put my fist through his teeth.

I let out a low growl, one that made the air between us thick with tension. He blinked, momentarily thrown off guard. Good. He needed to remember who he was dealing with.

I closed the space between us, my body pressing closer to Layla's, my protective instinct kicking in. "Keep your eyes forward," I said, my voice hard but calm. "Don't look at him. Don't speak to him."

I could feel her shuddering under my hand, the fragile remnants of her composure starting to break. She'd been doing so well—she'd been laughing, feeling like herself again—but one encounter with him, and I could see the cracks starting to form. I wasn't about to let her regress now, not when we were so close to getting her back on track.

I was just about to usher her out when I felt a shift in the air—someone else moving between Dash and me. The werewolf barista had stepped forward, towering over Dash with a fierce look in his eyes.

"Do we have a problem here?" the barista asked, his voice steady, pressing a finger into Dash's chest like it was an everyday occurrence.

Dash scoffed, a dismissive gesture I could feel radiating off him. "No problem here," he said, brushing the barista's hand away as if it were a pesky fly, then turning on his heel and heading toward the counter.

The audacity. The complete and utter lack of self-preservation.

I used this chance to scoot Layla out of the coffee shop and before I could get through the exit myself, I could hear Dash yelling at me, "You can't protect her, man. She's a basket case. She's broken."

I wanted to snap, to end him, to drag him into the street and make him regret every second of the past few months. But Layla was still with me, and I couldn't let her see me lose control like that. Not now. Not in front of her.

Instead, I took a deep breath and placed a hand on Layla's back, guiding her toward the door. I could feel her anxiety building, the way her body was trembling ever so slightly. I wanted to reassure her, but my mind was already racing. Dash was still out there, roaming free, and that made him a threat. I couldn't allow him to get close to her again.

I turned my gaze over my shoulder one last time to see Dash still at the counter, acting like nothing had happened, his posture arrogantly relaxed. He was too comfortable, too confident in his freedom, and it made my blood boil.

"Are you okay?" I asked quietly, my voice softer now, as I led Layla outside into the cooling air.

She didn't answer at first. I could feel the weight of her fear pressing down on her, and I hated it.

"Yeah," she muttered after a long pause, but I could hear the cracks in her voice, the tremor of uncertainty she was fighting to hide.

I stopped walking for a moment, turning to face her fully. "Don't let him get to you, Layla. You're stronger than this."

I could see the conflict in her eyes—she wanted to believe it, wanted to trust that things could be okay, but the damage had already been done. Dash's presence had chipped away at her, and it was going to take more than just words to pull her back together.

I gently cupped her face in my hand, forcing her to look at me. "He's not worth it. You're better than him, and I won't let him hurt you again."

She blinked a few times, and for a moment, I saw the flicker of heat in her eyes. That was the part of Layla I needed to see—strong, determined, and capable of fighting back.

But I wasn't going to leave her alone to fight her battles. Not when Dash was still a looming threat.

"Let's get out of here," I said, my voice firm again, as I wrapped my arm around her shoulders and began walking. "You don't need to worry about him anymore."

It wasn't a promise—it couldn't be. But I meant it all the same. Dash Madden had made the mistake of crossing paths with me, and now he would learn just how serious I was. He wouldn't hurt her again. Not as long as I drew breath.

And if he tried?

He wouldn't walk away the same.

She cried the entire walk back. Every step we took was heavy, each one sinking deeper into the pain she didn't deserve. Her sobs were quiet, but I could feel the weight of them pressing down on her fragile soul. I kept my grip on her hand, steadying her with gentle tugs, guiding her through the quiet streets like a beacon.

I wanted to fix this, wanted to erase the hurt that had crawled under her skin, but I couldn't. I couldn't make her forget what Dash had done, or how his presence had shattered what little peace she'd managed to grasp. But I *could* keep her safe. I could be the shield that she didn't know she needed, even if she wasn't ready to lean on me completely yet.

She hasn't left the bed since we got to her home. The tears have long since stopped, but the heaviness lingers. I'm on the floor beside her now, leaning against the bed so she can feel me, so she knows she's not alone in the silence. One of the promised boundaries was that I wasn't allowed to lay on Sadie's side of the bed, and though I've never been the type to linger on the floor, this time, it's different. I'm here for her. I don't want her to feel abandoned, even though it feels like that's all I can offer—my presence, but it's not *enough* to fix what's broken inside her.

I can't change the way she feels. I can't snap my fingers and take the weight of the world off her shoulders. What I *can* do is wait for her. I can stay, even if she doesn't ask. I want her to heal, to find herself again. To feel like Layla again. The sarcastic, sharp-tongued, fiery woman who could challenge me with nothing but a raised eyebrow and a well-placed insult.

Right now, she's not her. And that kills me more than I'd like to admit. I want her back—the Layla who would roll her eyes at me, who would banter with full confidence, the one who didn't seem so... fragile.

But she's not ready. And that's okay. I can wait.

"I'll be fine," she whispers, but I can hear the cracks in her voice. She doesn't believe it. She's saying it for me.

I'm not fooled.

"Layla, baby girl," I murmur, my voice soft but deliberate, trying to break the silence. "The dust bunnies down here are terrifying me. Any longer and I'll be forced to name them."

She doesn't answer, but I see her shoulders stiffen slightly, the tension in her back lessening. She's listening. Maybe she won't laugh, not yet, but the fact that she's still hearing me means something. Anything. And that's enough for now.

I stretch my legs out, crossing them at the ankles, trying to settle in for the long haul. I can't leave her. Not when she's like this. Not when she's a broken puzzle piece, unsure of where she fits. She can't see it, but I do. I can see the pieces of her that are still whole, the bits of her that *are* still Layla. They're buried right now, but they're still there. I just need her to realize it.

She shifts, pulling the covers tighter around her, curling into herself, but she doesn't push me away. She's too proud to admit she needs anyone, but I can tell she doesn't want to be alone.

My thoughts race ahead, wondering what more I can do to make her feel better, what words I could use to make her understand that she's not broken beyond repair. I want to tell her everything will be okay, but those words feel like a lie, like something I can't promise. The truth is, I can't change the world for her. I can't make the demons in her mind vanish. I can't stop her past from haunting her.

What I *can* do, what I've just now decided to do, is stay. And I will.

I've faced countless enemies, but none of them compare to the one standing in the way of her healing: her own fear. The fear that Memetim feeds off of. That's what keeps her broken. What keeps her scared. I can protect her from the physical threats. The monsters that lurk in the shadows. But I can't fight her own thoughts for her. That's something she has to do herself.

And yet, I don't know how to give her the strength she needs to face it. All I know is that I'm here. I'll always be here.

Another sigh escapes her lips, and I want to say something, anything, to break the silence.

"I'm not going anywhere, Layla." It's a promise, even if it's one I can't fully keep. But it's the best I can offer her for now.

She turns slightly, just enough so I can see the top of her head, the light strands falling messily over her face. She's exhausted, physically and emotionally, but I can feel the flicker of her spirit still there. Barely. But it's there.

"You're not alone," I murmur again, just in case she needs to hear it. "Not while I'm here."

I lean my head back against the bed, closing my eyes for a moment. All I want is for her to be okay. For her to believe in herself again. For her to look at me with those eyes that could challenge the very heavens themselves. I need her to fight back, to stand tall, to be the Layla I have started to know and love.

But until then, I'll wait. I'll wait as long as it takes. Because no matter how long it takes for her to heal, I'm not going anywhere.

Not ever.

She pulls the blanket tighter around her body as if it could shield her from the world.

"Can you even breathe under there?" I ask, my fingers absentmindedly fidgeting with the end table handle, brushing over the spot where her rose toy lies.

"Stop touching my stuff," she mumbles, her voice muffled by the blanket. I can feel the slight shift of annoyance in her words, but it's not enough to break through the thick wall she's built around herself.

"Talk to me." The words leave my mouth before I can stop them, but I'm desperate, wanting something—anything—from her. "Tell me what I can do to make you feel better."

Her silence is louder than anything she could say. It presses on me like the weight of a thousand broken promises. My hands are still shaking, not from fear, but from the helplessness that I can't seem to fight off.

"Don't shut me out," I whisper to the space between us. I don't expect an answer, but I still wish for one, more than I should. "I'm begging you, Layla… please don't shut me out."

But there's nothing. Just the soft, rhythmic sound of her breath, even and shallow beneath the weight of that damn blanket.

"I thought Guardian Angels were supposed to be quiet and hidden," she says, her voice barely above a whisper, heavy with the exhaustion of everything she's been through. "Just leave me alone."

I swallow the lump in my throat. Her words sting, but they're not meant to hurt me. She's hurting, and I'm just here, the constant reminder that I'm not enough to fix it.

But I won't walk away. Not now.

"She prays on your vulnerability, Layla," I say, my voice low, trying to keep the calm that's been slipping away with every moment I don't know how to help her. "And my friend will be here soon." My eyes flicker to the door, knowing what's coming. "I need you to get up, tiny mouse."

I stand, my feet dragging as I step around the bed, but the blanket is already a weight, one I can't seem to lift for her. I grab the edge of it, pulling it down gently, but firm enough to show I mean it.

"We'll fix this Dash issue when I get Memetim," I add, the urgency clear in my voice. I need her to move, to see beyond the fog that's clouded her thoughts.

But she doesn't move.

The Sandman is coming, and I need her awake, alert, and fighting. I need her to feel the urgency that I can't fully explain. The world is on the edge of chaos, and Memetim is waiting for her to break. She has to stay strong for herself.

She's not going to get away from me that easily. I pull harder on the blanket, forcing the warmth to leave her, forcing her to face what's coming.

"You don't get to hide from this." The words slip out, harsh, but I don't care. I won't let her fade into the shadows, not when I can keep her here, with me. I need her to understand that.

She flinches, and for the first time in what feels like forever, I see something like resistance in her eyes. It's not much, but it's a start. I'm not asking for her to snap back to who she was for me earlier, but I need to see the fight inside her. I need her to feel the power that's buried beneath her grief.

"Get up, Layla," I say again, quieter this time. "Please. We can't fix anything while you're lying there, waiting for it to go away. I need you with me."

There's a long, painful silence, but I don't let go. I'm not going anywhere. Not until she's standing, not until I see her *fighting*.

"Remember when you told me I'm not allowed to watch you masturbate?"

The words hang in the air between us, and for a moment, I think she's going to bury herself under the blanket again, retreating from whatever fragile progress we've made. But instead, she shoots up from the bed, her eyes burning with a mixture of anger and confusion.

I don't flinch.

I just need her up, moving, even if it's not the way I want it. If pushing her, even with my words, gets her to be present, gets her *out* of that heavy fog of grief and fear she's drowning in, then I'll say whatever it takes.

Even if it means pushing her away from me. If it means that I'll never kiss her or hold her in the way I've dreamed of, I'll make that sacrifice. I'll keep my distance if it keeps her safe.

If protecting you, Layla, means I have to lose everything—*you* being my everything—then so be it. Nothing else matters if you're not safe. Even if I have to stand alone against both realms, I will fight to make sure you remain untouched.

I'd carry this pain for you if I could. Fuck, I'd take it all on myself if I had the power. It tears me apart to see her like this, to know I can't fix it, can't just will her back to the person she used to be. I hate that I can't shield her from Memetim, from Dash, or from the storms within her own mind. All I feel is helplessness.

I stand on the outside of this storm, watching it consume her, and I can't reach her. I can't pull her out.

But I'm not giving up.

"I might have a confession," I say, stepping to the foot of her bed, my hands wrapped tightly around the shredded purple blanket she had clung to like a lifeline.

"Why do I have the feeling you're about to piss me off?" Her voice is tight, her hands clutching the sheets beneath her.

I don't answer immediately. The moment is too heavy, and I can't waste it with a joke or a half-formed thought. What I'm about to say isn't easy.

"What if I wasn't just watching? What if—"

The pillow hits me square in the chest, cutting off whatever I was going to say. It's soft but somehow solid in its weight, and I can't help but let out a laugh, the sound rough in my throat.

"Really?" I can't help but smirk, watching her face flush with irritation. "That's how you're going to handle this?"

She doesn't respond with words, but the fiery look in her eyes tells me everything.

But I can't stop myself.

"I wasn't going to hurt you, Layla." The words slip out before I can stop them, the sincerity of my voice even surprising me. "I never would. But if you need me to back off, I will."

There's a beat of silence, and then she huffs, her expression softening just slightly.

"Just stop saying things that make me want to strangle you, Azrael." She slumps back against the pillows, her hands finally releasing the sheets.

I nod, stepping away from the bed. It's not the confession I wanted, but it's enough. Just seeing her fight back, even in the smallest way, is enough to breathe life back into my chest. She's still in there.

She's not gone yet.

And I'll keep fighting for her—*every* part of her—until she's safe again.

"You jerked off to me!" She screams at me, her face flushed with a mix of embarrassment and outrage.

I hold my hands up in mock surrender, a grin spreading across my face. "No. Not exactly." I grab the pillow she threw at me, tossing it back toward her with a flick of my wrist. "As a Reaper, I don't have a dick. Thank you very much."

Her eyes widen in shock, the sorrow that's been clinging to her is fading for just this moment. "You don't have a dick?" she exclaims, her voice full of disbelief.

I can't help the smirk that tugs at my lips. "I do right now." I wink, a playful gleam lighting up my expression.

She groans, covering her face with her hands. "You're a pig. Disgusting." She falls backward onto the bed, sinking into the mattress with a frustrated sigh.

I chuckle, standing there for a moment, just watching her, letting the tension between us shift. "Can I get in the bed yet and just... not touch you? Or are we barely on half base?" I ask, my tone light, teasing, but underneath it all, there's a soft vulnerability. The truth is, I just want to be close to her again, to feel like we're back on some kind of level ground.

I drop the blanket at the foot of the bed, about to sit down when, almost like clockwork, the air shifts. There's a subtle pull of energy, and then—he's here.

"Hello, Ashton," Orcus hums in greeting, his voice as smooth and relaxed as always. He's always had a soft spot for the Sandman.

Ashton steps into the room with his usual calm smile, his presence oddly comforting. "Hello, Orcus," he replies, his voice low and warm, a stark contrast to the tension in the room.

The sudden change in dynamic pulls me back into myself, the weight of the situation shifting as Ashton's arrival fills the space.

I look at Layla, still lounging on her bed, her irritation slipping into curiosity. This is just another day in this strange, unpredictable world I've dragged her into.

Chapter Seventeen

Layla

Enter Sandman - Metallica

I don't even have time to process anything I've learned in the last 24 hours. My mind feels like it's being bombarded with one insane revelation after another, and I just can't keep up. Azrael. Orcus. Guardian Angels. Vampires. Werewolves. And now, to top it all off, this guy—the Sandman—standing next to the fucking Grim Reaper.

I can't even wrap my head around it.

If I thought Azrael was striking, this guy is something else entirely. He looks almost... ethereal. Nearly as handsome as Azrael, if that were even possible. And if this were some romance novel, this would be the part where I melt under the weight of his gaze, maybe throw caution to the wind, and let both of these supernatural men plow me into oblivion. I can practically hear the dramatic music building.

But no. No, this is my reality now. And none of this makes any fucking sense.

"Ashton," Orcus calls him like we're all just supposed to know who he is. And I guess in this world, maybe we are supposed to know who he is.

He's standing there, and I can barely focus on anything else but the way he looks. Pale—almost translucent—and his eyes, deep and shadowy, are speckled with what seems like stardust. It's like looking into the night sky itself. His hair is dark, tousled, and just long enough to brush against his shoulders, with a few silver strands scattered here and there like he's been touched by time itself.

He's wearing a midnight blue robe that shimmers as if it's made of fragments of the night sky, something alive, something otherworldly. The robe moves with an ethereal grace, and there's this pouch hanging from his waist, decorated with delicate silver chains that catch the light in a way that makes them look like they were crafted by the stars themselves. It's a kind of beauty that's almost too much to comprehend, too perfect for a world like mine.

He looks at me like I'm some kind of puzzle to be solved, or worse, an object to be assessed.

"Is this Layla Simmons?" he asks, and I swear to God, he's speaking like I'm not even here like I can't hear them. His voice is soft, but it carries a weight, a deep, reverberating tone that settles in the pit of my stomach, making everything in the room feel more alive than it should.

Azrael nods, his face impassive, though I can see the flicker of something dangerous in his eyes.

"Memetim is in her mind?" Ashton asks, his gaze shifting between Azrael and me. His hand dips into the pouch at his waist, fingers moving with a kind of practiced grace as he starts rummaging around, as though this is just another routine part of his day. I, on the other hand, feel like my world is crashing down in real-time.

"Yes," Azrael responds simply, sitting down on the foot of my bed.

I don't even think. I just react. Without even realizing it, I go to shove him off the bed with my foot, desperate to get some space between us. His grip on my ankle is immediate, his fingers curling around my foot with startling gentleness, completely at odds with his usual cold, distant demeanor. And then, before I can even process what's happening, he starts massaging my foot.

What the hell?

I try to pull away, but he doesn't let go. Instead, his gaze stays fixed on Ashton, unblinking, completely unperturbed by my discomfort.

"Azrael, what the hell are you—" I start to protest, but he doesn't seem to hear me. Or maybe he's just ignoring me, which, frankly, seems more likely. His focus is entirely on Ashton.

I huff, exasperated, but the moment the words leave my mouth, a strange calm settles over me. Something is soothing about the way he's rubbing my foot, even if it's the most bizarre thing that's ever happened to me. It's almost like he's grounding me, keeping me in the present, and for that, I can't bring myself to argue.

"You're... you're giving me a foot rub?" I ask, disbelief creeping into my voice.

His eyes flicker to mine for just a second, as if acknowledging the absurdity of the situation. "You seem tense," he says, his tone almost casual, as though foot massages are just part of his job description.

I can't decide if I want to laugh, scream, or pass out from the sheer weirdness of it all.

Meanwhile, Ashton is still rifling through his pouch, oblivious to the ridiculousness of the moment.

I glance at him again, trying to keep my thoughts from spiraling too far into panic. This is all happening too fast. I just wanted to get through the day without having my mind completely shattered, and now I'm faced with god knows how many supernatural creatures, each one more overwhelming than the last. And I'm supposed to be the strong one? The one who handles it?

A surge of frustration courses through me, but I push it down. Now isn't the time for a meltdown.

Instead, I swallow hard and look at Ashton, my voice coming out steadier than I expected. "What exactly do you do, Ashton? Besides... looking like a walking, talking celestial body?" I can't help but add the sarcasm, a weak attempt at grounding myself in this madness.

His lips quirk in the faintest of smiles as if he finds the question amusing. "I'm a messenger of sorts," he says, finally pulling something out of his pouch—a small, glowing vial that seems to hum with energy. "I deliver dreams. And sometimes, I help clean up the messes other beings leave behind."

I blink, staring at the vial as the glow dances between his fingers. My head spins.

"I... I'm sorry," I murmur, trying to make sense of the words. "Did you just say you deliver dreams?"

Azrael finally lets go of my foot, though I can still feel the warmth of his touch lingering, even as he turns his full attention to Ashton. There's a shift in the air, the kind of quiet tension that comes before something big is about to happen, something I can't yet comprehend.

Ashton doesn't answer me directly. Instead, he holds up the vial, turning it in the light. "Memetim is doing something to your mind, Layla," he says softly, his voice dropping in tone. "Something that's going to make everything a lot worse if we don't stop her soon."

I swallow thickly, the weight of his words settling in my chest like a rock. I want to ask him more, and demand answers, but something about the way he's speaking, the way he's looking at me, makes me feel like I'm barely holding onto the edge of something too big for me to grasp.

I suddenly feel very small.

Ashton reaches into his pouch once more, pulling out a delicate necklace. The pendant is circular, trapping a moonstone in its center, the stone glowing softly, almost like it's alive. The chain is thin and silver, the kind that would catch the light just right, even in the darkness.

He steps forward and fastens it around my neck with a swift, practiced motion. "Never take this off," he says, his voice firm, though there's a softness to it. "Even when you shower. It will not rust."

I sit there for a moment, stunned, as he retreats back to his spot. I reach up to feel the necklace, my fingers grazing over the cool, smooth surface of the moonstone. The weight of it feels strangely comforting, even though I'm still trying to understand why any of this is happening to me.

I glance at Azrael, a thought that I can't shake sliding into my mind. I wonder if Azrael would ever give me jewelry. The idea hits me out of nowhere, and I feel my stomach flip. Why the hell would I think about something like that now? Ew.

I pull my gaze away quickly, feeling the flush creep up my neck as I inspect the pendant again. On the back, there's an engraving—"Schutz." I frown, turning the necklace over between my fingers, trying to understand.

"What does this mean?" I ask, looking around for Ashton, who is already rummaging through his pouch again.

"Protection," he answers without looking up, his voice drifting over to me like it's just another piece of information. He then points at the moonstone. "That's the moonstone," he continues. "It balances emotions, enhances intuition, and soothes. It wards off nightmares."

He finally looks at me, his lips curving up into a smile. "No more bad dreams. Ever."

I'm still holding the necklace, staring at the moonstone, and something about the whole situation doesn't sit right with me. Ashton is talking like this is just another task, like he's handed out enchanted jewelry to people before. But for me? This is all new, and the weight of it—literally and figuratively—feels far too heavy.

"Thank you?" I murmur, more to myself than to anyone else, still processing everything he just said.

Azrael, quiet and stoic as always, watches me, his expression unreadable. But his eyes flicker with something I can't quite place. I want to ask him more, to demand answers, but before I can, Orcus' voice cuts through the air, as sarcastic as ever.

"Ashton is a male of little conversation," Orcus says, his words accompanied by a flicker of red that dances across Azrael's fingers, the light casting odd shadows over the room.

Ashton merely nods in agreement, his gaze dropping to the vial he's pulling out of his pouch. "Now, sleep," he commands, his voice gentle but insistent.

I freeze, every muscle in my body locking up at the sound of those words.

"Oh, fuck no!" I shout, leaping up from the bed and yanking my foot away from Azrael. "Every time I sleep, she nearly kills me!" My chest is tight, my breathing quickening as the memory of the nightmares floods my mind—the suffocating, terrifying visions of Memetim twisting through my dreams, trying to break me down. The feeling of being helpless, trapped in my own mind, with no escape.

I look desperately at Azrael, my gaze pleading, silently begging him to stop this madness.

He stands up slowly, his tall frame looming over me. The calm in his eyes isn't reassuring—it's almost too calm as if he's already prepared for whatever's about to happen next.

"Layla," Azrael says, his voice low and steady, "I know it's hard, but we need you to rest. Memetim is only growing stronger the longer you resist. You need to sleep in order to heal."

The way he says it—like it's that simple—makes my chest tighten even more. How can he stand there and talk like this is just another part of the plan? How can I trust them?

"Azrael, you don't understand—" I start, but Ashton steps forward, interrupting me with a soft shake of his head.

"You don't have a choice," he says, his voice gentle but firm. "Memetim will not stop until she has you, Layla. And the only way we can fight back is for you to rest, to be stronger. This is the only way."

His words, while soft, feel like a weight on my chest. The realization that they might be right settles in, but I still don't want to give in.

"You can't force me to sleep," I mutter, my voice shaky with a mix of fear and anger.

Azrael's eyes narrow slightly, and his hand reaches out, fingers brushing the back of my neck where the necklace Ashton gave me rests. The touch is surprisingly gentle, almost reassuring.

"We're not forcing you, Layla," he says quietly. "But you have to trust us."

Trust. The word hangs in the air between us, and I wonder if I can. Can I really trust him? Trust them all?

I feel the cool weight of the moonstone against my skin, and for a moment, it almost feels like it's calling to me, like it wants me to close my eyes, to let go. But I'm terrified—terrified of what will happen if I do.

"Please," Azrael murmurs, his voice barely above a whisper. "For your own sake."

I stare at him for a long moment, feeling the pull of exhaustion creeping in despite myself. My body is screaming at me to rest, but my mind is locked in a battle of its own.

Finally, I take a shaky breath, my resolve crumbling just a little. "Fine," I say, my voice barely audible. "But if anything happens, I swear to—"

Azrael cuts me off with a soft look, his eyes deep pools of concern. "Nothing will happen, Layla. We're here. We'll protect you."

And for the first time, just maybe, I believe him.

Azrael turns his gaze toward Ashton, his expression serious. "The Underworld hired him to protect you and get Memetim out of your head, but to do this, you have to sleep so we can get her out."

Ashton doesn't say anything in response, just a brief nod, before walking toward me. I try to hold onto the last shred of control, but it's slipping, the weight of exhaustion too much to fight. I feel the anxiety shift beneath my feet, and before I know it, Ashton is sprinkling something cool over my eyes. It doesn't hurt. In fact, it feels strangely soothing, like the gentle pressure of a thousand tiny fingertips, massaging away the tension in my body.

A tingling sensation pulses through my eyelids, and despite my resistance, they begin to grow heavier.

Heavier.

Heavier...

The chaos that's been consuming me—the fear, the anxiety, the constant whirlwind of thoughts and memories—begins to fade. I can feel the panic draining out of me, slowly, almost like it's being pulled away by invisible threads. The shrieking terror that has lived in my mind for days, no—fucking months, begins to quiet as if someone has turned down the volume on a radio, fading to a dull murmur.

I no longer hear Memetim's whispers, the cruel laughter that's plagued me for so long. Instead, I hear something soft, gentle, a peaceful sound that wraps around me like a warm blanket.

The sound of waves.

A calm, steady rhythm. Waves crashing softly against the shore.

I open my eyes, but this isn't like my usual beach dreams. This place is different. More real. The air smells saltier, and fresher. I'm standing on a golden shoreline, the sand beneath my feet warm and inviting, the sky painted in hues of soft pinks and oranges as the sun begins to rise.

And there, standing just beyond the water's edge, is Ashton. He looks ethereal, almost translucent in the growing light. His gaze is calm, unwavering, as though he's been waiting for me to find my way here. But there's something else—something more.

Azrael steps into view beside him, his presence more commanding than ever, but there's a softness to him here. A tenderness. I want to run toward him, to leap into his arms and forget everything that's ever weighed me down.

It's an urge I know I can fight in the real world, but here? In this dream world where reality bends, I can't control it. I can't stop the pull that draws me toward him, closer and closer, like the tide drawing me into its embrace. Each step I take toward him feels lighter than the last as if the weight of my fears is dissolving, melting away with every inch of space I close between us.

The morning light begins to illuminate the scene around us, the colors growing brighter and warmer. The golden glow touches everything, spreading across the water, and painting the sand with warmth. For the first time in ages, I feel a sense of peace—a sense of safety I never thought I'd experience again.

When I finally reach Azrael, I don't think. I don't hesitate. I throw myself into his arms, pressing my lips to his. He stiffens at first, surprised, but there's something soft in his gaze that tells me he's not angry, not repulsed. He studies my face as if searching for something—before his lips meet mine, pulling me closer, deeper into the kiss.

I can taste him—his breath, the lingering hint of something powerful but comforting. It's not like the desperation I've felt before. This kiss isn't born of fear or need; it's born of something warmer, something softer. I let myself melt into it, the world around us falling away.

As our lips part, I pull back slightly, looking up at him, still caught in the haze of the moment.

"Memetim is gone," Ashton's voice cuts through the fog, his words light, almost too light. "You won't have nightmares ever again."

The weight of his words settles over me, and for a moment, it's hard to breathe. The constant ache that's lived in my chest—the constant knot of fear that's wound itself so tightly around my heart—begins to unravel.

"Ever?" I ask, my voice small, and hesitant.

"As long as you keep the necklace on." Ashton's voice is steady, but there's a hint of reassurance in it, something I never thought I'd hear. He gestures toward the pendant resting against my skin, the moonstone gleaming in the sunlight. "Sanctuary dreams bring safety."

The words sink in, and a strange warmth spreads through me, starting in my chest and radiating out. For the first time in... I can't even remember how long... I feel the fear lift. The gnawing terror that has clung to me for weeks, for months, is gone. It's like a weight has been lifted, a burden I didn't even know I was carrying, suddenly vanished.

I want to cry, but I don't. Instead, I let the peace of this moment wash over me. The world around me, this perfect dreamscape, feels like something I could stay in forever.

But then, just as quickly as it appeared, that peaceful calm is shattered by a voice. A loud voice.

"Wake up, Layla!" Orcus screams, his voice sharp, insistent. "Layla! Wake. Up!"

His words hit me like a physical blow, harsh and jarring, dragging me from the warmth of the dream and back into the cold, harsh reality.

"Wake up!" Orcus shouts again, the panic rising in his tone.

The world around me starts to dissolve, the edges blurring, the peaceful shoreline fading away like smoke. My body jerks, my eyes snapping open as the dream is ripped away from me, the weight of my fears crashing back down.

I jolt upright, gasping for air, my heart racing as I try to orient myself. My room is dark, familiar—yet everything feels off. My chest tightens as I scan the space, my eyes falling on the werewolf barista standing in the doorway.

Blood. There's so much blood.

His face is streaked with it, cuts and scrapes lining his arms. His full beard is soaked, and it drips steadily onto the floor, pooling around his feet. The metallic scent of it hits me like a wall. It's nauseating. My stomach turns, but I can't tear my eyes away from him.

"The shop," he rasps, struggling to breathe. His voice cracks as he looks around, his gaze locking onto Azrael with a kind of terror in his eyes. "They're all dead," he whispers, his body trembling violently.

And then, as if the reality of it all hits him at once, he collapses into himself, breaking down completely. His sobs fill the room, raw and guttural, and I can't even begin to imagine what he must have seen.

Ashton stands by the chair, still as stone. His face is unreadable, emotionless, but I can sense the weight of the situation in the way his hands twitch, the subtle flex of his muscles. He's trying not to show it, but it's there.

Azrael's face shifts, worry painting his usually stoic expression. His gaze flicks back to Ashton, then to the werewolf, taking in the damage with a quiet intensity that unsettles me.

Both men turn their full attention to the barista, whose breaths are shallow, and ragged, his chest heaving with the weight of everything he's seen and been through.

"What happened?" Azrael's voice is calm, but there's a noticeable edge of urgency beneath it.

The werewolf swallows hard, his hands shaking as he tries to steady himself. "A demon... swept through," he breathes out, each word painful, like it's costing him something to speak. "A demon killed everyone. I fought her as much as I could... before I had to retreat." His voice cracks, and then he collapses into tears. "I almost died. They died... I couldn't save anyone."

My stomach churns, the weight of his words sinking into my bones. A demon. A fucking demon, coming through and slaughtering everyone at the coffee shop. His guilt is palpable, thick in the air around us.

Azrael is silent for a moment, his hand twitching toward the werewolf as if to offer some form of comfort, but he doesn't reach out. Instead, his focus shifts, his attention narrowing.

"Ashton?" Azrael's voice is softer now, quieter as if he's trying to steady himself. "Can you guard Layla with your life?" His gaze flits to me, eyes full of warning and concern. "Call Sadie. I need Song here to protect you while I'm gone. Ashton can't leave until Song gets here."

I don't even have the time to process his words before I'm scrambling to pull myself together. My mind is whirling—Memetim, demons, the coffee shop massacre, and now Ashton needs to protect me? This is all too much, too fast.

Ashton, however, doesn't seem to have any urgency in him. He mutters a dry, almost sarcastic, "Above my pay grade."

I can't help the irritated snort that escapes me, but I'm too shaken to really give it any thought.

"Mine too," Orcus chimes in, his tone dry but carrying an undertone of amusement, like he's enjoying watching Azrael struggle with the chaos that keeps erupting around us.

Azrael's lips thin into a tight line, clearly frustrated by the situation. He stands, his movements measured and deliberate. "Stay here," he tells me, his voice firm as if trying to anchor me to this place in the face of the chaos outside. "Don't leave. Don't do anything until I get back."

I want to argue, to fight against the idea of being left behind while everything falls apart. But I know better than to protest now. The reality of what's happening sinks in. There's no time for hesitation, no room for fear. If anything, I need to be strong for the people around me, even if I'm shaking like a leaf on the inside.

Azrael looks at Ashton, a silent conversation passing between them before he turns to leave, his form already moving toward the door.

"Remember what I said, Layla," Azrael's voice calls to me. "Stay here."

I nod, but inside, a thousand thoughts race. Demons. Dead bodies. My connection to this world of supernaturals feels like it's growing stronger and more dangerous every second. I reach for my phone to dial Sadie, my fingers trembling slightly as I try to get her on the line.

And in the stillness of the room, Orcus' voice leans closer to me, his glow reflecting the turmoil that seems to be pulsing through the air. "You know, Tiny Mouse," he says with a sly grin cracking through, "the moment you start getting comfortable, that's when the universe decides to throw in something… interesting."

I glance at the ring form of Orcus on Azrael's finger, a shaky laugh escaping my lips despite everything. "Don't even start with me, Orcus," I mutter, my voice hoarse. "I can barely keep it together right now."

But deep down, I know that whatever happens next, nothing is ever going to be the same. And I'm not sure I'm ready for whatever the universe has in store for me.

Chapter Eighteen

Azrael

Seven Devils - Florence + Machine

The coffee shop, a place that used to feel like home to me, now stands as a macabre scene of death and devastation. Mortal police swarm the entrance, their presence a stark contrast to the familiar warmth and comfort that this place once provided. I move through the shadows, invisible, unnoticed in my true form. My form blends into the darkness, a mere wisp of presence beneath the blue-tinted crime scene tape that's been stretched tight across the door, keeping the civilians at bay.

I should feel something. Disgust, perhaps. Rage, even. But all I can do is focus on what's in front of me: the destruction of something that was once sacred.

In the far corners of the shop, two figures stand hunched over in glee, the Keres—my sadistic twin sisters. The air crackles with their malevolent energy, a sickening hum of predatory joy as they feast on the souls of the fallen. Their talons, long and cruel, rake through the invisible fabric of the world, tearing open the layers between the living and the dead. They pull the souls out, dripping with black energy, devouring them whole.

They don't even acknowledge me. Not a glance, not a word. Their hunger eclipses everything else. Even me.

I take a deep breath, the familiar scent of coffee that used to suffocate the air, welcoming me every time I entered, is gone. In its place, a thick, acrid stench of iron and death. The scent of blood clings to everything. The walls. The ceiling. Even the air seems saturated with it.

The shop that had once felt like my sanctuary is now a horror show. Blood splatters across the walls, streaking in twisted patterns from the violent struggle that took place here. Some of it has even reached the ceiling, like a grotesque artwork painted by chaos itself. Pools of blood are scattered across the floor, turning the once-welcoming space into a grotesque deathbed.

I step carefully around the bloodstains, my boots making no sound against the soaked tiles. The silence here is oppressive, too quiet for a place that once buzzed with life, with laughter, the hum of coffee machines, and the soft murmur of conversations. Now, only the echoes of death linger in the air.

My chest tightens, but I force it down. I can't afford to be affected by this. Not now.

I move deeper into the shop, my eyes scanning every corner, every darkened space. I need answers. I need to find out what the hell happened here. What twisted hand could be responsible for this level of destruction?

Then I see it. A message scrawled in blood, smeared hastily across one of the counters, as if whoever did this had been in such a rush they didn't care about being clean. The letters are jagged, and uneven. "Memetim."

My stomach tightens, a knot forming in my gut. She's been here. The thought of her presence here, in this space, fills me with an overwhelming sense of dread. Memetim is dangerous, and unpredictable, and now she's left her mark on this place, this sanctuary.

I take another step forward, eyes narrowing as I search for more signs, anything that could point me toward her.

This is terrifying.

I only left here a short while ago, taking Layla with me. I brought her here for a reason—a safe getaway. My safe haven. And now, it's gone. It doesn't exist anymore.

Who ruined my slice of peace?

The walls, once a comfort to me, now feel like a prison. I can feel Orcus, seething beside me. The energy from him is palpable, like heat radiating from an open flame. He's never been fond of this place—but now, it's something worse. He senses the souls. The lost ones. They cling to the air like shadows, mingling with the scent of blood that is far too thick to ignore. The once-welcoming aroma of coffee has been replaced by something foul, something darker.

"What happened here?" I ask the Keres sisters, my voice barely a whisper as the weight of the scene settles deeper in my chest.

The redhead, eyes gleaming with malicious glee, chimes, "Memetim."

The other one, with jet-black hair, sings softly, her voice lilting, like a lullaby of death, "She released the prison and set their target as this mortal coffee shop."

I glance back at the bloodstained walls. The floors, once polished and clean, are now soaked in red. It's as if the very building has absorbed the violence, the terror, the agony of those who were slaughtered. I could feel it before I even asked—the Keres have been feasting. This place is their banquet, and they are the guests of honor.

"Their lost," the redhead says flatly, as though recounting the obvious.

"Our feast," the other sings with unsettling excitement. It's almost like they're celebrating, and the horror of it claws at me from every direction.

I look at Orcus, who is still tense, still radiating that heat. He's not pleased, and neither am I. "Where are they going next?" he asks, his voice sharp and cold, cutting through the atmosphere like a blade.

I already have a bad feeling about this.

The Keres pause, their gazes shifting between one another, their smiles stretching wider. Together, they sing, their voices hauntingly in sync, "A mortal home."

I freeze. My chest, already tight from the chaos I've witnessed, drops like a stone. A mortal home? My thoughts rush back to Layla, to her safety, to her vulnerability. A mortal home.

Fear—raw and unfamiliar—grips me, choking the air from my lungs. This isn't just an attack. This isn't just a meaningless slaughter. This is calculated. This is personal.

The coffee shop... it was a decoy. Memetim didn't just strike here for the sake of it. She wanted me away from Layla. She wanted me to be far from where I needed to be.

I stand frozen, my mind spinning. Every instinct inside me screams, urging me to move. To run. To get to Layla before it's too late.

"Get to her," Orcus growls, he flashes a glow with urgency. I can feel the shift in him, the sudden awareness that something far worse is coming. He's never been one to care much for mortals, but Layla is different. He can sense the danger too, the risk to her life.

The Keres giggle, a chilling sound that echoes around the blood-soaked room, as though they know exactly what's coming. They know the devastation that is set in motion.

I transport myself back to Layla's home, my chest pounding as I burst through the door. The scene is a nightmare. Her furniture is destroyed, her bed shredded like it was torn apart by something vicious. I can't breathe. I run through every room, panic twisting my gut. My mind screams for her, begging to see even the smallest sign that she's okay—that she hasn't become my sister's next meal.

I return to her bedroom—the last place I saw her, the place where I didn't even get the chance to say goodbye because I was so damn sure I'd see her again. My throat tightens as I scream her name, and the world outside responds with a crack of lightning splitting the sky followed by a downpour that seems to echo the storm inside me.

"Where are you, Layla?"

I look around her room, my eyes desperate for any clue, anything that will tell me where she might have gone. There's nothing at first, just the destruction left behind. Then, my gaze falls on the little throne I sat in when I was with her. I throw the cushions aside, not caring about the mess. I need to know.

And there, beneath them, a piece of paper. My pulse spikes. Part of me hopes it's from Ashton, or maybe the werewolf. Anyone who could help. I rip it open, my hands shaking. If it's something Layla misplaced, I might lose it entirely.

I unfold it and immediately recognize the symbols—letters that only Ashton and I would understand. A secret code, one we created as kids to talk about the things we'd overhear, the things adults would never tell us. A code born of necessity and curiosity, and one that only the two of us could decipher.

I read every symbol, every letter, and with each one, a wave of relief crashes over me, washing away the fear that has gripped me since I arrived.

Ashton. He took both Layla and Sadie, and the injured werewolf, to safety. His home. In the Underworld.

The knot in my chest loosens. They're safe. They're alive.

I let out a shaky breath, trying to calm the panic that's still simmering beneath the surface. But then Orcus speaks, and the reality of the situation begins to settle back in.

"Layla is going to have a hard time processing this," he says, his voice low and grave.

I barely hear him. I'm already moving, my mind focused on one thing: getting to them. I can't afford to waste time. Not now. Not when every second counts.

Before Orcus can finish his sentence, I've already transported us to Ashton's home. To the Underworld.

The transition is as smooth as it is jarring, like stepping through a veil between worlds. One moment, I'm in the wreckage of Layla's home, and the next, I'm standing in a space that feels both foreign and familiar. The air here is heavy with the weight of the Underworld, the shadows darker, the silence deeper. It feels like the entire place is holding its breath.

I don't wait for my surroundings to fully register. My thoughts are with Layla—her safety, her well-being.

I'm standing at the door, my hand hovering over the handle, uncertain of what I'll find on the other side. The weight of the unknown presses against my chest, the familiar tension of war and survival creeping in, but I'm not prepared for this. The chaos is unfolding too fast, and I don't have time to process any of it, let alone come up with a plan.

Empathy for Layla and Sadie hits me in a wave—an ocean of emotions crashing over me. These two women, who thought they understood the world, are now drowning in something far darker and more dangerous. They've been thrust into a nightmare, one where nothing makes sense and everything is a lie. I can't even begin to imagine how they must feel.

I take a deep breath, steeling myself for what's ahead. I'm walking in as someone who's failed them already. I haven't protected them the way I promised. I haven't kept my word.

When I push the door open, I step past Ashton and the damned werewolf without a second glance, my eyes drawn to where I know Layla is. It's like a pull, a thread connecting us that I can't ignore. I know where she is, without question. I just know.

I find her in one of Ashton's quiet spare rooms, the kind that's far enough from the commotion to give her space, yet too close to the rest of the world to truly shield her from it. She's sitting alone on the edge of a couch, her posture slumped as if the weight of everything that's happened in the last 24 hours is too much to bear. Her hands are clasped tightly in her lap, her knuckles white from the pressure. Her head is lowered, her gaze locked on the floor like it's holding secrets that she's desperately trying to unravel.

The room is dim, the only light coming from the low glow of a lamp in the corner. It casts shadows across her face, making her look like a ghost of the woman I thought I was getting to know. There's a stillness to her, an emptiness that I can't explain, but I feel it deep in my bones.

She doesn't look up when I enter, even though I know she's aware of my presence. I feel it, the tension in the air, thick and heavy. But she doesn't move. She doesn't acknowledge me, and for a moment, I wonder if she ever will again.

"Layla." My voice is soft, almost too soft, like I'm speaking to someone who could shatter at any moment.

For a long, painful second, she doesn't respond. I think she's going to ignore me entirely. But then, slowly, she lifts her head. Her eyes meet mine—wide, unfocused, and distant. There's something wild in them, something frantic, as if she's seen something that no one should ever see and now she's trying to process it all.

"You're... you're not really human," she says, her voice barely above a whisper. Each word cuts through the silence like a blade. "I thought I was crazy, but you're real. All of this is real."

I feel the weight of her words settle on my chest like a boulder. The truth I've tried to shield her from is out in the open now, and there's no going back. I want to reach out to her, to hold her and tell her everything will be okay, but I know I can't. Not yet. Not like this.

I take a step closer, my voice trembling despite myself, "I wanted to tell you. I wanted to show you when you were ready. But I never meant for this to be your introduction to my world."

Her laugh is bitter, filled with disbelief. She shakes her head, the motion almost like a tremor. "My world. Your world..." She trails off, her lips curling into something that could almost pass for a smile, but it's empty—hollow. "There's just... no line between them anymore, is there? It's all one nightmare."

I feel something tighten inside me, something close to guilt. It's a sensation I'm not familiar with—one that feels like chains constricting around my ribs. I've been trained to guide souls to the next world, not to protect the living from the weight of the truths I carry. I was never meant to bear this burden with her. But now that it's here, now that she knows, I can't just walk away. I can't leave her to figure this out alone.

I feel the conflict deep within me. I've broken rules I didn't even know existed. This wasn't supposed to be my responsibility, and yet, here I am, caught between worlds—between what I am, what I should be, and what she needs me to be.

"I never wanted this for you, Layla," I say softly, my voice barely a breath. "This world... my world... it's not one you should ever have to see. But now that you have, I'll help you navigate it. I won't leave you to face it alone."

She doesn't respond right away, just stares at me with those wild green eyes. Her lips part, as if she wants to say something, but no words come. I can feel her struggling with it, with everything that's just been dumped into her lap.

And I can't help but wonder—will she ever be able to see me the same way again? Will she ever be able to trust me after all this?

But before I can continue, she speaks again, her voice trembling, barely audible. "I don't know if I can handle this, Azrael. I don't know if I can handle you."

The words hit me like a punch to the gut. My chest tightens, my throat closing around the ache that suddenly blossoms inside me. But I can't back down. Not now. Not when she's finally seeing the truth.

"I'm sorry," I whisper. "For everything. But I'll do whatever it takes to make sure you're safe. I'll protect you, even if it means losing everything else. I'm sorry, Layla." The words fell from my lips like lead, hollow and weightless. I could feel the emptiness in them, and I knew she could hear it. "If I could've spared you this, I would have."

She exhaled sharply, the tension in her shoulders loosening just a little. Her gaze softened, but there was still that flicker of fear, like a ghost behind her eyes, never fully gone. "Azrael... what... what else are you hiding? What else is out there?"

I hesitated, my chest tight with the gravity of the moment. I knew that once I opened this door, once I started revealing the things I'd kept buried, there would be no turning back. There would be no comforting veil between her and the darkness I'd kept her from. But there was no choice now. She deserved the truth, no matter how ugly it might be.

"Everything you've ever imagined," I said, my voice barely a whisper, "and more. Some of it... isn't kind. But I'm here, Layla. I will stand between you and the worst of it."

For a brief, fleeting second, I thought I saw a glimmer of trust in her eyes—just a hint, a spark—but it was quickly masked by the wariness that had already settled there. She nodded, her hands loosening just a little, but I could feel the hesitation in her. The uncertainty. Part of her was still seeing me as a stranger, someone she didn't fully understand, caught between the male she thought she was getting to know and the thing I had become.

I could feel her fear, thick and palpable in the space between us. She stood rigid across the room, her arms crossed tightly against herself like a barrier she wasn't sure how to let go of. Her eyes darted around Ashton's home, scanning every shadow as if the walls themselves might come to life, might turn on her in the blink of an eye. I knew that feeling, the one where the world feels like it's closing in, and every dark corner hides something you're too afraid to face.

Her breaths were shallow, and uneven, as if she were trying to steady herself, trying to convince herself that everything was real—that I was real. That what she was seeing, what she was hearing, was something she could trust.

"Layla," I said softly, stepping toward her, trying to close the distance between us. But she flinched, just slightly, enough to pull away from me.

I stopped. I didn't know if it was the right move to push closer, or if giving her space was what she needed. But I could feel the weight of her fear pressing against me, a living, breathing thing. It was almost suffocating.

"Look at me," I said, my voice gentle but firm. I needed her to see me, to see the fucking truth I have been running from.

She lifted her eyes to mine, and there it was—something raw, something new—fear, yes, but something deeper too. A realization that she couldn't outrun. Her gaze was searching me now, desperate for any shred of comfort, but also afraid of what she might find.

I took another step forward, and this time, she didn't flinch. I reached out, just barely, my fingers brushing against her wrist. It was all I could offer right now, a promise that I wouldn't leave her to face this alone.

"I'm not going anywhere, Layla," I said, my voice a low vow. "Not now. Not ever. I swear it."

Her breath hitched, and I saw her struggle, like the words I was offering her were too much to accept all at once. I could see it on her face, the battle between wanting to trust me and being so terrified of what it meant to do so.

She finally spoke, her voice fragile, yet firm in its own way. "I don't know if I can keep doing this, Azrael. I don't know if I can keep living in a world like this... with you, with *all of this*." She gestured vaguely around the room, as if everything—the truth, the danger, the strange pull between us——was all too much to handle.

I swallowed hard, feeling that same knot of guilt tighten in my chest. "I didn't want this for you, Layla. I didn't want to drag you into this world, but I'm not going to let you drown in it. Not if I can stop it."

Her eyes softened for a second, the weight of my words settling between us. But there was still that flicker of fear, still the question that lingered unspoken between us: *What if it's too much? What if I can't keep going?*

"I won't ask you to do this alone," I added, my voice thick with something unspoken—something I had no words for. "I'll help you. But you have to trust me, Layla. You have to trust that I won't let this world take you from me."

There was a long silence. She seemed to be weighing my words, considering them with a caution that told me how deeply this was all affecting her. She wasn't just scared for her own safety anymore. She was scared for us—for what we had, for what we might become in this twisted, dangerous reality.

Her breath was still shallow, but I could feel her steadiness returning, little by little. The tension in her shoulders began to ease, and I saw the slightest hint of a nod. A fragile sign, but one that told me she was still holding on.

The door creaked open, and Sadie walked in. She froze mid-step, her eyes locking onto mine before quickly darting to Orcus at my side, his form now in its true, terrifying glory. The mixture of disbelief and defiance in her expression was unmistakable.

"So... you're really telling me you're Death?" she asked, crossing her arms tightly, as if bracing herself for a revelation she didn't want to hear. Her tone dripped with skepticism, as though she were daring me to prove it.

Before I could speak, Orcus' deep voice rumbled through the air, amused and full of that ever-present confidence he carried. "Oh, she's a doubter. I like this one already," he drawled, a smirk evident in the way he spoke.

Sadie's gaze snapped to him, her brow furrowing as she took in the sight of the scythe, its ethereal form towering beside me. "And the scythe talks too? Right. Sure, why not?" She threw her hands up in exasperation and looked back at me, half-laughing, but there was no humor in her eyes. "You told us all that Grim Reaper stuff, but now we're supposed to believe *this* is real? This is a fucking dream, dude."

I met her gaze, calm, unshaken, the weight of my true nature settling in the silence between us. "I never lied, Sadie. This is as real as it gets. This isn't a dream."

She let out a short laugh, but it didn't mask the disbelief in her voice. Her arms tightened across her chest. "You mean to tell me you're actually... Death?" She looked me up and down, clearly struggling to reconcile the truth with the mortal appearance I was wearing. "No offense, but you don't exactly look the part. Where's the whole skeletal vibe?"

Orcus chuckled, a low and rich sound, his presence in the room palpable. "Expecting something more theatrical? I can assure you, Azrael is more than capable of inspiring terror when he needs to." His voice carried a sense of pride in my power.

Layla stiffened at the exchange, shrinking back just slightly, her gaze flickering between me and the world she was now trapped in. The fear in her eyes was heavier than before. "You... you should have told us what this would be like," she whispered, her voice barely audible, like the words were getting stuck in her throat. Her eyes were wide, shadowed with disbelief. "I thought... I thought I understood what you were, but this... this is more than I ever imagined."

Guilt twisted in my chest, the weight of her fear a reminder of how much I had failed to protect her from all of this. But I kept my expression steady. "Layla, I never wanted you to see this side of me, of my world. To see the Underworld, itself. I wanted to spare you from all of this."

She shook her head, staring down at her trembling hands. "But it's real, isn't it? And I'm here now, in the Underworld. This is... this is what I was afraid of all along."

Orcus' voice softened, though it still carried that deep resonance. His words seemed directed at both Layla and me, a reminder of the power of fear in this realm. "Fear is natural here, Layla. It's what keeps you alive. But fear can also be a guide, if you let it."

Sadie rolled her eyes, her gaze shifting between Layla and me as though she were watching a performance. "So, what? We're supposed to be reassured by the talking scythe?" She smirked, but I could see the doubt creeping into her eyes. "You know what, Azrael? Prove it. Show us why we're supposed to believe all of this."

Orcus chuckled darkly, thoroughly enjoying her challenge. "Oh, this one is bold," he murmured, his voice full of dark amusement. "She thinks she's beyond fear. I wonder how long that will last."

I felt the tension in the room shift, the weight of the challenge hanging in the air like a storm cloud. Sadie wasn't backing down. She was daring me to show her the truth, to prove everything I had said to her.

"Orcus," I said sharply, a warning to keep his jibes to himself.

Sadie tilted her head, a smirk tugging at the corners of her mouth. "What's the matter? Are you scared to show me your true side, Azrael? Or is it all just smokes and mirrors?"

A slow, almost predatory grin spread across Orcus' surface as he hummed darkly. "Azrael, I like this one. Feisty. Perhaps she'd make a fine addition to our entourage."

I shot him a sidelong glance, barely holding back a smirk of my own. "Trust me, you'd regret that decision within a day."

Sadie's brow shot up as she caught the exchange, her lips curling into a sly grin. "Oh, was that a joke? From *Death* himself?" She turned to Layla, the grin widening despite the surreal situation. "I think I'm starting to get used to this."

Layla managed a shaky smile, her eyes still cautious but softening slightly. "Sadie, maybe... maybe we shouldn't test him."

Sadie shrugged, unbothered. "Hey, I'm not testing anyone. I'm just saying... if I'm in the Underworld with the Grim Reaper, I might as well know what I'm dealing with, right?"

I couldn't help but shake my head, amused despite the tension. "You already know what you're dealing with, Sadie. I'm right here to protect you both. Nothing more, nothing less."

But the spark in her eyes didn't flicker as she crossed her arms, her gaze unwavering. "I'll believe it when I see it."

Chapter Nineteen

Azrael

Hurt - Johnny Cash

"I have to talk to Ashton and the werewolf and then report back to Hades. You two girls should be safe here. Do not leave Ashton's house. At all." I lock eyes with Layla, hoping she'll hear the urgency in my voice, the raw sincerity that I never wanted to put her in this position.

I never wanted her to experience any of this. I just wanted to free her from Memetim's grasp. But by doing so, I've thrown her straight into the path of every demon and monster that stalks this cursed world. Why did I have to fuck up and drag her into this nightmare? Protecting her has consumed me—blurring the lines of my mission, of my training. I've crossed a line I didn't even know existed. For her. Always for her.

Both girls shrug as if they're resigned to the chaos surrounding them, and Sadie plops down next to Layla on the bed. But Layla... she stares at me, her eyes glassy, tears threatening to spill. I feel the weight of them, even from where I stand. I wish I could absorb those tears, swallow her fear, and carry it for her so she doesn't have to. I wish I could take away every ounce of pain I've caused. Every little thing that's happened because of me.

If I could, I would rewrite everything. I would meet her properly, the way Fate intended. I wouldn't have her here in the Underworld, vulnerable, afraid, caught in the web of forces far bigger than anything she could comprehend.

A new hatred claws at my chest, sharper than anything I've ever known. Memetim. She is beyond termination. My thoughts spiral out of control as my blood boils. I want to kill her. I want to tear her apart, rip the life from her, and feed her bones to the hellhounds. She has no idea what she's started. What she's done to me.

She's fucked with my future. My Fated Mate.

I turn to leave, gripping the doorframe, but my eyes find Layla's one last time. She's still watching me, her expression a mixture of confusion and something else, something like quiet desperation. I feel it deep in my soul—the pull to her, the need to be close, to protect her.

"I hope you can forgive me, Layla," I whisper, the words a breath between us, so low I'm not sure if she hears them. My throat tightens as I add, "We weren't supposed to meet like this. We were destined to meet…" A tremor runs through my body, the next words slipping out, fragile and broken. "But not like this."

I walk away before she can respond before she can hear me fully. And if she does, I know it'll hurt her more. I'm forcing her to think about my words. To process all the weight I've just dumped on her fragile heart.

But it's too much. I'm too much.

Something inside of me snaps. I'm broken. I can't fix this. I can't undo what I've done. I've led her into a world of monsters, and now I fear for her. For the woman I love but can't fully protect. The fear of losing her before I ever had the chance to love her the way she deserves… before I ever had the chance to truly show her the male I am, the creature I'm meant to be.

How can I love her? How can I be obsessed with a half-mortal woman—my Fated Mate—when she doesn't even know who I truly am? When she doesn't know the depth of the darkness I carry with me? How can I protect her when every force in existence is gunning for her?

I'm not enough.

I am nothing but a broken tool—a Grim Reaper who barely passed the training. And now, I'm about to face the very demons my brothers and I locked away to protect our father's mortals. I'll have no protection. None. My father won't spare me. He'll let them tear me apart. He'll let them tear Ashton apart, and most terrifying of all... he'll let them tear *Layla* apart.

A Grim Reaper's tear falls freely as I walk down the hall, heading toward Ashton and the werewolf. I need to pull myself together. I can't let them see this. I can't show them how much I'm unraveling inside. They'll never trust me to lead them through this if they see the fear consuming me. I'm supposed to be one of the strongest beings in existence, the Scythe-bearing Reaper. I have to act like it.

No more weakness. No more hesitation. For Layla. For Ashton. For the world that's been thrown into chaos because of *her*—Memetim's *mess*.

But even as I tell myself to brace, to steel myself, the sting of Layla's face—her tears—lingers with me, gnawing at my core. And the darkness in my chest, the hatred for Memetim, just fucking grows. It burns hotter with each step I take until I feel like I'm walking through fire.

I can't save everyone. But I *will* save her. And if I have to rip this world apart to do it, I will.

But the fear of losing the love I've finally found gnaws at me like a festering wound—a scent so potent even Orcus would catch it, a weakness that both of them will sense. My love for Layla Simmons is the one thing that makes me tremble it's the one thing I can't control and it's the one thing that threatens to consume me.

I wipe my face, pushing back the sting of tears, but they burn in the back of my throat. The thought of losing her, of failing her, grips my insides like cold iron, tightening with every beat of what actually might be my heart. But wait, shit. I don't have a heart. It's fear I can't shake, no matter how hard I try to bury it beneath the weight of my duty.

A voice—low, cold, familiar—cuts through the chaos of my thoughts.

"Weakness," Orcus says, his tone unwavering, "is not found in love. It is found in fear."

I stopped mid-step, his words struck me with the force of a stone sinking into the churning waters of my mind. I almost don't want to hear them, don't want to acknowledge the truth in them, but I know better than to ignore him. Orcus has always been my grounding force, a constant presence when everything else feels like it's falling apart. A voice of reason in a world where nothing makes sense.

"You think your love makes you vulnerable?" Orcus continues, his voice cutting through the tension. "No. Your fear does. The love you have for her... it does not diminish you. It strengthens you. It gives you something to protect, something worth fighting for. Something that will burn in you like a fire when you face those who would seek to destroy it."

His words land like a balm on my tortured mind, piercing through the suffocating fog of doubt that's clouding my judgment. I close my eyes for a moment, letting them sink deep into my bones, letting them settle in the pit of my stomach.

I want to believe him. I want to think that my love for Layla can be a source of strength, not a weakness. I want to believe that I can protect her, that this obsession, this bond, is something worth holding onto, even when the world around me crumbles.

I clench my fists, feeling the familiar weight of Orcus' blade at my side, grounding me, and reminding me of who I am. Of what I'm capable of.

"I can't fail her," I mutter, barely more than a whisper, as if the very air might hear me and betray me. "I can't lose her."

Orcus' voice softens, but there's no mistaking the certainty in his tone.

"You will not lose her, Azrael," he says, his words unwavering. "Not while I am here. And not while you remember who you are."

I swallow hard, letting the gravity of his words settle in my chest. They feel like a lifeline, tethering me to something greater than my fear. Something more powerful than the doubts I've carried for so long.

"You are Azrael. The first of your kind. The one who walks through death's door. You are the scythe's keeper, the embodiment of balance. You will carry this weight, as you always have."

A deep breath fills my lungs as I steady myself. Orcus' presence, though something I don't always understand, feels like a solid foundation in moments like this—like a tether to something unbreakable. A reminder that I am not alone in this fight. That I am more than the doubts that plague me.

I stand tall, letting the weight of his words sink in, and for the first time in what feels like forever, I let go of my fear. I release it into the dark, where it belongs, and allow the steady rhythm of Orcus' voice to anchor me.

"Fear nothing." Orcus' final words echo in my chest, reverberating through me, an undeniable force pushing me forward.

I straighten my back, pushing aside the fog of uncertainty that has clouded my mind for so long. The fear no longer has control over me. I will protect Layla. I will not let them take her from me.

I am Azrael. The one who walks through death's door. The one who will never falter.

I pause, my voice thick with the weight of the question I've been carrying for too long. "Orcus. Did you know the entire time Layla was my Fated?"

There's a long silence, the air between us growing heavy. I can feel Orcus' presence beside me, the scythe's ominous hum almost like a heartbeat, steady and constant.

Finally, his voice breaks through the silence, calm but carrying a hint of something deeper. "I knew."

My heart tightens. The tension in my chest grows as I try to process his words, but I can't. "Then why didn't you tell me?" The frustration boils over. "Why didn't you warn me? Why let me... why let us go through all this without preparing me for it?"

Orcus' response is measured, carefully. "Because it wasn't the right time, Azrael. You weren't ready."

I stare at him, disbelief flooding my chest. "Not ready? She's my Fated! She's been in danger, and you let me—"

"I didn't *let* you do anything," Orcus interrupts, his voice firm. "You needed to meet her on your own terms, in your own way. You needed to come to this realization when you were strong enough to handle it. You couldn't have known the truth, not yet. The pull would've consumed you. You would have thrown yourself into the flames before you had the strength to stand in them."

His words hit like a slap, cutting through the fury and panic building inside me. I'm silent for a moment, my thoughts racing, trying to make sense of everything. My fists clench involuntarily.

"You could've warned me," I murmur, more to myself than to him. "I was already falling. It never felt like a choice. The bond between us... it was never a question of when, just how. And now, I'm supposed to protect her, knowing the kind of danger she's in? Knowing what's at stake?"

Orcus doesn't answer immediately. He waits, his silence hanging in the air like a weight. Then, when he speaks, his tone is softer but still resolute. "The timing wasn't right, Azrael. You need to learn what you're capable of. You needed to grow, to understand your own strength. To truly protect her, you had to understand who *you* are first. If I had told you earlier, if I had forced you into it, you would've broken. Your energy and mind, already in chaos from this mission, wouldn't have been able to handle the truth."

I take a step back, the truth of his words settling into the pit of my stomach. "You think I'm ready now?"

"I know you're ready," Orcus replies simply. "You've always been ready. But you needed to find that in yourself."

I feel a strange sense of clarity in his words, but also the gnawing tension. My Fated. Layla. She's more than I ever expected, more than I'm prepared for, and yet she's everything I never knew I needed.

I let out a long breath, the weight of it all threatening to crush me. "I don't know if I can do this. She deserves better than me."

Orcus' voice hardens like steel being tempered. "Don't you dare. You are more than capable of protecting her. You've already proved that. Now, you need to *believe* in yourself the way I do."

His words stir something inside me, a fire that's been smoldering deep in my chest. I can't afford to doubt anymore. I can't afford to fail her. The road ahead won't be easy, but if there's one thing I've learned, it's that I won't face it alone.

"Alright," I say, finally lifting my head. "I'll protect her. I'll do what I need to do."

Chapter Twenty

Azrael

Welcome to the Jungle - Guns 'N' Roses

I finally muster the courage to walk into the same room as Ashton and the werewolf. The weight of everything that's happened hangs heavily over me, and I know this conversation won't make it any lighter. The moment I step into the doorway, I catch Ashton's low voice murmuring to the werewolf.

I lean against the doorframe, silently observing Ashton as he wraps the wolf's hand with precise care. There's a tenderness in the way Ashton moves—careful, methodical—but it doesn't mask the tension in his shoulders.

"You got my message," Ashton mutters, his focus on the task at hand. His voice is thick with guilt. "Not long after Sadie got there, they came. I panicked. I'm sorry. This was the only safe place I could think of."

"It's all right," I say, stepping into the room. "I'm grateful you acted quickly. I can't take them to my place, not with Memetim lurking. She's bound to have eyes on me."

Ashton nods but doesn't look up. His hands move deftly, securing the last of the wrappings. The werewolf winces but doesn't utter a sound. His resilience doesn't go unnoticed.

I take a seat on the couch, letting out a slow breath as I turn to the wolf. His aura feels heavy, burdened with grief and anger. "What's your name?" I ask, my voice softer than I expected.

His reply is clipped, almost a growl. "Luca. My name is Luca Cross."

He refuses to meet my gaze, his body rigid like a coiled spring.

"Well," I say, inhaling deeply, "Luca, I owe you an apology. None of this should have happened to you. I'm sorry for the chaos I've brought into your life."

Luca's glare snaps to me, sharp enough to cut through the air between us. His golden eyes burn with barely restrained fury. "Don't you dare apologize. This isn't just about you."

His words hit harder than I expected, and I sit back, watching as the dam finally breaks.

"My family's coffee shop—it's gone. Burned to the ground," he says, his voice cracking despite the anger laced within it. "All of my customers—my friends—slaughtered in cold blood. I couldn't do a damn thing to stop it. I lost everything. Everything that was handed down to me."

There's a rawness in his tone that strikes a chord deep within me. He's not just mourning his losses; he's mourning his failure to protect them.

"I'm sorry," I say again, though the words feel feeble in the face of his grief. "If you'd like, one of us can take you home. You don't have to stay here and be dragged into this any further."

His head snaps up, and for the first time, his gaze locks with mine. The intensity in his eyes holds me in place. "No," he says firmly, his voice steady despite the storm raging beneath it. "My family's coffee shop is gone, and the blood of my pack stains the ground. But I won't run. Not when I can still offer my services."

There's a fire in him—a determination that demands respect. I nod slowly, acknowledging his resolve.

"You're Declan Cross's son, aren't you?" I ask.

His expression shifts, the anger giving way to a flicker of surprise. "You knew my father?"

"I did," I reply, as mall, bittersweet smile tugging at my lips. "He was a great werewolf and an even greater friend. Your family's name carries honor, Luca. You should be proud of that."

His jaw tightens, and he looks away, his hands clenching into fists. "I'm proud," he murmurs, though the pain in his voice tells me he's still coming to terms with everything he's lost.

Ashton clears his throat, breaking the silence. "Luca's right, Azrael. This fight—it's not just yours. We all have something to lose, and we all have something to fight for."

I glance between the two of them, their determination mirroring my own. For a moment, the crushing weight of responsibility feels a little less suffocating. But the fear of what's to come still lingers at the edges of my mind.

"Then we fight together," I say, my voice steady. "For the ones we've lost—and the ones we still have to protect."

"So, what's our next move since you've dragged me into this mess?" Ashton asks, leaning against the counter with a raised brow. His tone is light, but there's an edge to it, the weight of the situation creeping through his usual calm demeanor.

I sink deeper into the couch, letting out a sigh. "We have to tell Hades."

Ashton lets out a sharp laugh. "Oh, he's going to love that. You know how much he appreciates surprises, especially ones involving mortal women."

"They aren't entirely mortal," I reply, rubbing my temples. "Layla isn't, at least. But yes, I know. This isn't something I can avoid. I have to report any major changes to the mission." I drag my hands down my face, the exhaustion setting in. "And this is a huge change."

"You think?" Ashton's chuckle is laced with sarcasm. He pushes himself off the counter and moves to pour a shot of something dark and ominous from a crystal decanter. "We're going to need an army to deal with Memetim and whatever she's planning. And let's face it, Hades isn't exactly the type to rally the troops. So that leaves it up to us three..." He downs the shot in one gulp. "...and we three are far from being enough."

Luca huffs from his spot on the couch, arms crossed and gaze distant. "I'm just a coffee shop owner," he mutters. "I don't know anyone."

Ashton nods in understanding, though his expression tightens. "Azrael, what about you? Do you still have contact with any Reapers from training? Or maybe some retired ones who owe you a favor?"

I nod slowly, thinking back to the network I've carefully built over centuries. "Of course. Keeping a portfolio of names and alliances is part of the job. But convincing them to join us won't be easy."

Ashton smirks, histone turning playful to mask the tension. "And what about your trusty talking scythe? Any brilliant advice from that hunk of metal?"

Orcus is unusually silent.

Ashton and I exchange a glance. Orcus is never silent when Ashton addresses him, always quick with a sharp remark or some sardonic wit. This silence is unnerving.

After a moment, the familiar vibration hums through my grip. Orcus is still present—just listening. I sigh, his lack of input is a rare but notable occurrence.

"We need to talk to Hades," I say, rising from the couch. My words feel heavier now, the weight of what they imply pressing down on me.

Ashton scoffs, shaking his head as he sets the empty glass down on the counter. "You and Vassago—always the goody-two-shoes, eager to run to your father to explain everything."

I stop mid-step and turn, narrowing my eyes at him. "Excuse me?"

He crosses his arms, meeting my glare with his usual unbothered demeanor. "Forgive me if I'm not exactly rushing to grovel before Hades, begging for forgiveness because two mortal women are hiding in my house. That's not my idea of a good time."

The air between us grows tense, but I don't let his words derail me. Instead, I drop the bombshell I've been holding back. "Did you know Vassago is missing?"

Ashton's expression falters for a split second, his usual confidence slipping. "Missing?" he echoes, his tone quieter now.

I nod, watching as the realization dawns on him. "They can't find him. Memetim took him."

His lips press into a thin line as he processes this, his sharp mind working through the possibilities. After a moment, he speaks again, his tone grim. "She's smart. She would've put him somewhere no one would think to look."

"Exactly." My jaw tightens as I study his face. "Any ideas?"

He hesitates, then his eyes narrow. "Has anyone checked the prison?"

The suggestion hits me like a bolt of lightning. It makes so much sense. Barely anyone ventures into the prison these days; it's practically forgotten. We haven't had new supernatural prisoners in ages.

"What if..." I trail off, the pieces falling into place. "What if Memetim brought Vassago to the prison and released everyone else in the process?"

Ashton's expression darkens, the implications of my words sinking in. "If that's true, then your father already knows. He has to. Unless the guards were wiped out, he has to be aware that the prisoners are gone."

I don't wait for him to finish his thought. The urgency building in my chest is too overwhelming. I shoot up from the couch, my nerves pounding. "I have to go," I say, already racing toward the door.

Chapter Twenty-One

Azrael

House of the Rising Sun - Animals

I appear before my father in the cold expanse of his throne room. The air is heavy, suffused with the scent of burning ash and ancient stone. He sits upon his throne, unnervingly calm for someone whose realm and dominion are under such dire threat. His expression is unreadable, though his eyes burn with a restrained intensity. My nerves are a twisted mess, threatening to undo me as I prepare to deliver news he won't want to hear. Every word I'm about to speak feels like it will cut deeper into the tenuous thread of his patience.

He's surprised—no, intrigued—that I requested this meeting. The weight of my own inadequacies presses down on me as I bow my head in respect before speaking.

"Why did you call me here, Azrael?" His voice is cold, measured, and sharp enough to flay flesh.

I steel myself and begin. I recount my meeting with Ashton and the harrowing events at the coffeeshop. My words falter briefly when I describe the massacre, the innocent lives snuffed out, and Lucas's narrow survival. I move on to explain how Ashton took Layla, Sadie, and Lucas into hiding, choosing a location so secret that even Memetim's spies wouldn't discover it. I keep my voice steady, despite the raw edge of anxiety clawing at my throat.

"And you've brought mortals into my realm?" His tone is clipped, disdain dripping from every syllable.

"Layla is not fully mortal," I say, choosing my words carefully, "but yes, they are here—for their protection. Memetim targeted them."

He leans forwards lightly, his presence more oppressive than before. "You risk my throne and the delicate balance of my realm for mortals? Explain yourself."

I take a deep breath, meeting his eyes. "It's not just about them. It's about Memetim. She's escalating her plans. If we don't act swiftly, she'll dismantle everything. I suspect she's holding Vassago. It would explain his disappearance."

The mention of his "favorite son" elicits a flicker of reaction from him—an almost imperceptible narrowing of his eyes.

"You think she has Vassago?" he asks, voice low and deliberate.

"I do," I reply, keeping my tone firm. "We need to check the prison. It's the most logical place to hold him. Barely anyone goes down there, and if Memetim released other prisoners in the process, it explains the surge of chaos."

Before my father could respond, Exu steps forward from the shadows. His tall, wiry frame is cloaked in obsidian robes, his gaunt face impassive. Without waiting for his permission, Exu bows slightly and vanishes in a swirl of smoke, already moving to investigate.

The room grows heavier in Exu's absence. I've done all I can for now, but the weight of my father's judgment bears down on me.

"I am greatly disappointed in you," He says finally, his voice cutting through the silence like a blade. "I knew it was a mistake to entrust this mission to you. Only a rookie would allow Memetim to escape and bring such ruin upon us."

The sting of his words is sharp, but I force myself to remain composed.

"I underestimated her," I admit. "But I'm not the only one. No one saw this coming, not even you."

His gaze darkens, and for a moment, I wonder if I've pushed too far.

"Do not test me, Azrael," he warns, his tone icy. "You brought this chaos into my realm. You will clean it up. Do not forget the cost of failure."

"Your son did what he had to do," Orcus screeches, his voice slicing through the oppressive atmosphere of the throne room. "You, of all people, know the bond of a Fated Mate. Do you not recall, Persephone? Do you not remember the chaos you unleashed in both realms over her? Do you not even recall the hollow shell you became when you lost her?"

Orcus' words reverberate like nails on a chalkboard, grating and unyielding. "Your son has followed every law you instilled in him. He has played by the rules of your court and obeyed the codes you beat into him as a child—until now. And why? Because you sent him on this mission alone, knowing full well his instincts to protect his Fated Mate would override everything else. It is not his failure, Hades. It is *yours*."

His fingers tighten around the armrests of his throne, his expression shifting from controlled disdain to simmering fury. "I created you, Orcus. Do not force my hand in destroying you."

"You created me," Orcus fires back, his tone unyielding, "with all-seeing knowledge to aid your son. I was your experiment, the prototype for a new breed of Reapers. And yet, the one you claim as your perfect creation terrifies you, doesn't he? Deep down, you know the truth. Azrael could topple your throne without so much as lifting a pinky. That's why you can't love him. You're too afraid of what you've made."

I freeze, the weight of Orcus' words pressing down on me like a suffocating shroud. The room feels smaller, and heavier.

Orcus continues, relentless. "Azrael's power isn't the flaw you believe it to be. It's your greatest success. But rather than embrace it, you turn away from him, too cowardly to admit that you fear your own son. And yet, despite all of that, his loyalty to you remains unshaken. He loves you in a way you've never deserved. The least you can do is show him respect."

The air crackles with tension as Orcus pauses, the sharp edges of his words sinking into the oppressive silence.

"And let's not forget," he adds, his voice cold and deliberate, "you cannot destroy me. That is how you designed me. That is why Azrael will always be the *only* scythe-bearing Grim Reaper you have."

My father's expression flickers, a crack in his iron facade, though he quickly schools his features. My mind races, a mixture of shock, anger, and a strange, dawning clarity. Orcus' words feel like a blow to the gut.

All this time, I thought my father's disdain was born of disappointment in my failures. But Orcus has laid it bare—his fear, his insecurity. And now, in this moment, I see the truth for what it is.

Orcus shifts slightly at my side, the faint hum of his presence vibrating against my hand as if to remind me he's still here, still my ally. "Stand by your son," he finishes. "Because whether you admit it or not, Azrael is the only hope you have left."

My father's eyes narrow, and for a moment, I wonder if he'll lash out. But he doesn't. Instead, he leans back into his throne, the icy silence returning to the room like a tidal wave.

I remain frozen in place, my mind racing to process everything Orcus has said. This is why he was quiet at Ashton's house, I realize. He wasn't silent out of hesitation or doubt. He was planning this, orchestrating a way to force my father's hand.

Orcus' loyalty, unshakable and fierce, is more than a bond. It's a weapon, a shield, and for the first time in a long while, I feel a flicker of hope that perhaps, just perhaps, I am not as alone in this as I thought.

"Azrael," my father begins, his voice trailing off into a rare and uncharacteristic silence.

I take a steadying breath, my voice firm but measured. "Father, I do not want your throne. I never have. My intentions were always for Vassago to take it. All I want is a future where Layla is safe. I *need* her to be safe." I pause, letting the words settle. "I'm asking only for your help inbuilding an army to destroy Memetim and the escaped prisoners, so we can all move forward."

He regards me, his expression inscrutable as he weighs my words. Before he can respond, Exu reenters the room.

And he isn't alone.

At his heels is Vassago—beaten, tattered, his once-majestic wings missing large swaths of feathers. Blood and grime cling to his armor, a haunting testament to his captivity. My brother stumbles, but Exu steadies him, leading him further into the throne room.

My father's eyes widen in an instant of raw emotion I've never seen before. Tears spill freely down his face as he rushes forward, his composure breaking entirely. He throws his arms around Vassago, embracing him as though afraid he'll vanish again. The sight is both heartbreaking and beautiful, a rare moment of vulnerability from the man who *created* me.

"My son," my father breathes, his voice cracking. "My son is found... and safe."

Vassago leans into the embrace, his strength faltering, and I stand frozen in the doorway, a rush of conflicting emotions tearing through me. Relief, guilt, and gratitude swirl together in a chaotic storm.

After their reunion, Vassago and I retreat to stand before the throne. His face is drawn with exhaustion, but his voice remains steady as he recounts what happened.

"Dash," he begins, "had a tainted soul. Memetim manipulated him, and made promises she never intended to keep. When she attacked, I took most of the blows meant for Layla. I was weakened enough for her to trap me." He exhales heavily, his eyes distant. "Eight months. I was trapped for eight months, isolated, trying to heal enough to escape. I had to get back to her, Azrael. She was my charge. My purpose."

The weight of his words sinks deep, and I find myself clenching my fists. "She's safe now," I assure him. "You did everything you could."

Vassago shakes his head, a faint smile tugging at his lips. "You're supposed to take the throne," he whispers, his gaze shifting to our father, who lingers at the edge of the room.

"I don't want it," I say firmly, my voice unwavering.

"But why?" Vassago's question hangs in the air, genuine confusion etched across his face.

"Before Layla, I wanted it," I admit. "After Layla, I don't. The role of the Lord of the Underworld demands constant offspring to strengthen the army with the best bloodlines. I only want Layla. If she doesn't want me, then so be it—I will remain shackled to her side, enduring every rejection she throws my way. But I will never see her as an incubator for an army. She is my equal. My other half."

Vassago studies me, his expression thoughtful. "You mean that, don't you?"

"I do."

He nods slowly, turning to our father. "Layla is far from mortal," he says. "And she's no succubus, either. She's something far more powerful than anyone in this room can comprehend. But she's vulnerable because she doesn't know what she is. Her energy core is dormant."

I stiffen. "What do you mean?"

"She matches your energy," Vassago continues, his lips quirking into a knowing smile. "Almost like a puzzle piece. She's the first of her kind. Imagine my surprise when I was tasked with protecting her as an infant." He looks at me pointedly. "Her mother knew. She knew Layla was something extraordinary and made sure she'd survive to grow into her potential. Trust me, Azrael, I've fought off more threats than you can imagine to keep her alive."

The weight of his revelation crashes down on me, leaving my mind spinning. Layla—powerful, unique, and entirely unprepared for what she's about to face. And yet, even now, she doesn't fully understand the magnitude of what she is.

But I will protect her. No matter what it takes.

"What is she?" my father asks, his voice unusually soft, carrying an edge of caution.

Vassago doesn't hesitate, locking eyes with me as if the answer is for me alone. He gestures toward the horns father wears as a crown. "The bloodline you tried to erase—the one that once ruled the Underworld—never died out. Lydia Simmons, Layla's mother, is the direct daughter of Cronos and Rheas."

My father's face darkens. "The Sickle Reaper," he murmurs, his voice low with recognition. "I couldn't wield Cronos' sickle. He wouldn't accept me." His gaze flicks briefly to Orcus. "That's why I had you designed and forged."

Orcus hums audibly, vibrating with what I can only describe as mild indignation.

I glare at my father, my fists clenching involuntarily. "I was created—crafted—solely to shadow the male you destroyed? And now I'm *destined* to be with his granddaughter?" My voice rises, anger lacing each word.

The weight of it presses down on me, suffocating. Why am I only learning this now, after centuries of servitude and blind loyalty? Why was this hidden from me, buried under layers of lies and manipulation?

"Drepane," Orcus suddenly hums, his voice sharp and resonant.

All eyes turn to my scythe, his interjection slicing through the tension like a blade.

"Explain," I command, my tone harsher than I intend.

"The sickle's name," Orcus replies, his voice tinged with reverence. "His name is Drepane, crafted from rubies and diamonds. There's a legend, you see. It's said that Cronos hurled Drepane into the ocean. But that's far from the truth."

A heavy pause falls over the room, and I can feel Orcus savoring the moment before continuing.

"After Cronos killed his father to seize the throne, Drepane shut down—refused to be used for ill intentions ever again. When Cronos began devouring his children, the ones Rheas couldn't hide, Drepane refused him outright. Told him he'd eventually meet his end. That he would return only for the one destined to wield him—the sickle-bearing Reaper."

"And Rheas?" I press, my voice tight.

"Rheas had an affair with Hades."

The revelation lands like a thunderclap. All of us instinctively turn to him, whose face hardens as he slumps back in his throne.

"She seduced Hades to kill Cronos after hiding as many of her offspring as she could in the mortal realms," Orcus continues. "For protection. Drepane went silent after Cronos' death, waiting—waiting for the one he deemed worthy to wield him again."

"And you think that's supposed to be Layla?" I ask, trying to process the overwhelming flood of revelations.

"Her, or one of her offspring," Orcus hums, vibrating with what I can only describe as excitement. "It's hard to say for sure. I could... perhaps... convince Drepane to talk to me. For answers." His tone lifts with enthusiasm. "I must admit, I'm rather excited to meet him!"

I don't respond immediately. My eyes shift back to my father, and the fury that's been simmering now boils over. Lies. He's told me nothing but lies my entire life. Lies about my purpose. Lies about my origins. Lies about Layla's true nature.

"I only ever wanted to protect the Underworld," my father says quietly, almost as if to himself. "And yet..."

"But with Layla and Azrael being Fated Mates," Orcus interrupts, his tone growing sly and speculative, "my money's on her firstborn son. Or... perhaps Layla herself. Imagine it—Layla becoming the first female Grim Reaper." He vibrates with excitement again. "The plot thickens, indeed!"

I glare at my scythe, torn between exasperation and reluctant amusement at his dramatics. "Orcus," I snap, but his enthusiasm only grows.

"Just think of the drama, Azrael!" he chirps. "The betrayals, the forbidden bloodlines, the ancient artifacts with their secrets—this is the stuff of legends!"

I sigh, rubbing my temples as the pieces fall into place. Layla, her mother, my own creation…everything feels like a tangled web of destiny and manipulation. And now, the fate of the Underworld—and perhaps more—rests on unraveling it.

Chapter Twenty-Two

Layla

Sweet Dreams (Are Made Of This) - Emily Browning

I traced the strange, shifting shadows on the walls, my fingers grazing the surface of the chair's armrest as if it might offer some kind of comfort. But nothing here felt remotely comforting. Ashton's home—if you could even call it that—was suffocating. The air was thick, and heavy with something ancient and unsettling, like it had absorbed too many secrets over the centuries. I tried to ignore the creeping feeling that the darkness itself was alive, twisting along the walls in eerie patterns like it was watching me—waiting for me to slip up. I could almost hear the walls breathing with a life of their own.

The only thing that anchored me was the steady tick of the clock somewhere in the room, its rhythmic pulse was a reminder that I was still in the realm of the living. I clung to it, desperate for normalcy, but no matter how much I focused on the ticking, it couldn't silence the frantic buzzing inside my head. My heart pounded in my chest, erratic and fast, as if it, too, was trying to keep up with the madness swirling around me.

Across from me, Sadie looked completely unfazed, her body sprawled comfortably on the couch, every inch of her exuding that trademark confidence that never seemed to fade. If anything, the place seemed to fuel her energy, not drain it. She took it all in with an easy, knowing gaze—like she'd been waiting for this moment her whole life. She shot me one of her smirks, her eyes glinting with something I couldn't quite place, and I knew, without a doubt, that if there was any fear lurking beneath her surface, it was buried deep. Maybe too deep for anyone to ever see.

Luca sat near her, though not as relaxed. His face was pale. There was a quiet strength in him, an anchor of resilience I couldn't help but envy. He wasn't at ease here, but he wasn't losing himself either. He was holding on to something that kept him grounded in this suffocating place—something I couldn't seem to find.

And then there was Ashton. The one who owned this cursed place, who had led us all into this hellish den of shadows and mysteries. He was different from the rest of us—there was no panic in his eyes, no tremor in his hands as he casually flipped through the pages of an ancient leather-bound book. Yet every so often, his gaze flicked up, his eyes skimming over us, taking in our every move. I could feel the weight of his stare, like it was measuring me, weighing me against some invisible scale. His expression was unreadable as if he was hiding something. Maybe more than just a secret. Maybe something worse—something I wasn't ready to hear.

My breath caught in my throat as his gaze shifted toward me. For a moment, the room seemed to shrink, the oppressive weight of it pressing in, suffocating me more than ever. What was he thinking? Why couldn't I stop feeling like he knew something I didn't? It was as if he could see right through me, peeling back every layer, every fear I was too terrified to voice. The longer I sat there, the more I wanted to bolt—to run, to escape this place that felt like it was closing in on me, but I knew I couldn't. Not yet.

Every part of me screamed to move, to find an escape, but my body remained frozen, tethered to this spot. Was I afraid of Ashton? Or was I afraid of what might happen if I let myself truly see him? Every time our eyes met, it felt like something inside me shifted, like I was standing on the edge of a cliff, about to fall into a chasm I couldn't climb out of.

Azrael's absence gnawed at me like a persistent ache, a reminder of the fragility of the world I now found myself in. Against all logic, he had become my anchor in this twisted nightmare—a dark comfort in a place where everything felt unfamiliar like it might swallow me whole. The thought of him not being here twisted in my gut like a blade.

I tried to push the feeling aside, to focus on something—anything—to break the oppressive silence that seemed to stretch on forever. But no matter how hard I tried, the questions lodged themselves in my throat, stubborn and heavy, held back by a paralyzing fear. Fear of the answers I wasn't sure I was ready for.

So I waited. My breath was shallow, my heart racing, clutching to the only thing in this place that felt solid—the clock's ticking. Its steady, unyielding rhythm was the only thing keeping me grounded and drowning out the voices of fear that echoed relentlessly in my mind. They are whispers of doubt and confusion that I couldn't shake.

The shadows around me seemed to shift again, but this time it wasn't the room. It wasn't just the haunting flicker of darkness playing tricks on my eyes. No, this was different. This was Azrael.

I didn't hear the door open, but I felt him the instant he entered, his presence filling the room like a storm rolling in. A towering shadow, dark and inevitable, his scythe gleaming like a blade forged in the heart of midnight. His form was familiar, comforting in its own right, but it wasn't just him that stood in the doorway. Behind him, there was another figure.

Vassago. The sight of him sent a sharp jolt through my chest. The Guardian Angel looked like he had been through hell itself. His wings were tattered and torn, blood staining the feathers in streaks of crimson. His skin was covered in bruises, and dark patches that marred what looked like it once was a flawless appearance. Even from across the room, I could feel the weight of his exhaustion, the way his body trembled with each painful step.

My chest tightened with a wave of empathy and dread crashing over me. The sight of him like this—so broken, so far removed from the ethereal being I had imagined him to be—was almost too much to bear. I wanted to ask Azrael what had happened, to demand answers. But my body betrayed me, keeping me rooted to the spot, too afraid to move. I wanted to rush to his side, but the sight of his emotional suffering left me paralyzed, a pit of shame opening in my stomach at the thought of running toward him when I was so terrified of what it all meant.

"Layla," Azrael's voice cut through the haze of my thoughts, steady and grounding. It wrapped around me like a lifeline. But there was something else in his tone—an edge, a subtle tension, simmering beneath the surface. His gaze locked with mine, intense and unwavering. I wanted to speak, to tell him how much I was struggling, but the words stuck in my throat, choked by the weight of the situation.

And then there was Orcus. The scythe's low hum filled the room, a disapproving vibration that seemed to resonate through my bones. It was as though Orcus could sense the same thing I did—the deep anger, the quiet rage that Azrael was holding back. I could almost hear the weapon's irritation in the air, a simmering frustration at the state Vassago was in, at the way he had been treated, the way his body had been broken and battered. I didn't know if it was Azrael's anger, Orcus' resentment, or my own, but the air was thick with it.

Sadie straightened in her seat, her usual smirk replaced by a rare look of concern as she took in Vassago's condition. Luca, too, went rigid, his eyes narrowing as his protective instincts seemed to kick in. Ashton, ever the calm presence, allowed his mask to slip for just a moment. His gaze darkened a flicker of something—something colder, sharper—passing through his eyes.

But I couldn't look away from Vassago. He is nothing more than a broken, bloodied shell of the being I had once imagined him to be.

I wanted to ask what had happened to him, to demand answers from Azrael, from anyone who could explain the horror that had turned the once-glorious angel into this shattered version of himself. But the words never came. I stayed frozen, staring at the broken wings, the bruises, the blood, fighting back the instinct to *run*. I was ashamed of my fear, ashamed of my inability to step forward, to do anything but watch. I felt so small in this moment, my courage slipping away like sand through my fingers. And still, all I could do was wait.

"Layla," Azrael repeats my name, his voice deeper this time, more insistent. "We need to talk."

I glance at Sadie, searching her face for some kind of reassurance. She's quiet, her usual smirk nowhere to be found, but that's not enough to calm the frantic pulse hammering in my chest. I drag my eyes back to Azrael, feeling the weight of his gaze like an anchor pulling me under.

"We can talk later, alone," I start, my voice shaking more than I want to admit.

Azrael cuts me off, his tone heavy with something unspoken. "But we need to talk now." He says it again, and the way the words hang in the air, thick with tension, makes my skin prickle.

The silence stretches, thick and suffocating, until Ashton breaks it with a question that makes the air grow even colder. "What did Hades say?"

Azrael's eyes shift to the floor for a moment, as if gathering the strength to say something. When he meets Ashton's gaze again, it's like he's measuring the weight of his words. "Did you know?"

The question hangs there, unanswered, as we all stare at each other, the heaviness in the room mounting by the second. I try to make sense of what's happening, but it feels like I'm just being tossed around in a storm of information I can't catch.

"Did you know about the story of Persephone?" Azrael continues, his voice is tight with a strange mix of anger and sorrow. "About Cronos and Rhea? And the rumors of me being fated to the direct descendant from Cronos?"

Ashton looks so small in his own home, caught off guard by the weight of the question. There's a flicker of something in his eyes, something unreadable. He's trying to hide it, but it's there, and I can't look away.

Then Azrael's words take a darker turn. "She kidnapped Vassago and stuffed him in the prison. She tortured him." His gaze shifts to his brother then, and the raw emotion in it sends a chill straight through me. "I got permission today to build an army. We are now at war."

The words hit me like a punch to the stomach, and I felt the blood drain from my face. War. There's no mistaking what that means, and it leaves my mind reeling. But it's not just the threat of war that makes my heart race—no, it's the way everyone's eyes turn to me. The weight of their stares feels like a thousand pounds pressing down on my chest. It's as though they expect something from me, and I don't know what it is, but it makes the anxiety in my veins spike higher, twisting like a knot I can't undo.

I want to speak, to ask questions, to understand why this is happening, but all that fills my head is the sound of my heart pounding in my ears.

And then it hits me, a surge of jealousy so sharp, it's almost painful. The realization slams into me with a force I can't stop. Azrael—Azrael is spoken for. He's off the table. The one person I've clung to in this chaotic, dangerous world is already someone else's, and I feel the weight of that truth settle like a stone in my chest.

Any hope of locking him down, of making him mine, is out the window. Gone.

I swallow, my throat tight, but the tears won't stop. They swell in my eyes, burning with the sting of something I can't fully grasp. It feels so stupid—so petty, even—but it's like the world just knocked my legs out from under me.

My sense of safety, of peace, was snatched away before I could even hold it, and now I'm left with this ache, this emptiness that I don't know how to fill.

I look down at my feet, fighting the tears, trying to hide the vulnerability that's threatening to spill out. I don't want anyone to see me break down over something so insignificant when there are bigger, more pressing dangers at play. But it doesn't matter. The tears come anyway, hot and unchecked, and all I can do is stand there, silently, feeling like I'm losing control of everything around me.

"Do not cry, Layla." Orcus hums through the chaos of the room, his voice smooth and low, like the calm after a storm. "There's a plot twist."

I blink, almost not trusting my own ears. My mind's still reeling, but I swear there's a twinkle in his voice, something playful that doesn't belong in this heavy moment. It almost feels like he's winking at me, though I know that's impossible. But then again, Orcus is never *really* impossible, I am learning.

"I know things no one else knows," he continues, his tone laced with something both comforting and cryptic. "What I can tell you from what I know, and what I sense from your emotions—you will be okay, Layla."

I don't know why, but the way he says it, so certain, somehow makes my chest tighten less. His voice is an anchor in a sea of uncertainty, and for a moment, I feel like maybe, just maybe, I'll survive this mess. It's ridiculous how much that twisted scythe of his can ease my panic.

I take a shaky breath and look for Azrael's blue eyes. The sight of him is always a little soothing, but today it feels different. His gaze locks with mine, steady and soft, a gentle reassurance in his quiet smile. And when he gives me that shy little curve of his lips, I realize—he's just as nervous as I am. Maybe even more so.

It's strange, and comforting in a way I didn't expect. He's been the one with all the answers, the one who stays calm in the storm, but today, it feels like we're in this together, both of us fumbling through a world that doesn't make sense.

Sadie's voice cuts through the moment, loud and clear, her usual sharp tone a little softer in her confusion. "Why is it not hot here? Why is there no fire?"

Her question hangs in the air, and for a second, no one knows how to respond.

Chapter Twenty-Three

Layla

Mad World - Jasmine Thompson

Azrael leads me down a corridor, away from the others. The weight of his silence hangs heavily in the air, and with every step, my unease grows. I've learned to read him, to pick up on the subtle changes in his posture, the stiffness in his shoulders, and right now, there's something about him that feels... off. He's not the same Azrael who had been a twisted comfort to me. This one feels distant, haunted.

Back in the main room, Ashton had apologized over and over, his voice shaking with guilt as he admitted to withholding things from Azrael—things I didn't even fully understand. Azrael, still visibly upset, had hugged him and offered forgiveness, but the tension between them lingered. Vassago, looking worse for wear, had retreated to a room to rest, and I overheard something about "healing energy" that only made me more confused. Apparently, when supernaturals share their energy, they heal faster. Azrael and Orcus had already gone through their shift of exchange—whatever that meant—and now they were ready for me.

Luca's color is slowly returning, but his eyes are still haunted, distant. I can't blame him. As for Sadie, she's been relentless, throwing out flirtations toward Ashton that leave him looking both uncomfortable and... maybe overwhelmed. Sadie has never been the shy type, but it's clear Ashton isn't sure what to do with her bold advances—or maybe it's just the sheer number of people packed into his space.

We finally reach a door at the end of the hall. Azrael opens it and steps inside, his presence pulling me in after him. He closes the door behind us, shutting out everything that came before.

The room is small but neatly arranged, with two twin beds facing each other and a vanity with bright lights framing a mirror. Each bed has its own end table and lamp, the simplicity of the setup almost normal compared to the world outside these walls. But nothing feels normal in this moment.

Azrael walks over to one of the beds and leans Orcus against the foot of it before sitting down next to the scythe, his posture rigid, like he's bracing for something. I stay standing, unsure what to do with myself. The silence between us stretches, thick and uncomfortable. Then, he looks up at me, his eyes flicking nervously before he speaks.

"We need to talk," Azrael says quietly, his voice heavier than I've ever heard it. His hands tremble as they clasp together in his lap, his fingers wringing themselves like he's trying to hold onto something—anything. He swallows, his usual calm gone, replaced by something...raw. "I need to be one hundred percent honest with you. And from here on out, I promise, Layla, I will be honest with you. No more secrets."

The words fall into the space between us like stones, heavy and unsettling. I open my mouth to respond, but nothing comes out at first. I'm too busy trying to process what this means, what he's trying to tell me. I rack my brain for something—anything—that could explain his sudden need for this level of honesty.

"What are you talking about?" The words come out sharper than I intended, but I can't help it. My heart races, and I feel a sudden coldness spreading through me.

If we were in a relationship, I'd be prepared for a breakup speech. I'd expect the worst, something about how he couldn't do this anymore, how he'd found someone else, or maybe—just maybe—he had cheated. My stomach twists at the thought.

But that's not it. It can't be. Azrael doesn't belong to me. Not in that way.

The realization hits me like a wave. He belongs to someone else. He's always belonged to someone else. And no matter how much I've come to care for him, I know my place in his world—just another passing moment, another side story in a life that isn't mine to hold.

But the feelings I've developed for him... they don't vanish with logic. It's not that simple. His presence in my life has anchored me in ways I can't explain. He gives me a sense of peace, a temporary relief from the chaos that constantly swirls around me. The idea that I might lose that, that I might never have it at all, gnaws at something deep inside me.

Azrael's eyes drop to his hands again, the tremor in his fingers more pronounced now. He doesn't meet my gaze, and for a moment, I wonder if he even knows what to say next. It feels like everything that was once certain between us—whatever fragile connection we had—is slipping away.

"I'm not... I'm not good at this," Azrael murmurs, almost to himself. "I don't know how to... how to make this right. I don't know how to be what you need, Layla. But I have to be honest with you. And that means..."

He trails off, looking up at me with an expression that I can't quite read, a mix of guilt, regret, and something else. Fear?

I don't know what to say. Every part of me wants to reach out, to tell him that it's okay, that we'll figure it out. But I can't. I won't lie to him. And I won't lie to myself, either.

"You don't have to explain yourself," I finally say, my voice quiet, brittle. "I'm not... I'm not expecting you to be perfect. I don't even know what I'm expecting." The words feel hollow as soon as they leave my mouth. I don't know what I'm trying to say, but it feels like we're both trapped in this tangled web of unspoken truths.

Azrael shifts uncomfortably on the bed, his gaze never leaving mine. His lips twitch like he's trying to find the words to ease the tension, but nothing comes. I wonder if he's even capable of saying what he's thinking.

"I'm scared, Layla," he admits, the words coming out in a low whisper, almost lost in the silence. "Scared that I won't be enough. Scared that I'll hurt you, or worse, that I'll push you away when I need you the most."

His vulnerability hits me harder than I expected. I feel a lump form in my throat, the sudden urge to comfort him is overwhelming. But I can't. Not right now. Not with everything hanging in the balance.

"I'm here," I manage to say, though it feels weak, too small for the weight of the situation.

Azrael nods, his eyes flicking down to Orcus, then back up to me. There's a moment of silence, heavy with everything that's been left unsaid.

"This will be harder for her to process," Orcus nearly sings, his voice carrying a note of warning. He knows. We both know how fragile my state of mind is right now. And as much as I want to pretend otherwise, I feel like I'm hanging by a thread.

But deep down, I don't think anything else can phase me at this point.

"Just rip the band-aid off," I mutter under my breath, the bitterness seeping through.

Expect the unexpected. My best friend is practically throwing herself at Ashton, the Sandman, for crying out loud. There's a werewolf in the next room, and I've just met my Guardian Angel. Oh, and let's not forget Azrael and his talking scythe. Just another Tuesday in my life. Or at least, it should be.

Azrael opens his mouth, but Orcus interrupts, humming softly, "You and Azrael met prematurely, Layla. At the worst possible time…"

"You're breaking up with me and we aren't even together?" I scream at Azrael, cutting Orcus off, the words like an involuntary eruption.

Azrael throws his hands up in the air, waving them side to side in frustration. I can almost hear him thinking, *Why is this so complicated?*

Orcus laughs a dark chuckle, "You should know by now he has a disability where he can't properly talk to you. It's a wonder you two even made it this far."

Azrael's face falls. He looks like I just crushed whatever was left of his self-esteem. "This is really hard to explain, Layla," he says, his voice tight with hesitation. "And I know it's going to change everything for you. You have a choice to make, and whatever you choose, I'll stand by you."

"Now she has a choice?" Orcus' voice drips with sarcasm. "Where was her choice when you stuck—"

Azrael moves faster than I can blink. He grabs Orcus by the blade and places a pillow over it with a force that I can feel through the air. Orcus lets out a screech of indignation.

"What happened to being truthful?" Orcus wails from underneath the pillow.

Azrael's voice is quiet, barely a whisper, as he looks up at me, the sincerity in his eyes almost unbearable. "I want you to know everything. I don't want you to feel trapped, Layla. I don't want to lie to you anymore." He sighs heavily. "I understand if you're mad, or upset. I will give you space if I say something that makes you angry. But, I need you to understand. I didn't want any of this for you."

"I'm stuck here." My voice cracks as I admit it, the weight of the words sinking deep into my chest. "I can't go back home. This is my reality now. I'm stuck with you, Azrael. And with you, Orcus." The words feel cold like they shouldn't belong to me. But they do. I'm trapped here in this world I never asked for, with people who hold pieces of my fate, I can't comprehend.

I can't go home. I can't wake up from this nightmare. My mother will report me missing soon enough. I can picture it—her calling the police, confused, terrified, when I don't show up for therapy or when she finds my groceries untouched. My house ransacked and destroyed.

Azrael takes a deep breath, releasing some of the pressure off the pillow that's now holding Orcus' blade hostage. "I have a lot to tell you," he says, the words strained, as though they are physically painful for him to utter. His body is tense, like he's about to run but forces himself to stay. "I don't know where to start, but I think we should start with the things that won't make you hate me more." His voice cracks at the end of that sentence.

I give a small nod, trying to reassure him, though I feel the fear building inside me. I don't know if I'm ready for whatever comes next.

"Tiny mouse..." He hesitates, his words faltering as though he's testing each one. Then, as if he's finally giving in, he blurts it out. "You're not mortal."

The air around us stills. I can't even process what I'm hearing. His words echo in my head like they're not even meant for me.

"What do you mean?" I stutter, the confusion seeping through my voice. It's like everything I thought I knew about myself is suddenly being ripped away.

Azrael leans forward, his eyes wide with the intensity of his revelation. "Your mother is a succubus. A hidden one. Highly powerful. She's the direct descendant of Cronos and Rhea—the ones who once ruled the Underworld."

My blood runs cold. I can feel the room shrinking around me, my heart pounding in my ears. "What?" I can barely form the words. "My mother... a succubus? That's insane."

He nods, his face grim. "Cronos didn't want to pass on the throne. He killed every one of his children, every single one of them. But Rhea—your grandmother—she took what children she could, the infants, and hid them in the Mortal Realm before Cronos killed her for betraying him."

My mind spins. *This can't be real. It can't be true.*

"Hades," Azrael continues, "was having an affair with Rhea after losing Persephone. And before Rhea died, she had Hades...terminate Cronos."

My breath catches in my throat. "I don't understand," I whisper, my eyes locked on Azrael's. "This... this doesn't make sense."

He exhales slowly, as though bracing himself for the weight of my disbelief. "I know it's a lot, Layla. But your bloodline... it's ancient. Powerful. And you have a choice to make now. A choice that could change everything for you—and for the Underworld."

I search his face, looking for some sign that this is a joke, that he's not serious, that none of this is real. But I find nothing but the truth in his eyes.

"Memetim is targeting you because..." Azrael trails off, his eyes searching for the right words. "Remember when I told you she believed you took—or were taking—something that belonged to her?"

I nod, still trying to wrap my mind around everything he's just told me.

He continues, "Me. She wanted to go through with a marriage pact arranged by my father, but I refused. She asked her sister, Fate, why I would refuse. Fate told her..." Azrael pauses, locking eyes with me, as if this is the crux of it all. "I was fated to be with a woman named Layla."

The room seems to close in as the weight of his words settles over me.

"A fated mate bond that can only be broken by death," Orcus adds, his voice laced with something like finality.

But everything inside me is screaming that none of this can be true.

I'm just... me. Mortal. Fragile. *I'm nobody*. And yet this man, the one I've already become so attached to, is telling me I'm more.

"You were glamoured to appear mortal," Azrael says softly, almost gently. "You pass as a mortal to all supernaturals... even me." He exhales a deep, frustrated breath. "No matter what emotions are running through your head, I will respect them. You can set whatever boundaries you feel are right. I'll respect that. But all I ask is that you allow me to still be there for you. To still protect you.

To teach you about the legacy you don't know, the laws of the Underworld. My trainer is incredible—he can—"

"Azrael." I cut him off, my voice trembling. "This is all too much. I am human. I am mortal. I am a nobody. I think you have the wrong Layla."

Tears start to well up, the pressure in my chest rising until it feels like I might break open. They spill down my cheeks, my emerald eyes losing focus as the reality of it all crashes into me.

This can't be happening. *This can't be my life.*

"Baby girl," Azrael murmurs, his voice low as he reaches out for me. I allow him to pull me close, needing the comfort. The thought that I might be the *wrong* Layla fills me with a sharp, gnawing fear.

"To you, maybe," he continues, his fingers gently brushing my cheek to wipe away the tears. "But to me? I'd set both realms on fire and behead any entity that gets in the way of you being happy." He presses a soft kiss to my forehead. "I knew from the second I saw you walking past the coffee shop that I needed you in my life. It's I who am a nobody. I'm the underdog. The failure."

"What do you mean?" I ask, my voice small as I search his beautiful blue eyes for answers.

"Ready for the talk that's going to piss you off?" His sly grin creeps up again, trying to lighten the moment.

I push him away, frustration bubbling up. He's ruining the beautiful vulnerability of this moment.

"Remember when you thought I—" Azrael mimics a crude gesture, sprinkling me with imaginary jizz.

"He fingered you," Orcus hisses impatiently from across the room, voice dripping with sarcasm.

Without thinking, I punch Azrael as hard as I can, dead center in the face. The smack of flesh against flesh is satisfying, but his exaggerated whine makes me regret it immediately.

"Ow! I deserved that," Azrael whines, rubbing his cheek where I landed the blow.

Chapter Twenty-Four

Azrael

My Blood - Twenty One Pilots

I walk out of the room, still holding my nose. It's throbbing. But my conscience is clear. I don't know how much longer I could've kept looking at Layla without knowing that I crossed a line—one I shouldn't have. I never wanted to be a predator, like Orcus had called me. I'm not that. But I broke her trust, and I know it.

"Fucking boundaries, Azrael! Learn them!" Layla's voice follows me down the hallway, and I hear objects crashing against the wall as she throws whatever she can at me. I don't care. I deserve it.

I make my way back to the living room, joining the group. They all look at me with varying degrees of concern.

"Did... she... punch you?" Ashton's voice is laced with disbelief. "What did you do to her?"

I shrug, sinking into the empty recliner. It's strategically placed so that when Layla enters, she's forced to sit across from me, directly on the couch. I need to see her face, even if it means enduring the fury in her eyes. I have no idea how I'm going to fix this, but I'll do whatever it takes.

I will always be here for her—no matter how long it takes. Even if it never happens, I'll be here. I never thought we'd even have conversations, but here we are... and I still managed to mess it all up.

Layla stomps in, steam practically blowing out of her ears. Her eyes lock onto me, and I shoot her a grin, followed by a wink. The smile I offer is an attempt to diffuse the tension, but I know it's futile. She's beyond pissed.

"How many of you fucking knew I was fated to this creep or whatever it's called?" Layla's words strike like thunder, and my grin fades. I'm not sure what to say, but I sure as hell wasn't ready for this.

Luca stares at her, eyes wide, his gaze flicking nervously between her and me. He scoots further away from her on the couch.

"Above my pay grade," Ashton mutters, then quickly tries to walk out of the room. Layla doesn't let him get far. She grabs a heavy book from the coffee table and hurl sit at him. It collides with the back of his head with a *satisfying* thud.

Ashton winces, grabbing the back of his head. He spins around, his face twisted in mock outrage. "Let's not forget who freed you from the Angel of Death, ma'am."

Layla doesn't miss a beat. "You freed me to make me a pawn in your fucked-up supernatural drama!" Her words are sharp, her frustration clear.

Orcus chuckles from his corner. "Luca, we need popcorn. This is getting good."

"You can't even eat!" Sadie snaps, rushing over to rub Ashton's head where the book hit. It's her way of showing concern, but it's clear she's more amused than anything else.

"That's not all she wants to rub, Ashton," Orcus teases, his voice dripping with mischief.

"Stop being a shit starter, Orcus!" Layla yells, cutting through the tension. "You're not helping!"

I can't help but smirk, despite the mess I've made. If there's one thing about this chaotic, fucked-up family we've become, it's that no one knows how to navigate anger without a little humor to lighten the mood.

But Layla's fury still hangs in the air, thick and heavy. I take a deep breath and finally speak up. "I didn't want this for you, Layla. Not like this." My voice is steady, but there's an undercurrent of regret that I can't hide.

Her eyes snap to mine. "Well, maybe you should've thought about that before you—"

I can't help it; I throw my head back and laugh, every fiber of my being shaking with it. "We've never had this much drama in the Underworld. This is far more interesting than Vassago letting me take the throne."

Everyone freezes. Even Layla pauses in the middle of whatever she's doing to turn and stare at me.

"Are you taking it?" Ashton asks, his voice tinged with disbelief.

I shrug, my mind running through all the complexities of the idea. It doesn't feel real, and I don't know if I want it.

"Do you think you can handle giving up being a Reaper and breeding your own army?" Ashton scratches his head thoughtfully, then glances at Layla with a sympathetic expression.

I chuckle dryly, feeling the weight of the decision pressing on me. "I'm thinking if I do take it, the laws regarding that will have to change. This bag of bones belongs to one being and one being only. Even if she doesn't want me." I smile, but it's hollow, the ache in my chest far too deep to ignore. Layla is mine, but she's not fully mine unless she gives herself to me completely, willingly. And that...I don't know if she will ever do that.

She looks at me, her voice softer than I expect, but there's pain in it. "I never said that, Azrael."

I wait, holding my breath, hoping for something—anything—to tell me that I'm wrong. "I said I think you have the wrong Layla. I am scared of *dying*, Azrael."

The words hang in the air like a thunderstorm on the horizon, charged with the weight of everything we've been avoiding. Ashton, ever the one to cut through the tension, glances at Layla. "Your mother's name is Lydia? Correct?" he asks, confirming something we all suspected. Layla nods, and Ashton turns to me, his gaze understanding, maybe even resigned. "She's the right Layla."

He shrugs, making his exit toward the dark hallways, Sadie trailing after him to keep the peace—or maybe just to escape before Layla throws something at him again.

"I'm scared of death. So how can I be his mate?" Layla's voice trembles, raw and vulnerable. She looks at Luca, almost pleading for answers. But Luca, poor guy, is too terrified to offer anything, his eyes darting to me.

I study her, my heart twisting as her words feel like a blade sliding between my ribs. *I am scared of death, Azrael.* Her fear resonates with me in a way I didn't expect. It echoes in the room, making my chest tighten as if the air itself is too thick to breathe.

I want to tell her that being scared doesn't mean she's not the *right* Layla. It only means she's human, feeling the very thing that makes her mortal. But it's harder to speak than I thought. Every word I try to find feels too fragile, too broken.

I take a deep breath, feeling the weight of the moment press down on me. "It's not about being fearless, Layla." My voice comes out quieter than I planned, more vulnerable than I expected. "It's... knowing what's at the end of the road and still choosing to walk it." I step closer, my eyes locked on hers. "Besides, you're braver than you think you are."

Before she can respond, Orcus' voice cuts through the quiet, sharp, and familiar in my mind. *Azrael, you're not fooling anyone here. Trying to dress death as a choice? She's terrified, and you know it. If you want her to see things your way, just...*

I cut him off with a mental growl, my frustration building. *Enough*, I send back, and there's a brief silence before Orcus' presence retreats, albeit reluctantly.

I don't know if what I said will help. I don't even know if she believes me. But I won't stop trying to show her that there's more than just fear at the end of the road we're walking down together.

Layla was watching me, her eyes filled with a mix of pain and confusion. The weight of her gaze hit me like a ton of bricks. "I don't know if I can ever give myself completely to someone who brings death, Azrael. You walk between two worlds like it's nothing. For me, it..." She paused, her eyes flicking downward as if the words themselves were too heavy. "It's suffocating."

Her words stung more than I expected, but I nodded. "I understand," I said, though the words felt wrong, almost hollow. I didn't want to push her, didn't want her to feel cornered. "You don't have to give yourself completely, not yet. Just... don't close the door."

Orcus, his voice softer than usual, added with an unexpected gentleness, "Maybe there's no rush. Eternity's a long time, you know."

But I could see it in her eyes—the look that told me eternity wasn't what she feared. It was the unknown. And that was the one thing I couldn't protect her from. I couldn't shield her from the confusion of learning she was part supernatural, not when it was so deeply tied to everything she was.

I ran my hand over the back of my neck, searching for the right words to ease her, to make her feel less alone in this storm of uncertainty. "Layla, I..." I hesitated, knowing this wouldn't fix anything. "I know this is overwhelming, but you're not alone. You've got Sadie. You've got..." I stopped and the weight of the words I was trying to say are hanging heavy. "... You've got me."

She locked eyes with me, and for a moment, it felt like I could see every part of her—the pain, the frustration, the confusion. "But why didn't anyone tell me? You—Ashton—everyone's hiding things from me. You let me believe I was just..." She trailed off, her voice sharp, frustration lacing every word. "Human."

Orcus couldn't resist, his voice cutting in dryly, *I told you this would come back to haunt you. Keeping her in the dark like that? Real smooth, Azrael.* Sarcasm laces his tone.

I clenched my jaw, the irritation bubbling up, but I forced myself to stay calm. I couldn't let him derail this conversation. "Layla, I know it feels like a betrayal, but it wasn't by choice. If I could've told you sooner, I would have. I..." I sighed, closing my eyes briefly as the weight of it all hit me. "I felt like it would break you. You were barely holding it together already. I didn't want to overwhelm you more."

Her silence lingered, hanging between us like a wall. I could see her struggling with what I said, trying to process everything all at once. I could almost hear her thoughts spiraling, and I wished more than anything I could give her the answers she needed. But right now, all I could offer her was time.

Layla's brow furrowed, her emotions are a storm brewing beneath the surface—half anger, half hurt. "But if I am only part of this world... If I'm not fully human..." She shook her head, her voice cracking under the weight of everything she was trying to comprehend. "What am I supposed to do with that? Just accept it?"

Orcus, unusually quiet for a moment, then murmured with an unexpected tenderness, *Go easy on her, Azrael. She will break before she bends.*

I didn't need to think twice. For once, Orcus had a point. I softened my tone, leaning forward, trying to bridge the gap between us. "You don't have to accept anything right away, Layla. Take it slow. Step by step. I'll be here. I'm not going anywhere."

Her eyes softened—just a fraction—but it was enough. She nodded, though the storm in her gaze hadn't quite settled. It was something.

I paused, the weight of everything left unsaid pressing down on me. "I'm not rushing you, Layla. I know what I told you—about who you are, about us—probably feels like another battle, but I didn't want you to hear it from someone else. Someone who might twist it and use it against you."

She looked away then, her jaw tight, the muscles in her neck stiff. "And if I... If I can't handle it?"

The question hung in the air like a lead weight. My chest tightened with a sense of helplessness I couldn't shake. *If she can't handle it... if she can't handle me...*

I forced myself to focus on her, to push the doubt aside. "If you can't handle it now, that's okay. It won't change anything." My voice softened, the words almost too heavy to say. "But know this—war with Memetim is different. She doesn't care about boundaries or mercy. She will come for anything that matters to me."

She looked at me, the flicker of fear in her eyes burning into mine, but it quickly transformed into something else—something close to determination. "So you're saying I'm a target now?"

The bitter laugh that escaped me had no humor in it, just the sharp edge of reality. "You've been a target even before the moment I saw you."

Orcus let out a sardonic chuckle. *Romantic as ever, boss. Keep talking like that, and she'll fall right into your arms—running.*

I shot back at him, *Would you be quiet for once?* But his words stung in a way I hadn't expected. It struck a nerve—one I didn't want to acknowledge.

Layla folded her arms, her eyes searching mine, her posture defensive but still, she was waiting for something from me. "So what now?"

I met her gaze, steadying myself. My mind raced with a thousand thoughts, but only a handful felt worthy of her. I didn't want to over promise, didn't want to offer false comfort. "Now? Now, we stay close. We learn who we can trust. And we don't let Memetim—or anyone else—tear us apart."

She held my stare, a silent war between us. There was a flicker of something in her eyes—fear, uncertainty, but also a willingness to try. It was a fragile thing, but it was something. I saw it, and for a moment, I wondered if I could be enough for her. If I could protect her from everything that was coming.

I cleared my throat, breaking the silence. "Off to bed, tiny mouse." I tried to soften the mood, a hint of playfulness in my voice, but it wasn't for her benefit—it was for mine. "You too, Wolfy," I added, shooting Luca a smile to ease his nervousness. He hadn't said a word, but I could feel his tension creeping into the air.

Luca nodded, his eyes wide with relief, though he didn't look entirely convinced.

For once, I hated being a supernatural who couldn't rest. I wasn't human, and there were no sweet escapes for me, no peaceful slumber. While they slept, I would be wide awake, haunted by the weight of my responsibilities. By the knowledge that even in the quietest moments, the storm could strike again at any time.

Chapter Twenty-Five

Layla

Everybody Talks - Neon Trees

The scent of coffee and something sweet tugged me from my restless sleep, guiding me out of my room like a siren's call. My movements were slow, my thoughts still knotted from the night before. As I stepped into the kitchen, I paused at the doorway, surveying the scene before me like I had stumbled into some sort of sitcom.

Sadie was perched at the table, buttering a croissant with the intensity of someone whose breakfast had personally offended them. Across from her was Luca, who somehow managed to look even scruffier than usual, was halfway through a mountain of toast. Ashton lounged at the head of the table, looking way too regal for someone in pajama pants, while Azrael stood by the counter, pouring coffee like it was some sacred ritual. And then there was Orcus, leaning casually against the table—if a glowing scythe could lean.

The moment I entered, Orcus' voice cut through the soft hum of morning conversation.

"Azrael, I still don't understand why you insist on brewing coffee like a mortal. Do you enjoy torturing yourself, or is this some form of penance?"

Azrael didn't even look up as he poured. "Some of us appreciate the process, Orcus. You wouldn't understand."

"I wouldn't? You've dragged me through your endless brooding monologues; I know exactly how much you enjoy making things unnecessarily complicated."

Sadie snorted into her mug, drawing everyone's attention. "Wow. This thing's got more personality than half the people I've dated."

"You flatter me, mortal," Orcus replied, dripping sarcasm. "But I assure you, my standards are far too high for whatever atrocities you've called 'dates.'"

"Oh, please. Like you could even pull off dating. Do you even have a face?"

Orcus' blade shimmered faintly. "Do you even know how to shut the hell up?"

"Children," Ashton cuts in, raising an eyebrow so perfectly arched I couldn't tell if he was annoyed or entertained. "Can we focus on the food? Some of us prefer to eat before the insults start flying."

"They've been flying since I got here," Luca muttered, mouth full of toast.

"Don't talk with your mouth full," Azrael said, his tone laced with authority.

"You're not my dad," Luca shot back.

"Trust me," Orcus chimed in, "if he were your dad, you'd be wearing a sweater vest right now and apologizing for existing."

Luca swallowed and smirked. "Didn't realize the scythe was a comedian."

"More of a multitasker," Orcus replied, radiating smugness only a sentient weapon could pull off.

I leaned against the doorframe, feeling a little dazed as the banter swirled around me. Despite the chaos, there was an odd comfort in it. Maybe I wasn't ready to fully embrace it, but in that moment, it felt like they were my new strange, dysfunctional family.

I sat down quietly, hoping to blend in. My fingers wrapped around the mug of coffee that Sadie slid my way without a word. Her grin barely contained, she leaned over and whispered, "This is gold."

Out loud, she asked, "Are you all always like this?"

"Yes," Ashton and Azrael answered in perfect unison.

"It's exhausting," Luca added, stabbing his fork into a piece of scrambled egg.

"Speak for yourself," Sadie said, elbowing me lightly. "I'm loving this. It's like breakfast and stand-up comedy rolled into one."

Ashton sighed dramatically. "And I'm apparently the only grown-up here."

"You?" Azrael asked, his lips curving into a rare smirk. "You're the one who still eats cereal with marshmallows."

"I'll have you know," Ashton replied, completely unbothered, "those marshmallows are a perfectly acceptable part of a balanced breakfast."

"They're literally sugar," Azrael shot back.

"And this coffee you worship is literally just bean water," Ashton said with a shrug, "but I don't judge."

Sadie burst into laughter, and I couldn't help the small smile tugging at the corner of my lips. For the first time in days, the crushing weight in my chest felt a little lighter. These people—whatever they were—had a way of making the world seem less terrifying, even if only for a moment.

Sadie raised her mug. "Here's to mornings that don't completely suck."

"Cheers," Orcus said, his tone managing to sound both sarcastic and sincere at once.

Laughter filled the room, and for a fleeting moment, the chaos of my life didn't feel so heavy.

I glanced over at Sadie, who had been unusually chipper this morning. Her grin was just a little too smug. Suspicious. I tilted my head, narrowing my eyes. "Why didn't you come back to the room last night? Where did you sleep?"

Sadie froze mid-sip of her coffee, her cheeks turning crimson in a way that screamed guilty as charged. She avoided my gaze, muttering into her mug, "Ashton's room."

The room went silent. Too silent. Then Azrael, sitting across from us, let out a groan.

"Of course. Why wouldn't you?" he muttered, shooting Ashton an accusatory look.

Ashton, unbothered as always, raised his hands in mock innocence. "What? She said she needed somewhere to crash. I was being hospitable."

"Hospitable," Azrael repeated, his voice dripping with sarcasm. "That's what we're calling it now?"

"Is it so hard to believe I was a perfect gentleman?" Ashton asked, reclining in his chair with an infuriatingly smug smile.

"Oh, please," Orcus interjected, his voice cutting through the tension like a blade—quite literally, given that he was a blade. "You're about as gentlemanly as a wolf in sheep's clothing. Sorry, no offense, Luca."

"None taken," Luca mumbles with toast in his mouth.

"Admit it, you took her in to fuel your insatiable ego."

Ashton feigned offense, pressing a hand to his chest. "You wound me, Orcus. I'll have you know I'm a paragon of restraint."

"Restraint?!" Azrael barked a laugh. "You, Ashton, have the self-control of a toddler in a candy store."

Sadie, still blushing but clearly unwilling to let the guys steal the show, leaned back in her chair with an exaggerated yawn. "You all can keep speculating, but I'll let you know one thing."

Everyone turned to her, their curiosity piqued.

"What?" Azrael asked, clearly bracing for impact.

Sadie grinned wickedly. "None of your business."

Ashton chuckled, lifting his coffee cup in a mock toast. "A lady never tells."

Azrael rolled his eyes so hard I thought they might fall out. "You two are insufferable."

"Thank you," Sadie and Ashton said in unison, both of them smiling like co-conspirators.

I pinched the bridge of my nose, shaking my head. "I shouldn't have asked."

Before anyone could add another quip, the door to the dining room creaked open, and the air shifted. A heavy presence filled the room, and we all turned as Vassago stepped inside.

He looked... rough. His robes were torn and bloodied, his face was still pale and bruised. The sight made my stomach drop.

Azrael was on his feet in an instant, his chair scraping loudly against the floor. "Vassago," he said, his voice low and tight.

Vassago's piercing gaze swept over the room before landing on Azrael. His voice, though hoarse, carried an undeniable authority. "We need to talk."

"Nice of you to join us," Orcus quipped, though his usual sarcasm was subdued. "You're only missing breakfast and half a dozen insults."

Vassago ignored him, stepping further into the room. His eyes briefly flicked to me and then to Sadie, and I could swear there was a flicker of recognition—concern, even—but it vanished as quickly as it appeared.

"Is it bad?" Azrael asked, his tone clipped, already bracing for whatever grim news Vassago had brought.

Vassago nodded once. "It's bad."

The air seemed heavier as Vassago stepped into the room, his presence commanding attention without a word. His appearance was jarring. He looked like he'd walked straight out of a war zone, and maybe he had.

Azrael moved first, crossing the room in long strides, his usual composure replaced with something raw, almost frantic. "Vassago." His voice was tight, his hands hovering awkwardly, unsure if he should help or if Vassago would even allow it.

Vassago's lips pressed into a thin line as his gaze swept the room, cataloging each of us like he was assessing a battlefield. "Not here." His voice was hoarse but firm, the kind of tone that brooked no argument.

Orcus, as always, was the first to break the tension. "Oh, come on. You can't just waltz in looking like the cover of *Bruised and Broken Weekly* and not spill the details. You're killing the mood—and that's usually my job."

"Orcus," Azrael snapped, but Vassago held up a hand.

"It's fine," Vassago said, though his tone suggested otherwise. "The details aren't for mortal ears." His sharp gaze landed on Sadie, making it abundantly clear who he was referring to.

Sadie, never one to back down, raised an eyebrow. "Mortal ears, huh? Hate to break it to you, buddy, but I'm already in way over my head. Might as well keep digging."

Vassago's expression didn't change, but his eyes flicked to Ashton as if silently asking why he allowed this.

Ashton, to his credit, just smirked. "They're tougher than they look. But if you insist..." He gestured toward the door. "We can take this somewhere more private."

"No," I said, surprising even myself. My voice was steadier than I expected, though my hands gripped my coffee mug like it was the only thing anchoring me. "If this is about me—about us—I think we deserve to know."

Vassago's gaze snapped to mine, sharp and piercing. It felt like he was looking straight into my soul, peeling back layers I wasn't sure I wanted to be exposed. My breath hitched, but I didn't look away.

Azrael, still standing close to Vassago, spoke up, his voice softer now. "She's right. Whatever's going on, it's affecting all of us. They deserve the truth."

For a moment, Vassago looked like he might argue. Then he exhaled, a heavy, tired sound, and nodded. "Fine."

As he stepped further into the room, the tension thickened. Orcus, never one to let things get too serious, muttered, "Finally, some drama worth sticking around for. I was worried breakfast would end without anyone crying."

"Read the room, Orcus," Azrael hissed, though there was no real heat in it.

Vassago ignored them both, his focus entirely on Azrael now. "The Underworld is in chaos. Memetim's rampage was just the beginning. The prisoners she freed..." He trailed off, shaking his head. "They've taken over entire sectors. Ashton's home may be safe now, but it won't stay that way for long."

Ashton straightened, his usual easy demeanor slipping. "What do you mean it won't stay safe? This place is fortified."

Vassago's gaze was cold. "Not against what's coming. Memetim's army isn't just made up of prisoners. Something darker is rising with them—something we've only heard whispers about until now."

A chill ran down my spine, and I could see from the way Sadie's hand tightened on her mug that she felt it too.

"What kind of 'something' are we talking about?" Azrael asked, his jaw tight.

Vassago hesitated, his silence more telling than anything he could have said. Finally, he muttered, "The kind that makes even the ruler of the Underworld afraid."

The room fell silent. Even Orcus didn't have a quip for that.

After a moment, Vassago turned to me. "You're not safe here. None of you are."

The words hung in the air like a death sentence.

"Great," Sadie said, breaking the silence with her usual bravado. "So what's the plan? Hide? Fight? Or do we just hope this 'something' decides we're not worth the trouble?"

Vassago almost smiled, a flicker of dry amusement in his otherwise grim expression. "You're braver than you look, mortal."

"She's reckless," Azrael corrected, though there was a hint of admiration in his voice.

"Whatever I am," Sadie said, leaning back in her chair, "I'd rather go down swinging than sit around waiting to be picked off."

I wished I shared her courage. My hands trembled slightly, and I placed my mug on the table to hide it. "So what do we do?" I asked, my voice quieter than hers but no less desperate.

Vassago's answer was blunt. "We prepare. And we pray it's enough."

Vassago's words lingered in the air, heavy and unyielding. *We prepare. And we pray it's enough.*

Azrael's jaw tightened, and he began pacing, the weight of the moment etched into every line of his face. Finally, he stopped, turning to face me. His dark eyes softened, but there was a fear behind them that made my stomach churn.

"Layla," he said, his tone measured but firm, "it's time we stop running blind. You need to meet the part of yourself you've been avoiding—the supernatural part."

I blinked, his words not quite registering at first. "What?"

"You've felt it, haven't you?" Azrael continued, stepping closer. "The fear, the dreams, the sense that there's more to you than what you know. Memetim came after you for a reason. You have a role in all of this, and it's time we find out what that is."

"No," I said, my voice shaking. I pushed back from the table, standing to put some distance between us. "You don't get to decide that. I didn't ask for any of this!"

Azrael's gaze didn't waver, though something in his expression softened. "I know you didn't. But ignoring it won't make it go away. If we don't act now, you'll be vulnerable—and so will everyone else trying to protect you."

"You're asking me to—what? Be like you? A warrior? I'm not that person, Azrael!" My voice cracked, and I hated how small I sounded.

"No one's asking you to be me," Azrael said gently. "But you need to learn how to protect yourself. To understand what's inside you, so it doesn't consume you."

"I can protect her," Sadie interrupted, standing as well, her fiery determination cutting through the tension. "She doesn't need to become some supernatural soldier."

"Your loyalty is admirable," Vassago said, his voice calm but authoritative. "But you don't understand what she's up against. None of us can fight her battles for her."

"That's where Exu comes in," Azrael said, ignoring Sadie's glare.

"Exu?" I repeated, dread curling in my stomach.

"The spirit of crossroads," Azrael explained. "He's one of the few beings who can guide you to the truth of what you are. He'll help you confront the supernatural side of yourself."

"And if I don't want to?" I asked, my voice barely above a whisper.

"Then you'll never be ready for what's coming," Azrael said, his tone harsher than I'd expected. "I won't lie to you, Layla. What's inside you is powerful, but it's also dangerous—especially if you don't know how to control it. This isn't just about you anymore."

Sadie's glare burned into Azrael, her protective instincts flaring like a shield between us. "You're asking too much of her," she snapped, stepping closer to me. "She's human, Azrael! She's not your soldier, and she's not some pawn in your cosmic chess game!"

Azrael met her fiery gaze with his usual calm, though his jaw tightened. "She's not a pawn," he said quietly, but there was an edge to his voice. "She's more than you realize. More than even she realizes."

Sadie scoffed. "Oh, I'd love to hear this one. Enlighten me, Mr. Grim Reaper."

Azrael hesitated, his gaze flicking to me as if weighing how much to say. Then he exhaled, his shoulders dropping slightly. "You want the truth? Fine. Layla isn't just some mortal caught up in all this by accident. She's supposed to be... one of us."

Sadie blinked, thrown off her rhythm for a moment. "One of you? What does that even mean?"

Azrael looked directly at me now, his voice steady but heavy with the weight of his words. "Layla is supposed to be the first female Grim Reaper."

The room fell silent, the air crackling with unspoken tension.

"What?" I finally managed to whisper, the word barely forming on my lips.

"Excuse me?" Sadie added, her voice rising. She stepped in front of me like she could block the revelation from taking root. "That's the dumbest thing I've ever heard. She's *human*. She's not built for this supernatural crap."

"She's not just human," Azrael said, his tone firm but not unkind. "She's something more. She's always been more, even if she doesn't understand it yet. This is why Memetim is hunting her. Why the Underworld is stirring." He looked at me again, his eyes softer now. "You're not ordinary, Layla. You never were."

I shook my head, stepping back. "No. That doesn't make sense. I've never—none of this—" My voice cracked, and I clenched my fists to stop them from shaking. "I'm not a Grim Reaper. I don't even want to be a Grim Reaper!"

"You think I wanted this?" Azrael asked, his voice quieter now. "To carry this title, this burden? I didn't have a choice, either. But you do. If you train—if you embrace this—you can shape what it means. You could change everything."

Sadie's laugh was harsh, almost disbelieving. "So that's your big pitch? 'Hey Layla, your life's been a mess, but here's a shiny new destiny as Death's replacement! No pressure, though!'"

"Sadie, stop," I said, my voice trembling. "I can't—I can't deal with this if you keep—"

"Don't you see?" Azrael interrupted, his voice sharper now. "This isn't just about her. If Layla doesn't step into her role, Memetim will destroy everything. She's a key part of this balance, whether she likes it or not."

Sadie threw up her hands. "Oh, so now she's some chosen one? I was playing along with the sick joke of her being your *mate*. But now all of *this*? How convenient!"

"It's not convenient," Azrael snapped, his usual calm cracking. "It's reality. And if we don't prepare her—if we don't help her find her strength—we're all doomed. Not just her. All of us."

The words hung in the air, and for once, Sadie had no snarky comeback.

I sank back into my chair, my head spinning. "The first female Grim Reaper," I murmured, barely able to comprehend it.

Azrael crouched in front of me, his blue eyes searching mine. "I know it's a lot. I know you're scared. But you don't have to do this alone. I'll be with you every step of the way."

"And me," Orcus piped up, his tone unusually serious. "I might be a sarcastic piece of weaponry, but I've got your back. Besides, who wouldn't want a badass Grim Reaper with style?"

Despite the tension, Ashton chuckled softly. "He's not wrong. You'd definitely up the aesthetic around here."

Sadie's voice broke through the quiet. "I don't like it. I don't like any of this. But if Layla's doing this, then I'm staying by her side." She folded her arms, glaring at Azrael like daring him to argue.

"Good," Azrael said simply, standing. "She'll need you. Both of you." He looked at Ashton, who nodded in silent agreement.

I didn't feel strong. I didn't feel capable. But as their eyes turned to me, one by one, I realized I didn't have the luxury of running anymore.

"Fine," I whispered, my voice barely audible. Then louder, "Fine. I'll do it. I'll meet Exu, train, or whatever it is you think I need to do. But don't expect me to like it."

Azrael's lips twitched in the faintest hint of a smile. "I wouldn't dream of it."

Chapter Twenty-Six

Layla

Bad Habits - Ed Sheeran

"You could have told me you weren't coming back to the room last night, Sadie. I waited for you." My fingers brush over the frosted glass of the window, but it does nothing. It's still clouded, still blurred. The Underworld outside is nothing but endless darkness, a void, and it makes my chest tighten. I don't want to look at it.

Sadie shrugs, her usual nonchalance settling in like a comforting blanket. She says with a flip of her wrist, as though she's not dealing with an apocalypse or living in the depths of some hellish realm. "What do you think about Ashton?"

She smiles so wide I can practically hear it. It's like she's back in high school, crushing on some random guy. But Ashton? The Sandman? It's a different level of weirdness I'm not sure I'm ready for. Still, I don't miss the way her gaze softens when she says his name. It's... surprising.

"I don't even have time to register thoughts about him when I'm trying to comprehend all this weird shit going on!" My voice catches a little. It's all too much—too much to process. Too much for my brain to handle at once.

Sadie quirks an eyebrow. "Do you believe in that 'fated mate' talk? Or that you're supposed to be a Grim Reaper—like him?" She practically spits the word 'him,' and I can't help but notice the bitterness that sneaks into her voice.

I turn to face her fully, arms folded across my chest. "I don't know what I believe anymore. I thought my biggest problem was being a normal girl with anxiety issues, and now? I'm some how supposed to be a 'fated mate' for someone like Azrael? A Grim Reaper, no less? Like that's even real."

Sadie bites her lip, holding back a laugh, but then her expression shifts into something more serious. "I get it. I really do. But you gotta admit, it's... kinda hard to ignore all the signs, right?" Her voice drops, and for a moment, it's not Sadie being sassy or joking. It's her trying to be real.

I glance over at the window again, my stomach a mix of nerves and anger. "I don't even know what to believe anymore. My whole life is built on lies, and now this? My mom—she's some—some succubus? And I'm... I don't even know what the hell I am anymore. How do you even trust anything when everything's falling apart?"

Sadie's expression softens, and she scoots over to the edge of the bed, pulling her knees up to her chest. "You don't have to figure it all out today, Layla. I mean, I'm freaking out just as much as you are, but I think... you'll find a way to get through this. Just, don't do it alone, okay?"

For a brief moment, the world outside feels a little less suffocating.

"Hey," she whispers, her voice teasing, but there's a gleam of excitement in her eyes. "There are fine-ass men out there, and one has fucking wings! Sure, he's beaten up and all, but what kind of alternate realm are we living in?"

I roll my eyes but can't suppress the faint smile tugging at my lips. "You've got a weird way of coping, you know that?" I shake my head, my hands gripping the sides of the window trying to stare out at the black void that stretches endlessly beyond. The Underworld looks... *wrong*. It's so foreign, so completely opposite of everything I've ever known. And now I'm expected to belong here. To fit in, to *survive*.

Sadie gives me a playful shove. "Come on, Layla. You can't be all doom and gloom forever." She pauses, her gaze softening just slightly. "It's *okay* to enjoy the weirdness for a second. Just... *look* at the guys around here. One of them's literally an angel. *A beaten up* and bloody angel but still—" She shudders dramatically. "Wings, man. *Wings!*"

I can't help but laugh, though it's strained, caught somewhere between disbelief and resignation. "I'm still not sure what part of this is real," I admit, leaning my forehead against the cool glass. "Everything feels like a dream. A nightmare, maybe."

Sadie, undeterred by my less-than-enthusiastic response, flashes a grin. "I mean, nightmare or not, you have to admit there's something *kind of* hot about a guy who can pull off the whole 'Grim Reaper' vibe with that scythe of his." She raises her brows, her voice low, playful. "You've seen how he looks at you, right? Just saying."

I close my eyes for a moment, her words swirling in my mind. Azrael... there are these moments when his gaze lingers on me, his attention sharp and intense. And maybe it's that—maybe it's the way he sees me—that pulls me in more than I want to admit.

"Sadie," I murmur, half-laughing, half-exasperated, "I don't need to be thinking about that right now." But the truth is, it's all I can think about.

Sadie shakes her head, looking frustrated. "And that *scythe*..." she starts, her voice trailing off as she glares toward the corner. "Every time I try to say something, it's like it's got something nasty to say to me."

I raise an eyebrow. "What do you mean?"

Sadie throws her hands up, clearly exasperated. "It's like, every time I talk around him, he has some little jab, like 'Oh, look, another mortal thinks they know everything.' Or, 'Keep talking, maybe you'll actually make sense this time.' And I'm like... what did I do to deserve that?"

I frown, thinking it over. "Orcus can be... blunt, I guess. He's not exactly the warm, fuzzy type, and he doesn't seem to really like people trying to *impress* him, I guess."

"Impress him?!" Sadie snorts. "I'm just trying to get along! I'm not over here asking him to like me. But it feels like every time I say something, I get a 'How quaint' or a 'Do you even know what you're saying?' like I'm some sort of joke to him."

I wince, knowing exactly what she means. "Yeah, it seems like he doesn't do well with people who aren't *his* person, like Azrael. Everyone else is just... an annoyance to him."

Sadie crosses her arms, shaking her head. "It's not even that he's *rude* to me. It's the way he talks, like... he's just so unimpressed with anything I say. I could ask for the time and he'd make me feel like I just asked him to solve the meaning of life."

I laugh despite myself because I know she's right. Orcus has a way of making everything feel...trivial like nothing anyone else does or says can measure up. "Yeah, he's got a bit of a superiority complex, especially around people who aren't, well, Azrael."

"I swear, one more sarcastic comment, and I'm gonna lose it." Sadie's voice lowers, but there's frustration in her tone. "Why does he have to be like that?"

I try to give a reassuring smile, even though I can't fully explain Orcus' behavior. "I don't think it's personal. He's just... used to being around Azrael. Everyone else is kind of an afterthought to him."

Sadie tilts her head, eyes narrowing. "Yeah, well, I'm *not* his afterthought, and I'm not gonna be his punching bag for all his attitude." She lets out a deep breath, leaning back against the bed. "I don't know how you plan to put up with it."

I shrug, trying to keep the mood light. "Because it's easier to agree to disagree than fighting with a weapon that could cut me in half without even trying."

Sadie snorts. "I still think he's way too grumpy for my liking. If he's not careful, I might just throw a tantrum. Maybe that'll shut him up."

I nod, grinning. "Yeah, maybe a little tantrum is exactly what he needs. He could use a taste of his own attitude, but I'm not sure a tantrum is enough to rattle him."

Sadie rolls her eyes, but there's a mischievous glint in them. "It's worth a shot. I mean, who does he think he is, acting like he's the only one who can be sarcastic?" She crosses her arms, then leans back against the bed, her expression shifting to something more thoughtful. "I get it, though. He's loyal to Azrael."

"I know," I agree, sitting down on the edge of the bed next to her. "It's like he doesn't even care to make an effort to be nice or... human, really. He's all 'I'm better than you' and 'You're not worth my time.'"

Sadie lets out a huff. "Yeah, but what's the deal with him and Azrael? Is he really that much of a... what's the word... *puppy* for Azrael?"

I chuckle at her use of the word "puppy," but it kind of fits. "Pretty much. Orcus has been with Azrael for... forever. They've got this bond that doesn't exactly leave room for anyone else." I pause, thinking it over. "But I don't think Orcus dislikes you, Sadie. He's just... used to being the one in control around here."

"Yeah, well, control doesn't mean you get to treat people like they're invisible." She leans forward, her eyes narrowing in mock irritation. "If it were up to me, I'd be giving him a piece of my mind. Maybe then he'd understand how to talk to someone who isn't, like, an ancient scythe-wielding god."

I smile at her, amused. "You'd probably make him crack a smile. Just be careful—he might start *offering* you advice you didn't ask for."

"Ugh, great. As if I need more unsolicited advice from *that guy.*"

I laugh, but deep down, I understand how she feels. Orcus may not be out to make her life miserable, but his attitude definitely appears to have that effect on her. "Don't worry. I'm sure you'll figure out a way to handle him... or at least tolerate him."

Sadie groans and flops back on the bed dramatically, her arms sprawled out like she's about to stage her own funeral. "Dude. We are supposed to be getting ready to *train* for a war... and I still can't wrap my head around the fact that I'm even saying that sentence."

I glance over at her, a bitter laugh escaping me. "Trust me, you're not alone. I've been replaying it in my head over and over: 'training for a war in the Underworld.' It sounds like a bad video game plot."

She rolls onto her side, propping her head up with her hand. "And what does that even mean? Like, are we gonna be sparring with swords? Learning how to dodge fireballs? Is there a syllabus for this crap?"

"I doubt it's going to be that straight forward," I mutter, pacing near the window again. "This isn't some kind of medieval boot camp. They probably expect us to just... figure it out as we go."

Sadie snorts. "Great. Because I'm so good at figuring things out on the fly. What if I accidentally get turned into some weird demon's chew toy?"

I shoot her a look. "Sadie, focus. We don't have the luxury of freaking out anymore. If we're going to survive this—if I'm going to survive this—I need you with me."

She sits up, her expression softening. "I *am* with you, Layla. I always will be. I'm just... processing, you know? I mean, this isn't exactly the life we planned."

"Tell me about it," I say with a sigh, leaning against the frosted window. "I thought my biggest problem was going to be trying to focus on not tripping over shoes and dying trying to get to the bathroom, not how to swing a weapon in a battle for the fate of... whatever this is."

Sadie groans again, flopping back once more. "Fine. Training. War. Let's do it. But if someone asks me to run laps, I swear I'm quitting this supernatural life and becoming a ghost instead."

"Sadie, do you remember Azrael saying your dad is in the Underworld?" I asked her. "Do you think you might ask him to see your dad? Maybe?"

Sadie blinks at me, startled by the question. "Ask him to see my dad?" She leans back, her brows furrowing. "I mean... I've thought about it, but..." Her voice trails off, and she starts twisting the edge of the comforter in her hands.

"But what?" I press gently, turning fully to face her.

She hesitates, her fingers still fidgeting. "What if... what if he doesn't want to see me? Like, what if he regrets staying here for me? Or worse, what if he's disappointed in the person I turned out to be?" Her voice cracks on the last word, and she looks away, blinking rapidly.

I shake my head, a soft sigh escaping me. "Sadie, come on. Your dad stayed here because he didn't want to leave you. That doesn't sound like someone who'd be disappointed."

"Yeah, but you don't know that for sure," she shoots back, her voice sharp with insecurity. "What if I go to see him, and he's like, 'Oh great, you're still a mess, Sadie'? I'm not exactly winning Daughter of the Year awards here, Layla."

"Stop that." My tone is firm, but not unkind. "You're not a mess, and you know it. You're the most loyal, brave, and stubborn person I've ever met. And if your dad had even a fraction of your personality, I can promise you he wouldn't see anything but how amazing you are."

Sadie snorts, but there's no real humor in it. "You're just saying that because you're stuck in this weird death realm with me and don't have a choice."

I roll my eyes, nudging her foot with mine. "I'm saying it because it's true. Look, if you're scared, that's fine. But don't let fear be the reason you don't ask to see him. You deserve answers, Sadie. And I think your dad deserves a chance to tell you how much you mean to him."

For a moment, she's quiet, her fingers still. Then, finally, she looks up at me, her eyes shimmering with uncertainty. "You think Azrael would let me?"

I smile, soft but steady. "Yeah, I do. And if he doesn't, we'll find a way. Together."

Chapter Twenty-Seven

Azrael

Lovely - Billie Eilish & Khalid

The sharp edge of Orcus's sarcasm cut through the quiet of my thoughts. "You're being unusually sneaky," he said, suspicion lacing his voice like a shadow stretching across the ground. "Care to clue me in before I start thinking you're plotting something stupid?"

"Patience," I replied, letting a smirk tug at the corners of my mouth. My boots crunched against the dirt as the training grounds stretched ahead, alive with the hum of activity. The familiar scent of sweat, steel, and magic hung in the air like a promise of determination and chaos intertwined.

Orcus, my ever-vocal scythe, wasn't one for patience—or subtlety, for that matter. His huff of exasperation crackled through my thoughts like a spark on dry kindling. "You're enjoying this, aren't you? Leaving me in the dark. Again."

"Guilty as charged," I said, the smirk now tugging into a full grin. "What's the fun in ruining the suspense?"

He snorted, the sound almost human if not for the undertone of sharp edges and malice. "Suspense, my ass. You're just a showoff."

Ahead of us, the training grounds buzzed with life. Supernaturals of all shapes and sizes clashed in sparring matches, their abilities crackling in the air like fireworks.

But my attention wasn't on the recruits I have so far managed to gather. Today was for Sadie. She had known about Song for a while now but hadn't actually met her Guardian Angel like Layla got to meet Vassago. Meeting someone so intrinsic to your soul wasn't something to rush—or spoil with secondhand stories. Song wasn't the loudest presence, but there was a gravity to her, an unshakable calm that balanced Sadie's storm.

To ensure everything went smoothly, I'd sent Vassago cryptic notes and worked behind the scenes. Getting him to play along hadn't been easy; Vassago thrived on directness, not games. But the moment was worth it. I couldn't risk Orcus ruining it with his big mouth—or blade.

"Still no hints?" Orcus prodded, his tone sharper this time. "You know, for someone who wields me like a precision weapon, you sure do love being vague."

I rolled my eyes and slowed my pace, letting the moment hang in the air. "You're sounding awfully needy today, Orcus. Do you want me to hold your hilt and reassure you?"

The scythe practically growled. "You can take your jokes and shove them. I'm serious."

"I know," I said, softer this time. My gaze shifted to a far corner of the grounds where Vassago stood, his massive wings tucked neatly behind him. Song was with him, a delicate figure of silver and light against his imposing presence.

"You'll see soon enough," I added. "Try not to ruin it."

Orcus let out a dramatic sigh, exasperation coloring the cool breeze that swept past us. "I swear, sometimes I think you keep beings in suspense just to annoy me."

"Sometimes?" I teased, my voice carrying a playful edge.

"You're insufferable," he shot back, though there was no real venom in his words. It was his way of admitting he'd play along—for now.

The training grounds bustled with life, a chaotic symphony of movement and sound. Supernaturals of every kind moved in a fluid, almost choreographed dance, sparring in the soft dirt or honing their weapons with deadly precision. The clang of steel against steel mixed with the flicker and hum of magical energy, creating a palpable tension in the air. Each fighter, each burst of power, seemed to vibrate with purpose and determination.

At the edge of the grounds, Sadie stood out like a firework in a storm. Her wild black curls bounced with every emphatic motion as she animatedly talked to Layla. Even from a distance, I could hear her voice rising above the noise, punctuated by bursts of laughter and her expressive, sweeping gestures. Layla's smaller frame leaned in attentively, her lips quirking into a smile as she tried—and failed—to keep up with Sadie's energy.

I cleared my throat as I approached, the sound sharp and deliberate. It cut through the din like a blade, drawing both women's attention.

Sadie turned first, her dark eyes narrowing with playful suspicion. Her lips curved into a sly smile as she arched an eyebrow. "What's with the mysterious face, reaper boy? Planning to throw me into a pit of doom or something?"

Layla snorted softly but didn't say anything, though the way her gaze flicked between us spoke volumes.

"Not today," I said, letting my grin stretch just wide enough to hint at mischief. "Follow me. I've got a surprise for you."

Sadie groaned dramatically, throwing her head back as though I'd just suggested something dreadful. "Ugh, surprises? You know how I feel about those, right?"

"Vividly," I replied, stepping closer. "But you'll like this one."

"Will I?" she teased, already falling into step beside me. Her boots scuffed against the dirt, kicking up small clouds of dust with each step.

Behind her, Layla trailed along, her brow furrowed in curiosity. "This doesn't have anything to do with training, does it?" she asked cautiously, her eyes sparkling with a mix of suspicion and intrigue.

Sadie immediately latched onto the idea, groaning again but louder this time. "This better not involve more warmups," she muttered, her tone tinged with mock exhaustion. "I've been tortured enough by Vassago."

I shook my head, smirking. "It's not warmups," I said lightly, a teasing note creeping into my voice. "But if you'd rather I cancel..."

Sadie's head whipped toward me, her expression comically horrified. "Don't even think about it," she snapped, though the amusement bubbling under her words softened the bite.

"That's the spirit," I said, chuckling.

Orcus, always eager to stir the pot, chimed in from his place on my back. "Careful, Sadie. With him, a surprise could be a hug or a death match. And I'm betting on the latter."

Sadie glanced over her shoulder, her smirk widening as she met the scythe's invisible gaze. "I'll take my chances," she said with mock bravado.

Layla, who had remained unusually quiet, finally spoke up as we continued walking. "Are you actually going to tell us where we're going, or do we get to play the guessing game?"

"That ruins the fun," I replied, flashing her a quick grin. "Just trust me."

Sadie shot Layla a pointed look. "Famous last words, right?"

Layla nodded solemnly, though her lips twitched like she was fighting a smile. "Definitely."

"Keep up, ladies," I said over my shoulder, picking up the pace. "We're almost there."

Sadie's groan turned into a half-laugh, half-grumble, but she didn't argue. The promise of something worth her time, even if mysterious, was enough to keep her moving.

We reached a quieter corner of the grounds, a serene pocket untouched by the chaos of sparring and magic. The air here felt different—lighter, calmer, as if the energy had paused to take a breath. In the center of it all, standing like a dream made flesh, was Song.

Her long silver hair shimmered, cascading down her back like molten moonlight, each strand catching the light as though it carried its own gentle glow. She radiated an unshakable calm, a serenity that seemed to ripple outward, softening even the sharp edges of my thoughts. Her luminous eyes, impossibly large and filled with an ancient wisdom, contrasted with her youthful appearance. Despite her small stature, there was a quiet strength in the way she stood, her delicate wings folded neatly behind her. The feathers were so fine, they seemed to blur into the ambient light, like a painting come to life.

Sadie froze mid-step, her eyes widening as her breath caught in her throat. Her wild energy seemed to momentarily vanish, replaced by an almost childlike awe. "That's her, isn't it?" Her voice was barely above a whisper.

"Song," I confirmed, stepping aside with a small, almost theatrical gesture. "Your Guardian Angel."

Song tilted her head slightly, her warm gaze locking onto Sadie's as though the rest of the world no longer existed. Her soft voice carried across the stillness, gentle yet firm. "I've been waiting to meet you, Sadie."

Sadie blinked, her hands hovering awkwardly at her sides. "You have?"

Song stepped forward, her movements impossibly light, as if the earth itself softened beneath her feet. Her presence commanded attention without effort, an ethereal magnetism that drew us all in. "Of course. I've watched over you for a long time."

Sadie's emotions played out on her face like an open book—a mix of disbelief, curiosity, and something deeper, harder to define. Her mouth opened and closed once before she managed, "You're... smaller than I imagined."

Song's lips curved into a soft smile, one that radiated patience. "Many have said that," she replied, her tone carrying a gentle humor. "Appearances can be deceiving."

Orcus, naturally, couldn't let the moment pass without a comment. "And probably smarter, too," he quipped, his voice oozing dry amusement. "Maybe you should listen to her, Sadie. You might pick up a thing or two."

Song laughed softly, the sound pure and melodic, filling the space with warmth. Sadie, her composure slowly returning, glanced over her shoulder at Orcus, her lips quirking upward into a grin. "You've got a lot of nerve for a glorified stick," she shot back.

"Glorified stick?" Orcus huffed. "Careful, mortal, or I might decide to practice a little 'accidental' teleportation the next time Azrael swings me."

Sadie snorted, her gaze flicking back to Song. "See what I have to deal with?"

Song's smile deepened, and she stepped closer to Sadie, her expression now earnest and steady. "You're stronger than you think, Sadie," she said, her voice gentle but carrying an undeniable weight. "And I will be with you every step of the way, no matter what challenges come your way."

Sadie blinked, visibly touched, but she quickly masked it with a playful grin. "Well, I hope you're ready for a wild ride, because challenges are kind of my thing."

Song tilted her head, the corners of her eyes crinkling with a hint of amusement. "I wouldn't have it any other way."

Sadie hesitated, her breath catching in her throat. Slowly, as if afraid the moment might shatter, she reached out, her fingers trembling. When they finally brushed against Song's feathers, her eyes widened, and her lips parted in awe. "They're softer than I could have ever imagined," she murmured, her voice a whisper of wonder. "Like... like they belong in a dream."

Song tilted her head slightly, a faint smile playing on her lips. Her silver hair caught the dim light, shimmering like threads of moonlight cascading down her back. "They weren't always this way," she said softly, her voice filled with both sadness and pride. "Thanks to Azrael and Orcus, they were able to grow back as they should."

Sadie's fingers lingered on the feathers, her brow furrowing as she glanced at me. "What does she mean? Grow back?"

I folded my arms, leaning casually against a nearby post, trying to erase the memory of Song broken and destroyed when I first met her. "Let's just say not all Guardians are lucky enough to escape unscathed when protecting their charges," I said, my tone matter-of-fact. "Song's been through more than most. But she's resilient, just like you."

Sadie's gaze darted back to Song, her eyes filled with a newfound respect. "You mean... you were hurt? For me?"

Song nodded, her luminous eyes softening. "It's a Guardian's duty to shield their charge, no matter the cost. I've been by your side, Sadie, even when you couldn't see me."

Sadie stepped back, her arms crossing protectively over her chest as she processed the weight of Song's words. "That's... a lot," she admitted, her voice tinged with guilt. "I never even knew you were there. I didn't even know Guardian Angels existed."

"You weren't meant to," Song reassured her, stepping closer. "But now you do. And together, we'll face whatever comes next."

I watched the exchange, a strange mixture of pride and unease curling in my chest. There was something undeniably beautiful about the way they connected, like two puzzle pieces finally clicking into place. But even as the moment unfolded, the weight of the war ahead loomed, a constant shadow in the back of my mind.

"She's going to need help and guidance," I said, breaking the quiet with a tone that was more serious than I'd intended. Still, I couldn't help the smirk tugging at my mouth as I added, "Training's only going to get really hard from here."

Sadie groaned dramatically, throwing her head back like I'd just announced the end of the world. "Can't we have a bonding day first?" she whined. "You know, get to know each other? Maybe some snacks, a nap?"

Orcus, ever the opportunist, chimed in with a mocking laugh. "A nap? Oh, Sadie, you really are new here."

"Hey," she shot back, pointing a finger at the scythe as if scolding him. "Even you probably need some rest, buddy. Don't act all high and mighty."

"I don't need rest," Orcus retorted smugly. "I'm a weapon, not a mortal with weak bones and a penchant for whining."

Sadie rolled her eyes but turned back to me, her expression a mix of amusement and irritation. "You could've picked a friendlier sidekick, you know."

I shrugged, letting my grin widen. "Orcus grows on you. Eventually."

"Doubtful," she muttered under her breath before sighing dramatically. "Fine. No snacks, no naps. But if training kills me, I'm haunting you."

"You'll have to get in line," I teased, gesturing for her to follow me. "Welcome to the Underworld."

As we started back toward the training grounds, Sadie stole another glance at Song, who followed closely behind. Her voice softened as she asked, "Do you ever get tired of being so... perfect?"

Song chuckled, the sound light and warm, and shook her head. "Perfect? Hardly. But I appreciate the compliment."

Sadie grinned, the tension in her shoulders easing. "Well, perfect or not, I think we're going to make a pretty good team."

Chapter Twenty-Eight

Layla

Arsonist's Lullabye - Hozier

The tension in the air was thick, like the hush before a storm, but this wasn't just any storm. This was something otherworldly, something I couldn't quite comprehend. I could feel it buzzing beneath my skin, crawling up my spine, the anticipation heavy in the air. Azrael stood across from me, his scythe—his constant companion—resting against his side. His sharp gaze cut through the quiet, but it wasn't aimed at me. No, his focus was on Sadie, her eyes wide with a mix of curiosity and unease.

"So, you're telling me," Sadie started, her voice tinged with skepticism as she crossed her arms. "That we need to see this... thing... of yours?"

Azrael didn't flinch, didn't even blink. He nodded solemnly. "It's part of your training. You need to start desensitizing to the true forms of supernatural beings. So you can survive."

Sadie raised an eyebrow. "I thought I was just learning to fight them, not... get used to looking at their ugly mugs."

I caught Orcus' chuckle at the edge of my hearing. He had a way of finding humor in even the most terrifying situations.

"It's not about fighting," Azrael explained, his voice low and serious. "It's about surviving the things that can't be fought. The things that can break your mind just by being seen."

I could hear the weight in his words, but I wasn't sure I understood yet. A pit formed in my stomach as I glanced from him to Sadie. I felt something stir inside me—an urge to flee, to hide, to avoid whatever was coming. But deep down, I knew I couldn't. Not anymore. I had no choice but to face it, even if the thought terrified me.

I glanced at Sadie, her arms still folded, lips pressed into a thin line. But even she was starting to look less sure, less confident in her usual defiance. The bravado she wore like armor was starting to crack.

"Fine," she muttered, her eyes shifting toward Azrael. "Show us the monster."

Azrael's posture remained unmoving, but I could sense the moment he decided to give in. He didn't need to say anything—it was like he had to brace himself first. A shift in the air, barely perceptible, told me he was preparing. And then, without another word, the world around him seemed to change. The air grew heavier and thick with something ancient and suffocating. My breath caught in my chest as the atmosphere seemed to warp, bending under some unseen pressure.

His cloak—always a dark, flowing thing—began to billow around him, not in a natural movement, but as if the very shadows were alive, drawn to him. The fabric stretched and twisted, its edges blurring until it seemed to dissolve into the air itself. The darkness around him deepened, pulling at my thoughts, warping my perception. My heart hammered in my chest, panic rising in me like a tidal wave. I fought to breathe, to keep my pulse from racing too fast. But the sensation of drowning in this growing darkness was almost too much.

Then, with a subtle motion, Azrael raised his hand, and the shadows followed—curling, swirling, bending into something darker, colder. My chest tightened, the air grew so thick it was hard to inhale. My lungs burned, my hands trembling at my sides, but I couldn't look away. Not even if I wanted to.

The moment he shifted, everything in me recoiled. The cloak melted into him, fusing with his form as if it had always been part of him. And then I saw it—the thing standing before me wasn't Azrael anymore. It was... something else. Something raw and unapologetic.

Where his eyes should have been, there was only the smoldering, ember-lit darkness of his skull, glowing from within with a fierce, fiery light. The flames flickered like a living thing, dancing wildly in the hollow sockets of his skull, casting shadows that twisted unnaturally across our surroundings. The flames reflected off the jagged, sharp edges of the bone, and I could hear the faint crackling of fire, though there was no warmth. Only cold.

Azrael's true form was the embodiment of death itself—an unfeeling, endless force, untethered from the mortal world. His cloak, now consumed by the void, seemed to pulse like it was alive, alive in a way I couldn't fully grasp. I could feel the weight of it pressing on me, suffocating me, and I wanted to look away. But I couldn't. My eyes were locked, my body is frozen in place.

Every instinct in my body screamed at me to run—to escape—but my legs wouldn't move. My heart raced in my chest, thundering so loudly I thought it might drown out everything else. The air was thick, thick with his presence, and I could feel it in my very bones. This wasn't Azrael. This wasn't the man who had stood by me, had comforted me. This was something else. Something terrifying.

Azrael's voice came to me, distorted and distant, as though it didn't belong to him anymore. "This is what I am, Layla," he said, his words heavy with the weight of something ancient. "This is who I am. The truth you're not ready to see."

I couldn't speak. Couldn't move. The words were there, in the back of my throat, but they wouldn't come out. My body felt like it was made of stone, rigid and unyielding. The flames flickering from his skull seemed to grow, casting the Underworld in a deeper, darker glow.

And in that moment, I realized something—this wasn't just Azrael showing me his true form. It was a warning. A reminder. He was *death* itself. And I was standing in front of it, utterly powerless.

My heart pounded in my chest, but I forced myself not to look away, not to shrink back. This was the man I had to trust, no matter how terrifying his form was. I had to.

Sadie was staring, wide-eyed, but not in terror. I saw her jaw tighten, felt her shoulders stiffen, but she stood firm. If I was going to make it through this, I had to do the same. The weight of the moment pressed on me, and I fought to keep my breathing steady, to hold my ground. If I let fear consume me now, I would lose everything.

"I know it's a lot," Azrael's voice broke through the haze of my thoughts, his words hollow yet somehow alive in the space around us. "But you need to see it. You need to understand it."

A chill ran through me, the air around us thick with the power emanating from his form. My hands clenched at my sides, nails digging into my skin as if I could ground myself in the pain. But then Orcus' voice—low and steady—whispered.

"You're doing fine, Layla. He's not going to hurt you."

I gripped the edge of the table, leaning against it, as if it could anchor me to something solid in the chaos of what I was seeing. The tightness in my chest felt like it might suffocate me, but I refused to look away. *It's just him*, I reminded myself. *It's still him beneath all that. It's just him...*

I took a shaky breath. And another. The darkness in front of me seemed to pulse with energy, a tangible weight pressing on me from all sides. Slowly, with Orcus' reassurance echoing in my head, I forced myself to raise my eyes to meet

Azrael's gaze—or what used to be his gaze. The ember-lit sockets burned into me, but this time, it wasn't so painful.

I could do this.

With a voice softer than I meant it to be, I spoke, the words trembling on my lips. "Okay. Okay, Azrael."

There was a long moment of silence, the weight of everything hanging between us. Then, a shift. The warmth of his voice reached my ears again, softer than before, a quiet gratitude in it. "Thank you."

And for some reason, I believed him. In that moment, I realized I hadn't just accepted his terrifying form. I had accepted him—all of him. The being of fire and darkness standing before me wasn't just a Grim Reaper. He was Azrael—the one who had saved me, the one who had sacrificed so much for me. And despite the cold terror his form had first invoked, I could feel it: this was still the man I was learning to trust. The fear didn't completely fade, but it became something else—a recognition of the depth of what he was, what he carried with him. And I could accept that. I think.

The raw, jagged edges of his skull still sent a shiver through me, but it no longer felt like a threat. It felt like something more complex, something I couldn't fully understand, but something I was beginning to.

A wave of heat washed through me, and I found my voice again, desperate to sound more confident than I felt. "So, what's next in this training?" I asked, trying to keep my tone steady, even as the tremors of unease still lingered beneath the surface.

Azrael's ember-filled gaze softened just a little. The fire in his sockets flickered, almost like a spark of understanding, but there was something else there too—something ancient and powerful. "Now... we prepare you for what's coming."

And with that, I finally exhaled, the weight of everything I had just witnessed settling on me. I wasn't sure if I was ready, but I knew I had no choice. Whatever the supernatural world was about to throw my way, I had to face it.

Sadie, still visibly processing the unsettling sight of Azrael's transformation, shifted her gaze to the corner of the field where Ashton stood. He looked remarkably unfazed by the whole exchange, like this was just another day for him. Sadie raised an eyebrow, her usual defiance returning with full force. "So, does he have a true form too? The Sandman, I mean."

Ashton blinked slowly, his posture relaxed as ever, his eyes half-closed like he hadn't a care in the world. He gave a small, knowing smile that somehow managed to be both comforting and slightly unsettling. "I do," he replied, his voice as smooth as ever, though there was a slight amusement in it, like he was humoring her.

Sadie tilted her head, lips curving into a half-smirk. "Oh, really?" she challenged, leaning back slightly, clearly intrigued despite herself. "What's it look like? Let me guess—spooky dust and endless nightmares?"

Ashton chuckled softly, a sound that resonated in the air like a low, distant echo. His smile widened just a touch, but there was something ancient in his eyes—something that made me shiver. "Not quite," he said, his eyes glinting with an almost otherworldly light. "But you could say my true form is... a little more abstract. A collection of thoughts, dreams, and shadows that come together to create something a bit beyond what your eyes could handle."

I felt the tension shift in the air as Sadie stared at him, her curiosity piqued despite her usual bravado.

"Abstract?" she repeated, clearly skeptical. "So, you're telling me you're like... a walking metaphor or something?"

Azrael's dry laugh broke the silence, his skeletal form still looming nearby, his voice a calm contrast to the strange weight in the air. "Ashton's not that cryptic," he said, voice dripping with dry humor. "It's just that his true form is... not something you'd want to see all at once. Not unless you're prepared for the weight of dreams themselves."

Sadie frowned, her arms folding again as she cast a glance at Ashton. "I thought I was supposed to be desensitizing to that too," she muttered, her usual bravado faltering just a little.

The Sandman's smile never wavered, but there was a softness to it now, a flicker of something—understanding, maybe? "You are. But like I said, some things are best seen when you're ready."

Sadie opened her mouth, but I could see the hesitation in her eyes. Even she, the one who rarely backed down from a challenge, wasn't sure if she wanted to know more. I didn't blame her. What Ashton was talking about, what I could almost feel just from his words, seemed more dangerous than anything I'd faced so far.

But maybe it was a good thing. Maybe it was all about preparing us for the unknown. And if that meant facing things that didn't make sense, things that were beyond comprehension, then I would have to trust that there was a reason for it. Just like I was learning to trust Azrael.

I watched their exchange, the tension between curiosity and wariness hanging in the air, and I couldn't help but feel a little comforted by Ashton's calm presence. I hold the pendant necklace Ashton gave me, hoping it would ground me. If anyone could make it through the supernatural chaos we were facing, it was probably Sadie. But even I wasn't ready for the things I'd yet to see.

"Well," Sadie said, with a smirk that was more about bravado than confidence, "guess I'll just have to take your word for it. No rush on that, huh?"

"Not unless you want it," Ashton replied, his tone still light. But I caught the faintest edge of seriousness behind it.

Chapter Twenty-Nine

Layla

Blood // Water - grandson

The moment's awkward pause was broken by the sound of lightning striking the ground, followed by a cool breeze that swept through the air. I felt a shift in the atmosphere, a presence that seemed to *hum* with power, and my gaze flicked toward the sound.

There, standing before us all was a man who *had* to be Exu.

He was everything I didn't know I needed to see.

Exu wasn't like Azrael's heavy, looming presence or Ashton's ethereal, dreamlike quality. He was sharp, charismatic, and... *alive* in away that made the air crackle. His skin, deep and rich like mahogany, seemed to shimmer under the low lights of the Underworld, as if his very essence was absorbing the world around him. His hair, a crown of long, thick locs, cascaded down like rooted vines, each strand a testament to strength and untamed elegance. His eyes glowed—bright, fiery amber, piercing through the dimness of our surroundings, but it wasn't just the color that caught your attention. It was the *fire* in them.

As he stepped further into the group, the scent of burning incense and something sweet but sharp, like spiced rum, followed him. His presence was a mix of fire and smoke, control and chaos—almost overwhelming, but not entirely unpleasant. His smile was easy, too easy, like he was amused by everything, especially *us*.

"So," Exu drawled, his voice deep and teasing, "this is the group I'm supposed to whip into shape? I must be slumming it today."

Sadie blinked, clearly taken aback by his confident, almost cocky entrance. But then, her usual sharpness kicked in, and she leaned forward, sizing him up. "And who exactly are *you* supposed to be? The one who's going to teach us how to handle all this crap?"

Exu's smile widened, flashing a set of perfect teeth. "In a sense, yes," he replied with a smoothness that made my heart race. "Name's Exu. I'll be guiding you through your... *training*." He glanced over at Azrael, his expression shifting, just for a moment, to something more serious. "I've been sent to make sure you understand the rules of the game. And trust me, it's a game you want to be good at, or you're out."

Sadie gave him as low once-over before scoffing, clearly unimpressed. "Right. So, you're some kind of... supernatural trainer?"

"Something like that," Exu said, running across through his locs. The motion was casual, but it was all too graceful, as though his every move was choreographed for maximum effect. "I'm here to teach you what the rest of the world won't show you. What you can't see on your own. But don't expect it to be easy, girl."

I felt a tightness in my chest. Something about Exu's presence unsettled me, though I wasn't entirely sure why. Maybe it was the way he seemed to hold everyone with just his eyes, as though he already knew all our secrets. Or maybe it was the way he seemed so *unaffected* by everything. There was a weight to him, a *presence* that lingered even after his words had passed.

Sadie tilted her head, clearly trying to figure him out, but I could tell she was no longer the confident, outspoken woman she'd been a second ago. Exu seemed to have a way of disarming people without even trying.

"What's your deal?" she asked, voice still tinged with skepticism.

"My deal?" Exu repeated with a low chuckle. "I'm just the one who makes sure you're prepared for the things that want to tear you apart."

There it was again—that cold shiver, the sense that everything we were about to face was far beyond what any of us had truly prepared for. Exu, unlike Azrael, didn't offer comfort or strength. He offered truth—brutal, unwavering truth. And something told me it would hurt to face it.

"You're all going to need it," Exu continued, his gaze sweeping over the group. "Because the training isn't just about the physical. It's about your mind. Your soul. And I don't think either of you are ready for what's coming. But I'll get you there. No matter the cost."

I swallowed hard, feeling the weight of his words settle on my chest like a stone. Exu's eyes flicked to me then, as if sensing my hesitation. His smile softened, but it didn't make the air any warmer. If anything, it made the whole situation worse.

"You're Layla, right?" he asked, his voice now calm, but still holding that sharp edge.

I nodded, unsure of what to say, or if I even wanted to say anything.

"You're going to be the hardest of them all," Exu said, his gaze flickering to Azrael for a brief moment before returning to me. "You're the one who has to unlearn everything. But don't worry," he added, his smile twisting into something more knowing. "I'm good at breaking beings."

I didn't know how to respond to that. My mind reeled with all the things I'd already faced, and yet, I wasn't sure I was ready to face this—Exu—or whatever truths he planned to expose about us.

Azrael's stance didn't shift, but I could tell he was just as wary of Exu's presence as I was. His eyes flickered for just a second, his grip tightening around the hilt of his scythe.

"If you're done with the introductions," Azrael said, his voice low, "maybe you can start with the training. These beings—*my beings*—are going to need all the help they can get."

Exu gave a slow, deliberate nod. "Oh, we're just getting started."

Exu's eyes never left us as he moved into the center of the field, the air around him almost crackling with energy. I couldn't help but notice how everyone seemed to instinctively take a step back, as though something about him commanded space. Even Azrael, usually so steady, seemed to shift his weight as if preparing for whatever was coming next.

Sadie, still skeptical but undeniably curious, stood with arms crossed, studying Exu with a sharp eye. "So, what exactly are we doing here? You're not just going to tell us to 'close our eyes and think happy thoughts,' are you?"

Exu chuckled, a deep, dark sound that was anything but reassuring. "If only it were that easy, girl. Training isn't about positive thinking. It's about facing the truth—*all* of it. The parts of you that want to curl up and hide, the parts that make you want to scream and run away. And trust me, when you face what's coming, you'll want to run."

"Sadie. My name is Sadie." She raised an eyebrow. "So, what are you supposed to do—scare us into being better fighters?"

"No," Exu said, his voice still smooth and calm, "I'm going to *show* you what you're really dealing with. I'm going to make you *feel* it. *That's* how you become strong."

My throat tightened. I didn't know if I was ready for that. For whatever he planned to show us.

"You," Exu said, turning his gaze to me, his amber eyes glinting with something unreadable, "you have the hardest road ahead. You can't just fight what's coming. You'll need to understand it, learn how to accept the darkness inside of you *because* it's already there."

I felt my heart hammering in my chest. The *darkness* inside me? What was he talking about? I had enough darkness of my own, didn't I? Was he saying there was more?

He must have seen my uncertainty because his smile softened, just a little, but it didn't take away the weight in his words. "You're not just training to fight, Layla. You're training to survive. To *live* in this world."

I swallowed hard, trying to steady myself. "How... how do I do that?" I managed to ask.

"You're going to learn how to *embrace* it," Exu said, his voice low, like a whisper meant only for me. "The supernatural. The otherworldly. The terrifying. And yes, even the things that will break you. You have to accept them. It's the only way to stay grounded when everything is falling apart around you."

Azrael shifted beside me, and I felt his presence more strongly now, as though he was somehow trying to offer me the strength I didn't know I had. His words from earlier echoed in my mind: *I'll protect you*. But could anyone really protect me from this?

Exu took a step closer, his eyes never leaving mine. "You've already seen the worst, Layla. But you haven't felt it yet. That's what I'm here for. I'm going to make sure you *feel* what's out there. That way, you'll be ready when it comes."

I didn't want to ask. I didn't want to know. But somehow, the question slipped out. "What... what do you mean by that?"

He let out a soft, almost pitying laugh. "You'll understand soon enough."

Exu gestured toward a tree at the far corner of the field, where a series of intricate, glowing symbols had appeared on the ground, runes that hadn't been there moments ago. My heart skipped a beat as I recognized them for what they were—*wards*, traps, protections.

"This," Exu said, voice casual as though we weren't standing in the middle of a mystical ritual, "is where it begins. You're going to step into this circle and face what's waiting for you. And trust me, you're not going to like it."

Sadie raised an eyebrow. "What's in there?"

"Something you're both going to have to deal with," Exu replied. "And it's the first step to training your mind."

I glanced at Azrael, searching his face for any hint of reassurance, but there was nothing. His expression was unreadable, his posture rigid as ever.

"Layla," Exu said, his tone softer now, almost coaxing. "You'll go first."

My pulse quickened as I took a hesitant step forward.

"I don't know if I can do this," I murmured, my voice a bit shakier than I'd intended.

"You don't have a choice," Exu replied simply. "But don't worry. We'll start slow."

He extended his hand, palm up, and suddenly the runes on the ground began to pulse with an eerie light, casting a glow that made the shadows of the Underworld dance. As if on cue, I felt the air around me grow thicker and heavier. Something *otherworldly* was beginning to slip into the air—something that was going to test everything I thought I knew about fear.

"You're going to feel it," Exu said again, his voice a steady whisper in the growing silence. "You're going to feel everything."

I stepped into the circle, and the world *shifted*.

As soon as I crossed the threshold of the circle, the temperature in the air seemed to drop—like stepping into an open freezer. The air itself felt dense, almost oppressive, and my breath caught in my throat. It was as though the weight of everything, every moment of fear and uncertainty I'd been carrying, had condensed into a single, suffocating force.

I forced myself to take a deep breath, though it came out shaky, and uneven. My skin prickled, the hairs on the back of my neck standing on end. Every part of me wanted to step back and run.

But Exu's voice cut through the fog of my panic, calm and unyielding. "You're going to face it now, Layla. Trust me, you don't want to be weak when it comes for you. This is where you find out what you're made of."

I felt his gaze on me, burning through the dark space between us. His words were laced with something I couldn't quite place, a warning, yes—but also something deeper. Something that said he *knew* what was coming, and whatever it was, he wasn't afraid of it.

I couldn't say the same for myself.

The runes beneath me flared brighter, casting an eerie, shifting light across us. The symbols began to rotate slowly, like gears in a clock, each pulse of energy making my heart skip a beat. And then, like a veil being lifted, the *presence* hit.

It wasn't just the cold. It was something worse—a hunger, a depth, a twisting *void* that seemed to crawl beneath my skin. My chest tightened as if invisible hands were wrapping around my ribs, squeezing the air out of my lungs. I gasped for breath, my thoughts scattering as something *dark* surged forward.

It wasn't a shape, not exactly. But it *felt* like a shape—massive, consuming, the kind of thing that whispered promises of oblivion. The darkness pressed against me, crawling through my veins, filling my mind with jagged edges, with screams, with despair.

I forced myself to stay still, my feet anchored in the circle as though it could protect me from what was slipping through the cracks of reality. The darkness felt *alive*, hungry for me, testing me, clawing at the edges of my sanity.

This was what Exu meant. This was the *feeling*.

It was the *fear* that made you weak. The kind of terror that stopped you in your tracks, that *paralyzed* you, that made you forget who you were.

But somewhere, buried beneath the weight of it, was something else. A flicker of defiance. A *spark*. I didn't know where it came from, but it was there, a tiny flame in the storm of dark energy swirling around me.

"Stay with it, Layla. Focus." Orcus' voice was deep and reassuring. It wasn't a shout or a command. It was a steady presence, like the hand of a guardian pulling me from the edge of the abyss.

"Focus," Exu repeated, his voice now like a thread of light in the suffocating dark. "You need to *accept* it. Don't let it break you. The fear is part of you. Control it, or it controls you."

I clenched my fists at my sides, feeling the tremors run through me. "How?" I managed to choke out, the word barely leaving my throat.

Exu didn't answer right away. He just watched me, his eyes unwavering, a sharp intensity there that was hard to ignore. "Stop resisting it. Let it *touch* you. But don't let it consume you."

I squeezed my eyes shut for a second, swallowing the bile that rose in my throat. *Let it touch me?*

The darkness clawed harder, but there was something different this time. The fear had always been there, lurking just beneath the surface of my thoughts, the *what-if*s, the unknowns that gnawed at me every day. But as it swirled around me, threatening to overwhelm my senses, I felt... not just fear. I felt *something else*.

It was as though I had tapped into a hidden part of myself, a deep well of emotion I didn't know existed, one that wasn't just about fear but about *acceptance*. A strange calm washed over me as I realized something: I couldn't outrun it. I couldn't hide from it. The darkness, the terror, the *unknown*—it was part of the world I now inhabited. Part of the power I had to learn to control.

It didn't make the fear go away, but it made it bearable. I wasn't fighting it anymore; I was... *living* with it.

I opened my eyes, and the darkness receded just a fraction. The pressure lifted, but the heaviness remained, like an old, familiar weight on my chest.

Exu was watching me closely, but there was a flicker of something—approval?—in his eyes. "You're getting it," he murmured. "Not everyone can face it this quickly. But you're not *everyone*, are you?"

I shook my head, still breathing heavily, but the panic had faded. It wasn't gone entirely, but it was manageable, a shadow in the corner of my mind instead of a raging storm.

"That's what this is about," Exu continued, his voice quieter now. "It's not about defeating the fear. It's about *existing with it*. Letting it fuel you instead of breaking you."

I nodded, the weight of his words sinking in. I wasn't sure if I was ready for everything that was coming, but in this moment, I knew I had to keep going. I couldn't give in to the darkness. I couldn't let it win.

Exu gave a single, approving nod. "Good. You're learning."

But before I could process what had just happened, I felt a shift again. Something *stronger* this time—like a door opening, a crack in reality. The darkness wasn't gone. It was just... waiting. And in its place, something new *loomed*. Something I wasn't prepared to face, something that felt even *worse*.

As the darkness swirled around me again, threatening to consume every inch of my mind, Orcus' presence cut through the fog like a bolt of lightning. His voice—low, rich, and unmistakably *there*—it was a lifeline in the suffocating chaos.

"You're stronger than you know, Layla. Don't let it swallow you whole."

I could feel his *words*, reminding me that I wasn't alone even when it felt like the world was closing in on me. His voice didn't come from any specific direction. It was everywhere anchoring deep within me.

"I know it's hard. It's supposed to be. But you're not made of glass. You won't break."

I took a shaky breath, pushing against the oppressive force of the darkness. The fear was still there, gnawing at the edges of my thoughts, but Orcus was right. I wasn't broken. I had been bent, and twisted, but I was still standing. Still *breathing*.

"You've faced worse than this," Orcus continued, his voice never faltering, "but this is different. It's not just about survival. It's about knowing that the fear will always be there, and choosing to keep going anyway."

I clenched my fists, letting the pain of the pressure surge through me. Orcus' words were like a steady anchor, pulling me back from the brink.

"You think Azrael can protect you from everything?" Orcus' tone shifted slightly, a knowing edge creeping into his voice. "He can't. No one can. But you, Layla? You've got the strength inside you to face it—all of it. The shadows. The darkness. The unknown."

I swallowed hard, focusing on Orcus' words as the swirling energy threatened to drag me down again. I could feel it all—my heart pounding in my chest, my legs trembling from the strain, but there was something else now. Something I hadn't realized before.

I had *control* over this fear. Not full control, not yet—but enough to stand firm.

The darkness pressed harder, curling around me like a living thing, but instead of succumbing to it, I met it head-on.

"That's it," Orcus whispered in approval. "Feel it. But don't let it possess you."

His voice seemed to grow louder, clearer as if he were standing next to me, guiding me through the storm of sensations. I could still feel the terror, the overwhelming pressure of everything trying to claw its way into my soul, but now, it was just *noise*. Just static.

"You think you're going to make me fall?" I muttered to the darkness, my voice shaking but determined. "Not today."

The cold didn't letup, but I felt a spark of something else—something *warmer*—flicker to life in the pit of my stomach. A fire, maybe. Or was it the slow burn of defiance?

The darkness seemed to recoil slightly, as though it didn't expect the challenge.

"Good." Orcus' voice hummed, low and darkly satisfied. "That's how it starts. Every time you push back, you get a little stronger. Don't let it overwhelm you. Use the fear. Make it your weapon."

The runes beneath me pulsed again, the light more intense now. I was holding my ground, feeling the heavy weight of Exu's gaze as he watched me, his expression unreadable, but there was a flicker of something in his eyes—something I couldn't quite place.

"Now," Exu said, his voice cutting through the tension. "You're ready to begin training for real. The fear doesn't just go away, Layla. But you'll learn to use it."

I nodded, trying to steady my breathing, but there was a strange sense of pride swelling inside me. I'd done it. I'd *stood* in the face of the darkness, and I hadn't let it crush me. Not yet.

"Thank you," I whispered to the empty air, though I knew Orcus could hear me.

"Anytime," he replied with a low chuckle that echoed softly.

Exu stepped forward then, a slight smirk playing at the corners of his mouth. "Not bad, Layla. But the real work starts now."

I turned to look at him, feeling the adrenaline coursing through me, a strange mixture of exhaustion and exhilaration.

"Yeah," I said, swallowing hard but standing straighter, "I'm ready."

Chapter Thirty

Layla

It's My Life - Bon Jovi

I leaned within the kitchen chair with my book in hand and watched Azrael as he paced in front of the counter like some caffeine-crazed maniac. His movements were quick, purposeful, like the fate of the universe hinged on his coffee routine. To him, maybe it did.

It was barely dawn—too early for me to function, let alone deal with this ridiculous display. Sadie, perched on the edge of the counter with one leg swinging, had no such qualms. She sipped her drink with the kind of casual amusement only she could pull off, her wild curls bouncing as she shook her head.

"You're really doing this again?" she asked, half-laughing.

Azrael didn't even glance her way as he reached for the coffee pot. "What else am I supposed to do? Coffee is life."

"Coffee is obsession," I muttered under my breath, but apparently, I wasn't quiet enough.

He shot me a glare, the kind that could wilt a flower. "I heard that."

"Good." I smirked and went back to pretending I cared about the book in front of me.

Azrael poured the dark liquid into his favorite mug—a black monstrosity with "Death Before Decaf" scrawled in bold white letters. Fitting, really. He held it reverently, like it was the Holy Grail, and took a slow sip, his eyes fluttering shut as though it were the nectar of the gods.

I couldn't stop myself. "You're the Grim Reaper, Azrael. How can you possibly feel sluggish? Your literal job is to collect souls. You'd think that would keep you on your toes."

His eyes snapped open, and he fixed me with that deadpan look he'd mastered over centuries. "Sluggish in spirit, Layla. You wouldn't understand."

Sadie nearly choked on her drink. "Oh, please," she said between sputtered laughs. "Sluggish spirit? You make it sound like you're about to become a zombie or something. Maybe you need a coffee intervention."

Azrael's response was immediate, his tone dry as the Sahara. "Try existing for centuries and dealing with the weight of countless souls on your shoulders without something to make it less miserable."

Sadie raised an eyebrow, the mischievous glint in her eyes unmistakable. "So, you've been drinking coffee for centuries? Like, even in the underworld? How does that even work?"

Azrael stirred his coffee with the same intensity of someone plotting world domination. "You wouldn't believe what I've had to do to get good coffee down there. And yes, centuries. It's one of the few things that makes immortality tolerable."

I couldn't help it—I laughed. Loud and unfiltered. "Maybe it's not the souls that are the problem, Azrael. Maybe it's the coffee."

He froze mid-sip and turned to me, his expression one of pure, unfiltered offense. "If you think I'm giving up coffee to save myself from whatever fate you're suggesting, you're delusional."

"Listen to the tiny mouse," Orcus chimed in, his voice echoing from where he leaned against the wall. "She might be onto something. The last thing we need is a jittery Grim Reaper. You're already impossible to deal with."

Azrael glared at his scythe, his jaw tightening. "Impossible? I'm the epitome of restraint."

I snorted again and closed my book with a thud. "Sure you are. And I'm a Zen master."

Sadie cackled, sliding off the counter. "This is why I love mornings with you two. It's like breakfast theater. Now, someone pass me a muffin before I die of hunger."

Azrael ignored her, muttering something about "heathens" as he stalked out of the kitchen, his coffee firmly in hand.

"Drama queen," Sadie said with a grin, tossing me a muffin.

"Tell me about it," I replied, already planning to weaponize this story later.

Sadie hopped off the counter with a grin that practically screamed mischief. She tilted her head at Azrael, who was guarding his mug like it held the secrets of the universe. "Alright, Reaper, if I can't take away your coffee, how about a decaf for once?"

Azrael froze, his eyes widening in sheer horror. For a moment, I thought he might drop the mug. "Don't you dare suggest such a thing. That's not coffee. That's... blasphemous bean juice."

Sadie barked a laugh, poking his shoulder like a pesky little sister. "It can't be that bad. At least it wouldn't make you jittery."

Azrael straightened, his voice dripping with indignation. "Jittery? I don't get jittery. I *am* the jitter."

I was mid-sip of my own drink and nearly spat it out, coughing instead. "You *are* the jitter," I repeated, snorting.

"He's not lying," Orcus chimed in from his spot on the wall. "I've seen him on a caffeine high. It's like watching a thunderstorm try to figure out how to rain sideways."

I couldn't stop the laugh that bubbled out of me, and even Sadie doubled over, wheezing. Azrael, of course, was unamused. He glanced between us with a frown, as though trying to decide whether we were laughing with him or at him.

Definitely at him.

"I think someone needs a nap," I teased, leaning back in my chair and crossing my arms.

Sadie smirked at me, then turned back to Azrael. "Oh, he definitely does, but there's no point wasting time convincing him. He's a lost cause."

Azrael arched a brow, his expression calm but his tone sharp. "I'm not the one who's far gone. You don't even know the true power of coffee."

Sadie's eyes sparkled, that dangerous glint of hers in full force. "Sure, sure. Whatever helps you sleep at night, Azrael."

He took a deliberate sip from his mug, savoring it like it was the blood of his enemies. "Sleep? I don't sleep. Reapers do not sleep. Plus, I have coffee."

"Oh, yeah?" Sadie crossed her arms, her voice light but challenging. "And you think that's a good thing?"

Azrael didn't even hesitate. "Better than needing a nap every two hours."

"The Reaper and his caffeine. World's worst combo," I muttered, shaking my head.

Azrael's sharp ears caught my words, and his gaze snapped to mine. "I heard that."

Sadie's grin only widened as she clapped a hand on his shoulder. "Good. You should probably hear it more often, buddy."

Azrael let out a long-suffering sigh, his fingers curling tighter around his mug. "You mortals have no respect for the things that keep me sane."

"Respect?" I raised a brow. "Azrael, you just claimed to be the jitter. I think sanity left the building a long time ago."

Orcus snorted—a strange sound coming from a sentient scythe. "And she's right. Again. You're not going to live this one down, my friend."

Azrael groaned, looking genuinely tempted to chuck his coffee at someone—probably me or Sadie. But he didn't, instead taking another slow, deliberate sip. The man had priorities.

For a moment, we all fell silent. Azrael kept sipping his coffee, as if nothing in the world could faze him. The quiet felt unusual, almost foreign, in the lively chaos that usually surrounded us. Then, with a sigh, he broke the stillness, his tone unexpectedly soft. "One day, Sadie, you'll thank me when you need a cup to survive."

Sadie rolled her eyes so hard I was surprised she didn't pull something. "Right. When that day comes, I'll just skip the coffee and take a nap instead."

Azrael chuckled under his breath—a rare, almost fond sound that seemed to soften the sharpness of his presence. "You can nap all you want. I'll be the one getting things done."

"Yeah, by drinking your body weight in coffee," Sadie fired back without missing a beat.

"At least I'm productive," Azrael said, pausing dramatically. Then he turned to Orcus. "Back me up."

"Oh, I'm sorry," Orcus said with mock sincerity. "Did you want me to lie for you? Because no, drinking coffee and pacing isn't exactly my definition of productive."

I couldn't help the smile that tugged at my lips. This was so typical. Azrael with his unwavering devotion to caffeine, Sadie never letting him have the last word, Orcus throwing in his signature snark, and me—always caught in the middle of the whirlwind. It was exhausting and comforting all at once.

Sadie tilted her head at Azrael, her expression softening slightly. "Doesn't it get old?"

Azrael shrugged, completely unfazed. "No. It never does."

The room settled into another brief silence before Sadie shifted, her playful energy dimming. She set her mug down and glanced at Azrael, something more serious flickering in her eyes.

"Hey," she started, hesitating for a moment. "I have a question."

I glanced up from my book, the shift in her tone pulling me from my faux reading.

Sadie took a breath, her fingers fidgeting with the edge of her sleeve. "Do you think you can take me to see my father? You said he was in the Underworld, right?"

The air in the room changed, the kind of stillness that pressed against your chest and made you hyper-aware of every sound, every movement. Azrael froze, his mug hovering midair. Slowly, he lowered it, his sharp, piercing gaze softening as he looked at her.

Sadie's confidence wavered for a moment, and she stared at the floor. When she spoke again, her voice was quieter, more vulnerable. "I know he's in the Underworld. I just... I need to see him. I need to know he's okay."

Azrael placed his mug on the counter, moving deliberately, his expression unreadable. Finally, he nodded, his voice calm but firm. "I can take you there. But the Underworld isn't a place for casual visits. You can't just wander around. There are rules."

Sadie nodded quickly, her determination steadying her posture. "I understand. I just... I need to see him."

I couldn't look away from the exchange. Sadie didn't ask for much—not from me, not from anyone. Seeing her like this, raw and resolute, hit something deep inside me. She wasn't just asking; she was trusting Azrael with a part of herself she rarely showed.

Azrael studied her for a moment longer before he nodded again. "Alright. We'll go. But you need to be ready for what you might find."

Sadie offered him a small, grateful smile, her eyes glistening with relief. "Thank you."

"Oh, don't thank him yet," Orcus chimed in, his voice cutting through the tension like a knife. "Wait until you've seen the place. Not exactly a tourist attraction."

A small laugh escaped me despite the heaviness in the air. I smiled at Sadie, hoping it carried a fraction of the reassurance I felt. Whatever she found there, she wouldn't face it alone.

Azrael stood, his commanding presence shifting the energy in the room once again. He glanced at both of us, his tone sharp but not unkind. "Let's go. No time to waste."

Sadie followed him, her determination evident, though I could see the uncertainty lingering in the set of her shoulders. My heart tightened.

And then there it was—that fluttering in my chest that I couldn't quite explain. It wasn't jealousy, not really. It was something deeper, something I hadn't yet untangled. Watching the way Azrael moved so quickly to help Sadie, to make her happy without hesitation, did something to me. It made me feel something I wasn't ready to name.

Chapter Thirty-One

Azrael

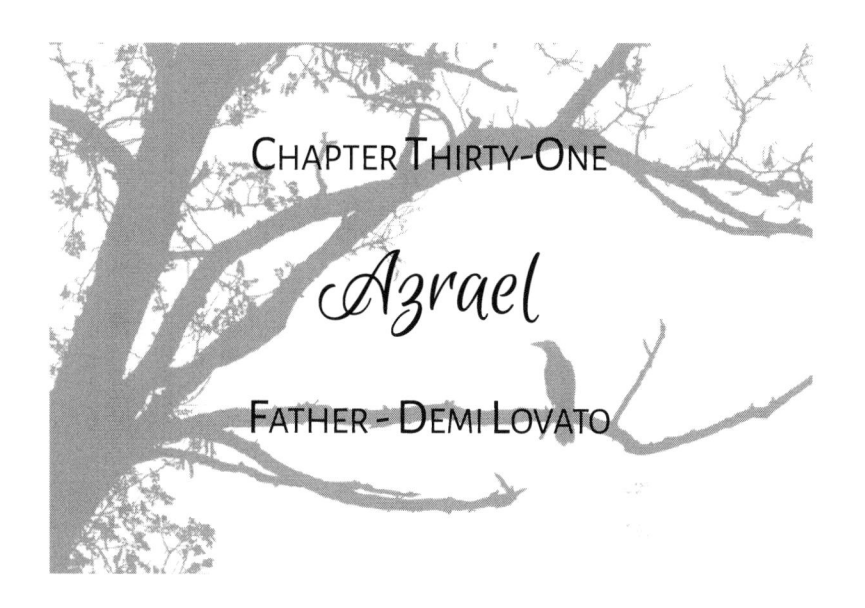

Father - Demi Lovato

The air in the Underworld was suffocating, thick with a cold that gnawed at the bones—a place suspended between the realms of the living and the dead. Here, time had no meaning, and neither did the passage of souls. I walked beside Sadie, the heavy weight of her presence pulling at the silence between us. We were in the lower districts now, where the streets twisted and coiled like the lost memories of the damned. The pulse of dark energy buzzed through the cobblestone paths, an undercurrent of despair that was impossible to ignore.

This was a place where nothing belonged, not even the souls wandering aimlessly, their hollow gazes fixed on nothing in particular.

Sadie walked in step with me, though I could feel the tension in her every move. She had asked to see her father, and I had agreed. It wasn't a decision I took lightly. I owed her this. I owed her this for uprooting her mortal life. She'd spent too long in the dark, wondering what had become of him after I first brought her here.

The street ahead twisted with dark energy, and the city's pulse felt more oppressive the further we walked. Finally, we stopped in front of a small, unassuming shop—*Dante's Goods*. The name seemed out of place for a place that sold nothing but ancient relics and the souls of the lost, traded as slaves, maids, and servants.

Sadie hesitated in front of the door, her uncertainty palpable. I stayed silent, arms crossed, watching her as she stared at the entrance. I could feel the storm of emotions brewing inside her, but there was nothing I could say to prepare her. The Underworld was unforgiving, and so was the afterlife her father had chosen.

"You ready?" I asked, my voice low, but carrying the weight of my own unspoken conflict.

Sadie gave me a tight nod, her lips pressed together in an effort to suppress the rising tide of emotions threatening to overwhelm her.

I opened the door, the bell above chiming with a soft, hollow sound as we entered. The shop was dim, the shelves lined with trinkets that held stories of their own. But it wasn't the oddities of the place that held Sadie's attention. It was the figure hunched over the counter in the far corner, sorting through forgotten things. His back was turned to us.

Her father.

Sadie froze, the breath in her throat catching. I felt the tension in her build, the rapid beat of her pulse as she stood, unsure whether to move or remain still. But it was too late—he had already sensed us. He looked up from his work, eyes widening slightly before narrowing in suspicion. The recognition hit him like a wave, and I saw the flicker of guilt and fear in his eyes. He hadn't expected this.

"Daddy?" Sadie's voice cracked, soft and fragile, as she spoke.

For a moment, there was no movement, no sound. Then he stood slowly, painfully so, his body stiff as though the very act of standing had become a monumental task. His face was gaunt, and his eyes—the same eyes Sadie had—were older, worn down by the weight of the Underworld.

"Sadie..." His voice was rough, thick with regret. "You... you're really here?"

Sadie's eyes were filled with an emotion I couldn't quite understand, but I suspected it was hope. And then, like a dam breaking, the tears started. "Oh my god, Daddy... I didn't know if I'd ever see you again. I—" She stopped, her breath hitching in her throat as she took a step forward.

He hesitated, his gaze flicking from Sadie to me, uncertainty clouding his features. He didn't seem to know what to say.

I stayed silent, arms still crossed as I watched the scene unfold. Sadie needed this. She needed the answers she'd been searching for, even if it was painful for both of them.

Finally, he muttered, his voice breaking with sorrow. "When I died... they pulled me here. They put me to work, made me a servant in this damn shop. It's the only thing they allow us to do here."

Sadie's lips trembled as she took another step forward. "But... why here? Why did you stay? You could've gone through another cycle. You didn't have to stay in the Underworld."

His eyes flickered with something that almost looked like regret, but there was a deeper sadness there. "I didn't want to do another cycle, Sadie. I couldn't stand the thought of being born again, losing all memory of you. I chose to stay here, to watch you grow up, to be with you in some way."

Sadie's breath hitched. Her father's words, his choice to remain in the Underworld to watch her from afar, hit her like a punch to the gut. I could see the conflicting emotions in her—love, grief, and anger all tangled together.

"Azrael told me you were here," Sadie said, her voice unsteady. "I didn't know. I thought you were gone, and... and that he was lying."

His face softened, but there was an unmistakable weariness in his eyes. He wasn't lying. I'm here. Just a servant to this shop.

Sadie's tears flowed freely now, her pain spilling over. "I... I never stopped thinking about you. I didn't know what happened to you. I thought you were gone forever."

"I'm sorry, Sadie," he whispered, his voice thick with emotion. "I'm so sorry."

The silence stretched, heavy and suffocating. Sadie wiped her eyes, sniffling. "I... I just wanted you to know that I didn't forget you."

"I know," he said softly. "I know, sweetheart."

There was nothing more to say. Sadie didn't need more words from him—what he had given her was enough. She knew now, and she could carry that knowledge with her.

I glanced at her, then back at her father. It was time for us to go. I moved to the door, gesturing for Sadie to follow me. She didn't hesitate this time, but I could see how heavy her heart was.

She paused for a moment, giving her father one last look. Then, with a final glance back at him, she turned and walked toward me. Without another word, we left the shop, the door closing softly behind us.

She didn't speak as we walked back through the Underworld's streets, and I didn't push her to say anything. There was nothing left to say. Sometimes, in the Underworld, silence was the only answer we had.

But then Sadie stopped, her back straight, her hands trembling at her sides. Tears streamed down her face as she spoke, her voice strained and broken.

"Azrael."

"Yes, Sadie?"

"Get my father out of there. Now."

Her brown eyes, flooded with emotion, locked onto mine, and for the first time, I saw the full weight of what I had cost her. Not just her father, but a piece of herself, lost in this place she never chose.

"I don't care how long it takes, what you have to do," she added, her voice trembling with a mix of sorrow and defiance. "You fucking owe me this, Azrael. You tore me from everything I know. My family. My life. I want my father safe. With me. No more games."

The blow hit me harder than I expected. I had never truly taken the time to understand Sadie's emotions. My primary focus had been on Layla, on the larger battles ahead. But Sadie had been forgotten, even by her own companion, since coming here.

I swallowed hard, the weight of her plea pressing down on me. I knew the complexities of this place, but in this moment, none of that mattered.

"You have my word, Sadie. I'll get to work on it."

She nodded, her back to me now as she turned, walking toward Ashton's home.

Chapter Thirty-Two

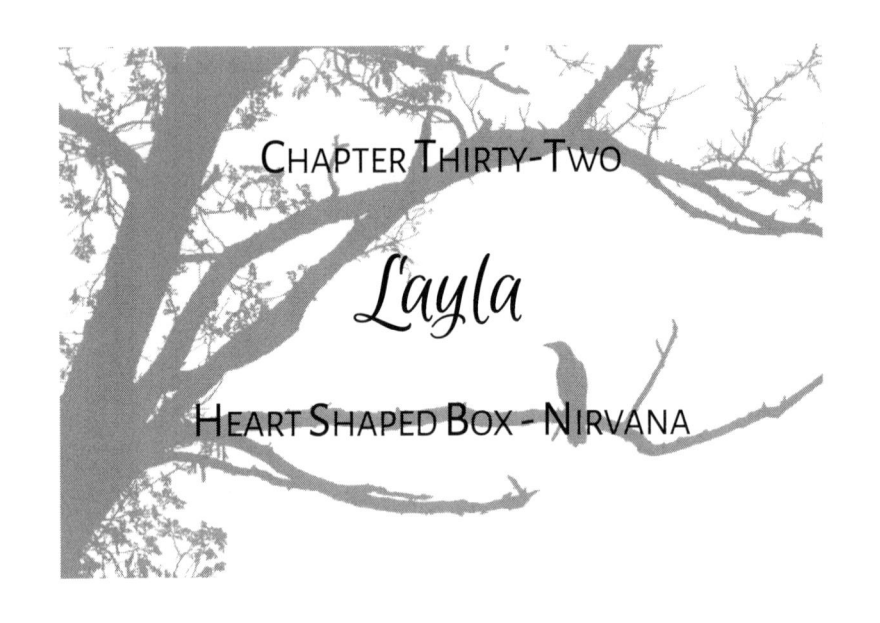

Layla

Heart Shaped Box - Nirvana

"Wake up, tiny mouse."

Azrael's voice sliced through the haze of my dreams, a familiar, dark rumble that should have been comforting. But this time, I didn't feel like facing him—or anything else. The covers felt like a safe cocoon, a barrier between me and whatever came with the day. I burrowed deeper, hoping he'd just give up and let me sleep a little longer.

"Layla," Azrael called again, this time with an edge of amusement, as if he enjoyed teasing me more than he let on.

"Go away," I groaned, rolling onto my side, pulling the blanket tighter around me, willing him to just leave.

"Oh, this is going to be good," came the dry, sharp voice of Orcus, cutting through my annoyance. "She's ignoring you, Azrael. Maybe I should take over. Hey, Layla! It's your favorite homicidal scythe here to ruin your morning!"

I groaned inwardly. I could feel a headache starting already, but there was no avoiding it. I threw the blanket off my head and shot Azrael a glare. He was standing at the edge of my bed, looking entirely too smug for someone who just interrupted my peace. Orcus hung casually across his back like a silent, menacing shadow.

"What do you want?" I managed to mumble, though I knew I didn't want to hear the answer.

Azrael shrugged, completely unfazed by my death glare. "I thought you'd like to see the city before training. You've only seen bits and pieces, but the real heart of the Underworld... it's worth seeing."

I blinked, trying to push myself upright. His invitation was tempting, in a strange, impossible-to-resist way. But my body felt sluggish, and my mind was still tangled in the remnants of sleep. "I'm not even dressed," I said, more to myself than him.

"She's not even dressed yet," Orcus chimed in, ever the troublemaker, his voice light and mocking. "You're bad at this romance thing. You've got to ease her into your creepy death realm, not drag her out of bed like a kid late for school."

Azrael let out a long sigh, clearly used to Orcus' antics. "Ignore him."

"No one ignores me, Prince," Orcus shot back with a glint of challenge in his voice. "I'm the charming part."

I couldn't suppress the smirk that tugged at my lips. Even if I hated admitting it, Orcus had a way of making the whole 'Underworld' thing a little more bearable. "You're something, all right."

"See?" Orcus said triumphantly. "She gets it."

A reluctant laugh bubbled in my chest as I swung my legs over the side of the bed. It was too early to be this awake, but here I was, caught between the strange pull of curiosity and the overwhelming need for more sleep. I threw on some clothes quickly—whatever was closest—and followed Azrael out into the dry atmosphere of the Underworld.

The air was heavy, the kind that made your skin feel too tight, but still, I felt the pull to see more. We followed a narrow path through the woods, the dense fog swirling around us, lit from within by faint lights, as if the trees themselves were alive. The deeper we went, the more alive the world felt. It was beautiful, and terrifying, and everything I'd ever thought the Underworld would be—and somehow, I couldn't quite stop the wonder that bubbled up inside me.

"Well, look at that, Azrael," Orcus drawled. "A real Prince of Darkness. Just look at you—glowing with that 'I'm going to conquer the world and brood in a dark corner about it' aura. Very regal."

Azrael didn't even look at him. "Keep talking, Orcus. I'm sure you have more profound commentary about the city's 'vibe.'"

"I'm just saying," Orcus continued, his tone unbothered, "this place is basically the 'hottest' tourist destination for anyone with a serious case of existential dread. Look at the architecture—gothic, gloomy, and about as welcoming as a tomb. Definitely not a place you want to bring your grandma for her birthday. Or, you know, *anyone* with a pulse."

"Orcus, shut up," Azrael muttered.

"Oh, so now you want me to be quiet?" Orcus feigned hurt. "What happened to all that 'I'm in charge here' energy? Where's the intimidation factor, hmm? I was expecting a little more flair from the Prince of Death. You're making me look bad."

"I told you, no one listens to you, Orcus," Azrael replied dryly.

"You're breaking my heart, Azzy," Orcus mocked, his runes lighting up with amusement. "Don't you worry, though. I'll keep entertaining myself while you keep pretending this place is *romantic*. Next, you'll say the rivers of liquid gold are perfect for a stroll. Maybe we'll stop at one of the 'gothic cafes' for a latte, yeah?"

I couldn't help but laugh at Orcus' antics, despite the eeriness of the city around us.

"Are you ever serious about anything?" I asked, raising an eyebrow.

"Why be serious when you can be *fabulous*?" Orcus retorted with a dramatic flourish of his blade. "Just ask Azrael. He's been brooding in this place for centuries and still hasn't figured out how to crack a smile."

Azrael grunted, clearly unaffected by Orcus' teasing.

"Well, if we're done with the comedy show," Azrael said, his voice shifting back to its usual tone, "we should continue."

"Fine, fine. But I'm going to need some more material for my stand-up routine," Orcus shot back. "Maybe Layla here can help me out. After all, she's living the dream—practically a tourist in the Underworld, getting the grand tour and all." He turned toward me with a grin. "If you ever need a tour guide, I'm your guy. The best part? No long lines or overcrowded buses. Just *good old-fashioned* terror and the occasional soul-crushing void."

I couldn't help but roll my eyes, though I was secretly amused. "You're something else."

"I know, right?" Orcus smirked, clearly pleased with himself. "It's exhausting, really. But I do it for the fans."

I couldn't help but laugh, despite the ominous surroundings. Azrael might not get it, but Orcus had a way of making even the darkest of places seem... a little less heavy.

The Underworld stretched out before us like a living, breathing entity. As we walked further into its depths, the black stone beneath our feet shifted, reacting to our presence, as though the very earth here was conscious. The air was thick with an unsettling calmness, the oppressive silence broken only by the distant sounds of creaking chains and the occasional flicker of supernatural energy rippling across the landscape.

The city itself was an organic blend of twisted architecture and nature's decay. Towering obsidian spires rose like the jagged teeth of some ancient, long-dead beast, their surfaces etched with centuries of forgotten history. There was no natural sunlight here, only the flickering glow of molten skies and rivers of fire, veins of light pulsing with an eerie energy that seemed to call out in a language I couldn't quite understand.

Above, the sky was a swirling canvas of red and orange, like the last remnants of a dying sun caught in a perpetual state of twilight. The clouds moved with purpose, sometimes still and other times swirling into ominous shapes, as though they were sentient and observing our every move.

As we walked deeper into the heart of the city, the streets grew wider, more imposing. The architecture around us became more intricate—gothic arches stretching toward the sky, windows that glowed with an unsettling greenish hue, and gargoyles perched high above, their eyes seeming to track our every step. The buildings were impossibly tall, stacked upon each other in a way that seemed more like a vertical labyrinth than a city.

In the distance, the sound of distant roars echoed through the fog, only adding to the growing sense of unease. As if drawn by the very essence of death and darkness, the souls of the damned drifted through the streets, their ethereal forms blurred by the constant mist. They were trapped here, stuck in a limbo of eternal restlessness, their once vibrant lives now reduced to whispering echoes that brushed against my mind like a cold wind.

"Those souls," Azrael said softly, his voice cutting through the silence. "They are echoes—remnants of those who were lost here, bound to the Underworld but unable to move on. Their memories are all they have left, drifting through the city like shadows."

I couldn't help but shudder as one of the figures brushed too close, a chill sweeping through me as if it had passed right through my bones.

The rivers of liquid gold that wound through the city were no less unsettling. The glowing liquid surged with a strange vitality, like the lifeblood of the world itself. As it wound through the streets, it gave the city an almost otherworldly glow, casting flickering shadows on the walls of the structures surrounding it.

As we approached the heart of the Underworld, the air grew thicker, heavier with the weight of history. The massive, looming structure of the castle ahead was like something out of a nightmare—its dark stone walls stretched endlessly upward, and its towering spires seemed to pierce the very clouds above. Each tower was adorned with dark runes that pulsed with a faint, ominous glow, giving the entire structure an aura of ancient power.

To the left of the castle stood the prison, an even darker and more forbidding structure. It looked alive, as though it were some ancient beast struggling against its chains, its massive gates adorned with sigils of containment. I could feel the weight of whatever horrors lay within. Even from this distance, a sense of malevolent energy emanated from it, as if the souls imprisoned there were crying out in fury and despair.

"This place," Azrael said quietly, "it holds everything—every dark secret of this world. The castle is where my father rules, but the prison... that's where the worst of the worst are kept."

I nodded, the weight of it all sinking in. This wasn't just a place of punishment—it was the very heart of chaos, of those who had been cast aside by the laws of the living.

From the balcony, I could see the endless expanse of the Underworld stretching beyond the city's limits. The mountains in the distance were jagged and bare, their peaks obscured by swirling clouds. Beyond that, the land fell away into a vast, blackened void, where only the faintest glimmer of light from the cities below illuminated the darkness.

The world was alive, but it was alive in a way that was... wrong. It was a reflection of the death that lingered here, of the suffering and chaos that had come to define this place.

"This is your world," I said again, but this time, there was a greater understanding in my voice.

"It's ours," Azrael replied softly, the weight of his words carrying more meaning than he let on.

The Underworld wasn't just a place. It was a living entity, full of memories, regrets, and power. It was a kingdom of death, and its rulers were just as bound to its rules as the souls that drifted through its streets. And somehow, despite everything, it felt... like home.

Azrael sighed heavily and turned to leave. "Come on, tiny mouse. I have something else I want to show you."

I lingered for a moment, staring at the castle and the prison beyond it. The Underworld was alive.

"Layla!" Orcus called, his runes flaring as Azrael slung him over his back. "You're going to get left behind! Someone has to teach you how to survive, and it sure as hell isn't going to be Mr. Broody over here!"

I laughed, jogging to catch up. Whatever the Underworld had in store, at least I would never be bored.

Chapter Thirty-Three

Layla

Disturbia - Rihanna

"Where are we going now?" I asked, trailing behind Azrael as we walked through the castle's cold, echoing halls. The air was cool, carrying the faint scent of old stone, and something earthy—wood smoke maybe, or something ancient that clung to the walls.

He glanced over his shoulder, the corner of his mouth quirking upward in that way he did when he was about to drop a little bomb. "There's someone I think you should meet."

"Another sarcastic weapon?" I teased, only half joking.

"Ha!" Orcus barked from his perch across Azrael's back. "She thinks I'm irreplaceable. Smart girl."

"Not quite," Azrael replied, clearly not bothered by Orcus's comment. "This one's a bit more... intense."

I frowned, quickening my steps to keep up with his long, confident strides. "Intense? Should I be worried?"

Azrael smirked, his eyes flicking to mine. "Not unless you plan to threaten me."

"Threaten you?" I repeated, my brows knitting together in confusion. "Why would I—"

Before I could finish, we arrived at an enormous set of doors, each one made of dark, weathered wood, towering above us. The intricate carvings on the surface seemed to come alive in the flickering torchlight, snarling faces of beasts etched so deeply into the wood they almost seemed to shift, watching us as we approached.

I instinctively took a step back, my heart rate picking up. The door was unsettling in a way I couldn't explain. "Uh, what's behind the fucking door, Azrael?"

Azrael's gaze softened as his fingers traced over the carvings, his posture relaxed as if he'd been through this a thousand times. "Cerberus."

My eyes widened. "The three-headed dog?" I blurted out before I could stop myself.

"Guardian of the Underworld," he corrected me, his voice almost reverent. "And my oldest companion."

Orcus chuckled from behind Azrael, his voice oozing with mischief. "Oh, this will be fun. Nothing like meeting a giant death dog to make your day interesting."

I shot him an exasperated glance but couldn't suppress the chill that crawled up my spine. "You could've warned me."

"Where's the fun in that?" Azrael quipped, pushing the door open with a fluid motion that seemed effortless despite the massive size of it.

The room beyond was like something out of a dream—or a nightmare. It stretched out in front of us, cavernous, with a ceiling so high it vanished into shadows. The flickering torchlight cast long, distorted shadows on the stone floor, and the air was thick with something ancient, like time itself was suspended in this space. The coolness of the room pressed in around me, but it wasn't the cold that made my skin prickle—it was the weight of the silence, the way the very air felt charged with something I couldn't name.

Then, I heard it—a low, rumbling growl that vibrated through my chest. It wasn't threatening, not exactly, but it was a sound that made my heart skip a beat. I didn't even have to look up to know it was him.

Cerberus.

I swallowed hard, keeping my gaze fixed on the floor as Azrael led me further into the room, his footsteps echoing against the stone. Cerberus was massive—massive in a way that no words could quite capture. The ground seemed to tremble beneath my feet as a pair of glowing red eyes flashed in the darkness. Then another pair. And another.

I didn't look up until I heard Azrael's soft voice calling out. "Cerberus."

The massive creature moved, his enormous body shifting through the shadows. My heart skipped, and my breath caught in my throat. He was... enormous. Even from where I stood, I could make out the sheer size of him—his dark coat blending seamlessly with the shadows, his three heads turning toward us as if they were synchronized. Each one was adorned with glowing red eyes, their intensity enough to make my stomach churn.

"Holy shit," I whispered under my breath, unable to stop the words from tumbling out.

Azrael didn't seem phased, his voice calm and reassuring. "Cerberus, come."

And come he did.

As we walked deeper into the room, the shadows seemed to stretch longer, pulling at the edges of my nerves. The massive form of Cerberus loomed in the center like a dark omen, and I couldn't shake the unease crawling along my spine. Despite Azrael's reassurances, I still had a hard time trusting the intimidating creature. The air in here felt thicker, charged with an energy I couldn't quite understand.

Azrael's footsteps echoed off the stone floor as he moved confidently toward Cerberus, his back straight and posture relaxed. It was clear he was used to this. Me? I was feeling a bit less confident.

"You're awfully calm about this," I muttered, taking another cautious step forward.

Azrael glanced over at me, his lips curling into a smile that didn't quite reach his eyes. "He's not going to bite you, tiny mouse. Unless, of course, you give him a reason."

I hesitated for a moment longer, but the curiosity gnawing at me finally won out. I took another slow step toward Cerberus, my gaze fixed on the middle head, the one that seemed to be the most engaged with me. The creature's black fur shimmered faintly, its texture seeming to change with every movement of the light, as though it were woven from the night itself. Despite my nervousness, I couldn't help but admire the way it rippled across his massive form. Each of his three heads seemed to hold its own quiet power, their red eyes glowing like embers, but it was his sheer size that truly took my breath away.

He was enormous. Every movement felt like the earth shifted beneath him, the ground trembling slightly with his weight. His three heads were each easily the size of a small horse, their jaws wide enough to swallow me whole if he so pleased. And yet, despite his imposing stature, he moved with a grace that belied his size. It was like watching the shadows themselves stretch and contort in his wake.

Cerberus's middle head leaned in toward me, and I instinctively held my ground. His enormous, wet nose brushed against my shoulder, and I flinched—not because I was afraid, but because I was unprepared for how cold it was. It was an icy, sharp sensation that ran straight through me, a stark contrast to the warmth of my own skin. I sucked in a breath, my body tensing slightly as his nose lingered there, just a few inches from my neck.

But as soon as I expected to feel the bite of teeth, Cerberus shifted, pressing his nose gently against me instead, the coldness somehow less intense now that I had gotten used to it. The touch was curious, almost affectionate, and I relaxed, though my fingers still trembled as I reached out.

"Whoa," I whispered, my hand hovering near his fur. "You're cold." I wasn't sure if I was saying it to him, or to myself.

Azrael's quiet chuckle echoed in the space around us. "He's a creature of the Underworld. Cold is kind of his thing."

I nodded slowly, still trying to process the sensation of this giant creature so close to me. Tentatively, I brushed my fingertips against the soft fur of his head. It was unlike anything I had ever felt before. It was silky—so much softer than I expected for something that looked like it could tear me apart in seconds. There was a strange warmth beneath the fur, like the heat of something burning far down in the depths of the earth, but the texture was velvety, almost like the finest cashmere.

The moment my fingers made contact, Cerberus shifted slightly, his head tilting ever so slightly in response. His eyes glowed brighter, but it wasn't a threatening light. It was almost... affectionate? I wasn't sure, but it didn't feel like danger. His fur was like the night sky, deep and unending, and as I slowly moved my hand along it, I realized that the further I went, the more I could feel the tiny, crackling energy humming beneath the surface, like static electricity. It was warm, but not in the way a living creature's warmth would be. More like the kind of heat you feel from something ancient and powerful—something that has seen centuries, if not millennia, of the world's ebb and flow.

I gave a soft laugh, letting my hand rest on the side of his massive head. "You're not so scary up close," I said, more to myself than anyone else.

Azrael raised an eyebrow, his lips quirking in amusement. "Cerberus is far more than just a dog. But I can't blame you for thinking he's terrifying."

As Cerberus's other two heads leaned in, the air around us seemed to shift. The middle head nuzzled my shoulder again, the coldness of its nose sending another wave of chill through me, but I felt an unexpected twinge of something else—something oddly comforting. His nose was soft, not rough like I expected, and it had a gentle, almost affectionate pressure against me. His fur, as soft as it was, was thick and plush, almost like a blanket, though it didn't hide the raw power that lurked beneath.

I laughed softly, the sound shaky but real. "You're huge," I murmured, stepping back slightly to get a better look at him. "I feel like I'm staring up at a mountain."

His towering height made me feel like a small child standing before something that belonged in a myth. Which didn't make sense because Cerberus is supposed to be a myth. The size difference was so vast that it felt almost comical, like I could have curled up at the base of his paws and disappeared entirely. He wasn't just large; he was overwhelming. His massive paws, each as big as my torso, were silent as they shifted on the stone floor, but I could still feel the vibration of his movements through the ground.

Cerberus' three heads lowered again, and for a brief moment, I was caught in their gaze. There was something ancient in those eyes, something that made me feel like he had lived longer than I could possibly imagine. The sheer power he exuded was undeniable, and yet, there was a strange gentleness in the way he looked at me.

I dared a small smile, my voice barely above a whisper. "Okay, maybe I was wrong. You're kind of... amazing."

"Told you," Azrael said with a hint of pride in his voice. "He's more than just a guardian. He's family. Cerberus has been with me longer than anyone else."

"Except Orcus," I teased, trying to mask my nervousness with sarcasm. But in the pit of my stomach, I felt the weight of Cerberus's presence, the ancient power swirling in the space between us.

One of Cerberus' heads let out a soft rumble, and I could've sworn it was a purr. The noise rumbled deep in my chest, vibrating through the air, and I blinked, startled.

"I think he's a bit of a giant puppy, in his own way," I murmured, eyes widening slightly at the sound.

Azrael gave a small laugh. "If you say so."

I took a deep breath, my fingers brushing one last time against the soft fur of Cerberus's head, feeling the static charge tingle beneath my touch. It was a strange sensation—one that rooted me in place, like I could feel the weight of his entire existence pressing against me. The experience was... surreal, but there was a warmth in it that I wasn't prepared for.

"Well," I said, taking another slow step back, "I think I'm officially convinced you're not here to eat me."

Azrael's smirk grew wider. "Not unless you give him a reason."

"Right," I said with a dry laugh, giving Cerberus one last look. The creature seemed to watch me, his eyes still glowing with that eerie, intelligent light. "See you later, Cerberus," I said softly, offering him a small wave. The creature huffed, and I swore I saw one of his heads roll its eyes in a way that was almost... amused.

As we turned to leave, I felt an odd sense of peace settle over me. Cerberus had been terrifying, but now, in the quiet moments of reflection, I could appreciate the depth of what he truly was—a guardian, a protector, and somehow... a little bit of a soft giant in the end.

Chapter Thirty-Four

Layla

The Edge of Glory - Lady Gaga

The following days have been a blur of sweat, pain, and exhaustion. Training has been so grueling that my bones feel like they've been through a meat grinder. I can't remember the last time I felt this sore—if ever. I'm not going to lie...There were a few days where I just lay in bed, too drained to move. Azrael, ever the perfect gentleman, hovered over me during those moments, bringing me plates of food, massaging my back or feet, and just sitting beside me, cracking sarcastic jokes or offering that maddeningly unreadable smirk.

It was oddly domestic—too domestic. And for a man wielding the power of death itself, Azrael was surprisingly good at fluffing pillows.

Meanwhile, Sadie has practically moved into Ashton's room. She spends so much time with him that the only time I see her is when she's sprinting by to grab a snack or dragging Ashton into some ridiculous game of "how much sugar can you add to your cereal before it becomes dessert?" Their laughter echoes through the halls, reminding me of something I used to feel: normalcy.

I try not to let the isolation get to me. I try not to regress into the old version of myself—the one who was afraid of her own shadow.

Afraid of death.

Afraid of... Azrael.

Afraid of myself.

But some days, the fear creeps back in like an unwelcome guest. Especially when I think about the possibility that I might actually be the first female Grim Reaper. That I migh tbe... death itself.

Spending time with Vassago has been enlightening, though not in the way I expected. He's as cheerful as a thunderstorm—storm clouds and bitter winds with no hint of a rainbow. All doom, no joy. But he doesn't fool me. I see through the cracks in his armor because I'm broken, too. I hear his screams at night, the raw, unfiltered terror that echoes through Ashton's home. We all hear it. But we pretend we don't, because what would we even say?

I see the way he flinches when someone moves too quickly near him or how he gasps when a loud noise startles him. It's heartbreaking, but the worst part is watching Azrael. The helplessness in his eyes. The way his jaw tightens when Vassago startles, like he's blaming himself for not saving his brother from whatever horrors he endured. Azrael wears guilt like a second skin, and the pity in his gaze when he looks at Vassago is enough to shatter anyone.

Then there's Song. She carries her own burdens, though she hides them better than Vassago. She agreed to join the army, but only because she wants to protect Sadie. I catch her watching Sadie sometimes, her lips pressed into a thin line, like she's mentally preparing herself for every possible scenario. For every possible loss.

Even here, in the Underworld, Song and Vassago still have their Angelic duties. That weight never leaves them.

And then there's my mother.

The thought of her lies churns in my stomach, a toxic cocktail of betrayal and confusion. She hired Vassago to protect me, but she hid this entire world from me. The truth of who—or what—I am. The pieces are there, scattered like a broken mirror, but I can't see the full reflection.

No one is telling me everything. I know it. I feel it in my gut. Azrael, Vassago, Ashton—they're all keeping pieces of the puzzle hidden.

But I want the truth. Not fragments. Not half-answers wrapped in cryptic riddles.

I want it all.

I stumble into the hallway, each step a jolt of pain radiating through my body. Training has left me battered, my muscles protesting even the smallest movement. But staying in bed feels worse—alone with my thoughts, the silence pressing down on me like a heavy blanket. I need a distraction.

Wobbling like a newborn deer, I follow the faint sound of voices, hoping to find some semblance of life under this roof. The smell of coffee draws me to the kitchen, where I find them—all the male supernaturals gathered.

Azrael is the first thing I see.

He's in his true form, a sight that still sends a shiver down my spine, though I've learned to suppress it. His hollowed eyes glow faintly, and his skeletal frame seems more imposing in the dim light of the kitchen. The edges of his form blur slightly, like he's not fully tethered to this plane, a reminder of what he truly is.

It took time to adjust to this version of him. But he was patient, using his true form during mundane, positive moments—foot rubs, back massages, quiet evenings spent talking about everything and nothing. I know he did it intentionally, to associate his appearance with comfort rather than fear.

I'm no idiot, though.

I also know why he prefers to touch me in this form. It's his way of hiding what I do to him, of avoiding the awkwardness of... reactions he can't control in his human body, frequent boners and all. It's a strange sort of courtesy, and I haven't decided yet how I feel about it. About him. About us.

The whole "fated mate" thing looms over me like a storm cloud I can't escape. Azrael hasn't pressured me—if anything, he's been careful not to—but his occasional sly comments and knowing smirks still manage to make me blush.

And damn it, he's great. Frustrating, but great.

"She's planning something," Vassago mutters, his voice low but clear.

I freeze in the doorway, the pain in my legs momentarily forgotten.

Ashton leans casually against the counter, his arms crossed and one ankle resting over the other like he hasn't a care in the world. "Well, when she shows up, we'll be ready."

"She wants Layla," Azrael says, his tone sharper, questioning.

Vassago nods, pacing back and forth. His steps echo faintly in the kitchen, a sharp counterpoint to the tense silence. His wings are rested, dragging on the floor as he paces.

"But why?" Azrael asks, his frustration evident in the way his jaw tightens.

Vassago stops mid-stride and turns to face him. "The throne. If Layla dies, you'll need a female—either to rule beside you or to breed an heir to take her place." His words are blunt, cutting through the air like a blade.

My stomach twists, the weight of the truth crashing down on me.

This is it. The whole truth. The thing they won't tell me to my face.

Azrael's hands curl into fists at his sides. "We can hire guards to watch her," he says, his voice tinged with desperation.

Vassago shakes his head. "Guards aren't enough. You know that."

Azrael's shadow seems to lengthen, his frustration radiating like a tangible force. "I won't let anything happen to her!"

His outburst silences the room, the air thick with tension.

He's so desperate to make sure nothing happens to me, he forgets how he is potentially putting everyone at risk.

I'm not worth numerous beings dying over.

"But he thinks so."

I jump at the sound of Exu's voice, spinning around to see him leaning casually in the doorway. He's got that infuriating, all-knowing look on his face—the one that screams he knows too much about everything.

Exu can do everything. Feel emotions, sense the truth, see the ugly parts of people they try to hide. He can even read minds when no one gives him permission to do so.

"I taught you about mental shields," he says, flashing a toothy grin against his caramel complexion. "Not my fault if you're too lazy to make sure they're there."

I glare at him. "I thought we discussed boundaries and rules."

He chuckles, shaking his head. "Sorry, didn't know my name was Azrael. Don't forget to remind Memetim of your boundaries before she tears you apart—mentally, before physically." His grin fades as he glances toward the kitchen, where the faint hum of voices continues. "He loves you, you know. More than you can imagine. He can't fight his instinct to protect and worship you." His gaze softens as he looks back at me.

"I just don't understand why," I whisper, my voice cracking. "I'm so broken. He's getting the worst version of me—damaged, destroyed. I don't even know if I can love anyone ever again."

Exu sighs deeply. "Eh. Have you ever really loved someone?"

I blink, confused. "What do you mean?"

He leans against the wall, crossing his arms. "I'm not talking about fleeting feelings or silly crushes. I mean the kind of love where being away from them physically hurts, like there's an emptiness inside you that nothing else can fill. It's not butterflies or sparks—it's a deep, grounding comfort. When they're in the room, it's like the whole world makes sense."

I swallow hard, my eyes drifting to the kitchen. To Azrael.

Azrael gives me all of that.

From the moment I met him—not the dream version, but the real one—he's made me feel safe, secure. When he leaves to train or stand before the council, I ache until he returns.

"You two weren't supposed to meet for a few more years," Exu says, breaking my reverie. "You can thank Memetim for that."

"What do you mean?"

Exu pushes off the wall and moves to the living room, gesturing for me to follow. I hesitate, then trail after him, my curiosity outweighing my reluctance.

"Hades arranged it all," Exu says as he sinks into the couch. "The marriage, the timeline, everything. He hoped it would keep Azrael distracted—focused on anything but the throne. Hades doesn't like anyone meddling with Fate but himself, and Fate told him one of his sons would come for his throne and kill him."

I sit beside him, staring in disbelief.

"He put Vassago on a pedestal," Exu continues, his tone dark. "Angels are less likely to kill their parents. But Azrael? Hades beat him every chance he got, set him up to fail. Hell, he even designed Orcus to be Azrael's demise. Didn't realize Orcus would grow a personality and turn against him. Funny how that works. You could say Orcus is more like Azrael's guardian angel than his weapon."

I stare at him, trying to process the weight of what he's saying.

"No matter how many times Hades tried to kill Azrael, Fate wouldn't allow it," Exu says, his voice dropping to a near whisper. "Eventually, Hades gave up—kind of. He matched him with Memetim, knowing Azrael would reject her, hoping she'd destroy him out of spite. Fate never told him how it would play out, though, so Hades is stuck in this constant state of anticipation and fear. And let me tell you, watching the so-called 'great ruler' squirm is far more entertaining than anything Memetim could cook up."

I'm speechless. How could a father do such heinous things to his child?

"Because he's a piece of shit. That's why." Exu laughs, the sound rich and deep.

I shake my head. "How do you know all of this?"

Exu leans back, smirking. "Because I helped Azrael's sisters torture Fate until she spilled everything. Hades coerced her into telling Memetim about you. We just left out the details when we told Azrael. He doesn't need that weight on top of everything else."

My mind spins as Exu's words sink in.

"Azrael is stronger than any of us," Exu says, standing up and stretching. "All he'd have to do is raise his pinky, and Hades would be dead. But watching the old bastard squirm is too good to pass up... more entertaining than Memetim sending crows to eaves drop on the boy band in the kitchen."

I start to get up, intent on confronting the group in the kitchen, but Exu grabs my wrist.

"Don't bother. They knows she's there. Everyone except Luca does. I've trained them all since they were toddlers—they're more aware than you think." He lets go, his expression softening. "Azrael will die to keep you safe. That male loves you."

He stretches again, heading toward the door. "Today's lesson? Mental shields. You're terrible at them. Sadie's already outdone you. You're supposed to be our queen. Start acting like it."

"Fuck you," I mutter under my breath as he disappears down the hall.

Chapter Thirty-Five

Azrael

Dodged a Bullet - Greg Laswell

I don't even want to think about "if Layla dies." That's not an option. It's not going to happen.

I glance at Luca, now seated with a plate of food he's been fussing over this entire time. I'm not going to lie—it's been great having him here. It's like having my own personal barista. He's been experimenting with new flavors, and I've been more than happy to play taste tester.

We've been talking about rebuilding the coffee shop once this war is over. Bigger, better, with an improved menu. A dream, sure, but it's a nice one.

"I'm not saying anything will happen to Layla," Vassago says, breaking my thoughts. He sighs, his usual calm cracking under the weight of the conversation. "I'm just saying we need to be prepared for what Memetim is planning."

"So, what's the game plan?" Luca asks, his voice muffled by a mouthful of bagel.

Luca doesn't know about the crows. He wasn't trained for this. He should be with Sadie and Layla, learning how to fight, and how to survive. But, I've kept him here. Maybe because it feels good to have something so normal in the middle of all this chaos because I can't fathom telling him werewolves are useless in the Underworld armies.

But we can't talk openly. Not with the crows listening. We'll have to keep the conversation light, toss in some lies for them to take back to Memetim, and fill Luca in on the truth later.

The room falls into a heavy silence as we all exchange wary glances. Luca, oblivious, just stares back at us, still chewing.

"We are being watched," Orcus hisses, his voice sharp enough to pierce the quiet.

"What do you mean?" Luca's head swivels, scanning the room. "There's no one here."

Vassago stiffens beside me, his gaze darting to the corners of the room like he's expecting something to lunge from the shadows. Ashton leans against the table, casual as ever, but the tension in his jaw betrays him.

I rub a hand over my face, trying to hold on to my patience. "Not someone. Something. Memetim's crows."

Luca blinks, his confusion obvious. "Crows?" he repeats, looking toward the windows. "What, like...birds? I haven't smelled anything."

"They're not ordinary crows," Orcus snaps, his tone dripping disdain. "They're her spies—shadow-bound and silent. They perch where you won't see them, hear everything you say, and carry it back to her."

"I don't see anything," Luca mutters, peering into the haze outside the window. "I would've smelled them."

"You weren't trained to sense them," Vassago says, his voice low, almost apologetic. His eyes never stop scanning the room, lingering on every shadow. "You wouldn't know what to look for."

"I can handle myself," Luca says, his posture stiffening. "I don't need special crow-sensing powers to fight."

"Unless you plan to wrestle them out of the shadows bare-handed, that's not exactly helpful," Ashton quips, his tone dry as sandpaper.

"Enough."

My voice cuts through the room, sharper than I intended, but their bickering isn't helping. My grip on Orcus tightens as I glance between them.

"If Memetim knows we're even considering a plan, she'll strike before we're ready. We need to deal with this. Now."

Ashton nodded, his eyes narrowing. "First, we need to confirm they're here. If Memetim's crows are listening, they won't leave without something useful."

Luca folded his arms, jaw tightening. "And how do we do that exactly? I'm guessing they're not going to just hop out and announce themselves."

"They're already here," Orcus said, his tone low and grim. "They've been listening this entire time."

The room fell into a tense silence. My gaze swept the walls, the ceiling, every corner cloaked in shadow. Orcus' ominous words hung heavy, pressing down like a weight I couldn't shrug off.

"Then we'd better give them something worth hearing," I murmured, my mind already spinning through the possibilities.

Ashton cocked an eyebrow at me, a small smirk tugging at the corner of his mouth. "Oh? Planning to put on a show, Azrael? I didn't realize you'd taken up theatrics." His voice was low, teasing, but there was an edge to it—a readiness.

"Not theatrics," I muttered. "Misdirection."

"Explain," Vassago said, his voice steady but firm, his eyes boring into mine.

I stepped toward the center of the room, letting my eyes fall half-closed as I focused. The shadows seemed to pulse faintly at the edges of my vision, but nothing stood out—not yet. "If the crows are here, they're listening for anything that sounds like a strategy. So we give them something. A decoy."

"A fake plan?" Luca frowned, his skepticism clear. "What happens when she figures out it's bogus?"

"She won't," I said, my tone clipped. "Not until it's too late."

"And if she does?" Ashton asked, his smirk fading into something more serious.

"Then we're no worse off than we are now," I shot back, my gaze darting to Vassago. He gave a small nod of agreement, his expression unreadable but resolute.

"Fine," Luca said, though his arms stayed crossed and his brow furrowed. "But how do we know it's working? How do we know when the crows are gone?"

"You don't," Orcus answered, his voice cold as steel. "Not unless you can sense their absence—and you can't."

"Then what's the point?" Luca asked, frustration creeping into his voice.

"The point," Vassago said evenly, "is that Memetim can't act on bad information. If we control what she hears, we control her next move."

I nodded. "Exactly. We'll make her think she's one step ahead while we set the real plan in motion."

"And what happens to me?" Luca asked, his voice quieter now but no less tense. "Am I just supposed to sit here and play dumb?"

"You're already doing that beautifully," Orcus said dryly, earning a glare from Luca.

"Enough," I snapped, cutting off the brewing argument. "Luca, you're staying here. Out of sight, out of reach. It's safer for everyone that way."

He opened his mouth to argue, but Vassago stepped in. "Azrael's right. If Memetim thinks you're uninvolved, she won't target you. That's the best advantage you can offer right now."

Luca grumbled something under his breath, but he didn't argue further.

"Alright," Ashton said, his voice softer but still sharp. "Let's give them their show. Azrael, lead the way."

I nodded, a plan already forming in my mind. If Memetim wanted to play games, then we'd play. But I wouldn't let her win.

Not this time.

Luca winced, muttering something under his breath that I chose to ignore.

"Ashton," I whispered, turning to him, "You're the best liar here. Can you make it more convincing?"

"Flattered, truly." Ashton drawled, though his smirk returned, "But if we're doing this, I'll need details. Something believable enough to lure Memetim into a trap of her own."

Vassago crossed his arms, his expression was thoughtful. "Make it sound like we're planning an ambush. Something aggressive. She'll want to act preemptively."

I nodded, gesturing for Ashton to proceed. "Spin your story."

Ashton stepped forward, his entire demeanor shifting. The air around him seemed to change as if he'd slipped into another skin entirely. "Listen," he began, his voice steady, commanding. "We strike at dawn. Memetim won't expect us to act so soon. We'll hit her fortress from the eastern ridge, where her defenses are weakest. Azrael and I will lead the charge—Vassago, you'll flank from the south. Luca—"

"Wait, wait," Luca interrupted, holding up a hand, "Why am I in the fake plan? I thought you said I wasn't trained for this?"

"Because it has to sound real," I whispered, my tone sharp. "Memetim knows your strengths—or lack thereof. If we leave you out, it'll sound suspicious."

Luca's jaw tightened, but he didn't argue further.

Ashton resumed without missing a beat, weaving a tale of coordinated strikes and carefully timed maneuvers, his voice steady and unwavering. Even I almost believed it; the picture he painted was so vivid.

"We'll need the element of surprise," Ashton continued, pacing slowly as though deep in thought. "Luca, you'll stay at the ridge with Layla to cut off any reinforcements. Vassago, you'll make the first move to draw her attention. Azrael and I will take the direct approach once the defenses are distracted. By the time Memetim realizes what's happening, it'll be too late."

Luca shifted uncomfortably, his brow furrowed. "This sounds like a real plan, not a fake one. What if—"

"What if nothing," I snapped. "It's not real, Luca. You just have to play along."

"I don't like it," he muttered, his voice barely above a growl.

"No one asked if you liked it," Vassago said flatly.

"Enough," I said, louder this time, silencing the brewing argument. My gaze swept the room. "This isn't about comfort. It's about survival."

The room fell into a tense silence.

"How long do we have to keep this up?" Luca finally asked, his voice low.

"Until they're convinced," I replied.

"And how do we know when that is?"

"You don't," Orcus hissed. "Unless you want me to carve the truth out of the shadows, but something tells me that's not subtle enough for you."

Ashton's smirk returned, though it was less amused this time. "Not subtle, no. But satisfying? Definitely."

"We can't risk it," I said firmly. "The moment we show our hand, Memetim will act. We need to stay ahead of her."

"Which means more talking," Ashton said with a shrug. "I can do that. Shall I recount my many glorious exploits?"

"By all means, embellish," I muttered, rubbing my temples.

Ashton chuckled, launching into an exaggerated tale of one of his supposed adventures. His voice filled the room, laced with humor and charm, masking the tension that lingered beneath the surface.

Luca leaned closer to me, his voice a whisper. "You're sure this is going to work? Don't you think they can hear it's fake?"

I met his gaze, my expression unwavering. "No, it's going to work."

Luca shoots be glare of annoyance.

"Still here," Orcus muttered, his tone dark, the faint hum of his sentience resonating through my grip on the scythe. "They're waiting to hear more."

I let out a low growl, frustration bubbling beneath the surface. Memetim's spies wouldn't be so easy to shake, but we couldn't risk staying exposed much longer. Every second they lingered was another opportunity for them to glean something we couldn't afford to lose.

"Ashton," I said sharply, my voice low but commanding, "Give them an exit point. Make it sound like we'll regroup somewhere isolated after the strike."

"Easy," Ashton replied, his grin sharp and predatory. "But if this works—and that's a big if—we're going to need a real plan. Fast."

"I'm working on it," I muttered, though the truth gnawed at me. My mind was racing, possibilities tumbling over one another like a deck of mismatched cards. We were running out of time, out of options. If Memetim's crows got away with even a shred of truth, we'd be at her mercy.

Ashton shifted his weight, his smirk replaced by a serious expression that didn't suit him. "Fine. Let's play." He leaned forward, his hands resting on the table. "The eastern ridge is a diversion. We'll regroup at the Forgotten Catacombs after the first wave hits. It's remote, and hard to navigate. Perfect for planning the second phase."

"Forgotten Catacombs?" Luca repeated, his confusion evident. "That's...that's real?"

"It's real," I confirmed grimly, my eyes scanning the room for any flicker of shadow out of place. "And abandoned. Which makes it a perfect lie."

Vassago's gaze narrowed, his jaw tight. "We're betting everything on the hope that Memetim falls for this. If she doesn't..."

"She will," Ashton interjected confidently, his voice cutting through the tension like a blade. "She's arrogant, always has been. If she thinks we're scrambling to regroup, she won't hesitate to press her advantage."

"Unless she sets a trap of her own," Vassago countered, his tone heavy with warning.

"Then we'll deal with it," I snapped, my patience wearing thin. "Right now, we have to assume this works. If we second-guess every move, we're already beaten."

Orcus growled softly, his voice curling around my thoughts. "They're lingering. Listening. But they're hesitant. Feed them more."

I exhaled slowly, forcing my mind to focus. "Ashton, embellish. Make it sound desperate. Are treat with a flicker of hope they can't resist exploiting."

Ashton nodded, his grin returning like a mask. "Desperate, I can do." He straightened, his voice rising just enough to sound deliberate. "We'll regroup at the Catacombs. The eastern ridge strike will buy us time to regroup and reinforce. It's our best shot. If we don't make it work, none of us walk away from this."

"Nice touch," Orcus murmured approvingly.

The room fell into a strained silence, each of us acutely aware of the weight pressing down.

"Still here," Orcus finally said, though there was a faint edge of uncertainty to his tone.

Luca glanced at me, his expression tense. "What if they don't leave? What if they're just waiting to confirm more?"

"Then we keep giving them scraps until they choke," I said coldly, my grip tightening on Orcus. "But they won't stick around forever. Memetim will demand answers. If we stay the course, they'll leave soon."

Ashton's gaze flicked toward me, his voice dropping. "And if they don't?"

I met his eyes, my voice low and steady. "Then we cut them down."

Chapter Thirty-Six

Layla

BELLYACHE - BILLIE EILISH

The pages smelled like dust and parchment, a scent that somehow comforted me despite the unease I felt with every word I read. Ashton's library was an endless maze of knowledge, most of it written in languages I didn't understand. But this book—this one, I could manage. It was a history of something called the *Hierarchy of the Underworld*, detailing supernatural politics that made human governments look tame.

I traced a finger down the faded ink, trying to absorb the sprawling complexity of it all. The words swam in front of me, cryptic and tangled, but I was getting better at this—reading between the lines, piecing together the cryptic ways. Still, it wasn't helping much. The weight of it all made my head spin.

The quiet was broken by the soft creak of my door. I didn't flinch this time.

"I was starting to think you'd gotten lost," I said, not looking up from the book.

Azrael chuckled, his voice low and familiar now, like a song I hadn't realized I missed. "I'm not Ashton. I don't wander around like I'm allergic to knocking."

I closed the book, laying it on the bed beside me as I finally met his gaze. He leaned casually against the doorframe, Orcus resting across his back. There was something different about him lately—something less guarded, though he still carried the same weight that seemed inseparable from who he was.

"Let me guess," I said, arching an eyebrow, "You're here to check on me."

His lips quirked into a half-smile, though there was a glimmer of something more serious in his eyes. "That obvious?"

"It's all you seem to do lately." I teased lightly, though I wasn't entirely sure if I minded it.

He pushed off the doorframe and stepped inside, shutting the door behind him. "I can't help it. You're one of the only beings I care about here. Either check on you or hear Ashton complain about the lack of decent wine. It's a tough call."

I laughed softly, shaking my head. "And here I thought the Grim Reaper would have better things to do."

"Not today." He pulled the chair from my desk and turned it backward, sitting with his arms draped over the backrest, looking more casual than I'd ever seen him. "What are you working on?"

I gestured to the book on the bed. "Just trying to make sense of how this world works. Ashton's books are helpful, but they're... intense. I'm barely keeping up."

"That's one way of putting it," he said, glancing at the worn leather cover. "But you don't need to figure everything out in one sitting." His voice softened slightly, almost thoughtful. "There's no rush."

"Maybe not," I admitted, leaning back against the headboard, "But it beats sitting around doing nothing. Besides, I need to be prepared. If Memetim shows up again, I'm not going to just stand there and let her do whatever she wants."

Azrael's expression shifted, something unreadable flickering in his eyes. "You've come a long way already," he said, his voice quieter, almost surprised. "More than anyone could have expected."

"Even you?" I asked, tilting my head slightly, half-teasing, half-curious.

He hesitated, then nodded slowly, as if he wasn't sure whether he should admit it. "Even me."

The honesty in his voice caught me off guard. For all his wit and charm, Azrael didn't often let his guard down. Moments like this felt rare—precious, even.

"Thanks," I said softly, looking down at my hands, the weight of his words sinking in deeper than I expected.

"Don't thank me yet," he said, his voice low and steady. "You're doing great, Layla. But there's more to learn still. And more to face."

"I know," I said, meeting his gaze again, and for the first time in a long while, I felt like I was looking at someone I truly understood. "But I'm not afraid anymore. Not of this place, not of you, not even of Memetim. If she wants a fight, she'll get one."

Azrael smiled, but it didn't quite reach his eyes, the weight of what he knew pressing down on him. "Good. Just don't forget—there's a difference between courage and recklessness."

"I'll keep that in mind," I said, my voice steady, but the reality of his words lingered in my mind, reminding me of how fine that line was. How easy it could be to cross it without even realizing it.

There was a long silence as he studied me, the air thick with something unsaid. I wanted to fill it with words, with something to push past the weight of what we were facing, but for once, I couldn't think of anything to say. So I just nodded.

Azrael let out a breath, his eyes softening just a little. "You're stronger than you think, Layla. Don't doubt that."

I wanted to argue. I wanted to remind him how far I still had to go, how much I was still learning. But his words, simple as they were, made something warm bloom in my chest. Maybe, just maybe, I could do this. Maybe I wasn't as lost as I thought.

"Then let's make sure we're ready," I said quietly, finally letting the silence stretch between us, feeling the calm of his presence settle in the space I hadn't realized was so heavy until now.

Azrael nodded, a flicker of approval in his eyes. He stood, his posture shifting back to the familiar, stoic form that he so easily wore. "I'll be here if you need me."

The Underworld might not feel like home yet, but it doesn't feel like a cage anymore. There's a strange sense of belonging here—something deeper than I've ever experienced. But it's complicated.

He leans in closer, and I can smell him. That lingering aroma of freshly brewed espresso, the worn leather of his jacket. It's human, but also otherworldly, as if he carries the essence of a thousand mornings with him. I wouldn't have thought it to be an intoxicating smell, but damn. The heat swells in me, and I suddenly realize just how close I am to doing something I'll regret.

I could jump him right now and ride out my pleasures until I couldn't feel anything else.

His gaze sharpens, his brow arches as if he can sense it, and I swear he can. "Are you okay, Tiny Mouse?" His voice drips with that sly grin, like he knows exactly what I'm thinking.

That grin. It's maddening. It reassures me that he knows what I want, even if he won't say it. But damn, if I'm not wishing he would.

And what I want to do is kiss him—something I haven't done since he and Ashton kicked Memetim out of my head. I want to taste him again, feel the warmth of him against me. I want to drown in him.

I look up at him through my lashes, biting my lip. I should be studying. I should be training. But all I can think about is what it might feel like to have him inside of me. To have him fill me, make me whole in a way nothing else can.

I shouldn't be thinking about this.

This is so wrong on so many levels.

But I am. I can't help it. And I don't know how to tell him to undress me, to worship my body like he worships the ground I walk on. How do I say it? How do I ask him for something I've never even been able to voice to myself, let alone to him?

Then, just like that, a thought flickers into my mind that completely kills the moment.

He always carries Orcus.

Where would Orcus be while he's... with me? Would Orcus judge me? Watch us?

And just like that, I dry up like a desert, the heat in my chest dissipating. I fall back on the bed, staring at the ceiling as if it might provide some answers.

"What's wrong?" His voice, once teasing, shifts to a worrisome tone. He moves to sit on the edge of the bed, his brow furrowing in concern. "Did I do something wrong again?" He asks, his voice softer than I've ever heard it.

The fear in his eyes hits me harder than I expected. It's not a fear of me, but a fear of pushing me away. Of losing me. I can see it in the tension of his jaw, the way he holds himself a little too rigidly.

This man—this male—is in love with me. Obsessed with me, if I'm being honest, and it's terrifying. I can see it in the way he's willing to risk everything for me. He'd give up the throne of the Underworld if it meant I'd be safe. He'd burn everything to the ground just to see me smile.

He's never judged me. Never once made me feel broken. And I've never once told him how grateful I am for that. How much it means that he's stayed patient with me, letting me heal at my own pace. He's never pushed me to be "normal"—to be anything other than who I am.

I think I'm falling in love with Azrael.

I'm fucking falling in love with the goddamn Grim Reaper, and that scares me more than anything else I've ever experienced. More than Memetim. More than the uncertainty of our futures. More than anything I've ever faced in my life.

319

I sit up, pressing my palms into the mattress. "It's nothing," I say, though the lie sticks in my throat.

Azrael watches me with those dark, fathomless eyes of his. I can feel him weighing every word, every breath. "You sure?" His voice is almost a whisper, but it carries more weight than any command I've ever heard.

I nod, though I know I'm not fooling him. But it's too much, too overwhelming, and I don't know how to say it. Not like this.

He leans closer again, and my heart stutters in my chest. There's a softness in his gaze that disarms me—something that makes me feel like I'm the only person in the world. And for a moment, I forget about everything. The world outside. The looming threat of Memetim. The impossible odds that are stacked against us.

For a moment, it's just me and him.

And I want nothing more than for this moment to last forever.

But it can't.

Not when I'm this broken. Not when I'm still so scared of what it means to love him.

"Just—be patient with me," I whisper, and I'm not sure who I'm saying it for anymore. For me, for him, for both of us.

Azrael's gaze softens, and I see the understanding there. The patience that has carried us both through this strange, confusing journey.

"I will," he promises, and in that moment, I believe him.

"Azrael," I mutter, closing my eyes because that will make it easier to speak, and less embarrassing. If I close my eyes, I can pretend I'm talking to the walls. Like no one is here and no one is listening. I can act like I'm alone.

"Yes?" His voice is soft, almost a whisper, and it's so fucking intoxicating. My heart skips at the sound, but I push through it, trying to focus.

"If we…" I trail off, struggling to find the courage. My pulse is thumping in my ears. "Do the deed… what does Orcus do? Like…" I take a shaky breath, "Does he watch?"

The words are out before I can stop them, and I instantly regret asking. Azrael's stillness is deafening, and I feel like the entire room is closing in on me. Did I go too far? Did I fuck this up?

Azrael stiffens, his expression caught somewhere between shock and disbelief. "Does he watch?" He repeats slowly, as if testing the absurdity of the words.

"Well, yeah," I say, my voice awkward, squirming under his gaze. It's hard enough to talk about this without adding the weight of his stare. I'm not sure what I expected—maybe reassurance? But it's not coming. At least not from him.

Before Azrael can respond, Orcus bursts out in laughter, his tone exasperated but oddly warm. "Layla, do you think so little of me that you feel I would intrude on such an intimate moment without an invitation?"

I blink, caught completely off guard by his question. What the hell?

Azrael drags a hand down his face, muttering something unintelligible. But Orcus, as usual, doesn't seem to care about the discomfort radiating off of Azrael. He's completely undeterred.

"Let me put your mind at ease," Orcus continues, his voice surprisingly gentle despite the amusement lacing his words, "I am always aware, but I do not pry into matters that are of no concern to me. When it comes to matters of intimacy, where I am not *invited*, I recede." His tone shifts, almost comforting, as if this is a conversation he's had before. "I assure you, Layla, I have no desire to linger in unwelcoming situations."

"You can recede?" I ask, narrowing my eyes in disbelief. "You mean, you can just... not exist for a while?"

"Not quite," Orcus replies, the smoothness in his voice never faltering. "But I can become, for lack of better terms, 'dormant.' I've had years to master the art of 'selective ignorance.'"

I glance at Azrael, who looks like he's about to crawl into the nearest hole and die. "And you couldn't have told me this before?" I ask, my voice laced with frustration. "This would have been useful information to have."

Azrael mutters, "I didn't think we'd be having this conversation." His ears are tinged a deep red, and his embarrassment is palpable. He looks like he wants to bury himself in the floorboards and never come out.

But there's something in his expression—something vulnerable—that makes my heart ache. It's like the walls he's built are cracking, and I don't know what to do with the knowledge that I'm the reason for it.

With a hint of amusement, Orcus adds, "For the record, I find this conversation far more embarrassing for Azrael than for myself. His expression is priceless."

Azrael groans, covering his face with his hands. "Why do you *talk* so much?"

Orcus, unphased, responds smoothly, "To torment you a little, perhaps."

Despite myself, I laugh—a short, startled laugh that bubbles up unexpectedly. It feels good like the tension is melting away. The air in the room feels lighter, the pressure easing and I'm almost grateful for Orcus' odd, relentless presence.

Azrael glances at me, still slightly red but with a faint, crooked smile on his lips. I can see the relief there, too—like this awkward conversation has lifted a weight from his shoulders. He's not quite so tense anymore.

Orcus, sensing the shift, offers something more sincere. "I have seen Azrael endure centuries of loneliness and pain. If you are his solace, his anchor, then I am honored to step aside for the sake of his happiness—and yours."

His words hang in the air, full of an unexpected depth. I blink, realizing that this... weird trio we've become is something far more intricate than I'd ever understood. Azrael and Orcus have shared more than just centuries of torment—they've shared this bond, this unspoken understanding that's hard to wrap my mind around.

I'm not sure what this all means. I'm not sure where I fit into it yet. But in this moment, it feels like the world is just a little bit less complicated than it was before.

And maybe, just maybe, I'm starting to believe that I could find a place in it. A real place. A home.

I look at Azrael. He's not going to make the first move. He's been clear about that—he wants everything to be my choice, my decision. And right now, that's what scares me. The weight of it, the responsibility of deciding something this big. Something that could change everything between us.

I drag my gaze over his body, feeling the heat creep through my skin as I gather what little courage I have left. I can't help but notice the way he moves, the strength in his frame, the way his muscles shift beneath the dark fabric of his clothes. My heart beats faster, a rhythmic thud that echoes in my chest. I just want to know what it feels like to have his body on top of mine, how it would feel to have him inside of me. The thought makes my breath catch, and an ache starts deep within me, one that I can't ignore.

The thought of how experienced he must be stirs something inside me—how he could teach me things I've never known before, how he could take care of my body like no one has, like I've always needed but never realized. I want to surrender to him, to lose myself in the intimacy of it all.

But the fear, the hesitation, still holds me back. I want it, but I don't know if I'm ready. And the last thing I want is to feel overwhelmed.

"Can we make a word up that hints for you to go away?" I ask, my voice barely above a whisper as Azrael and I lock eyes.

Azrael doesn't move, his gaze steady, watching me with an intensity that's almost suffocating.

"Sure," Orcus chimes in, as if this is a normal request. "If that's what makes you more comfortable."

"Pineapple," I say, my voice steady. There's no smile on my lips, no playful glint in my eyes. Myexpression is a mask, hiding the wild thoughts racing through my mind. The need for Azrael is growing stronger, a hunger building within me that I don't know how to quell.

"So, pineapple, Orcus," I repeat, my voice firm now.

Without a word, Azrael shifts Orcus into his ring form, the scythe's presence retreating into something smaller, quieter. And then, in the same fluid motion,

Azrael leans in. His body is so close to mine now that I can feel the heat radiating from him, the raw desire rolling off him in waves. We're nose to nose, and I can feel the hunger in his eyes, the way his lips barely part in a silent invitation.

His breath brushes against my skin, and I tremble, unable to hide the effect he has on me. His gaze doesn't break from mine, as if he's waiting for me to decide, to take the next step.

The tension between us is thick, a tangible thing that wraps around my chest and squeezes. It's all I can focus on. The only thing I can think about is him.

His hands are still at his sides, his body tense with restraint. He's waiting for me. I can feel the weight of it—the pressure to move, to decide, to finally give in.

"I want you," I breathe, the words slipping from my lips before I can stop them.

Azrael's gaze darkens, his breath catching at my admission. For a moment, I think he might pull back, might wait for me to change my mind, but then he closes the distance between us, his lips capturing mine in a kiss that's everything I've been craving, everything I've been too afraid to ask for.

It's slow at first, tentative as if we're both testing the waters. But then the hunger takes over, and all I can feel is him. His warmth, his strength, the way he presses me into the bed with a gentleness that belies the intensity of his desire.

I can't think anymore. I don't want to. All that matters is him and the way he makes me feel, the way he touches me, the way he seems to understand exactly what I need, even before I do.

And for the first time, I let myself sink into it.

I embrace his face, pulling him close as I kiss him passionately, my tongue dancing against his in perfect rhythm. Azrael stands, shifting just enough to move the chair from beneath him. His hands grab my waist, urging me to feel the length of him, my fingers tugging at his jeans and boxers, desperate to have him exposed. I can feel his pulse racing under my touch, a quiet moan escaping his lips, and it sends me into a feral state. My body screams "yes" while my mind whispers "not yet," but the need surges through me, overwhelming all reason. I can't stop now.

His hands explore my body, pulling me closer as he slides his jeans and boxers down, freeing himself. I break the kiss, trailing my lips down his neck, his chest, until I'm lowering to my knees. I reach for him, taking him in my mouth, every inch of him, savoring the taste of him, feeling the heat of him against my tongue. Azrael's head falls back, a low growl escaping from deep within him. "Tiny Mouse," he rasps, "I've been waiting for this moment."

He pulls me away, licking the remnants of him from my lips before lifting me onto the bed. My sweatpants are yanked off with a swift motion, and his fingers find the waistband of my panties, teasing me with the slow pull as if he's savoring the moment. The tension builds between us, and I feel my heart race, my anticipation rising with every inch he draws them down. Our eyes lock, and his intense gaze makes my stomach flutter, sending a surge of heat straight to my core.

I'm on the edge, ready to explode, aching for him to take me, for him to fill me completely. He kisses me once more, and I can feel the heat of his body pressing against mine, his length brushing against my stomach, guiding me toward the promise of more. My breath catches in my throat as he rubs his hardness against my thighs, teasing, pushing me further into the desperate edge of hunger I can no longer control.

He moves lower, his lips brushing against my skin, his tongue teasing its way down to the sensitive folds of my body. One leg is thrown over his shoulder, and he spreads me open with one swift motion, locking eyes with me as he spits, rubbing the moisture into my clit. "You're so wet, Baby girl," he murmurs, and the sound of his voice sends a shiver of need coursing through me.

He lowers his mouth to me, and his tongue begins its work, sweeping across my skin, licking, sucking, exploring every inch of me. I clutch the sheets beneath me, my body writhing in pleasure, unable to hold back. He doesn't stop; he's relentless, his fingers joining his mouth as he thrusts deep into me, curling them, hitting every sensitive spot within. My breath hitches as I feel the pressure building, my body bucking instinctively against him.

"Please, don't stop," I beg, my voice a mix of need and desperation.

He pulls back, his eyes burning with dark intent. "Beg me again, Tiny Mouse. Like your life depends on it."

"Azrael," I moan, barely able to breathe as I watch him, my body trembling under his control." Please, don't stop. It feels so fucking good…"

And then here turns, devouring me with his mouth again, pushing me to the edge, until the fire inside of me bursts. A scream threatens to tear from my throat, but I'm lost in the sensation, gasping for air as I ride the wave of pleasure.

But he doesn't give me a moment to catch my breath. Before I can fully process what's happening, I feel him at my entrance, the tip of his cock teasing me, driving me wild." Azrael," I moan, feeling the tension in my body break, a mixture of pain and pleasure as he eases himself inside. "You're so big…"

He groans in response, and I feel him, deep inside of me, stretching me, filling me completely. His head falls to my shoulder, his breath hot against my skin as he starts a slow rhythm, pushing in and out. Every thrust is deliberate, each one more intense than the last. I can feel the tension building again, the pressure rising within me, and I lock my legs around his waist, pulling him deeper.

But then, just as I think I can't take anymore, he pulls back, his fingers moving between us to taste us both, before returning to me with a forceful thrust. His hand covers my mouth, his eyes dark with desire as he murmurs, "If you scream again, Tiny Mouse, I'll stop. Do you want me to stop?"

I shake my head desperately, the need coursing through me, the fire in my core threatening to consume me whole. "No," I whisper. "Don't stop."

The pace quickens, and I feel him swelling inside me, his cock filling me even more, and I know he's close, I can feel it, that hot rush about to break through us. My body clenches around him, my orgasm building as his thrusts become more powerful, each one sending a shockwave of pleasure through my body. And then, with a final, earth-shattering thrust, I feel him release, his warmth flooding inside me, and I can't help but tremble, feeling the aftershocks of both of our climaxes surge through my body.

He collapses beside me, his chest rising and falling with his heavy breath, his body pressing into mine, holding me close as the room falls into a quiet, post-orgasmic haze. The world outside may still be waiting, but for now, I'm lost in the quiet of the moment, the warmth of his skin against mine.

Azrael pulls away after a while, moving to the bathroom, and when he returns with a warm, wet wash cloth, he gently cleans me, the tenderness in his touch completely contrasting the intensity of what just transpired. This is what the romance novels don't talk about enough: the aftercare, the moments when he's not just using me, but caring for me, showing me that I belong to him—not in a degrading way, but as a lover who cherishes me.

He didn't treat me like a conquest. He didn't make me feel like a "personal slut," as some would say. No, Azrael made love to me. He didn't just fuck me—he took his time, he savored every inch of me, and in return, I gave him every part of myself. He owned me in the way that only a male who truly cares for his partner can.

As he pulls away, I feel a sudden coldness, a void where his warmth had been just moments ago. My mind swirls with thoughts, not doubts, but questions—questions I don't know how to answer. What does this mean for us? What happens next? The war is still out there, the threat of Memetim's forces still looming. How long can this fragile peace last?

I draw the blanket up to my chest, my voice soft as I finally ask, "Azrael?"

He turns to face me, his eyes searching mine, as if he can sense the uncertainty swirling inside me. "Yea?" he says, his voice low, almost hesitant.

"What happens now?" I ask, my tone fragile, but I need to know. Not just about us, but about everything. The war. The crows. Memetim. This moment—how long can it last?

He crosses the room and sits at the edge of the bed, brushing his hand against mine in a gesture so simple, yet so comforting. "Now?" he says, his voice warm, steady. "Now, we take this one step at a time. Together."

I want to believe him. I want to trust that this can work, that we can face whatever comes next, but deep down, a small part of me still whispers that I don't belong here—that I am just a human, a mortal, trying to survive in a world of gods, monsters, and wars that I barely understand.

Before I can spiral further, Orcus' voice cuts through the silence, a deep rumbling sigh that seems to echo in the room. "If I may interrupt," he begins, his tone far too calm for the moment, "I'd like to point out that whatever steps you take, they should involve less lying in bed and more preparing for battle."

I blink, startled by the intrusion, my fragile bubble of peace bursting in an instant. "Orcus, seriously?" I ask, half-annoyed, half-amused.

"Seriously," he replies, his voice unwavering. "You may think the world has paused for this little... bonding moment, but I assure you, Memetim's forces have not. They're moving. Planning. And so should we."

Azrael groans, rubbing a hand over his face, clearly frustrated. "You couldn't give us a moment?"

"I gave you several." Orcus retorts with a knowing smirk. "And I only intervened because someone has to remind you both that the stakes are a bit higher than pillow talk."

Despite myself, I can't help but let out a small laugh. The absurdity of the situation makes the tension in my chest ease, if only for a moment. Azrael shakes his head, the irritation on his face flickering for just a second before he softens, torn between exasperation and amusement. "He's not wrong," Azrael admits, his tone reluctant but genuine.

I let out a sigh, the weight of everything crashing down on me again. I push myself up, wrapping the blanket around me like armor, as if it could protect me from everything I don't understand. I glance at Azrael, the raw vulnerability in his gaze, and I know he feels it too—the overwhelming burden of what's coming, the uncertainty of how we'll handle it all.

"We'll deal with it," I say softly, more to myself than to him, trying to convince myself that this, whatever this is, can still work.

Azrael reaches out, his hand brushing mine. "We will," he agrees, his voice low and steady. But the doubt lingers, even in his words.

Chapter Thirty-Seven

Layla

In the Night - The Weeknd

I barely had time to process what had happened between Azrael and me when the door to my room slammed open.

Ashton stormed in, his usually composed demeanor nowhere to be found. His face was pale, his movements rapid as his coat billowed behind him like a storm cloud. "We have a problem," he barked, his voice thick with urgency.

"Ashton?" I sat up quickly, clutching the blanket around me, still reeling from the intensity of the moment. Azrael, already alert, was on his feet in an instant, his expression sharpening into one of steely focus.

"What happened?" Azrael's voice was calm, but I could see the tension in his shoulders, the way his body stiffened in response to the gravity of the situation.

"The crows," Ashton said, his voice low and serious. "They've taken Luca."

"What?" I blurted out, my heart dropping into my stomach. "How? Why?"

Ashton met my gaze briefly, his expression grim. "Memetim's crows aren't just spies. They manipulate shadows, open portals... take beings. They've been watching Luca, waiting for the right moment. And they didn't wait to hear a damn battle plan."

Azrael's jaw tightened as he moved, already gathering his clothes, and getting dressed with quick, efficient movements. "Where did they take him?"

"That's the problem," Ashton said, pacing the room, his hands running through his hair in frustration. "They didn't leave a trace. With the Underworld being so vast, and the crows' ability to slip between shadows and beings, they're nearly impossible to track. She must have a plan—using Luca as leverage or bait."

I stared at him, my stomach twisting into knots. Luca, the guy who cared more about perfecting his coffee art, was now in the hands of Memetim's forces. The thought made my skin crawl, the horror of it sinking in deeper with each passing second.

"Why Luca?" I asked, trying to keep my voice steady, though it wavered at the edges. "He's not... he's not even involved in all of this. He's just..."

"A werewolf?" Ashton interrupted sharply, his tone much harsher than I expected. "Memetim doesn't care about that. She cares about hurting us, hurting Azrael. Luca's important to him, and that makes him a target."

Azrael's eyes darkened as he looked away, his hands clenching into fists at his sides.

The silence that followed felt heavy, suffocating, until Orcus' voice broke through the tension. "This is no coincidence," he said, his voice cutting through the room with precision. "Memetim knows exactly when to strike and who to take. She's playing a game, and we're the pieces."

I felt a chill at his words. The realization that we were caught in the crosshairs of someone who could manipulate so much—someone so calculating—sent a wave of dread through me. The stakes were rising, higher and higher with every passing moment, and the world I'd stepped into was more dangerous than I could've ever imagined.

Azrael's face hardened, but his gaze remained unwavering. "We don't let her control the game," he said, the authority in his voice clear. "We take the fight to her."

Ashton nodded, a flicker of determination crossing his features. "Right. First, we need to figure out how to track Luca. And then... we end this, once and for all."

But even as he spoke, I could feel the weight of the unknown bearing down on us. This wasn't just about rescuing Luca anymore. This was about taking a stand. Against Memetim. Against everything she represented. And against the terrifying unknowns that lay ahead.

"Then we find her." Azrael's voice was like steel, unwavering in its resolve. "We find Luca, and we stop her."

"Easier said than done," Ashton replied, his tone darkening. "The crows are already gone. But I might have an idea—a risky one."

Azrael narrowed his eyes, his expression turning calculating. "How risky?"

Ashton stopped pacing, meeting Azrael's gaze head-on. "Risky enough that if it doesn't work, we might lose more than Luca."

A silence hung in the air as Azrael processed the words, his face growing colder with the weight of the situation. Before he could respond, a knock at the doorframe drew our attention, breaking the tension.

Vassago leaned casually against the wall, his golden hair slightly disheveled, his wings tucked tightly against his back. Behind him, Song stood like a shadow, her quiet intensity radiating from her. Her expression remained unreadable, but her presence was impossible to ignore. Not far behind her, Sadie followed, her usual bubbly demeanor tempered by the weight of the moment. She had been training with Song lately, learning whatever she could about the Underworld, and though her confidence still shone through, there was an underlying seriousness in her every step.

"You needed me?" Vassago's voice was tinged with weariness, as though he'd been roused from sleep. "The crows have Luca?"

Ashton nodded curtly. "They've taken him. Likely to one of Memetim's shadow lairs, but pinpointing where is the issue. The Underworld is too vast to search blindly."

"And you expect us to solve that?" Song asked, stepping forward, her voice calm but laced with the same steel that had marked her every move since her arrival. "Do you think angels are designed to sniff out shadows like hounds?"

"No," Azrael interjected before Ashton could respond, his voice firm but measured. "But I trust you two to handle this better than anyone else."

Vassago raised an eyebrow, crossing his arms over his chest. "That's quite the compliment, brother. I assume you mean us to track the crows' trails?"

"Yes," Azrael replied, his gaze steady and unwavering. "You're the fastest among us, and Song has the precision we need. Together, you might be able to follow their path through the shadows. If you find Luca, don't engage unless absolutely necessary. Just get his location and return here."

Song glanced at Vassago, her wings rustling slightly with the movement. After a long moment, she spoke. "Fine." Her voice was resolute. "But I expect a proper strategy once we return. No more rushing in blind."

Vassago smirked, his usual cocky charm coming through. "Don't worry, Songbird. I'll keep him inline."

Song shot him a glare at the nickname but didn't respond, instead focusing on the task at hand.

Vassago paused, his gaze shifting to me. There was a softness in his eyes, a fleeting vulnerability that caught me off guard. "Layla," he said, his voice gentle. "You'll be okay?"

I blinked, startled by the question. In all the chaos, I hadn't thought to consider how I was feeling. The weight of everything that had happened pressed down on me—Luca gone, Memetim's ever-growing influence, the war that loomed just beyond the horizon. "Me?" I echoed, unsure of how to answer. I tried to offer him are assuring smile, though it felt hollow. "Yeah, I'll be fine. Just... find Luca."

Vassago nodded, his expression hardening once more. "We'll be back soon."

Before Song could step through the door, Sadie blocked her path, her wild black curls more disheveled than usual, her eyes glistening with unshed tears.

"Don't," Sadie's voice cracked, her raw emotion spilling out. "Don't leave me."

Song hesitated, her fists clenching at her sides. "Sadie, this isn't about leaving you. This is about doing what's necessary."

"I don't care!" Sadie snapped, stepping forward, her desperation palpable. "You're my Guardian Angel. You're supposed to stay with me, to protect me. Not go running off into danger!"

Song's expression softened, a flicker of something unspoken in her eyes, but her voice remained steady, unwavering. "I am protecting you, Sadie. If we don't find Luca, Memetim gains the upper hand. You think I want to leave you? You think this doesn't tear me apart?"

Sadie's lip quivered, but her anger seemed to burn brighter than the pain. "Then stay. Let someone else go. Vassago's fast enough on his own. You don't have to go with him."

"You know that's not how this works," Song said gently, her tone firm despite the softness in her eyes. "Vassago needs me. He might be fast, but speed isn't enough to track shadows this deep. I have to go."

Sadie shook her head, her hands clenching into fists as if willing her emotions to calm. "I've already lost too much. My family. My friends. My life. If something happens to you—" Her voice cracked, and tears spilled over, her composure finally giving way.

Song reached out, cupping Sadie's face with both hands, her touch tender but insistent. "Nothing's going to happen to me." She spoke with a quiet resolve. "I promise, I'll come back. But I have to do this."

Sadie's sob turned into a bitter laugh, a mixture of disbelief and sorrow. "Don't make promises you can't keep."

Song didn't respond immediately. Instead, she leaned forward, pressing her forehead against Sadie's. Her voice was barely a whisper, but there was a deep sincerity in it. "I'll keep this one," she whispered, her words laced with a quiet strength.

For a moment, the room was still, the only sound being Sadie's quiet sniffling, the weight of the situation hanging heavy between them. Slowly, reluctantly, Sadie stepped back, her hands falling to her sides, the fight draining out of her.

"Be careful," Sadie's voice was barely audible, but the fear and love in it were unmistakable.

"I will." Song's response was steady, her gaze hardening as she turned to Vassago. "Let's go."

With a final glance at Sadie, Song and Vassago disappeared in a burst of light, their forms swallowed by the shadows as they left us behind in the stillness of the room.

Azrael's voice broke the silence that followed, his tone a soft reassurance. "She'll be back, Sadie."

Sadie didn't answer, though. She just stood there, staring at the empty space where Song had been, her gaze fixed as if willing her to reappear as if refusing to let go of the fragile hope that Song would return.

I walked over, still wrapped in my blanket, and placed a hand gently on Sadie's shoulder. "She's strong," I said softly, offering what comfort I could. "And she's not alone."

Sadie's fiery gaze snapped to Ashton, her eyes burning with a mixture of grief and fury.

"This is your *fault*!" She spat, her voice trembling with raw anger. "You didn't have to send her! You could've sent someone else, but no—you just had to drag her into this."

Ashton, who had been leaning casually against the doorframe moments ago, straightened, his usual calm demeanor cracking for the first time. "Sadie, this isn't about—"

"Don't you *dare*!" She cut him off, stepping closer, her voice rising with fury. "Don't you dare tell me this isn't about her! You don't get to act like her life is just another pawn in your stupid fucking chess game."

"She's not a pawn," Ashton replied sharply, his usual smooth tone gone. "She's a *warrior*, and she *chose* to go."

Sadie's bitter laugh echoed in the room, her hands trembling at her sides as if the weight of the situation was too much to bear. "*Choose*? You mean you gave her no choice! You sent her because you *knew* she'd do it without question. Because that's what angels do. Right? *Obey* orders and damn the consequences."

"Sadie—" Azrael started, but Sadie didn't listen, her focus now entirely on Ashton.

"You don't even care, *do you*?" She accused, her voice cracking as the anger mixed with sorrow. "You sit here, playing puppet master, while the rest of us lose *everything*." Her voice broke, but she pressed on, the pain of loss consuming her. "Do you know what it's like to lose someone who's supposed to protect you? To be left behind over and over?"

Ashton's eyes narrowed, and for the first time, his usually collected voice dropped, filled with an edge that spoke to the weight of his own burdens. "Do you think I don't understand loss, Sadie? Do you think I don't feel the weight of *every* decision I make?"

Sadie's tears streamed down her face, her voice shaking as she demanded, "Then why her? Why not someone else?"

"Because she's the best chance we have of finding Luca!" Ashton's voice rose, the frustration seeping through his calm exterior. "Do you think I wanted to send her? That I wanted to risk her life? If there was another way, I would have taken it. But there isn't."

The room fell into a heavy silence, the tension thick. Sadie's breathing was the only sound, her tears now silent as she absorbed the raw truth of what had just been said.

"Sadie," Ashton said after a moment, his voice softer now, "I know what she means to you. I know you're scared. But Song is strong. She's capable, and she will come back."

Sadie shook her head, her voice breaking as she whispered, "You don't know that."

"I do," Ashton insisted, stepping closer. "Because she loves you, and beings like Song? They don't leave the ones they love behind."

Sadie stared at him, her lip trembling. Then, without a word, she turned and stormed out of the room, slamming the door behind her.

Azrael let out a heavy sigh, pinching the bridge of his nose. "You handled that well," he muttered under his breath.

Ashton shot him a glare, his usual calm cracking for a moment. "If you've got a better way to reassure a mortal terrified for her Guardian Angel, I'm all ears."

I stayed quiet, my thoughts a storm in my head as I watched the door Sadie had disappeared through. Her anger was justified, but Ashton wasn't entirely wrong either. He spoke the truth; Song was strong, but even angels had their limits.

Still, I couldn't shake the gnawing feeling that we were losing too much already.

"We've bought ourselves a little time," Ashton said, running a hand through his hair as he exhaled sharply. "But if they don't come back with something useful, we'll have to consider more... drastic options."

Azrael's jaw tightened at the mention of drastic measures. "They'll find him."

I wanted to believe him. I wanted to believe that, despite all the darkness around us, Vassago and Song would find Luca, and bring him back safely, and that all of this would be a distant nightmare in the end. But there was something in Azrael's gaze—flickers of doubt—that made me wonder if even he believed the certainty in his own words.

I looked down at the ring on Azrael's finger, a strange sense of clarity washing over me. "Orcus," I said, breaking the silence. "Do you think they'll find him?"

The weapon's voice, usually so sarcastic and biting, was unusually calm. "If anyone can, it's those two. But Memetim's crows aren't just creatures of shadow—they're intelligent. If they've hidden Luca somewhere even I can't sense, it'll be because they planned for this."

I swallowed, the weight of Orcus' words sinking in. If the crows were one step ahead of us, we could be in more trouble than we thought.

Azrael's expression darkened, his eyes locking with mine, the gravity of the situation settling between us. "Then we'd better plan for what happens next," he said grimly." Because no matter where Luca is, Memetim's not going to stop there."

I nodded, understanding the truth of his words. Memetim wasn't one to back down. This was only the beginning.

Chapter Thirty-Eight

Azrael

Elastic Heart - Sia

I watched Layla closely, the tension in the atmosphere palpable as she glared at Orcus, her arms crossed tightly across her chest. She was stubborn, determined, but the frustration in her eyes spoke volumes. The pressure was starting to get to her, and I couldn't blame her. The weight of Drepane's legacy, the sentient sickle that would either make her stronger or break her, was a lot to bear.

"Let me get this straight," she said, voice sharp, her eyes narrowed. "I have to turn into ... *that*"—she waved vaguely in my direction, her hand sweeping over my true form—"because some old talking blade needs to approve of me? Are you serious?"

I couldn't help but let a small smile curl at the corner of my mouth. Her defiance was part of what made her... her. But this wasn't some trivial task, and she was starting to grasp the weight of it.

"Not just 'some old, talking blade,'" Orcus replied, his usual cocky tone absent for once, replaced by something closer to respect. "Drepane is ancient—older than me, older than Azrael. He was wielded by gods before the Underworld even had rules. If you want his help, you'll need to prove you're worthy of it."

Layla huffed, her breath sharp with frustration. "Why does it even matter? Can't we just... ask nicely?"

Orcus laughed, and the sound was cold, like metal scraping across stone. "Ask nicely? That's rich. Drepane doesn't do *nice*. He does *worthy*. And, right now, you're about as worthy as a damp towel."

Her face flushed at the jab, her frustration rising in tandem with her irritation. "Gee, thanks for the pep talk," she muttered under her breath, clearly not appreciative of Orcus' bluntness.

Sadie, who had been lounging at the picnic table, snorted, her voice carrying a touch of sarcasm. "He's not wrong, though. You do kind of flinch at anything spooky. Might want to work on that if you're trying to be Grim Reaper 2.0 over there."

I shot her a warning look, though it didn't have much effect. Sadie just grinned, clearly entertained by the situation.

"Sadie," I said, my voice low and a touch more dangerous than I intended. "Enough."

She just shrugged, unfazed by my warning. "What? I'm just saying what everyone's thinking."

I turned back to Layla, my expression softening, though the situation remained as dire as ever. Orcus had a point, even if his delivery was... less than gentle. Layla was being tested, and this wasn't going to be an easy journey for her.

Orcus ignored the interruption and continued, his tone now more serious. "Layla, you're not just here to impress Drepane. He's more than a weapon—he's a force. If you wield him, you're not just borrowing his power—you're binding yourself to his purpose. And trust me, he doesn't take that lightly. He'll want to see what you're made of—literally."

Layla flinched at the implication, her eyes dropping to her feet as she shifted uncomfortably under the weight of Orcus' words. She wasn't afraid to face challenges, but this was different. Drepane wasn't just some tool. He was a living force, and to wield him would mean changing the course of her fate, whether she was ready or not.

"But why me?" she asked softly, her voice barely above a whisper, her gaze still fixed on the ground. "Why does it have to be me?"

I felt a pain in my chest, knowing exactly what she meant. It was the same question I'd asked myself when my fate had been thrust upon me. The weight of responsibility, the terror of what lay ahead—it was too much for anyone to carry alone. But the answer, as much as I hated it, was clear.

"Because you're the one who can handle it," I said, my voice firm but gentle. "You've already proven that, Layla. Drepane isn't just choosing you because you're strong enough—he's choosing you because you're willing to fight for what matters. And if you can't see that yet, you will soon enough."

She didn't look up at me, but I saw the subtle shift in her posture. The frustration was still there, but there was a flicker of something else, something deeper. Maybe she wasn't sure of herself yet, but I knew her better than she gave me credit for. Layla had more strength in her than she realized.

Orcus' voice broke the silence again, softer now. "It's not just about strength, either. It's about heart. And if you want to stand beside us—if you want to be more than just a scared mortal—you need to find that heart, Layla. Drepane won't settle for less."

She finally looked up, her eyes locking with Orcus' surface, and for the first time, I saw something shift in her. The doubt wasn't gone, but it had been replaced with a quiet determination. She wasn't backing down.

"I'll do it," she said, her voice steady. "I'll prove I'm worthy."

I nodded, the tension in the room easing slightly. Orcus let out a low chuckle, a slight edge of approval in his tone. "Good. That's the first step."

As I watched Layla, I felt the weight of the situation shift slightly. There was still so much to do, so many obstacles in our path, but for the first time in a while, I allowed myself to believe that maybe, just maybe, we could pull this off.

"Without Drepane, you're screwed," Orcus said bluntly, cutting through the tension in the room like a blade.

"Always the charmer," Sadie muttered under her breath, not bothering to hide the sarcasm in her voice.

Layla sighed, her fingers pinching the bridge of her nose in frustration. "So, let me get this straight. I have to turn into my 'true form', and convince this... ancient sickle that I'm badass enough to wield him? And if I don't, we're all doomed?"

"Pretty much," Orcus said, his voice cheerfully unbothered.

"Great. No pressure or anything," Layla grumbled, her eyes rolling as she paced in small circles.

I couldn't blame her. This was a heavy burden to place on her shoulders, but I knew she had it in her. She just didn't see it yet.

"Hey," Orcus said, his tone shifting, more encouraging now. "You've got this. You're already stronger than you think, and I'll be here to guide you through it. It's not about being perfect—it's about showing him you won't break under the weight of what's coming."

Layla hesitated, her arms crossing protectively over herself, her fingers twitching nervously at her sides. "And what if I do break?" she asked softly, almost afraid to voice the fear.

"You won't," I said firmly, stepping closer to her, my gaze steady and unyielding.

She looked up at me, her expression unreadable. Her eyes were searching mine for the certainty I had in my voice, and I held it there, unwavering. After a long pause, she finally sighed, letting the weight of the moment settle over her. "Okay, fine. Let's do this. But if I end up a pile of bones on the floor, I'm blaming all of you."

Orcus chuckled at that. "Fair enough. Now let's get started before you lose your nerves."

The room felt smaller, the air heavier, as the weight of anticipation pressed down on us like a second skin. Layla stood in the center, her posture rigid, the occasional sharp intake of breath betraying the unease she was struggling to hide. I could see the nerves gnawing at her, even if she was trying to steel herself against them.

"Layla," I said, my voice softer than I intended, my gaze steady on her. "You don't have to be afraid of this. It's part of you."

She turned her head slightly, her eyes narrowing as they locked into mine. "Easy for you to say. You've been... whatever you are forever. I've been human for 23 years. This?" She gestured vaguely to herself, the motion quick and restless. "This isn't natural. None of this is."

"Death rarely is," Orcus quipped, his metallic voice laced with a strange, dark humor. "But you're handling it better than most."

Sadie crossed her arms and rolled her eyes. "Great pep talk, talking sword. Really inspiring."

Orcus emitted a low hum of irritation. "Scythe," he corrected, his tone sharp. "Not sword."

Exu chuckled from his perch, arms folded. "You'll forgive her ignorance. Sadie isn't used to weapons that talk back yet."

"Neither of us are," Layla muttered, her tone dripping with dry sarcasm.

I ignored the banter and stepped closer to Layla, my gaze focused entirely on her. The room felt quieter with just the two of us. "You're stronger than you think," I said, my tone deliberate, leaving no room for doubt. "This form isn't a punishment. It's a reflection of your purpose."

Layla tilted her head, doubt flickering in her gaze. "And what's my purpose, exactly? To some half-dead monster?"

"No," I said, my voice firm and unyielding. "To bridge the gap. To remind the living, supernatural, and the dead that they're not as different as they think. You're proof that the line between them can blur. That it *should* blur."

Orcus huffed from where he hovered nearby. "Azrael, you make it sound so... *poetic*. She's got bones for a reason. Let's not sugarcoat this."

Layla's lips quirked upward for a fraction of a second before she caught herself, the tension in her face returning. "So what? I just... will it into existence?"

"Yes," I said simply. "But it's more than that. You have to feel it. Your true form isn't just a look; it's a part of your essence. You have to let go of what you think you are and embrace what you actually are."

Sadie scoffed from her spot. "Sounds like a load of cryptic crap to me."

"Sadie," I said, casting her a warning glance, my patience for her sarcasm wearing thin.

"What?" She threw her hands up, completely unbothered by my glare. "I'm just saying. If someone told me to '*embrace my essence*,' I'd think they were selling self-help books."

Exu snorted, clearly enjoying himself, leaning against the wall with an amused grin. "Can't say I blame you, Sadie. This whole 'essence' talk is a bit much for me too."

Layla's gaze flickered between us all, a small, tired smile curling at the corners of her lips. I could see her trying to fight the tension, trying to find some space to breathe between the weight of the moment and the oddball dynamics of the people around her.

"You'll get there," I said, my voice steady. "But you have to take that first step. You have to believe that this is your path. And no matter how difficult it gets, you won't break."

She nodded, but there was still a glimmer of hesitation in her eyes. The fear wasn't gone—it never would be—but the determination to rise above it was starting to shine through.

"Alright," she said, her voice a little steadier than before. "Let's do this."

"Close your eyes," I instructed, stepping back to give her some space. "Focus on the parts of you that feel... different. Alien. That's where your form starts."

Layla hesitated, her breath shallow, but eventually, she did as I said. Her eyes slipped shut, and the tension in her posture softened, though it didn't vanish entirely. The room held its breath with her, waiting.

"Good girl," I murmured, my voice soft but steady. "Now let yourself feel the shift. Don't fight it."

For a long moment, nothing happened. The air was thick with anticipation, yet stillness ruled. Then, faintly, a shimmer began to surround her, like heat waves rising from the asphalt on a scorching summer day. It was subtle at first, just a faint pulse in the air.

Her body jerked, her eyes snapping open with a sharp breath. "It's... it's not working," she said, frustration lacing her words.

"It is," I assured her, my voice firm. "You're holding back. Let go of the fear, Layla."

"I'm not scared!" she snapped, her voice betraying the edge of panic that had crept in. The slight quiver in her tone was all the confirmation I needed.

"You are," Orcus interjected bluntly. "But that's okay. Everyone's scared the first time they do something seemingly impossible."

"Not helping," I muttered under my breath, knowing that Orcus wasn't one for soft encouragement.

Layla's hands clenched into fists, her jaw tight. She closed her eyes again, breathing deeply, and the shimmer around her intensified. This time, the transformation began to take shape, slow at first, but relentless in its pursuit.

Her legs remained human for the moment, but from the waist up, her body began to fade. Her flesh rippled and melted, leaving bone in its place, the pale structure glowing faintly with an eerie, silvery hue. It was a grotesque beauty, mesmerizing and terrifying at once. Her face shifted last, her skin peeling back as though the universe itself was forcing her to shed the shell of her humanity.

Her skull remained exposed, and the empty sockets of her eyes burned with a haunting purple light.

She opened her mouth, attempting to scream, but no sound emerged.

"It's working," I said, stepping closer, my voice steady despite the eerie sight. "You're doing it."

Her skeletal hand twitched, curling into a fist as she struggled. "It feels... wrong. Like I'm being torn into two!"

"It'll get easier," Orcus said, his tone unexpectedly gentle. It was strange to hear him speak like that, but Layla needed it. "This is who you are. The rest is now pretense."

Layla swayed, her balance faltering, and I reacted instinctively, my hand reaching out to steady her. "You're okay," I said quietly, my voice soothing. "You're okay."

Her skeletal jaw moved, the words forming slowly, painfully. "It doesn't feel okay."

"It will," I promised, my voice low and confident, though a small part of me understood her discomfort. I wasn't sure how long this would take for her to fully accept, but I knew we didn't have the luxury of time.

Sadie, who had been silent up until now, finally spoke. "Well... that's terrifying."

Layla let out a noise that could have been either a laugh or a sob, the sound rough and strained.

"Perfect," Orcus said, his voice ringing with approval, the edge of a wicked grin in his tone. "You'll impress the hell out of Drepane."

"Or scare him off," Sadie muttered, her voice laced with skepticism, though there was a twinkle in her eye.

"Drepane doesn't scare," I said, standing taller, my gaze never leaving Layla. "But he will judge, and we'll be ready."

The tension in the room was palpable. Layla's form wavered, her skeletal structure still not fully in sync with her human consciousness, but she stood tall, unwilling to let herself falter.

And I knew, deep down, that she would get there. She had to. There was no other choice.

Orcus' voice broke through the silence once more, softer now. "The hardest part is over. The rest is just finding the rhythm."

Layla's eyes, glowing with that haunting purple light, met mine. "I don't know if I can do this," she said, her voice quiet but filled with a mixture of fear and resolve.

"You already are," I replied, my words firm but gentle, the weight of them settling between us.

Chapter Thirty-Nine

Layla

Can't Hold Us - Macklemore

The room is silent except for the sound of my breath, steady and deep, as I grip the wooden training sickle. The weight still feels strange in my hands. I try not to think about how unprepared I feel. This is supposed to be natural, but it's anything but.

Exu stands beside me, his massive presence a constant reminder of what I'm up against. His caramel skin glistens faintly under the dim light, and his dark locs seem to move slightly as though alive with his energy. He's silent for a moment, watching me carefully, then speaks. "You're gripping it too tight."

I glance at him, my fingers reflexively tightening around the handle. "I need control," I say, my voice strained, as if I can convince him—and myself—that I have it.

"You have control when you can feel the weapon, not when you're trying to dominate it." His tone is calm, patient. He's been telling me this for days, but it's harder than it sounds.

I try to relax, but the sickle feels so foreign, so dangerous in my hands. Control. Let the sickle flow. His words echo in my mind, but it's hard to stop fighting against the weapon. I have to get it right—because if I don't, I could let our entire found family down.

I exhale, letting go of the tension in my grip. The sickle doesn't feel any less powerful, but it does feel... lighter. Not physically, but emotionally. For the first time in this whole training session, I'm not forcing it into submission.

Exu's voice breaks the silence. "Better."

I give him a quick, tight nod, though I'm still not sure. The sickle feels more at ease in my hands, but that doesn't mean I have control. It means I'm simply trying to follow what it wants, instead of forcing my will on it. There's a difference.

"Now," Exu says, stepping back slightly, "remember what I taught you. You're not fighting to land a blow. You're fighting to move, to flow. That's what will make you dangerous."

I take a deep breath, trying to focus. Trying to get my body to listen to the rhythm Exu keeps telling me about. I raise the sickle again, trying to mimic the fluid movements he showed me. The second I swing it, though, everything feels off. The motion feels clumsy, jerky. I stumble, misstep, and the sickle barely even cuts the air.

Frustration wells up, hot and sharp. My breath catches, and for a moment, it's all I can do to not let the panic take over. I can't do this. I'm not ready. This weapon will never listen to me.

Then Exu's voice cuts through the frustration, low and steady. "It's okay. You're still learning. But your mind is the one holding you back. Focus on your breath. Feel the rhythm. Let the sickle follow it."

His words sink in slowly. I force my eyes closed, pushing aside the doubts and the fears swirling inside me. Inhale. Exhale. I try to sync my breath with my heartbeat, slow and steady. I feel the sickle in my hands again—its weight, its curve, its purpose. I stop thinking so much and start feeling.

And that's when it happens. I feel it. The rhythm. The sickle follows my movements, almost as if it's alive, shifting with my body instead of against it. It's strange, but... right. The awkwardness lessens, just a little. I swing it again, and this time, it feels more like an extension of me than an object I'm trying to control.

Exu doesn't say anything, but I catch the faintest quirk of his lips, a subtle sign of approval. It's all I need. I keep going, moving in the rhythm, the sickle finding its path, its purpose, just like he said it would.

I take another deep breath, this time more confident. I'm not perfect, not yet, but it's a start. I can feel the progress in my arms, in the way my body moves with the sickle instead of forcing it.

Exu moves beside me, silent as ever, but his presence is a steady anchor in this sea of uncertainty. "Good," he says, breaking the silence. "Now let's do it again. And again. Until you stop thinking and start moving."

The challenge lingers in his words, but I know he's right. This isn't just about physical strength. It's about trust—trusting my body, trusting Exu's lessons. And trust takes time.

So, I lift the sickle again, focusing on the rhythm, on the flow. And I keep going, step by step, until the weapon and I are moving as one.

Chapter Forty

Layla

Castle - Halsey

As much as I have the urge to jump Azrael for round two, it doesn't feel right. The last time, while we were... well, *doing that,* Luca was being kidnapped by strange shadow crows. I'd be lying if I said that didn't scare me off from the act, but honestly, it's not even about that anymore. These past few days, Azrael has been consumed with worry—not just about Luca, but about Vassago and Song, too. I can see it in the way he moves, the constant tension in his shoulders, the way his eyes flicker to the shadows like something's about to spring from them.

The past week has been a whirlwind of vigorous training—mentally, physically—trying to pull out my true form. The form that's half-human and half-supernatural, the one that is supposed to symbolize hope for others like me. Half-bloods. And that thought, the idea that I'm not truly human, makes my stomach twist. I hate it. I hate what I am. I'm not a freak, but being caught between two worlds—being neither here nor there—sickens me. It makes me feel less real, less... whole.

Still, I've been working on it. I can hold my true form for a decent amount of time now. But Azrael says the only way I'll ever truly master it is if I get my own Reaper tool—like Drepane, the one my mother's father used to overthrow the throne. Drepane has been sleeping ever since.

Orcus believes that Drepane might accept me, or at least give me a chance to prove I'm worthy. He's stronger than Orcus, more cocky too, but who wouldn't be when you're that old and that powerful? The whole idea makes my head spin. How could I, of all people, be worthy of wielding something so—*legendary*?

And yet, here I am.

Today's the day. The day I stand before the Grim Court, ask for permission to meet Drepane. The Court's role is to protect him, to weed out the worthy from the unworthy, deciding who deserves the chance to even meet him. I don't even know what I'm doing here, but I have to. For the Underworld, for everyone, for the balance between life and death that's slipping away.

The Grim Court is nothing like I imagined. It's not the darkness, or the heavy silence, that unnerves me—it's the feeling of being seen, really *seen*, in a way that leaves no secrets untouched. The floating orbs of light above each throne illuminate everything. The thrones themselves—massive structures of obsidian and bone—tower over us, arranged in a semi-circle that makes me feel like prey under the gaze of hungry predators.

Azrael strides ahead, calm and composed, Orcus slung casually over his shoulder. He looks like this is just another day at the office. Meanwhile, my heart is hammering in my chest, my legs like lead. With every step, it feels like the weight of a thousand eyes is pressing down on me. I'm out of my depth. I don't belong here.

"Steady," Orcus says, his tone cool and deliberate. "They don't need to know you're scared out of your mind."

"I'm not scared," I mutter under my breath, mostly to myself, but my voice betrays me. I am scared.

Azrael glances back at me, his expression unreadable. "It's okay to be nervous. Just speak plainly when the time comes. They value honesty."

That makes one of us. I'm not sure I can be honest about why I'm here. Or about myself. About the fact that I don't believe I *belong* in *this* world. I'm a half-blood. A dirty mortal. I was never meant to stand in a room like this.

We reach the center of the room, and the thrones loom high above us. The judges start introducing themselves, their voices like distant echoes in my mind. Judge Thanocles, the tallest and most imposing of them all, leans forward in his seat, his skeletal frame cloaked in deep shadows.

"Layla Simmons," his voice rings out, low and commanding, like the toll of a distant bell. "You stand before the Grim Court, seeking permission to meet Drepane? Give us a damn good reason for that purpose."

My throat tightens, and for a moment, I forget how to breathe. I can't think. Can't speak. The weight of the Court's eyes bears down on me, cold and unrelenting.

"Fae have your tongue?" Lady Morvina's voice cuts through the silence, dripping with disdain. Her silver hair gleams like frost, her hollow eyes narrowing as she surveys me. "She speaks for herself, doesn't she? Half-bloods rarely have the courage to do so."

"I'm not—" I stop myself, fists clenched tight at my sides. *No*. I won't let her bait me. I won't give her the satisfaction of seeing me break.

"Enough," Azrael says sharply, his voice carrying the weight of authority. "Layla is here because the Underworld is falling apart, and we need Drepane to restore the balance. If she wasn't capable, she wouldn't be standing here."

Thanocles raises a bony hand, silencing Morvina before she can respond. His gaze turns to me, sharp and piercing. "And what do you say, Layla Simmons? Why should we allow you to awaken the Sickle of the Ancients?"

I draw in a deep breath, the air cold in my lungs. For a moment, I just stand there, unsure of what to say, but then the words come, and they're firmer than I expect. "Because this isn't about me," I say, the phrase sounding like something

I've heard from my supernatural counterparts more times than I care to count. "It's about fixing what's broken. The Underworld, the balance between life and death—everything is falling apart. If Drepane can help us stop Memetim, then I'll do whatever it takes to prove myself. Even if you think I don't belong here."

I swallow hard. Because I *don't* belong here. But I have to. I have to be enough.

The silence that follows is deafening, and I wonder if I've said something wrong. If I've crossed a line. But when Thanocles speaks, it's as if he's considering my words with the weight of centuries.

"You will face the test of worthiness," he declares, his voice chilling. "Only the past wielders of Drepane may judge whether you are worthy to stand among them."

I nod, my stomach turning into knots and I grasp my pendant around my neck to ground me. This is it. This is where I find out if I have what it takes.

Thanocles raises a bony hand, and the air shifts. Shadows coil and twist in the room, and from the darkness, figures emerge. Tall, imposing, undeniably otherworldly. The figures of Drepane's past wielders flicker into existence, their translucent bodies glowing with an ethereal light.

I brace myself. They're here. The judgment begins.

"Layla Simmons," one of them spoke, their voice icy, reverberating off the cold walls of the Grim Court. "Do you truly believe yourself capable of wielding Drepane? Do you think yourself worthy to fight for the Underworld?"

I swallowed, my breath catching in my throat. "I—" My voice faltered, uncertainty gnawing at me.

Another figure emerged from the shadows, their glowing eyes narrowing as they studied me like a piece of prey. "You're mortal," they hissed, their voice sharp like a dagger. "Weak. Afraid. What right do you have to stand where we once stood?"

I could feel the sting of their words, the weight of their judgment pressing down on me, suffocating me. But I clenched my fists at my sides and held my head high. "I'm not... mortal. I'm not weak," I managed, though the words felt hollow, even to my own ears.

The air shifted, and suddenly a towering figure loomed over the others, his presence swallowing the light. His aura was unlike anything I'd felt before—ancient, unyielding, full of wrath. The others seemed to recoil in his presence, and I could feel my pulse quicken.

"Cronos," Orcus hissed, his voice filled with distaste.

I froze. The name hit me like a physical blow. Cronos. The god of time, the one who had destroyed his own bloodline to protect his throne. The one who was my— *grandfather*. My mind spiraled, my thoughts a jumbled mess as his cold eyes locked onto mine.

"Do you dare stand before us?" His voice was low, venomous, each word like a whip. "You, the spawn of my disgraceful daughter? The bastard bloodline that should have ended eons ago?"

The words hit me with the force of a hammer. The breath rushed from my lungs, but I refused to back down. I wouldn't let him break me. Not now.

Cronos took a slow, deliberate step toward me, his skeletal fingers curling around the spectral form of Drepane that floated beside him. "Do you even know who you are, girl?" he sneered. "What you represent?"

"I..." My voice faltered, but I forced myself to keep my gaze steady.

"You are nothing," he spat, his words dripping with disdain. "An abomination that should have never existed. I destroyed my children to protect my throne. Your mother was a mistake, and you are *shame* incarnate. You don't belong *here*."

The room seemed to close in on me. His words felt like daggers, each one cutting deeper than the last. But I stood firm, my body trembling, but my resolve unyielding.

Azrael, standing beside me, bristled with anger. His hand tightened on Orcus, and his voice rang out, sharp and commanding. "That's enough."

Cronos turned his gaze to Azrael, his lips curling into a mocking smile. "And what are you to her, Reaper? A crutch? A distraction? She'll never stand on her own if you keep shielding her from the truth."

"Her mate!" Azrael's voice roared through the chamber, his fury palpable.

Cronos's golden eyes flickered with malice as he sneered. "Son of Hades? The one who *murdered* me and took my throne?" His mouth twisted in distaste. "How disgraceful to *my* legacy."

"Because you—"

"Stop!" The word burst from my lips before I could stop it. My fists clenched tightly at my sides as I stepped forward, ignoring the tremors in my legs. I wouldn't let them control me. I wouldn't let Cronos bury me before I had the chance to prove myself. "I don't care what *you* think of me," I growled. "I didn't *ask* for your approval, Cronos. I'm here for Drepane. Not for you."

Cronos chuckled, the sound dark and unsettling. It vibrated through my bones. "Bold words for someone so... fragile," he mocked, his voice thick with venom. "Do you even understand what it means to wield Drepane? To shoulder the weight of the Underworld's fate?"

I felt the anger boiling in my chest, an inferno threatening to consume me. "Then let me prove it!" I shouted, my voice loud, the words spilling out like a challenge. "I didn't ask to be born, Cronos. But I am here, and I'm not going to let your hatred stop me from doing what's right."

Cronos's laughter echoed again, hollow and cold. "What's right?" He sneered. "You are nothing more than a half-blood mortal pretending to *play* with gods. You think Drepane will choose *you*? A broken girl who denies her own nature?"

His words stung, but they no longer had the power to paralyze me. I wouldn't let him. I wouldn't let anyone stop me.

"Prove your worth," he commanded suddenly, his voice deep with finality. His fingers flicked, and the spectral form of Drepane appeared between us, its sickle gleaming with an ominous, ghostly light. "If you dare."

The challenge hung heavy in the air, and for a moment, I hesitated. My fingers trembled as I reached for the sickle, its aura buzzing with power. The moment my fingers brushed its surface, a jolt of energy shot through me, filling my mind with visions of destruction. I saw Cronos wielding Drepane, cutting down his enemies with ruthless precision. The weight of his rule, the countless lives he destroyed—each swing of Drepane a death sentence.

"You will never endure this burden," Cronos's voice was a whisper in my mind, but it felt as if he were speaking directly into my soul. "You lack the strength. The resolve. The blood."

"I'm *not* you," I bit out through gritted teeth, forcing myself to hold on, even as the visions of blood and destruction pressed down on me. "I don't need to be like you to make a difference."

"Difference?" Cronos stepped closer, his golden eyes glowing with a twisted hunger. "You think the Underworld will bend for you? That Drepane will kneel to your weakness? You are *nothing*. Less than nothing."

Something inside me snapped, a breaking point I didn't know existed. The power, the weight, the fear—they all swirled together into a storm, but I gripped the sickle tighter. I pushed through the pain, through the fear, through every insult he had thrown at me.

"I don't care what you think," I hissed, my voice shaking but firm. "I'm not doing this for *you*. I'm doing this to protect the beings I care about. To fix what *you* and others like you broke."

Cronos's expression darkened, his golden eyes narrowing. But he said nothing. The other wielders shifted, murmuring among themselves. I couldn't hear the words, but I could feel the change in the air—the shift from contempt to curiosity.

"You deny your nature," Cronos said after a long, tense pause. "Yet you speak with conviction. Perhaps you have inherited more than I thought. Or perhaps you are simply foolish."

Before I could respond, the battlefield dissolved around me. The visions faded, and I was standing once again in the Grim Court. The wielders of Drepane stood in their ethereal forms, flickering in and out of existence.

Thanocles's voice broke the silence, steady and commanding. "What is your judgment?"

Cronos stepped forward, his gaze locked on mine, his eyes glowing with ancient hatred. He studied me for a long moment, his lips curling into a cold smile.

"She is unworthy," he declared, his voice ice. "But perhaps desperation is what the Underworld needs. Let her bear the burden of Drepane's judgment. Maybe he will kill her for us all."

I didn't flinch. I didn't say a word. Let them believe what they wanted. I was still standing, and that was all that mattered.

Chapter Forty-One

Layla

Shatter Me - Lindsey Stirling ft Lzzy Hale

The Grim Court led us down a long, dimly lit hallway, its stone walls towering above us like silent sentinels. The air was thick with ancient power, every step we took echoing like a distant warning. The door at the end loomed, a cold, imposing figure that marked the beginning of the test I had to pass. I glanced up at Azrael, his expression unreadable, his cool demeanor unbroken.

"Why did you tell him I was your mate?" I finally asked, the question bubbling up from the pit of my stomach. The thought of Azrael claiming me so openly, despite my hesitation, weighed heavily on my chest.

He didn't even look at me as we walked. "Because you are," he replied, his voice smooth, but there was a hint of finality in his words.

I frowned, pushing harder. "How am I supposed to prove myself if you keep using your name to get me further?"

Azrael's lips twitched into a smirk, his eyes never leaving the door ahead. "You're not. But the world will see you differently because of it."

Frustration built up in me, and I couldn't hold it back any longer. "I didn't even accept the mating bond," I said, raising my voice just a little to get his attention. "Hello? Azrael, are you even listening to me?" My hand waved in front of his face, but he didn't flinch.

Before I could even process what was happening, Azrael's hand shot out, pushing me gently but firmly against the cold stone wall. His face was inches from mine now, his icy glare piercing through me.

"Despite you not accepting the bond," he hissed softly in my ear, "it doesn't erase the fact you are my mate. We are fated. No matter how long you try to ignore it, no matter how many times you push it down and use me as a 'curiosity fuck', I'll be here. I'll always be here—treating you no less than the queen you truly are. Reap the benefits of our bond, or throw my name out there. Use our connection to your advantage. Because at the end of the day, I don't care how you use me. I'll just be thankful to be here—to be near you, to breathe the same air you breathe. It's a privilege, one I didn't truly earn."

His words hit me like a wave, crashing over me, leaving me breathless. Azrael pulled away, a smirk playing at his lips, before turning and continuing his steady march toward Drepane's room.

The silence stretched between us, thick with tension, as we reached the door. I pushed it open slowly, revealing the ancient sickle resting on a stone table, bathed in an eerie spotlight. Drepane lay there, dormant, silent—waiting.

Shadows shift subtly, casting moving patterns across the walls, as though the room itself is alive. The air is perfumed with the bittersweet scent of roses mixed with a metallic tang, creating a haunting allure.

The obsidian-black walls are entwined with dark ivy, its tendrils seemingly alive, creeping and curling across the surface. Crimson roses bloom sporadically along the ivy, their petals edged in black, as if kissed by decay. Glowing runes in a purple pulse faintly between the vines, adding an ethereal touch.

The ceiling mimics a twilight sky, swirling with deep purples and silvers. Roses and ivy cascade down from the edges, intertwining with iron sconces shaped like skeletal hands, which clutch glowing flames of ghostly light.

I turned to Azrael, who seemed unfazed. "Just talk to him," he said with a shrug, a casualness that only made me more nervous.

"How did you get Orcus, anyway?" I asked, trying to keep my mind occupied.

Azrael rubbed his neck, sighing as if the memory weighed on him. "My father handed me Orcus when I was five and said, 'Good luck.'" He chuckled darkly.

I took a deep breath, stepping closer to the sickle. "Drepane, I wish to speak to you," I called out, my voice shaky despite my best efforts to sound steady.

Silence. Nothing. The sickle remained dark, still, its power dormant.

I tried again, desperation creeping into my tone. "Please, Drepane. It is dire."

Still, no response. My heart pounded in my chest, and I turned to leave. But then, the air in the room shifted—like a sudden pulse—and a faint hum vibrated through the ground. I froze, turning back to see the sickle glowing with a soft, purple light. His voice, when it came, was smooth and authoritative, yet it carried a chilling edge.

"What do you want, Cronos' child?" Drepane asked, his voice resonating in the room.

"I need your help," I said, my voice rising in conviction. "Memetim is wreaking havoc and destroying the Underworld. We need your help to restore peace."

"Peace?" Drepane's voice was laced with disdain. "There was peace before Cronos used me to destroy the previous ruler. There was peace before Hades turned it into a cesspool, breeding worthless armies. What can I do to bring peace when you come from the very blood I banished from wielding me?"

The sting of his words cut through me, but I refused to let it break me. "I am not Cronos," I said, my voice steady despite the fire building inside me. "Yes, I am his descendant, but I am not Cronos. And he"—I turned, placing a hand on Azrael's shoulder—"is not Hades. We are fated, but we can't fix the Underworld until Memetim is gone."

Azrael's voice was quick and urgent, as if trying to pull me back into reality. "Terminated," he corrected, his eyes flicking between Drepane and me.

Drepane's silence stretched out, his presence in the room growing heavy. Finally, after what felt like an eternity, he spoke again. "Return to me when you feel worthy. When you are confident enough in your power to face the challenges ahead. Until then, do not disturb my slumber."

I felt my stomach churn. "What do you mean?" I asked, my voice trembling.

"You are weak. Scared. You need to train more, grow stronger—physically and mentally," Drepane's voice turned cold, almost mocking. "Only then will you prove your worth."

I felt the weight of his words pressing down on me like an iron hand, suffocating my resolve. But I couldn't give in. Not now. Not when I was so close.

Before I could respond, Azrael grabbed my arm and started pulling me away, his grip firm, but I wrenched myself free, standing my ground. "No!" I shouted, my voice raw, breaking with emotion. "I'm sick and tired of everyone telling me who I am and what I am. I am worthy!"

My voice cracked with the force of my conviction. I could feel Drepane's energy wrapping around me like a vise, testing my limits. But I wasn't going to let it break me. Not again.

Drepane's presence was overwhelming, as if the sickle were staring directly into my soul. For a moment, there was nothing but silence. A heavy, suffocating silence that seemed to stretch forever. Then, Drepane's voice rang out once more, sharp and commanding.

"Words mean nothing. Prove it."

The air shifted again, colder this time, and I felt my pulse quicken, the challenge in his words echoing inside me. My heart pounded, but I didn't waver. "How?" I asked, my voice steady despite the whirlwind in my chest.

Drepane's blade gleamed as it pulsed with dark energy. "You have always run from who you are. Face it. Show me that you are not bound by your fear."

Azrael's voice cut through the tension, low and desperate. "Layla, this isn't a fight you can win right now. Drepane is ancient—he doesn't see things like we do. He's not trying to be fair."

I spun to face him, my voice sharp with frustration. "Fair?" I threw a hand toward Drepane. "Do you think my life has been *fair*?" I turned back to the sickle, standing tall. "If this is what it takes to get him to listen, then I'll do it. I'll prove to him I'm worthy."

Orcus' voice rumbled in my ear, his tone filled with warning. "The kid's got fire. But fire alone won't be enough. You want to stand before Drepane? Brace yourself. He'll strip you down to your very core. There's no hiding here."

I swallowed hard, but his words only fueled the fire inside me. I wasn't afraid anymore.

"Fine." I squared my shoulders, looking Drepane in the eye. "I'm not afraid."

The sickle's presence grew even more suffocating, a cold, invisible pressure that seemed to crush me from all sides. But I refused to back down.

"We'll see," Drepane's voice echoed, cold and unconvinced. "To wield me, you must prove yourself worthy, Layla. You cling to a mortal shell, denying your true nature. If you want my power, you must embrace it—body and soul."

Before I could speak, the room shifted violently, the ground cracking beneath me as I was pulled into another reality. I stumbled, my hands catching me just before I hit the ground. When I looked up, the world around me had vanished. I was no longer in the Grim Court.

Instead, I stood on the edge of a vast, desolate battlefield, the wind howling around me. Azrael's voice and Orcus' presence faded into silence. I was completely alone.

"What is this?" I whispered, my breath visible in the freezing air.

"That is your truth," Drepane's voice echoed from everywhere and nowhere, filling the space around me like a growing storm. "Your challenge is to shed your denial and face what lies within you. Only then, will you be able to claim me."

I glanced down at my hands. My skin felt wrong—too heavy, too fragile. The wind carried whispers, growing louder with every passing second. It spoke of fear, of failure, of the mortal life I refused to let go of.

"No," I muttered, clenching my fists until my nails bit into my palms. "I'm not weak."

The battlefield shifted, the landscape around me warping into something grotesque. And then, I saw it—my reflection, twisted and monstrous. Its upper half was skeletal, glowing faintly with an eerie, otherworldly light, while the lower half remained human. The figure's hollow eyes burned with an intensity that sent acold shiver down my spine.

"This is what you are," Drepane's voice rumbled, deep and final. "A half-truth, trapped between worlds. Fight it, or embrace it. The choice is yours."

The reflection took a step toward me, its hollow gaze locking onto mine. I could feel the pull of its energy, its weight, trying to sink into my very bones.

Without warning, the creature lunged at me. Its bony claws swiped through the air, and I barely dodged, my heart hammering in my chest. I scrambled backward, but it was relentless, its claws outstretched like death itself.

"You can't run from yourself," it hissed, its voice a warped, mocking version of my own.

I stopped, panic threatening to take over, but I planted my feet, forcing myself to stand my ground. "I'm not running." The words came out more as a command than are assurance, my voice tight with defiance.

The creature paused, tilting its head, as if it was trying to read my resolve.

"I'm not running," I repeated, louder this time. "I've been training, fighting, surviving. I'm not weak, and I'm not afraid to face what I am."

The creature's hollow eyes narrowed, its skeletal face twisting into something almost human—something malicious. It charged again, this time faster, more furious. I could feel the power behind its movements, but this time, I didn't flinch.

I reached deep within myself, tapping into something I had buried for far too long—strength I hadn't even known I possessed. My body hummed with the energy of it.

When the creature struck, I grabbed its skeletal arm, holding firm. A surge of raw power shot through me like lightning, and in that instant, I felt the shift—my body transforming, my essence changing. My skin turned translucent, revealing the glowing bones beneath. I wasn't just transforming; I was awakening, embracing all that I was.

"I am both..." I said, my voice steady and sure, echoing with newfound conviction. "Mortal and supernatural. I don't have to choose."

The creature's hollow eyes widened, and it let out a deafening scream, but it was too late. My strength exploded outward, and the creature dissolved into ash, scattering to the wind. The battlefield around me dissolved as well, replaced by the cold, familiar walls of the Underworld.

Drepane's blade gleamed in the dim light, and his voice resonated with a new tone—one of respect, and perhaps something more. "You've taken your first step."

Azrael's hand was on my shoulder, steadying me as I swayed, disoriented by the intense surge of power that had just ripped through me. I felt a familiar weight in the air, and Orcus' voice—gruff and sardonic—broke the silence.

"You didn't die. I'm impressed."

I turned to find Azrael's eyes scanning me, a mix of concern and pride in his gaze. His voice cut through the silence, hard but filled with an edge of hope. "Well? Did she pass, old blade, or are you going to keep us waiting?"

Drepane's voice reverberated around the room, low and solemn, like the toll of a bell. "She has faced the truth of herself and embraced it. I accept her."

The sickle's blade shimmered, its surface glowing faintly in the dim light. A sudden warmth filled the room, washing over me like a quiet affirmation, a recognition of my struggle and triumph.

I glanced at the weapon, its presence now no longer cold or distant, but steady—patient, waiting.

"You mean—" I started, my voice trembling.

"You are worthy to wield me," Drepane said, his tone unwavering, ancient. "*But* wielding my power is no easy burden. Remember this, Layla: Strength is not just what lies in your body, but what lies in your heart and mind. You must continue to grow, for the war ahead will demand everything of you."

A mixture of relief and anxiety coursed through me. The weight of what I'd just accomplished began to sink in, but with it came the reality of the responsibility I was now carrying.

"However," Drepane continued, his tone turning sharp, commanding. "My power is not meant to linger in mortal hands. You can wield me under one condition, Layla."

My throat tightened, a wave of unease washing over me. "What condition?"

"You *must* provide a successor," Drepane's voice echoed, as if his words had been etched into the very air. "A male offspring—one who can take me when the time comes. That is the price for wielding me."

A cold knot formed in my stomach, and the words hit me like a blow to the chest. "A... child?"

Azrael stiffened beside me, his jaw tight as a muscle. He leaned in, his voice low and furious. "You can't just demand something like that from her," he growled, his tone darker than I'd ever heard it.

Drepane ignored him, his voice growing colder, more authoritative. "The choice is yours, Layla. If you refuse, I will not serve you. But if you accept, I will stand by your side in the battles to come."

I turned my gaze to Azrael, then back to Orcus, my heart thumping in my chest. This wasn't just about the power to defeat Memetim. This was about the Underworld, about the future I had yet to fully understand but was bound to protect.

My voice was quiet but unwavering. "I accept."

Azrael's hand tensed on my shoulder, his eyes searching mine. He didn't speak, but the intensity in his gaze spoke volumes—love, worry, and something else I couldn't quite name.

"Then it is done,"Drepane said, his voice final, sealed in the air. "For now, you may wield me. But remember your promise, Layla. I will hold you to it."

A sharp, sudden pain stung my wrist, and I looked down to see a large birthmark appear, its shape unmistakable—a sickle, burning into my skin.

The weight of Drepane's words settled over me like a heavy cloak. As Azrael guided me out of the chamber, the silence felt suffocating, the tension thick in the air.

Orcus broke it, his voice low and almost amused. "Well, that escalated quickly."

I shot him a shaky smile, my mind spinning, still trying to process everything that had just transpired. One challenge was over, but a far greater one loomed ahead—our missing werewolf, and of course, that bitch, Memetim.

Chapter Forty-Two

Layla

Rise - Katy Perry

"I can't believe you would make a fucking deal like that with Drepane! Are you out of your mind?" Azrael's voice is like a whip cracking in the tense air.

I wince, guilt and panic swirling in my stomach. I knew how much it meant for all of them if Drepane agreed to let me wield him, and I was desperate to bring back good news. Vassago and Song are still missing, and the fear—no, the anxiety—clings to us all, tightening our chest with every passing moment.

"I just wanted to help…" My voice trails off as I stare down at my feet, which seem to shuffle of their own accord as we exit the Grim Court.

"Helping would've been proving your worth, training more, and showing us you're ready. Not jumping into something you barely understand." Azrael's sigh carries the weight of his frustration, but there's something softer in it too, something that tells me he cares. A lot. Maybe too much at times.

I don't fully understand the mating bond—what Exu told me echoes in my mind: Azrael has a primal instinct to protect me at all costs, no matter what.

Even if it means putting everything he's known for centuries at risk, including his friends, who he loves like family.

Family.

I involuntarily set that in stone when I agreed to Drepane's condition. Azrael and I will have a family of our own—eventually. So many things I don't understand about this world, about the bond between us. It's all overwhelming. *When will I stop feeling so damn lost?* When will this world feel like second nature to me?

I don't know. I can't see the path ahead, and the uncertainty is gnawing at me.

"I didn't mean to yell." Azrael's hands gently cradle my face, his touch so tender it almost makes me forget the sting of his words. His gaze locks with mine, his beautiful blue eyes full of something I can't quite decipher. "You promised offspring when you aren't even sure if you will accept the mating bond—accepting me..."

I swallow hard as he releases his grip, and with it, the dam I've been holding back finally bursts. The tears come, fast and hot, pouring down my cheeks. "I'm sorry!" I choke out, my voice breaking under the pressure of everything I've been holding inside. I didn't mean to yell—I didn't, but I needed to say it! I needed to push through the choking in my throat...

My words tremble as I try to gather myself. "I don't understand all of this, Azrael, and I don't know if you're truly okay with me being so damn broken."

Azrael doesn't hesitate. He grabs my face again, his fingers warm and firm, pulling me closer, his lips crashing against mine in a kiss that sets my body alight. The world shifts around us, the pain, the confusion, the fear—it all fades away with that single kiss.

"You. Are. Not. Broken." His words press against my lips like a vow, and then he presses our foreheads together, his breath mingling with mine. "The cards you were dealt were not yours to hold. I love you, Layla. Even if you don't believe me. Even if you can't understand why, I would do *anything* for you, without a second thought. Without a guess, or even a question. If I have to wait an eternity for you to believe in yourself, to see that my intentions are true and real, I'll wait for you. As long as it takes."

His words sweep through me, washing away some of the guilt and doubt, leaving something stronger in their wake.

"I promised a stupid weapon a fucking child, Azrael!" I sob, my heart breaking as the consequences of my actions finally begin to sink in. "How can we bring a child into this kind of world?"

Azrael's gaze softens, his thumb brushing a tear from my cheek. His voice is calm, steady, as he speaks. "We make it safe enough for him to survive it." He exhales slowly, the weight of his own thoughts pressing on his shoulders. "Together, we will make this world safe for *our* son. Drepane can wait for his wielder, however long it takes. He can wait, and he will be patient."

I can see it in Azrael's eyes—the frustration he won't voice, the fear he refuses to let show. But I can feel it. And above all, I can see how much he cares for me, even as I wrestle with my doubts. I would give anything to understand what mess I've just gotten us into—the danger, the consequences, the inevitable start of a relationship I've been running from.

The one time we had sex—*was that the reason?* Did I cloud my judgment with something that felt so right but wasn't the real thing? It was supposed to be curiosity, nothing more. But now... I do care about him. I do. But love? Am I ready to love someone else when I'm still struggling with who I am?

Azrael pulls away slightly, his expression hardening into something resolute, the burden of the situation pressing on him as much as it does me.

"You need to meet Exu and get back to training," Azrael says as we step outside the Grim Court, the harsh atmosphere of the Underworld crashing over us like a cold wave.

I shiver as I try to adjust to the air, the weight of it pressing into my chest.

"Where are you going?" I ask, my voice quieter now, almost too small for the chaos inside me.

"Ashton is back from his errand," Azrael replies, his eyes darting briefly to my lips, then back to my eyes. He's hoping for something, I can tell. But I'm not ready. Not yet. *Not yet, Azrael.*

"I'll be fine," I say, nodding before turning away. I can't give him more right now, and I know it hurts him. But the truth is, I don't know how to love him. Not yet.

Chapter Forty-Three

Layla

Uprising - Muse

I swung the fake blade again, the awkwardness of it almost unbearable in my hands. It felt too light, too stiff, a hollow imitation of what I needed. Frustration bubbled in my chest, threatening to spill over. This cheap replica of Drepane didn't respond to me the way the real one would, and I wanted to scream.

Exu's calm, measured voice broke through my thoughts. "Relax, Layla. You're too tense. Trust the weapon. Let it become a part of you."

I shot him an annoyed look, the frustration bleeding into my tone. "Trust the weapon? Exu, it's fake. It's not even close to the real thing, and you want me to trust it?"

"Trust yourself," he corrected gently. "You're focusing too much on what it isn't instead of what it could be. Stop forcing it. Breathe, Layla."

I let out a long, exasperated sigh and dropped the blade to the ground. Wiping my sweaty palms on my pants, I muttered, "Easy for you to say. You've been doing this for centuries. I got thrown into this mess without even asking for it."

Exu stepped closer, his gaze steady. "What mess are you talking about?"

The words spilled out before I could stop them. "Azrael. This whole thing with him. The mating bond, his name—he keeps throwing it around like it's supposed to mean something to me, like I'm just a pawn in some game I never agreed to play."

Exu's expression didn't change, but something softened in his eyes. "You're not a pawn, Layla. But I understand why you feel that way."

I shook my head, my frustration boiling over. "It's not just that. He's mad because I promised Drepane whatever it took to bring him to our side. He's mad because I made a decision—one I thought was best for us. It's always about what Azrael wants. What about what I want?"

Exu studied me for a moment, his silence heavier than words. Finally, he spoke. "Azrael is... complicated. He's not the easiest to understand. But you have to realize, the Underworld isn't a place you can walk away from. There are forces at work here much bigger than either of you."

I ran a hand through my hair, my frustration bubbling up again. "I don't care about the Underworld! I care about making it on my own. I want to be my own person, not just 'Azrael's mate.' I'm tired of him making decisions for me, then getting angry when I make one myself."

Exu's gaze didn't waver. "I hear you. But Azrael is fighting something too, Layla. He's not the only one with a burden. His name, his title—they come with expectations that weigh heavier than you realize."

I scoffed, crossing my arms. "I get it, Exu. He's the Grim Reaper. Everything's supposed to be about him. But why does that have to be at my expense? Why does he get to decide everything just because of this bond? I didn't ask for any of this."

Exu placed a firm but gentle hand on my shoulder. "I know you didn't. But Azrael... he's not trying to hurt you. The weight he carries isn't just the Underworld. He's carrying you, too, whether you realize it or not."

The words hit me like a punch to the gut. He's carrying you. For the first time, I saw Azrael's actions in a different light. Maybe he wasn't trying to control me. Maybe he was just overwhelmed, just like I was. But that didn't make it easier.

"I don't want to be a burden," I said quietly, more to myself than to Exu.

"You're not a burden," Exu replied firmly. "But you need to let him in. And you need to let yourself be who you are, even in the face of all this. That bond isn't just a chain. It's a connection, and it's stronger than either of you realize."

I took a shaky breath, my frustration giving way to something softer, though no less tangled. "I don't know if I'm ready for that. I don't know if I'll ever be ready."

Exu's lips curved into a small smile. "You don't have to be ready. Just take it one step at a time."

His hand lingered on my shoulder as the weight of his words settled in. Before I could respond, the air around us seemed to shift, the world tilting ever so slightly.

A low, unsettling noise filled the air. It wasn't the usual rustling of wind or distant sounds of the Underworld. It was something darker. Closer.

I froze, instinctively reaching for the blade at my side—well, the fake blade—but it felt so ridiculous in my hand, like a toy compared to what I'd need. My stomach tightened, a shiver crawling down my spine.

Exu's expression shifted instantly, his eyes narrowing. "Get back, Layla," he said, his voice low and dangerous.

"What is that?" I demanded, my heart thudding in my chest.

Before he could answer, the air around us darkened. A shadow flitted across the sky. It was fast, too fast to be anything natural. Then, a scream—high-pitched, eerie—echoed through the air. The first of them.

I gasped as a mass of black wings descended, blocking out the little sunlight that had remained. The crows came in droves, their sharp cries piercing the air as they swarmed around us.

I could barely process what was happening. The crows were everywhere, their wings whipping through the air in an overwhelming frenzy. I heard Exu shout something, but his voice was drowned out by the cacophony of shrieking birds and flapping wings.

The first crow struck. It was large, its claws slashing at Exu's arm before he could react. The impact knocked him back a step, and I saw the flash of blood in the air.

"No!" I screamed, my legs moving before I even had time to think. I rushed toward him, but Exu's eyes locked onto me, sharp and commanding.

"Get back!" he snarled. "Run!"

But I couldn't leave him. I couldn't just stand there while they attacked him. Exu staggered, blood staining his arm as more crows dove toward him. He swung his arm to try and ward them off, but his movements were slowing, and I could see the toll it was taking on him.

"No!" I shouted again, more desperate this time.

I gritted my teeth and dashed toward him, trying to help—do something, anything—but the crows were relentless. They came at us from all sides, their beady eyes gleaming with malice. One of them flew too close, and I swiped at it with the fake blade, but it barely made contact.

Exu was trying to fight them off, but he was outnumbered, injured. And I could see it now—he was weakening, the blood staining his clothes darker by the second.

"Exu, we need to get out of here!" I shouted, panic rising in my chest.

With a grunt, Exu shoved me back. "No, Layla. I'll hold them off. Go! Get to safety."

I shook my head violently, my heart hammering in my chest. "I'm not leaving you!"

I knew this wasn't the time to argue. He was hurt, badly. I wasn't sure how much longer he could hold out. But I wasn't going to leave him behind.

My mind raced as I looked around. The crows were everywhere. There was no way I could fight them off. I had to get help.

Without thinking, I grabbed Exu by the arm and hauled him to his feet, ignoring the shock on his face. "You're not doing this alone, Exu. I'm getting you out of here!"

He tried to pull away, but I wasn't going to let him. Blood poured from his wound, his face growing paler by the second. I felt a surge of adrenaline—I had to get him to safety.

I didn't care how many crows swarmed us. I had no time to think of anything else. I grabbed Exu's good arm and dragged him behind me, moving as quickly as I could, stumbling over the uneven ground.

The birds screeched behind us, and I could hear their wings beating louder as they followed, but my only focus was getting Exu out of danger.

A distinctive screech shredded through my mind. "You, bitch! Azrael sent Vassago to my home."

I wasn't sure how far I ran, but I didn't stop until I saw the familiar outline of Ashton's house in the distance. It felt like a lifetime since I'd seen it, but the sight of it gave me a sliver of hope.

I could feel Exu's weight growing heavier in my arms, and I knew we didn't have much time before the crows caught up. The thought of leaving Exu behind—of losing him—was something I couldn't even entertain.

Just a little farther...

The screech came back like nails on a chalkboard. "I will get you, Layla."

With a final burst of strength, I managed to pull him through the door to Ashton's home.

I slammed it shut behind us, locking the door with trembling hands.

The house was too quiet, too still.

Exu collapsed against the wall, gasping for breath, his face pale and covered in sweat. His injury was worse than I thought—his arm was drenched in blood, and his eyes were beginning to glaze over.

I couldn't breathe. I was frozen, staring at the man who had always been a father figure to Azrael, the one who had always been there to guide me... now fighting for his life.

"Exu, stay with me," I said, my voice shaky.

Chapter Forty-Four

Azrael

This is War - 30 Seconds to Mars

I walk through Ashton's home, each step weighed down with the tension that has been building in me for days. The uncertainty, the fear, the raw, gnawing need to protect Layla—it's like a storm inside me, threatening to burst at any moment. She's my mate, and I still don't fully understand what that means for us, for me. But I know this much: I will destroy anyone who dares threaten her.

When I reach Ashton's study, I pause. I can hear his voice—low and steady—mingling with another, one I don't recognize. There's an edge of something in the conversation, something too serious to ignore.

I push the door open just enough to see inside. Ashton stands near the fireplace, leaning casually against the wall, his arms crossed over his chest. But it's the woman beside him that catches my attention.

A woman, tiny with sandy blonde hair and the kind of light emerald eyes that haunt me. They are hers. *Layla's eyes.*

The confusion hits me like a punch. I glance at Ashton, my mind spinning. This wasn't supposed to happen—not like this. Why the hell is she here?

"Ashton," I greet, my voice a little more clipped than I intended. My mind is already racing through a thousand possibilities.

His gaze flicks to me, calm as ever. "You're back. Good. This is Lydia," he says, nodding to the woman beside him. "Lydia—"

"I know who he is," she interrupts softly, stepping forward with a small smile, extending her hand to me. "It's nice to finally meet you, Azrael."

I shake her hand, my thoughts still swirling. I can't put my finger on it, but something about her unsettles me. A cold knot forms in my chest, but I force myself to focus. There's too much happening, too many pieces I need to understand.

"Lydia has agreed to join the war with us," Ashton continues, his voice never changing. "But she has some interesting information to share."

I sit down, trying to suppress the storm of emotions swirling inside me. The tension in the room grows heavier, and Lydia follows me to the seat, her gaze never quite leaving me. Ashton, however, remains calm, detached. It's as if he's waiting for something to fall into place.

"My daughter's fight is my fight," Lydia starts, her voice quiet but firm. "I didn't know she was meeting you this soon. You were supposed to be pushed toward her when she was older."

I can't make sense of her words, and it's not just because of the strange way she's speaking. There's something deep, something dark, lurking behind every syllable. I open my mouth to ask, but she's already looking at me, her gaze flicking from her feet to Ashton, then back to me.

Ashton stays silent, allowing the tension to build, and that only heightens the gnawing feeling in my gut.

"Hidden succubus, why are you *really* here?" Orcus' voice rings in my ears, sharper than it's ever been before. He's pissed—just as confused, just as furious.

I can almost hear him pacing in the back of my mind, urging me to listen carefully, to dig deeper.

Lydia doesn't flinch, but there's a momentary pause before she answers, the weight of her words heavier than they should be. "Because, right under my nose, I didn't realize what was happening to my daughter. Hades is to blame."

"What do you mean my father is to blame?" My voice feels tight in my throat. My father. Every time I think of him, every time I have to deal with his twisted plans and his hatred, it makes my blood boil.

She looks at me like I'm an idiot. "Azrael, your father is *terrified* of you, and for centuries, he's been trying to find ways to destroy you—to terminate you." Her eyes darken as she speaks, her voice soft but sharp like a blade. "He knew the moment you were bonded to her, but he couldn't find her."

That fucking realization hits me like a freight train. My father was already trying to control my fate before I even knew what was happening. "I presume that's why I could only sense that she was mortal when I first saw her?" I ask, though part of me doesn't want to know the answer.

Lydia nods, but there's something in the way she does it—something sad, something resigned. "Yes," she whispers.

The silence stretches between us as my mind reels. Every piece is coming together, but it's all tangled, like a web I can't untangle. "Why did you choose Vassago, my brother, to be her Guardian Angel?" I ask, needing something to anchor myself to reality.

"Because, despite *your* jealousy of your brother," Lydia's gaze sharpens slightly, but there's no malice behind it. "He loves you unconditionally. He would die for you. And he would die to ensure your mate would live a full life—a life that would lead her to you. Your father couldn't stand the thought of that."

I swallow hard, my jaw tight. I never understood why Vassago was chosen. But this?

Lydia looks at Ashton, as if seeking permission to continue. Ashton just nods, still watching her carefully. His eyes are unreadable, but there's something sharp in them now, something that tells me he's been waiting for this too.

"Your father has spent your entire existence trying to kill you, trying to set you up for failure. And when *he* failed—when you kept defying him, kept surviving—he started pushing you toward Memetim, taunting her to try to find Layla." Her voice drops to a whisper, as if the weight of her words has crushed her spirit.

All of this... was part of his plan?

I can't help it. The disbelief in my voice cuts through the air. "All of this...was part of his plan?"

Lydia's eyes go distant, her face betraying the painful memories. "Before Layla was even born, I knew exactly what her future was going to be. It was more than just a maternal instinct—it felt like I was her servant, bound to her. My purpose was to protect her, guide her, nurture her... so she could eventually become the Queen of the Underworld."

I lean forward, my heart pounding. "What is Layla?" I demand. I need answers. I need to understand what she means, what I'm supposed to protect.

"A new breed of supernatural," she replies softly. "I figure a dormant gene from either my father or mother woke up. I don't know. But I do know this—Hades will kill Layla as soon as he finds her, Azrael. Because he knows... he's one step closer to losing his throne."

I'm frozen in place. Her words slice through me, and Orcus growls low in my mind. *This is more than I thought. She's more than I thought.*

I can feel Orcus shift, his rage and frustration pouring into me like molten lava. "He's going to try and take her from you, Azrael. From us."

I feel the rage boiling inside me. My father—the one who's hated me, who's never seen me for what I am, what I could be—he's *terrified* of me. Terrified of Layla, of the power we'll wield together. *And now... he's going to try to destroy her.*

I close my eyes, the weight of it all sinking in, but I can't—I won't—let him take her. Not now. Not ever.

"I will destroy him," I mutter to myself, and Orcus echoes the thought, louder, sharper.

Lydia's gaze flicks to me, understanding flashing across her face. She knows what I'm thinking. *And she's right to be afraid.*

"Why didn't you choose Vassago?" I can't help but ask. The question just spills from me before I can stop it, but something in me needs to hear it. "I don't know how much you've studied on me, but I'm a failure compared to my brother." My voice rings with bitterness I can't disguise.

Lydia doesn't flinch, not a single muscle in her face betrays what I just said. "He's not as powerful," she starts, her tone matter-of-fact. "Yes, he is cunning, smarter than you—"

"Ouch," Orcus hisses in my mind, his voice dripping with sarcasm.

Lydia doesn't even acknowledge him, her eyes steady on me. "But his energy and power are *nothing* compared to yours. You've held back for so long because you wanted Hades to love you." Her eyes narrow just slightly, the words cutting deeper than they should. "Now you need to run forward, Azrael, because if you don't—my daughter will die, and I will *fucking kill you.*"

She says it with such a sweet smile, as if the threat didn't just settle like a lead weight in my chest. I blink, stunned, and it takes me a moment before I can respond.

"I'm just having a hard time processing all of this," I say, my voice strained as I look at Ashton, hoping for some sort of explanation. Instead, he just shrugs. He's always so damned calm, like nothing shakes him. It's both comforting and unnerving in equal measure.

How does he do that?

Lydia turns her attention back to me, her smile never wavering. "It's nice to meet you," Orcus hums in a sing-song voice, his tone dripping with faint amusement.

"Likewise, dear Orcus," she replies, the sweetness of her words almost unnerving. "I've heard so much about you. All good things."

"Of course," Orcus purrs in his usual, condescending way.

I lean back in my chair, the weight of everything crashing down on me. This woman—*this mother*—has been playing a dangerous game with her daughter's life, and now she's sitting here like she's already won. Like the world is hers to control.

"I just wish we could have met under better terms," she says softly, her tone turning a little more somber.

I don't know what to say to that. The weight of everything she's just revealed—*my father trying to kill me, trying to kill Layla, trying to control everything*—is too much for me to process all at once.

"So when were you planning on telling Layla she wasn't a mortal woman?" I ask, my voice softer now, though it still carries the undercurrent of frustration. I sit up in my chair, folding my arms over my chest, trying to rein in the swirling thoughts in my head. "You knew what she was, and you kept it from her?"

Lydia looks down for a moment, her fingers tightening into fists. "I didn't know how to bring it up without risking my husband finding out as well. I was planning to tell her when I found out Dash was going to propose." Her voice catches briefly, and she shakes her head. "Before Memetim worked a deal with him to kill Layla."

Memetim. I can't stop the growl that rises in my chest at the mention of her name.

"Is that so?" I hum, a dark amusement in my voice that doesn't match the growing fury inside me. "You knew Memetim was close to her? And you did… what? Nothing?"

I can feel Orcus bristling in my mind, just as enraged by this whole situation. *The fucking audacity.*

Lydia's expression falters for just a moment, and she looks down at her hands, as if regretting the actions she failed to take. "And you and Ashton failed to quarantine her once you threw her from Layla's mind. We all make rookie mistakes that lead to detrimental endings. All we can do now is try to right our wrongs."

I can feel Orcus' rage flare, and mine burns just as hot as he scoffs, *Rookie mistakes?*

What the hell does she think this is? A game? Layla's life is at stake here, and we've all been dragged into this mess because of mistakes made by people who should have known better. *Should have done better.*

I want to scream at her, to demand why she didn't do more, but before I can form the words, the door to the study bursts open with a force that makes the room feel like it's shaking.

"Azrael!" Layla's voice cuts through the chaos, sharp with panic, and my heart seizes at the sound. I whip around, rising from my seat, and see her standing there, blood smeared across her chest and face, her breath coming in desperate gasps from struggling to hold Exu's dead weight the best she can.

Chapter Forty-Five

Layla

Shadow of the Day - Linkin Park

The moment I step into the study, it's chaos. Ashton and Azrael rush towards me, grabbing Exu from my trembling grip. I barely register my mother moving swiftly across the room, emptying the desk to make space for them to lay Exu down. My mind is a fog of panic and disbelief.

"What the hell happened?" Ashton's voice cuts through the noise, but his calm tone only seems to heighten the rush of terror in my chest.

"Memetim!" I barely manage to choke out, my voice raw and broken. Tears sting my eyes, but I refuse to let them fall. I wasn't strong enough. I couldn't help Exu fight her—couldn't help him fend off the crows. The image of him shielding me, taking blow after blow from them, is burned into my memory.

"She came for Layla," Exu gasps, his breath shallow, strained. "The crows were trying to take Layla..." His words are punctuated with coughing, and he tries to sit up, but Ashton, always so steady, pushes him back down gently.

"Easy!" Azrael snaps, his voice sharp with authority, his gaze locked on Exu, as though he can will him to heal with his focus alone.

The blood pools onto the table, dripping onto the floor, and I can't stop staring at it. The blood, the crows—everything is tangled together in my mind, so intertwined that I feel sick. I want to run, to escape the images flooding me, but my feet feel like they're rooted to the floor. My breath is shallow, like a fish out of water, my chest tight with panic.

"Layla," my mother's voice cuts through the chaos, sharp and insistent. She's suddenly beside me, gripping my arm, and it startles me. "What happened?"

"I-" My voice cracks, and I swallow hard, trying to steady myself. "They came out of nowhere. The crows. Memetim—she..." The words catch in my throat, and suddenly, my knees give out. I sink to the floor, clutching my arms to my chest like they can hold me together.

My mother's hands are on me in an instant, one of her arms going around my shoulders as she kneels next to me, her voice a mix of urgency and gentleness. "What did she do, Layla? Tell me."

"She was relentless," I whisper, my voice barely audible, but the words feel like they're tearing through my chest as I say them. My gaze drifts to the blood beneath the desk, pooling like a reminder of what just happened. "Exu tried to protect me, but... there were so many of them. She... she said it was a message."

"A message?" Azrael's voice cuts through the heavy silence, calm, yet there's something dark in it, something that tells me he's not as unaffected as he seems. His hands are glowing, his focus never leaving Exu as he pours his energy into him, but I can see the tension in his jaw, the strain in his every movement.

"She said..." I hesitate, fighting to push past the images of the crows and their beady eyes, the memory of their blood-stained talons raking through flesh. "She said this was only the beginning. That it was retribution—for sending Vassago and Song to her lair."

The room falls silent, the weight of my words sinking into the air like a heavy fog. Azrael stares at Exu, his concentration unwavering as he heals him, but I can tell that the words hit him harder than he's letting on. Ashton's surprise is obvious now as he exchanges looks with my mother, his voice breaking the silence.

"Are they alive?" he asks, his tone low, like he doesn't want to hear the answer.

My mother leans forward, her brows furrowing as she takes in what I said. "How long have they been gone?"

"A week, nearly." Azrael's voice cracks slightly, his forehead beading with sweat as he presses harder into Exu's injuries. His hands pulse with light, but it's obvious the effort is taking everything he has. "They were supposed to go and retrieve Luca," he adds, as if the words are slipping from him without thought.

"Who is Luca?" My mother asks, her confusion evident.

"A werewolf barista," Ashton answers, his voice flat, like he's used to this madness by now.

"A... what?"

I glance between them, my mind still trying to make sense of it all.

"Look, can you shut the fuck up?" Azrael growls, his voice low and furious. "Ashton, *fucking help me!*"

Exu's body is limp, his breath shallow. The sight of him so lifeless is like a punch to the gut. My heart races. *I can't lose him. Azrael can't lose him.* Exu is more than just Azrael's friend—he's family, and if anything happens to him, I don't know what Azrael would do.

Exu slips into unconsciousness, his body still but for the faint rise and fall of his chest. My stomach plummets at the sight, my thoughts scattering like leaves in a storm.

"Is he going to be okay?" The words escape my mouth before I can stop them. I don't want to hear the answer. I don't want to know that Exu might be beyond saving, but the fear is choking me, making it impossible to stay silent.

But as the blood pools around us, the memory of the crows returns to me in full force. The blackbirds, their eyes glistening in the dim light, the sharp, cruel talons that shredded through Exu's body as he shielded me. Their screeching fills my ears, and I can almost feel their cold, dead gaze on me once more. Their cries echo in my mind, relentless, haunting.

I couldn't protect him. I couldn't stop them.

I clamp my hands over my ears, as though it will silence the memory, but it only makes it worse. *Their screams...* They'll never leave me. I can still hear Exu's voice, desperate, as he fought to keep them off of me. His blood staining the ground.

My heart pounds in my chest as I cling to the memory of his sacrifice, my mind swirling with terror and helplessness.

"He should be," Azrael mutters, wiping the sweat from his forehead. His focus never wavers from Exu's body, but his voice is tight with exhaustion. "We really need Vassago here to help, but at this point, we can only take turns so we don't exhaust ourselves." His eyes flick to me briefly, a silent question lingering between us. Then he looks at my mother, exchanging a look that speaks volumes.

But before we can say anything else, a scream shreds the tense atmosphere. *Sadie.*

"No!" The scream is raw, filled with panic and grief, and it cuts through the air like a knife.

Without a second thought, Ashton pushes past us, his expression already set with determination. I'm right behind him, my heart racing, but when we reach the living room, the sight that greets me makes my stomach drop, my breath catching in my throat.

Vassago is kneeling on the floor, battered and bruised, missing feathers, his usually immaculate appearance tarnished by the damage he's sustained. In his arms is a figure so small, so lifeless, that it sends a wave of nausea through me.

Song.

Her body is pale, her once vibrant form now lifeless in Vassago's arms. The room falls into a heavy, suffocating silence as Sadie's broken sobs fill the air.

Luca limps into the room next, his ear torn, his right arm in a sling. He looks every bit the warrior who's been through hell, and the guilt in his eyes is almost palpable.

"I'm so sorry, Sadie," Vassago says quietly, his voice strained with regret. "I tried to save her. I tried to protect her. There were far more beings waiting than we bargained for."

Sadie's cry is a raw, guttural sound, and I feel my own heart ache for her. She's barely holding herself together, her hands trembling as she clings to Song's lifeless body. "Song!" she screams, her voice breaking with the weight of her grief. "I told her to fucking stay. Why didn't she listen to me?" She howls in anguish, her body wracked with sobs.

Without a word, Ashton rushes to her, wrapping his arms around her waist, offering her the comfort that only he can. But his face is strained, his jaw clenched, and I can see the tear tracks cutting through the dirt and sweat on his face.

The sight of Song's body, once ethereal and filled with light, now lying so still on the living room floor, is too much for me to bear. My eyes sting with unshed tears, and I feel my throat tighten. This is real. This is happening.

Ashton rushes to Vassago and pushes him down causing Azrael and Luca to both ferociously growl his way. "Don't you *dare* fucking touch my brother like that again!" Azrael growls.

"It's time we fight back, Azrael," Ashton says, his voice broken with emotion. There's a fierceness in his words, a need to do something, to take action, but I can hear the pain in them too. He's drowning in it.

I turn to Azrael, watching the expression shift on his face. Something clicks in him, something I can't quite place, and he straightens, his jaw tightening as the weight of it all settles in. His gaze locks with Vassago's for a moment before he says, "You proposed a mating bond, and she accepted."

Vassago stands, wincing as he limps toward the liquor bar, and pours himself a shot of something dark. The glass clinks as he raises it to his lips, his eyes never leaving Azrael's as he takes the shot in one fluid motion.

"I hope your army is ready, Azrael," Vassago says, his voice low but steady, a stark contrast to the chaos around us. "You're going to need it, plus some. She has ancient supernaturals on her team." He pauses for a moment before downing another drink. "News on Drepane?"

The room is still. It feels wrong to be talking about war, about strategy, while Song's body lies cold and silent on the floor, but this is the reality we're in now.

Sadie's next scream shatters the fragile quiet, her voice full of raw emotion. "How the fuck can you guys sit around Song's dead body and casually talk about war?" She stands abruptly, her fists clenched at her sides. "Do you have *no* decency?" She points a shaking finger at Azrael, her eyes filled with rage and grief. "How fucking *dare* you not mourn her before we lose more lives to this. This is *your* fault."

Her words hit like a slap to the face, and for a moment, the room is so still that I can hear the blood rushing in my ears.

"*You* did all of this! If you never came into our lives, this wouldn't be happening!" Sadie's voice is trembling with fury, her face flushed with anger and heartbreak.

The words hang in the air like a weight, and Azrael's expression flickers for a moment. There's a brief flash of something—regret, guilt, or maybe even acceptance. But then, it's gone, buried beneath the mask he's perfected over the centuries. He doesn't answer her right away. He doesn't need to.

Instead, he turns to Vassago, his eyes hardening. "We don't have time for this. We need to focus. We'll mourn later."

I want to scream, to argue with him, but all I can do is stand there, my hands shaking as I clutch onto the edge of the doorway. The room feels like it's closing in on me, like I can't breathe. There's too much at stake. Too much happening all at once.

But for a brief, fleeting moment, I let myself feel the weight of it all. The loss, the pain, the fear.

This war is here, and it's costing us everything.

My mom moves swiftly behind Azrael, her presence a quiet but steady force. She reaches Sadie just as her knees buckle, catching her before she collapses to the floor in a heap of grief. "Baby girl," she says softly, her voice warm but firm. She strokes Sadie's hair, her fingers gentle but insistent. "This isn't Azrael's fault. Or Vassago's. This was Memetim, and *we will* avenge her death."

Sadie's sobs only intensify as my mother kisses her forehead, her voice filled with the quiet authority that I'd always relied on growing up. "I know this hurts. Song loved you *very* much, but she wouldn't want you to stand by crying. We need to stop Memetim, and we need to do it now."

Sadie doesn't respond right away, just curls into herself even more, the weight of it all crashing down on her. But my mother's words are like a balm to her aching soul. Slowly, very slowly, Sadie begins to calm, the sobs turning to shaky breaths ass he leans into my mom's embrace.

"We leave in the morning," Azrael announces, his voice cutting through the room like a blade. His words are final, resolute, like there's no room for discussion.

Before anyone can respond, he turns and walks out, leaving us in stunned silence.

"Layla," his voice calls from the hallway, and I turn just in time to see him glance over his shoulder. "You need to retrieve Drepane before war."

His words hit me like a ton of bricks. Retrieve Drepane. Before war. I swallow hard, a knot tightening in my throat. I don't even have time to process it—he's already gone.

The door clicks shut behind him, leaving us behind in the living room, standing in the aftermath of it all. The room feels suffocating now, the air thick with grief, anger, and confusion.

Sadie's cries still echo in the air, each one like a knife twisting in my chest. My mom continues to hold her, trying to soothe her as best as she can, but I know it's not enough. Nothing will ever be enough to ease the pain of losing someone so close, so loved.

Vassago is at the liquor bar, pouring drink after drink, trying to drown the pain. His gaze is distant, unfocused, and I know he's blaming himself for Song's death, just like everyone else in this room.

Luca is standing off to the side, looking dazed, his mind likely processing everything too slowly to make sense of it all. His broken arm and torn ear are barely noticeable in the chaos, but I know it's all he can think about right now.

Ashton is pacing, his fists clenched, his anger almost palpable. He's seething, barely holding it together. The tension in the air is suffocating, thick with emotions we're all trying to bury deep inside.

And then there's me. I stand there, my mind racing, my thoughts spinning, and all I can think about is how much I hate that we're here, in this mess, in this moment. Why is my mother even here? Why did she come to all of this?

Her presence is unsettling. She's been trying to keep things calm, trying to soothe everyone's pain, but I can't help but feel like this is all out of place.

I know why she's here. She's my mother. She wants to protect me, just like always. But I don't know how to feel about her being in the middle of this war.

I want to yell, to demand answers, to scream at Azrael for leaving me with this impossible task. Retrieve Drepane. *Before war.*

But all I can do is stand there, my fists clenched at my sides, my chest tight with unspoken fear and frustration.

Sadie's cries have softened now, and my mom continues to comfort her, speaking in soft, soothing tones. But all I can hear is the distant sound of my own breath, the weight of what's coming bearing down on me.

War. It's not just a word anymore. It's the future, it's the *reality*. And I don't know if I'm ready. I don't know if any of us are.

Chapter Forty-Six

Azrael

Bury Me Alive - We Are The Fallen

I retreat to my room in Ashton's home, the weight of everything crashing down around me. The door clicks shut quietly behind me, and I lean Orcus against the wall, my fingers trembling as I try to calm the storm inside of me. I can feel it, a burning fury rising from deep within, and I can't control it.

I roar, unleashing the pain I've been holding back for so long. The grief, the guilt, the anger—they all mix together in a violent explosion. I saved Song only to put her in more danger, to watch her die in front of us. How could I have let this happen? How could I not have known it was coming?

Something inside of me is growing—fiery hot, something that feels like it could tear me apart if I let it.

"You need to calm down, Azrael," Orcus hums from where he rests, his voice calm but firm. "You're going to release a secluding channel of energy if you keep this up, and right now is not the time for that."

"Yeah, well, what do you know about losing a comrade?" I snap at him, my voice hoarse with frustration. "You insufferable piece of metal. Do you even have the emotions to care about *anything* but yourself?"

"Azrael," Orcus replies, his tone a mixture of irritation and something else—something that almost sounds like concern. "I care or you wouldn't be standing before me. You and I both know that. Mourning over a lost loved one can bring the worst out of an individual. Don't let this be what breaks you."

I grit my teeth, my chest tight with emotion. "What if I lose Exu? How can I live with myself then?" The words break from me, raw and desperate, and I hate how weak they sound. Tears sting at the back of my throat, but I fight them back. I refuse to let them fall.

"Exu will be okay," Orcus hums, his tone surprisingly soothing. "Everything seems so scary and so unclear right now, but I assure you, Azrael, everything is working as it should. We will lose a lot more with the war. You need to prepare for that."

I swallow hard, trying to steady my breath, but his words don't ease the panic clawing at my chest. I know he's right, but the thought of losing someone like Exu—someone who's been by my side for so long—*it destroys me.*

A knock at the door interrupts my thoughts, and before I can say 'go away', the door creaks open. Layla peeks in, her eyes wide with concern, and a shy smile plays on her lips before she steps into the room and closes the door behind her.

"Are you okay?" she asks quietly, her voice laced with worry.

No. I'm not fucking okay. But I can't tell her that. She's already carrying so much weight, and I can't add to it. She leans on me for answers, for reassurance, and I can't afford to be the one who breaks. Not now. Not when she needs me.

"I'll survive," I say, forcing a small, reassuring smile, though I know it doesn't reach my eyes. "Are you okay?"

Layla shrugs, her gaze distant for a moment before she answers. "I could be better, but somehow I feel like losing Song is just going to be the tip of the iceberg. It's going to get worse from here on out, huh?"

"It will, Tiny Mouse," I say, the nickname slipping out before I can stop it. She hates it when I call her that, but it's the only thing that makes me feel like I'm still in control. It's my comfort, my way of holding onto something familiar in the chaos.

She looks at me, a faint smile tugging at her lips, but it doesn't quite reach her eyes. "So, Ashton brought my mother to the Underworld. Was that his risky plan this entire time?"

"Yes," I reply, watching her carefully, trying to gauge where this conversation is going.

Layla's lips quirk into a small, knowing smile. "Brings a whole new meaning to 'go to hell'. I used to tell her that all the time growing up, not knowing this was her world, was *my* world... I never even knew it all existed."

"She wants to help with the army. With the war." I walk over to the small red velvet loveseat in the corner of the room and sit down, my body heavy with exhaustion. Layla follows me, sitting at the foot of the bed, her gaze fixed on me with a mixture of curiosity and concern.

"And you're going to let her?" she asks, her voice quieter now, the weight of her words hanging in the air between us.

"I'd be stupid if I turned down her help," I answer, leaning back and turning slightly so I can see her face. I try to keep my tone light, but the weight of everything is pressing down on me, making it hard to keep my composure.

Layla's brow furrows as she looks at me. "What if something happens to her?"

I don't answer right away. What if something happens to her? The thought is enough to send a chill down my spine. I can't protect everyone, no matter how hard I try. "We will try to keep that from happening," I finally say, my voice low. I don't promise anything because I can't. Not in a world like this.

Mortals. Their thoughts are hard to retrain and comfort, Orcus hums through my mind, his voice laced with a strange kind of amusement.

Layla's voice pulls me back to the conversation. "What did you mean when you said Ashton and Sadie have a mating bond?"

I blink, startled by her question. I hadn't expected that. "I haven't asked him yet, but I can tell it's happened."

"How?"

"He's attuned with her emotions," I explain, shifting slightly to look at her more fully. "It's a fairly new bond. They're still figuring out how to feel their own emotions, but right now, if Sadie is sad, Ashton will feel sad. The bond is like that. But there are numerous perks."

"Like?" Layla presses, her curiosity piqued.

I pause for a moment, considering how much I want to tell her. "He can track her. He'll always know where she is. They can communicate telepathically, no matter where they are, no matter the distance. They'll always know the other is safe. Alive." I smile softly, my gaze softening as I think of Ashton and Sadie. "Your friend is safe and happy. That's all that matters right now, right?"

Layla nods, but there's something else in her eyes, a question lingering beneath the surface. "If I accept our mating bond, would that be a comfort we would have?"

The question hits me like a bolt of lightning, and for a moment, I don't know how to respond. Something in my chest drops, and I find myself at a loss for words. I'm not ready for this. I don't know if I'm ready for this.

"Yeah," I reply softly, my voice barely above a whisper. "I think it would be."

She stares at me for a long moment, and I feel her gaze weighing on me, measuring me, wondering if this is the right choice.

"How would one accept the mating bond?" Her voice is quiet, but there's a certainty there, as if she's already made up her mind.

I don't know how to explain this to her. "Just by accepting me for who I truly am..." My words trail off, and I feel an uncomfortable tightness in my chest. "Sealed with..."

"Sex," Orcus hums through the air, his voice laced with dark amusement. "By accepting Azrael and me as the bond affects me as well."

Layla's cheeks flush slightly, but she doesn't shy away. "Is that all it takes?" she asks, her voice barely above a whisper.

I look at her, my breath catching in my throat. I don't have an answer. Not one that feels like enough.

For a moment, there's nothing but silence between us. But it's not uncomfortable. It's the kind of silence where everything seems to hang in the air, a suspended breath. Waiting.

She blinked at Orcus, surprised by his words.

"I have to have sex with a scythe?" she asked, her voice a mixture of disbelief and confusion.

"Well, Sadie had to have sex with—" Orcus started, but I quickly cut him off with a sharp cough. I didn't even want to think about that. The idea of Ashton and Sadie... the thought alone made me uncomfortable—itchy, even.

"Azrael, why do you hide things like this from me?" She looked at me, her emerald eyes full of questions. "Why don't you just tell me everything?"

I rubbed the back of my neck, avoiding her gaze for a moment. "Because I want to protect you," I said quietly, my voice softening. "I want to shield you from the darkness, from things I know will hurt you. I don't want to scare you away."

She took a deep breath, then looked at me with a quiet understanding that made my chest tighten. "I have nowhere to run, Azrael. I'm already so deep in this. It's like my future was set in motion for me... before I even knew it."

I sighed, my fingers running through my hair as I thought of what to say. "You talked to your mother, didn't you?"

Her gaze was steady, no surprise in her voice. "You didn't tell me anything."

"I didn't want to overwhelm you," I muttered, unable to meet her eyes. "I was still learning everything myself before you came barging in with Exu." I tried to laugh, but it came out weak, forced.

She was silent for a moment, her expression softening as she processed what I said. Finally, she spoke, her voice quiet but steady. "Is Exu going to be okay?"

Her question hit me harder than I expected. I wanted to reassure her, but I had no guarantees. I couldn't lie to her. Before I could answer, Orcus' voice cut through the silence.

"He'll be fine, Layla," Orcus said, a surprising warmth in his tone.

Layla nodded slowly, accepting his words, though I could see the doubt lingering in her eyes. She was trying to hold it together, but I could feel the weight of everything pressing on her. I wanted to take it all away—make her world lighter, safer—but I couldn't. Not yet.

After a moment of silence, Layla spoke again, her voice barely above a whisper. "I want to accept the bond, Azrael... but I'm scared about how it will change everything. What if I'm not ready?"

I was stunned. She was willing to consider this, to accept a bond she barely understood, despite all the fear and uncertainty. In that moment, I felt an overwhelming rush of affection for her—this beautiful, brave woman who, despite everything, was willing to step into the unknown with me.

I took a slow step toward her, my hand reaching for Orcus, gently laying him beside her on the bed. I stayed close, my eyes never leaving hers. "We'll take it slow. At your pace. Whenever you're ready, Tiny Mouse."

Her scent—vanilla, fear, and something deeper...lust—filled the air around us. It made my mind race, and my body reacted instinctively. This was about trust, about her accepting everything that came with me and with Orcus.

"Whenever you're ready," I whispered again, my voice low and steady, my gaze locked onto hers. "We'll move at your pace."

Her breath hitched, pupils dilated, and for a moment, hesitation flickered in her eyes—before it melted into something darker, something hungry. She dragged her gaze over me, slow and deliberate, lingering where my need for her was most obvious. Heat simmered between us, thick and electric, and when she met my eyes again, the silent challenge there unraveled what little restraint I had left.

Leaning in, I brushed my lips along the delicate curve of her neck, my hands trailing down her sides before slipping beneath the hem of her shirt. The fabric lifted easily, and as it hit the floor, I traced my mouth lower, pressing kisses to the soft swell of her breasts. A shiver rippled through her, and she exhaled a quiet, needy sound that sent fire straight through me.

Her fingers fumbled at my belt, urgency threading through every touch, while I hooked my thumbs into the waistband of her sweatpants and panties, dragging them down in one swift motion. Impatience burned through me—I needed her, now.

She tugs my pants down, and the moment I'm free, her fingers curl around me, her touch warm and deliberate. Before I can position her, she leans in, wrapping her lips around me with a slow, agonizing heat that steals the breath from my lungs. A shudder wracks through me as her tongue glides from tip to base, teasing, tasting, before she takes me back into the wet heat of her mouth, sucking with a pressure that has my head tilting back.

A groan escapes me, raw and unfiltered. "Fuck, Mouse... that feels so fucking good." My eyes flutter shut, every nerve in my body drawn tight, threatening to unravel under her touch. But then—instinct kicks in. The bond.

My fingers tangle in her hair as I pull her away, the loss of her mouth making my pulse hammer. She barely has time to react before I lift her, tossing her onto the center of the bed with effortless strength. The way she lands—breathless, wide-eyed, waiting—sends a wicked thrill through me.

I reach for Orcus, my fingers wrapping around his hilt as I lift him, the room's dim light catching along the curve of his blade. His voice hums in my mind, ever the amused spectator.

I look down at my Tiny Mouse, laid out before me, her breath coming in soft, uneven pants. She parts her legs without hesitation, offering herself fully, and the sight alone has my pulse hammering. She's drenched, slick with need, and every part of me aches to claim her.

Dragging my fingers through her warmth, I stroke along her folds, gathering the proof of her desire before bringing them to my lips. The taste of her coats my tongue—sweet, intoxicating, entirely her.

A low growl vibrates in my chest as I settle between her thighs, pressing a kiss to the soft skin there before diving in, licking my way from her entrance to the swollen bundle of nerves that has her hips jerking in response. I catch it between my teeth, teasing, before sucking deep enough to pull a broken moan from her lips.

For a fleeting second, I consider muffling her, pressing my hand over her mouth to keep her quiet—but no. Not this time. This time, I want every soul in this house to hear her. To hear that she's mine. That she's finally accepted me.

To hear that their Queen is being worshipped.

"Take her, Azrael," I hear Orcus nearly moan, "Mark her."

I pull back, wiping my mouth with the back of my hand, savoring the taste of her as I grip Orcus with the other. His presence hums in the air, a silent observer to the claim I'm about to make.

With deliberate slowness, I drag the flat of his blade along the inside of her thigh, watching as a shiver ripples through her. The contrast of cool steel against heated skin makes her breath hitch, her body caught between anticipation and surrender.

I trail the edge along her folds—not enough to break skin, just enough to make her gasp, to make her nerves spark with pleasure laced with something sharper. A test. A tease. The moment the tip of the blade grazes her clit, she jolts, a whimper slipping past her lips as her fingers tighten in the sheets.

"You're trembling, Tiny Mouse. Is it from pleasure... or anticipation?" Orcus utters.

My grip shifts, turning Orcus so that the hilt now faces her. With my free hand, I tease her, circling her clit with slow, measured strokes before slipping two fingers inside. Her body clenches around them, desperate, needy. I start slow, savoring the way she writhes beneath me, before quickening my pace, curling my fingers just right—searching for the spot that will send her over the edge.

Her moans build, coming faster, breathless and pleading, her body tightening around me as the pleasure coils, ready to snap. I add a third finger, pushing her higher, drawing her out, watching as she trembles beneath my touch.

Lowering my head, I taste the evidence of her pleasure, letting my tongue linger before finally positioning Orcus' hilt at her entrance. I move it against her, slow, controlled, watching her face for any sign of discomfort—ready to stop if she so much as flinches.

"Does that feel good, baby girl?" My voice is thick, rough with need.

She meets my gaze, eyes hazy with pleasure, and nods.

As I push him deeper, a sharp, breathless moan tears from her throat, echoing off the walls, raw and unrestrained. Her legs fly open wider, her body arching in surrender as I hover over her, watching, savoring the way she unravels beneath me.

"She's holding onto me like she never wants to let go. Do you think she likes me better, Reaper?" Orcus' dark chuckle fills the rooms.

Orcus vibrates within her, the wicked hum pulsing against her, teasing, tormenting. A strangled gasp escapes her lips, and I swallow it with a kiss, capturing her moans as I drag my tongue against hers. She meets me with urgency, raking her tongue along my teeth before plunging deeper, taking what she needs.

"You're dripping all over me, girl. Such a good little thing, making a mess like this." His voice lingers in the moment.

I trail my lips down the curve of her throat, tasting her, teasing her with playful nips that have her body trembling beneath me.

"If you don't put her on her back and fuck her properly, I just might."

A growl rumbles in my chest as I rip Orcus away, tossing him onto the bed beside us. I can't wait. I won't. The need inside me is too sharp, too consuming. Orcus is right. I need to be inside her now.

My hand finds my cock, hard and aching, and with a single thrust, I sink into her—hot, tight, perfect. A strangled curse rips from my throat as she clenches around me, her body gripping me so fiercely I nearly lose control right then and there.

No. Not yet.

I grit my teeth, gripping her hips to keep myself grounded, to keep from giving in too soon. But she feels too good, too right.

"Don't hold back, Reaper. Give her everything you got."

I feel it—the bond between us snapping into place, not just forming but strengthening with each thrust, each breath, each shared moment of pleasure. It's more than a connection; it's a force, a pull so strong it threatens to consume me entirely.

Her arms tighten around my neck, her legs lock around my waist, dragging me closer, as if she's trying to merge us into one. And in a way, we already are.

Metaphorical strings weave between us, binding our souls. A surge of energy rushes through my veins, a power I've never experienced before. I feel her—her thoughts, her memories, her emotions flooding into me, bare and unguarded. I hear her, not in words, but in sensations, in desperate, unspoken pleas.

Rub my clit.

I obey.

My fingers find that sensitive bundle of nerves, working her in sync with my thrusts, pushing her higher, pulling her apart. She shatters around me, and as she clenches down, as her cries fill the air, something *clicks*.

I see her.

Not just the woman beneath me, not just my mate—but *everything* she is, everything she was ever meant to be.

Her bloodline is chaos and creation. A perfect storm of supernatural genetics, interwoven into something greater. Fate. Fortune. Reaper. Reincarnation. *Destiny.* A being beyond comprehension, beyond limitation.

And she is *mine*.

With one final thrust, I surrender, spilling into her as she wrings every last drop from me, her body milking me in perfect rhythm. The world fades into a haze of ecstasy, but the weight of what just happened lingers, settling into my bones.

I hover above her, breathless, pressing my forehead against hers as my gaze drifts down to where our fingers remain entwined.

A mark begins to take shape on our skin, inked by something beyond mortal comprehension—a supernatural binding, a declaration that cannot be undone.

Matching thorn-laced roses bloom along our fingers, a single stem twining around us like a vow. Red as blood, dark as fate, glistening with sweat, scented with sex.

I brush my lips against her temple, my voice a whisper against her skin.

"The Queen has arrived."

Layla doesn't belong to me.

I belong to *her*.

We *both* do.

Chapter Forty-Seven

Azrael

I stare across the room at the throne—my throne. Hades sits upon it, watching me, his cold gaze a mirror of the disdain he's always had for me. I've had enough of this, enough of him. This is the last time we'll face each other.

I step forward, the weight of Orcus' handle grounding me, as it always does. The scythe's presence is a constant reminder of what I am, what I've become.

"Well, well," Hades drawls, his voice rumbling like distant thunder. "The prodigal son finally returns. I've been waiting for you to come crawling back to give me updates."

I meet his gaze without flinching. "Crawling? I must've missed the part where I ever needed you. I'm done with you, old man."

His eyes flash, narrowing to slits. "Watch your tongue, boy. I still hold power over you. You would do well to remember that."

I step closer, leaning on Orcus for a moment. "You don't hold power over me. Not anymore."

Orcus hums, pleased.

I grip the scythe tighter, the words cold and cutting. "I'm not one of your pawns. I don't need your approval. You're not my ruler. You never were."

For a moment, the air between us crackles with tension, the silence thick and oppressive. Hades rises slowly from the throne, looming over me, his anger palpable.

"You dare speak to me like this?" he growls, his voice a low rumble that shakes the ground beneath our feet. "After everything I've done for you—everything I've sacrificed—"

I cut him off before he can finish, my voice low but firm. "Sacrifices? You didn't do anything for me. You used me, you beat me, lied to me... Father, you used me, just like you've used everyone else. And I'm done being your tool."

The air grows colder, the very walls of the room seeming to pulse with his fury. Hades clenches his fists, and for a moment, I think he might lash out. But I stand my ground, the only sound in the room the faint hum of Orcus.

"You're nothing without me," he spits, his eyes blazing. "You think you can just walk away and become your own man? You're my son, Azrael. And you will always be mine."

I feel Orcus stir, as though he's preparing to strike, but I keep my focus on Hades. My voice is steady, resolute. "Not anymore. After the war with Memetim, I'm not just taking my throne—I'm taking this war to you, father. I'm going to rid the Underworld of your tyranny."

Hades steps forward, his fury rising. The temperature drops, and I can feel the chill of his rage seeping into my bones. "War will be a fitting end for you."

I don't flinch. I don't even blink. My smile is dark, the edge of it cutting like a razor. "If you want war, father, then war is what you'll get. But know this: I'm no longer fighting for you. I'm fighting for Layla and me—our future. You've had your time, Hades. The throne, the power, the games. But not anymore. I'm taking what's mine."

His eyes widen, realization flickering across his features. "Layla," he murmurs, the word slipping from his lips with an undertone of disbelief. His gaze sharpens, narrowing as his fury turns to something darker, more personal. "You've secured the bond with her."

I don't respond, but the truth hangs in the air, thick and undeniable.

Hades sneers, his lips curling into something cruel, something malevolent. "Then you'll lose, just like everyone else who's ever defied me."

I chuckle, the sound bitter and hollow. "We'll see, won't we?"

I turn on my heel, stepping away from him and toward the door. Hades calls out, but I don't turn back. I don't need to. The decision has been made.

He thinks he can still control me, I think as I step into the hall, the doors swinging shut behind me. But I've made my choice. This ends now. His throne belongs to Layla and me. I will retrieve her throne.

Orcus hums softly, his voice laced with amusement. *I've always said you'd be the death of him, Az. And now, I get to watch it happen. How delightful.*

I let out a soft, bitter laugh. I'm done with him.

Chapter Forty-Eight

Layla

Centuries - Fall Out Boy

I nod to the Grim Court as we pass them, making our way down the long hall toward Drepane's quarters. Each step feels heavier as I walk beside Azrael in his true form. A surge of emotions rushes through me from our bond thread, and I can't help but feel a flutter in my chest. This male—this terrifyingly powerful, unwavering, fierce male—is mine now, for all eternity.

Pride. Happiness. But beneath it all, there's a sharp, unfamiliar fear—his fear—not mine. The overwhelming torrent of emotions swirls inside me, and for a moment, I feel disoriented, like I'm standing on the edge of something huge. Something that could swallow me whole if I'm not careful. But I also feel his love, raw and deep, and that anchors me.

Through the bond, I can sense his unease, his worries. He's terrified—terrified of losing me, of standing before his father and what it might cost him. His father's hatred burns through as a dark, cold anger, one that chills my soul. My heart clenches in response. The bond connects us on a level deeper than I could have imagined, and in moments like this, I can feel everything—his rage, his fear, his love, his guilt. All of it.

I try to shake off the unease, focusing instead on the path ahead. The beings around us—they used to feel so distant, like strangers in a strange world. But now, they're mine. These are my beings now. My court. The Grims bow their heads as we pass, some more respectfully than others. Lady Morvina still walks around with a stick up her ass, but even she can't help but acknowledge me now.

Azrael walks beside me, lost in thought as always. I know he doesn't sleep, he doesn't rest, and yet, he was there beside me—holding me through the night, whispering soft, reassuring words while I slept, his fingers gently playing with my hair. For the first time since I arrived here, I felt a sense of safety that I never thought I would experience. A fleeting peace.

I belong here now.

Not just as "Layla Simmons," the girl who was thrust into this world by fate, but as *Layla*, the wielder of Drepane, the Queen of the Underworld. The weight of it presses on me. I don't yet fully understand the responsibility that comes with this, but I will. I have to.

I haven't even completed the *Hierarchy of the Underworld* yet, still learning the intricacies of the world I'm now a part of. But I'll learn. And soon, I'll be ready to rule beside Azrael. I can feel it in my bones.

Azrael reaches out and touches the doorknob to Drepane's room. With a soft click, the door opens.

"Hello, young one," Drepane's voice echoes through the room.

"Hello, Drepane," I answer, my voice steady despite the anticipation bubbling inside me.

"What do I owe the pleasure of this meeting?" he asks, his tone light but there's an edge of curiosity beneath it.

"Memetim killed an angel," I state, my words sharp. His aura flares with anger at the mention of her name. "It's time we act."

His energy shifts, and I can feel his intense displeasure. "Understood... but you must know, once we bond, the pain will be immense. I will shift, find my place among you and Azrael and Orcus, and entwine my lifeline with yours. You're freshly mated, so this will be painful. Congratulations, Queen of the Underworld."

"Thank you," I murmur, my throat tight with emotion. "But I can't lose anyone else. Not after everything."

I glance at Azrael, and I can feel the tug of his emotions through the bond. His pain—sharp, raw, and laced with guilt. His grief over Song's death is consuming him, and the guilt cuts even deeper. He let her go on a mission, sent her into danger without knowing what awaited her, without preparing for it. He blames himself for her death.

I reach for his hand, my fingers closing around his. He stiffens at first, but then his grip tightens, grounding both of us in this moment. I don't speak, but my touch says everything. *I see you. I am here. We will get through this. Together.*

Drepane's voice calls me back to the present. "Come here, my Queen," he hums, his tone gentle but firm.

I release Azrael's hand, taking a slow, steady step toward Drepane. The sound of my heels clicking against the marble floor echoes in the vast room, a rhythmic pattern that steadies my nerves. The room is beautiful—roses and green ivy adorn the walls, creating a contrast of life in this otherwise dark place. I reach out for Drepane's diamond-encrusted handle, and the moment my fingers brush against it, a jolt of electricity shoots through me.

Pain. Pleasure. Power.

The energy courses through my body, and I scream as my whole being is set alight. The sensation is overwhelming—intense and wild, like I'm being torn apart and rebuilt all at once. My body freezes, then heats up. Purple energy pours from every pore, filling the air with a vibrant, pulsing aura. My head spins with the force of it, and I can feel my life bond stretching, tugging, pulling in new threads.

Azrael's presence at my side flares with concern, his worry sharp through the bond. I know he's feeling this, feeling my pain, but I don't pull away. I can't.

Drepane is with me, keeping me steady, tethered. I can feel the connection growing stronger, the bond forming between us—between *me* and the sickle I now wield.

As the pain begins to recede, I open my eyes, and for the first time, everything around me feels *alive*—alive in a way I've never felt before. I glance down at myself and realize—I've shifted. My true form is here, glowing, radiant. My body pulses with purple energy, the same energy that now flows through Drepane. *We are one.*

I turn to look at Azrael, and the awe in his eyes takes my breath away. His jaw hangs open, and his pride—his pride is overwhelming. The bond thread swells with it. He's proud of me. Orcus is proud of me.

I used to doubt myself. I used to wonder if I was worthy of all this. But now... I know. I'm worthy.

I am the sickle-bearing Queen of Reapers. The Queen of the Underworld. Daughter of a mortal and the Hidden Succubus. Fated mate of Azrael, Prince of Death.

And Memetim will pay for what she's done to me. To all of us.

"Are you ready, my Queen?" Drepane's voice hums through the air, and I can feel the weight of the war ahead. "It is an honor to finally serve someone worth serving."

"Thank you," I reply, my voice a little shaky as my body still pulses with the aftershock of the bond.

Azrael reaches for my hand, pulling me closer. The weight of the task ahead is heavy, but I'm not afraid. With Azrael by my side, with Drepane at my back, I will face whatever comes.

We turn to leave the room, our weapons in hand—sentient, deadly, and unyielding.

"This is a plot twist, one Memetim wasn't banking on," Orcus vibrates in my mind, his voice full of amusement. "Memetim today. Hades tomorrow. Our throne by Friday... just in time to enjoy the weekend."

I can't help but smile, my heart lightening despite everything. Azrael squeezes my hand, and I know—this war? This is ours to win.

Chapter Forty-Nine

Azrael

Warriors - Imagine Dragons

"How old are you?" Orcus asks, breaking the silence that's settled around us.

"So old, I forgot," Drepane replies nonchalantly, his tone laced with a touch of sarcasm.

I feel the weight of the moment settle over me as I glance at Layla beside me. It seems like peace and quiet are things we can't afford anymore. Now that we've got two talking weapons to deal with—one a smartass and the other who acts like he'd rather be left alone—our days of calm are over.

"It's not that I don't want to be bothered," Drepane continues, his voice like a low hum vibrating in my skull, "I'm saving all my energy for war. How many prisoners are we going against?"

"972," I reply without missing a beat, my eyes scanning the battle plans laid out on the desk in front of me.

"That's some numbers." Drepane's tone sharpens, his curiosity piqued. "A lot of hybrids and ancients? A few shifters?"

"All of the above," I say, rubbing a hand over my face as I stare at the list of soldiers I've recruited. It's a daunting task, even for someone like me. "It's a diverse army. And I'm not sure we have enough to handle just the ancients alone."

"How many?" Drepane presses.

"Roughly 1100," I sigh, the weight of it all sinking deeper into my chest.

"Far from enough," Drepane mutters. The weight of his words is not lost on me. He's right. We're up against more ancients than I'd like to admit.

I glance at Layla, who stands beside me, her calm demeanor almost unnerving. I know better than to trust the stillness on her face. Through the bond, I can feel the tremors of uncertainty running through her, but she hides it well. She's trying to keep me steady, to keep us both from spiraling into panic. But I have a bad feeling about this war. A gut instinct that's never steered me wrong before.

"Is that counting the Grim animals?" Drepane hums, his curiosity still growing.

"Not many Grim beast keepers these days," I answer, my tone a little darker than usual, "But, yes. Including Cerberus."

I place the paper down on the desk with a heavy sigh. My thoughts are a tangled mess, but I push them aside as Vassago enters the room, his presence filling the space like a storm on the horizon.

He looks worse for wear, but today, he's sharper than he's been in weeks. His gaze locks onto Layla with an almost reverent bow of his head before he turns to face Drepane, his eyes narrowing slightly.

"Ashton has my briefing of the territory. He will be in there shortly. I managed to find Angels who didn't have charges currently to join. They don't mind leading us into war." He glances at Drepane. "She always goes above expectations, huh?" Vassago's voice is soft, but there's an edge to it as he stares at Drepane. "We have Drepane fighting alongside us now."

Drepane's aura ripples in response, a hum of energy that seems to reach into every corner of the room. "My power is your power. My energy is hers," he says, his words carrying an undercurrent of promise.

Layla raises an eyebrow, her voice cautious. "What does that mean?"

"It means…" Vassago steps forward, his tone serious as he meets her gaze. "You will never be tired during the fight. He will consistently replenish you while raising the dead and opening the Empty for his chosen past wielders to fight with us. You'll never run out of strength. That's the price of having him on our side."

Layla's eyes flicker with understanding, but I can see the questions still swirling behind them. Before she can ask more, Vassago turns to leave, giving a final, quiet thanks to Drepane.

"Thank you, Drepane," Vassago says, his voice soft with gratitude.

Drepane hums in response, his energy pulsing gently in the room. "I do what is necessary."

I turn back to the papers, my fingers brushing over them as I try to gather my thoughts. "So, then our numbers look decent?" I ask, my voice carrying an air of skepticism I can't quite shake.

"Might be just enough to pull it off," Vassago says as he exits, his words carrying an edge of uncertainty, even though he tries to mask it.

"Is 'just enough' good enough?" Layla's question hangs in the air, heavy with doubt.

"We'll see," Orcus chimes in from the side, his voice vibrating with the same unease I feel. His sarcasm doesn't do much to lighten the mood. If anything, it only adds to the growing tension in the room.

I gather the paperwork into a neat stack, the weight of it pressing down on my shoulders like a boulder. "We'll see," I repeat, my voice low and steady, though the pit in my stomach tells me otherwise.

I'm not sure if 'just enough' will ever be enough. But I have no choice but to push forward.

"Let's head to the dining room," I say finally, the words heavy with finality. Ashton's briefing waits for us, and there's no time to waste. The army is gathering, and we need to be ready.

But I can't shake this feeling of doom. This sense that something's off. That maybe, just maybe, no matter how hard we try, we're still not ready for what's coming.

Walking into the dining room, the overwhelming smell of breakfast and s'mores coffee instantly hits me.

Fuck, I'm so relieved Luca is back home and safe. He's got a few cuts and scrapes left to heal, but overall, he's in one piece. That's all that matters.

"I'm fighting with you," Luca announces as he places two plates of food on the table—one for Layla, one for me.

I can't help but scoff. "You aren't trained," I mutter as I sink into the chair, reaching for the coffee that's already been prepared for me.

Luca's eyes flash with anger, his jaw tightening as he crosses his arms over his chest. "Layla is barely trained and she's your mate. How is it you'll allow her to fight but not me?" His voice is low, but the underlying frustration is clear.

I take a sip of my coffee, the warmth doing little to settle the cold unease swirling in my gut. "Because werewolves have no power. No match. No chance at fighting the supernaturals that inhabit the Underworld." My voice sharpens, more out of necessity than anger. "If you want to chance that, Luca, then so be it. But Layla belongs here. You do not."

I see the sting from my words land, and it hits harder than I expected. I can feel his pain seeping through the bond, and I immediately regret being so harsh, but I won't apologize.

"I'm only trying to protect who I can," I mutter, my gaze faltering for a moment before meeting his again. "I apologize."

Luca turns to Layla, and for a brief second, I see the flicker of something soft in his eyes—a kind of hurt that he's trying to hide. Layla drops her head, avoiding his gaze.

Luca's jaw clenches, his fists curling at his sides. "So, that's it? I'm useless to you?"

"No," I say sharply, my tone hard and unforgiving. I see him flinch, and it only makes my words hit harder. "You're not useless. You're just…" I hesitate. The next part is harder to say than I'd like to admit. "You're mortal in a way they will exploit. If something happens to you down there, I can't save you. You'd be gone, and I…" My voice trails off, the words lodging themselves in my throat like a stone.

"You what?" Luca presses, stepping closer now. The intensity in his eyes is unmistakable. "You what, Azrael? Don't stop now. Just fucking say. You don't trust your life with me."

I swallow hard, my chest tightening at the weight of what I'm about to say. "I can't lose you," I admit, the words barely escaping my lips. My voice is a whisper, but it carries all the weight of the fear I can't escape. "I trust you, Luca, but this isn't about trust. It's about protecting the people who matter to me. And that includes you."

I pause, trying to gather my thoughts, but the emotions are crashing over me. "We almost lost you once. I don't want to go through that fear again. I can't."

The room falls into an unbearable silence, the air thick with unspoken words. Luca doesn't respond at first. His anger is still there, simmering, but now there's something else in his eyes—something I can't quite place.

"You're unbelievable." Luca mutters, shaking his head in disbelief. "You think keeping me out of the fight is going to protect me? If this war goes south, no one is safe. Not me, not you, not Layla. I'd rather die fighting than sit on the sidelines while everyone else risks their lives."

His words strike deeper than I thought they would. A cold sense of helplessness creeps into my chest, but I refuse to show it. I hold his gaze, the intensity of the moment burning between us.

"And I'd rather you hate me than see you dead," I say, my voice thick with emotion. "Do you understand?"

Luca stares at me, his chest rising and falling with the force of his emotions. He takes a step back, his fists unclenching, but there's no relief in the tension that lingers in the air.

Slowly, he turns to Layla, who remains silent at the table, her shoulders tense under the weight of the conversation. Her head is still bowed, but I know she's listening—she always listens, even when she doesn't speak.

"Do you agree with him?" Luca asks, his voice quieter now. The anger has faded, replaced by a vulnerability I wasn't expecting.

Layla's gaze flickers up, and she meets his eyes, her expression softening just a fraction. "I think he's trying to protect you," she says softly, her voice gentle yet firm. "Even if it doesn't feel that way."

Luca's face tightens, and he lets out a bitter laugh that echoes in the stillness of the room. "Protect me. Right." He shakes his head, glancing back at me, his expression unreadable now. "You're wrong about one thing, Azrael. I do belong here. Whether you like it or not."

Without another word, he turns on his heel and storms out of the room, the door slamming behind him with a finality that hangs heavy in the air.

The silence that follows is deafening.

I don't know what to say. I don't know if there's anything I can say. Luca's anger still lingers, but it's no longer aimed solely at me. It's a wild, untamed thing, and I don't know how to tame it.

I glance at Layla, who is still quiet, her gaze fixed on the empty space where Luca stood just moments ago. She says nothing, but I can feel the uncertainty in the bond, the pull of her emotions swirling between us. She's trying to make sense of everything, just like I am.

The door doesn't even have time to rest on its hinges before Ashton strides through, Vassago right behind him. "Family drama?" Ashton asks, raising an eyebrow.

"No." I take another slow sip of my coffee, pretending not to feel the lingering tension in the room.

"Ah, understood." Ashton leans against the edge of the table, his usual calm demeanor giving way to something more focused. He takes a seat at the end of the dining table, his posture commanding as he clasps his hands together.

Sadie enters shortly after, plopping down next to him with a smile, though it doesn't reach her eyes.

"So what we know so far," Ashton begins, eyes scanning each of us, "is that Memetim's forces are stationed at the Gates of Tartarus."

"The Gates of Tartarus?" Layla asks, brow furrowing in confusion.

"It guards the prison." Drepane mumbles, his voice low and almost sing-song in its rhythm. "Now, hush, young one."

Ashton shoots a side-eye at Drepane but doesn't address him directly. "They've fortified the surrounding area. Looks like they went back for Vassago, found out we already had him, and decided to set up shop there instead. Vassago reported seeing an army of demons, shades, and other ancient supernaturals loyal to Memetim—besides her crows. They're focused on two things: killing Layla and capturing Azrael. And... Orcus."

The room falls silent. Orcus hums faintly against the chair where I've leaned him. The sound is soft but unmistakably filled with a weight that presses down on all of us.

"They're after Azrael and Orcus?" Layla asks, her tone too calm, like she's already processed the threat. She's barely flinching at the idea they want to kill her; it's all about me and the scythe.

"They are," Ashton confirms. "Memetim is going to attempt a ritual to sever Orcus from Azrael. If they succeed, they won't just take the scythe—they'll control the balance of life and death itself."

"She can try," Orcus rumbles, his voice vibrating through the floor. "But she won't succeed. I am bound to Azrael. No one else can wield me. If Azrael doesn't exist, neither will I."

The weight of his words hangs in the air for a moment. My chest tightens at the thought of that kind of disruption, but Orcus' presence, as usual, calms me just enough to keep my focus.

"They don't know about Drepane yet," Vassago says, his voice grave. "The crows haven't returned since the attack on Layla and Exu. He's the element of surprise."

My eyes move to the sentient sickle resting at Layla's side, a faint pulse of energy radiating from it. I can almost feel Drepane's awareness stirring, responding to the mention of his name. Layla's fingers tighten nervously in her lap, but she says nothing.

"If the ritual progresses and Orcus' bond weakens," Vassago continues, "Drepane could disrupt the entire process."

Layla's hand brushes mine under the table, and it's like a grounding cord snaps into place between us. Her touch is warm, calming, even as the rest of me churns with a mix of emotions. I think I've flooded the bond thread, and I can feel her trying to carry some of it.

"Do you think we can pull this off?" Her voice is low, filled with a mixture of fear and determination that threads its way into mine.

I meet her eyes and see the same question reflected there. The weight of it all presses heavily against my chest, but I force myself to stay steady. I know what this is: the calm before the storm.

"Drepane chose you for a reason," I say, my voice firm, despite the unease gnawing at me. "I believe you can do this."

Ashton breaks into the conversation again, stepping forward with a plan. "We'll split into two teams. Azrael, Layla, and Vassago will infiltrate the stronghold to stop the ritual. The rest of us will engage the enemy at the gates and draw some of their forces away."

His gaze shifts to Sadie, then back to me. "Sadie will stay behind with Luca. I can't risk anything happening to her—she isn't like Layla. She's mortal through and through. I'll make sure the house is protected. Enough protection spells to keep them safe."

I nod, understanding the necessity of the decision.

"I understand completely," I say, my voice tight with the gravity of what's to come.

The silence in the room deepens as we all process Ashton's plan. There's an unspoken acknowledgment between us all—this won't be easy. And there's no guarantee we'll make it through unscathed.

But there's also something else in the air—determination. We're ready. Whatever comes next, we'll face it together.

Chapter Fifty

Azrael

Heathens - Twenty One Pilots

The sound of boots hitting the asphalt fills my ears, the steady rhythm accompanying the weight of what's ahead. Layla's nerves reverberate through our bond thread, thick and raw. I glance over at her, watching as she stands tense, fitted into her fighting armor. Her shoulders are stiff, her eyes fixed on the ground as if searching for some kind of answer, some sign of reassurance she's not finding. She clenches her fists, flexing her fingers against the gloves she hasn't even secured yet. Drepane stands beside her, leaning against the wall, the ancient weapon who says nothing but seems to sense the gravity of the moment.

"Relax," I call, my voice cutting through the thick air, firm yet soft enough to carry past the tension coiling around us. "You'll fight better if you're not wound tighter than a bowstring."

Her head snaps up, and our eyes meet. There's fire in her gaze, but it's buried beneath layers of doubt, making her look smaller than she is. The intensity in her eyes flickers, even as she retorts, "You're one to talk." The words lose some of their bite, her voice softer than usual. "You're practically vibrating."

I want to argue, to brush off her words, but she's right. The buzz beneath my skin isn't just anticipation—it's the awareness of the threads connecting us all, the fragile weave of fate that could unravel in an instant. Every choice feels like it could be the wrong one, but there's no time for hesitation.

Vassago strides past me, boots heavy on the floor, adding to the rhythm of movement around us. His wings are folded tightly against his back, but even so, the energy radiating off him is undeniable. "We don't have time for hesitation," he growls, voice gravelly. "Memetim's ritual won't wait for us to gather our courage."

He's right, but his bluntness grates on me, as if he's reminding us of something we already know too well. Memetim's plan to sever my bond with Orcus is a calculated strike, one that would turn the tide of this war. If she succeeds, it won't just weaken me—she'll kill both Orcus and me.

I glance at Orcus, the scythe resting across my back, and I feel him, the hum of his presence steady and constant. He's more than a weapon to me; he's my companion, my tether to this life. "They won't get the chance," I mutter, more to myself than anyone else, my resolve firming despite the doubt gnawing at me.

Vassago snorts, his expression unreadable, but he doesn't argue. "Let's hope your confidence isn't misplaced."

Behind him, Ashton emerges from the shadows of the room, his expression grim and taut, the calm strategist in the midst of chaos. Even he seems weighed down by the coming battle. "Everyone's assembled," he announces, his tone clipped, ready for action. "It's time."

Outside, the air is thick with unspoken fears, with anticipation and hesitation brewing like a storm. Supernaturals of all kinds fill the space, their eyes reflecting a mixture of determination and uncertainty. At the front of the room stands Lydia, her presence commanding despite the weight she carries. She's the glue that's held us together so far, but even she's feeling the pressure now.

"We know the stakes," Lydia begins, her voice cutting through the murmurs of the room. "Memetim's ritual is her play to tip the balance in her favor.

If she succeeds,she won't just weaken Azrael—she'll leave us vulnerable to a counterstrike. We can't afford that."

All eyes shift to me, and the weight of their expectations presses down on my chest like a boulder. I can't tell them the full truth—how severing the bond will kill Orcus and me both. It's something I can't bear to say, and it's something they need to avoid knowing. I step forward, meeting their gazes one by one, my shoulders square and my expression firm. "They're banking on our failure," I say, my voice steady despite the storm inside me. "On fear, on doubt, on division. But they've underestimated what we're capable of. She doesn't understand what it means to fight for something greater than yourself."

Layla steps up beside me, her presence a quiet strength as she adds, "She doesn't understand loyalty. She doesn't understand *us*."

The room shifts, the tension easing just enough to make room for resolve. Lydia nods, satisfied with Layla's words, then gestures for Ashton to step forward with the final plan.

Ashton doesn't waste any time. "We'll split into two teams. Azrael, Layla, and Vassago wil linfiltrate the stronghold to stop the ritual."

Chapter Fifty-One

Azrael

Iron - Woodkid

The air is thick, every breath heavy with the weight of impending violence.

Boots crunch against the rocky terrain as we approach the Gates of Tartarus, the jagged peaks looming like the fangs of some ancient beast. Around me, the army marches in grim silence, their weapons clinking softly with each step. The thread of connection between Orcus and me hums with tension, its energy a pulse against my spine. I can feel the weight of Layla's presence through our bond, a steady beat of determination laced with lingering apprehension.

"We're getting close," Vassago mutters, his voice cutting through the oppressive quiet. His wings twitch, restless, and his hand tightens around the hilt of his blade. "The ritual site should be just ahead."

I glance back at Layla, who's keeping pace beside me. Her face is set, her lips pressed into a thin line as Drepane's faint glow reflects off her armor. Despite her earlier nerves, she's composed now- a warrior ready to face whatever lies ahead. She catches my gaze and gives a slight nod, her resolve bolstering my own.

"Let's move," I say, my voice sharper than intended. I'm trying to suppress the unease curling in my gut, the nagging whisper that something just isn't right. Orcus hums again as if sharing the same thought, but there's no time to dwell on it. We have a mission: Stop Memetim's ritual and protect the bond.

The three of us break off from the main force, slipping into the labyrinthine passages that wind toward the supposed ritual site. The further we go, the darker and more oppressive the air becomes, as if the realm itself is trying to swallow us whole. Shadows twist and writhe along the walls, and the only sound is the faint echo of our footsteps.

"Do you feel that?" Layla asks, her voice barely above a whisper. Her hand brushes the hilt of Drepane, the weapon vibrating faintly in response.

I nod, the sensation of wrongness settling deeper in my bones. "Stay close." I murmur, my gaze scanning the darkened corridor ahead. "We can't afford any mistakes."

"This will be interesting," Orcus rumbles softly from my back. His voice feels like a whisper, but it's loud in my mind. The bond we share is alive with energy, and the weight of his presence keeps the nerves at bay, for now.

"You're always so cheerful," I mutter, trying to push the anxiety from my chest.

Vassago, a few paces ahead, pauses and looks back over his shoulder, his wings folded tight against his back. He's always been a quiet presence, but there's something in the way he stands now—alert, prepared for anything—that makes my chest tighten.

"Memetim will pay for underestimating us," Vassago says, voice laced with an edge of anger. "She may have forces stacked against us, but we're not going to fall that easily."

His words resonate, but I can't ignore the dread creeping into my bones. I'm a figure of power, the Prince of Death, but even I know the fragile nature of our existence in this war.

We move through the darkened landscape, the shadows long and the wind cold, and as we near the stronghold, the atmosphere shifts. The air crackles with energy, the veil between realms thinning. The Gates of Tartarus are close. Too close.

We emerge into a cavernous chamber, the walls glowing with an eerie, pulsating light. At the center of the room, runes are etched into the ground, their lines seeping with what looks like molten gold. A figure stands at the heart of the markings, her presence radiating malevolence.

Memetim.

Her dark hair glints in the dim light, and her red eyes gleam with a predatory hunger that makes my blood run cold.

"You're late," She purrs, her voice like silk wrapped around steel. "The ritual is already complete."

Orcus flares in protest, his energy searing through my mind, "She's lying." I hiss, but even as the words leave my mouth, doubt gnaws at the edges of my thoughts. The markings on the ground seem... wrong. Too pristine, too deliberate.

This isn't a ritual site- it's a stage.

"Azrael," Vassago growls, his stance shifting. He's noticed it too. "It's a trap."

Memetim's laughter fills the chamber, sharp and grating. "You're quick, I'll give you that. But not quick enough." Her gaze shifts, locking onto Layla with an intensity that makes my chest lurch.

A sudden shriek splits the air, a horrific sound that rattles through the earth beneath our feet. Shadows seem to form around us, growing longer, twisting and shifting into shapes that aren't quite human.

"Get ready," Vassago growls, spinning around, his wings unfurling as he prepares for what's coming.

I draw Orcus, feeling the familiar weight of the scythe in my grip, the cold steel warming under my touch. The moment I lift it, the bond between us flares to life, as though Orcus himself is coming to life with every swing.

From the darkness, demons pour forward—twisted creatures with horns and claws, their eyes glowing with malice. The first wave crashes into us, their bodies moving in a blur of blackness and claws, each more grotesque than the last.

A demon lunges for me, but before it can reach me, Orcus hums in my grip, the blade cutting through the air in a deadly arc. The demon shrieks as it's cleaved in half, its dark blood spilling onto the ground.

"Is that the best you can do?" I sneer, but I'm not fooled. There's more coming.

"Just keep your eyes open, Azrael," Vassago warns, a sharpness in his voice that reminds me of the battle ahead. His wings snap outward, and he dives into the fray with the ferocity of a warrior born. His fists strike like hammers, sending demons flying with every punch. He's a blur of power and speed, his form a constant motion of controlled violence.

Layla moves with determination by my side, Drepane gleaming in her hand. The weapon pulses with energy, his sentience alive, and I can feel the power flowing between her and the weapon as she strikes down demon after demon. There's no hesitation in her movements, no fear in the way she cuts through the enemy.

"You're doing great," I murmur, trying to keep the tension at bay.

"Save it for the big guys," she replies, her voice tight with focus. Her hair whips around her face as she ducks under a demon's swipe and brings Drepane down in a swift motion, the weapon slicing through its torso in one clean blow.

"I'm not impressed," Orcus grumbles in my mind, his voice a deep rumble. "We've faced worse."

"We're just warming up," I mutter, watching as more demons flood the battlefield.

The enemy's numbers are overwhelming, but we're holding our own, keeping the line steady. But then the shadows shift again, and I hear a low, bone-chilling cackle that sends a shiver down my spine. The ground trembles as massive shades rise from the darkness, their forms ethereal but powerful, each one wielding dark magic that crackles in the air.

"Shades," Vassago warns, his voice clipped. "They're strong. Don't let them get too close."

Layla grips Drepane tighter, her stance ready. "Bring it on."

I don't have to say anything. We're already in motion, each of us moving with purpose, with the knowledge that we can't afford to hesitate. I swing Orcus at the first shade that charges toward me, the blade slicing through its incorporeal form, but it reforms with a sickening, guttural growl.

"That won't work," Orcus warns. "These things can't be killed with mere steel."

"I know," I snap, swinging again. "We need to disrupt their magic."

"Good luck with that," Drepane's voice cuts in, sounding amused. "It's all about the power of belief, Azrael. These creatures are born from fear and darkness. You want to break their hold, you have to crush their foundation."

The next wave of enemies is relentless. The shades' magic starts to take its toll, the energy in the air shifting as they summon more of their kind from the shadows. But then Layla steps forward, her eyes blazing with determination, and with one swift motion, she channels Drepane's energy into a devastating strike. The sickle hums with power, and a blast of dark light explodes outward, scattering the shades like leaves in the wind.

"That's my girl," I murmur, watching in awe.

But even as the battlefield shifts in our favor, I feel the pressure mounting. The enemy's forces are relentless. Demons keep pouring from the darkened landscape, claws and teeth bared, a never-ending tide of destruction.

"Hold the line!" Vassago roars, his voice filled with authority. His wings spread wide, pushing back the oncoming demons.

I feel the weight of Orcus at my back, and the bond between us flares once more, the urgency of our mission pulsing through me.

Another wave of enemies surges forward, but we're ready. With each strike, the world around us becomes a blur of motion—swords, sickles, magic, and blood. The enemy is fierce, but we are fiercer. We'll fight through this. We have no other choice.

"We're almost there," I say, my voice steady despite the chaos around us. "Just hold on."

Chapter Fifty-Two

Ashton

Warriors - 2WEI

The sound of clashing weapons and the roars of demons overwhelms my senses. My boots crunch against the charred earth as I push forward, my body moving on instinct. Every strike, every block, every swing of my sand blade feels like an eternity.

The angels are holding their ground in the skies, but it's a struggle. Demons and shades pour out of the gates like a tidal wave, their twisted forms grotesque, their eyes burning with hatred. This isn't just a battle for the Underworld—it's a battle for everything we've built. For every soul, every life. If we lose here, everything goes with it.

"Push forward! Don't give them an inch!" I shout, my voice rising above the chaos. My command isn't just a plea—it's a demand. I can't afford any hesitation. Not when the stakes are this high.

A demon lunges toward me, its claws sharp enough to tear through steel. I sidestep just in time, letting it crash into the ground beside me. Without missing a beat, I drive my sword through its back, the tip sizzling as it hits the creature's core, before I drown it in a wave of sand.

"Push them towards the gate!" I call to the other soldiers, my eyes scanning the battlefield. The ritual that Memetim is trying to complete is still in motion, a sickening hum echoing in the air as the energy from her forces seeps through the ground. If we don't stop it, everything we've fought for will be lost.

I move forward, cutting through the enemy ranks, my thoughts momentarily drifting to Sadie. I can't help it. I've left her behind, trusting that she'll be safe while we face the battle. The weight of that decision presses on me like a boulder, but I have to believe that she's okay. That she's holding down the fort.

Sadie?

The telepathic connection is faint but there. I can feel her—her worry, her fear—filling the space between us. I don't want to disturb her— to worry her, not while she's waiting at the house, but it's impossible not to reach out.

Ashton, please be careful.

Her voice is a soft whisper in my mind, but it cuts through the noise around me. I hear the fear in her words, the same fear that's twisting inside me for her safety. I want to tell her everything will be fine. That I'll be back soon. That we'll win. But there's no guarantee.

I'm fine, Sadie. We're holding our own here. Just keep yourself safe. Don't leave the house.

I hate being stuck here, not knowing if you're alright. You promised you'd come back.

Her words hit me harder than I expect. I want to promise her everything—promise her safety, promise her I'll make it back. But there's too much uncertainty here, too many unknowns.

I will come back; I swear to you.

Song said the same thing.

There's a moment of silence, and I can feel her presence still lingering in my mind, though I know she's gone. The weight of her concern weighs on me as I push forward.

Suddenly, I'm slammed into by a shadowy figure—a shade, its insidious claws slashing at my chest. My armor holds, but the force sends me stumbling back. I grit my teeth, growling as I slice through the shade's tendrils, blood and shadow dripping from my blade. I form a shield of sand to help cover me from future attacks.

"Focus!" I snap to the nearby warriors, who are struggling to keep the horde at bay. "We can't let them overwhelm us. Stay sharp!"

I spin, cutting through another shade's throat, and I don't stop. There's no time to waste. We can't afford to let up.

Up ahead, Lydia's form is unmistakable as she leads a charge of angels. She's a force of nature on the battlefield, but I know she's not invincible. None of us are.

The ground shakes as another wave of demons rushes toward us. The air is thick with the stench of sulfur, the screams of the fallen, and the clashing of steel. I hear the screech of an angel falling from the sky, and I turn just in time to see the being plummeting toward the ground, engulfed by the mass of enemies.

I raise my hand, summoning a burst of energy to knock back the creatures closest to me. The blast reverberates through the field, pushing back the attackers long enough for our front lines to regroup.

But this isn't over. Not yet.

I can feel the pulse of the dark magic deep in my bones, the tug of Memetim's power trying to pull us into her web. I have to push forward. I have to reach the gate.

Stay strong, Sadie. Stay with me. I'll be back.

But even as I send the thought out, the battle rages on, and I know the fight is far from over.

The clang of steel against steel rings in my ears, drowning out all else. I cut down another demon, but my movements are becoming slower, more deliberate. The weight of the battle is pressing down on me. There are too many of them, and no sign of any relief in sight. The air is thick with the stench of blood and ash, the smell of burning bodies mixing with the sickly-sweet scent of dark magic.

The pulse of Memetim's magic is undeniable, rippling through the ground, thrumming beneath my feet. It's stronger now, a powerful current of energy that tugs at my soul, urging me to act, to stop whatever it is she's doing. But I don't know where to go, who to strike, or how to put an end to it.

The demon horde is growing, their numbers swelling as more pour through the gates of Tartarus, just as we feared. Demons, shades, and ancient supernatural creatures with loyalty to Memetim—these are not the typical enemies we face. They're ruthless, their power far beyond what we've encountered before. I can feel their presence, the way they move through the air like shadows.

"Don't let them push through!" I shout to the others, but my voice is lost in the chaos. It feels like we're drowning, with no lifeline in sight.

Lydia is nearby, her glowing weapon cutting through the darkness as she deflects attack after attack. Her sword slices through the air, leaving trails of light in its wake as she fights. But even she's showing signs of wear. Her movements are slower, her face drawn with exhaustion.

I don't have time to check on her. I can feel my own energy waning. Another demon approaches, claws sharp and eyes blazing. I slam my sword into its chest, but it doesn't go down immediately. The demon screeches, grabbing at my arm with ungodly strength. I wrench free, stumbling back just as another two rush me. The sound of claws raking against the metal of my armor is enough to make my stomach churn, but I hold firm. I can't show weakness. Not now.

Focus.

I push the thought into my mind, forcing myself to focus. The demons are relentless. They never stop. One after another, they charge, and with each swing of my sword, I can feel my own stamina draining. I can feel the weight of the world pushing against me.

Behind me, I hear a loud crack, followed by a blast of energy. I turn to see one of the angels drop to the ground, his wings singed, his body writhing in pain. "No!" I shout, but I'm too far to reach him in time. He vanishes in a puff of smoke before I can do anything. Another life lost. Cerberus jumps out from the puff of smoke and latches on to a nearby demon, each head shaking opposite direction from the other, ripping it apart.

The demon forces are surging now, and I can feel the pulse of Memetim's magic tightening, coiling like a noose around us. I know that if we don't stop it, everything we're fighting for will be lost. But I don't know where to strike. I don't know how to stop her.

I'll find a way, I tell myself, but the words feel hollow. I can't stop the growing sense of dread that fills me with every passing moment. Every swing of my sword, every shout to my army, feels like it's getting us closer to the edge of the cliff.

I glance to the side, seeking out Lydia, but she's lost in the thick of the fight, her focus entirely on the demon in front of her. I can't keep track of everyone, and that uncertainty gnaws at me.

And then, I feel it—a surge of energy from within the battle. *What the hell?* It's sharp, jagged, and unmistakable. It's the same feeling I got when I first encountered Memetim's magic. Only stronger.

Sadie...

I try to reach out to her, but there's no time. The air is thick with magical energy, and it's blocking the connection I usually have with her. The uncertainty eats at me. I know she's safe at home. I know she's protected by the spells I've put in place. But still, the doubt lingers. I have to push it aside.

A massive blast of dark magic pulses out from the heart of the enemy ranks, and the ground beneath us shakes. I stagger, my knees buckling from the force, but I catch myself. My eyes widen as the energy swirls above the battlefield. It's getting closer, threatening to devour everything.

Memetim's magic? It's near. We have to stop it. I have to stop it.

With renewed determination, I push forward. I'm so focused on the ritual, the magic, that I don't see the demon coming until it's too late. It lunges at me, and I twist just in time to avoid its claws, but its teeth sink into my arm, and a sharp pain lances through me.

"Damn it," I hiss, tearing my arm free and spinning around to finish it off. The demon's body crumples to the ground, but the pain in my arm is enough to slow me down.

Memetim's magic intensifies, and I know in my gut we're close to the endgame. *We don't have much time.* My grip tightens on my sword as I charge again, slashing my way through the oncoming hordes. The screams of the fallen, the howls of the demons, it all blurs together in a symphony of destruction.

I feel the energy again, stronger now. But I can't find its source. My breath is coming in ragged gasps. The more I push, the harder it gets to keep going. But I can't stop. Not when everything is on the line.

And then, as the battle rages, the truth begins to sink in. The ritual Memetim was supposedly carrying out? *It's not real. The rumors... they were just that—rumors.*

Chapter Fifty-Three

Azrael

I Will Follow You Into the Dark - Deathcab for Cutie

"You brought her right to me. How thoughtful!" Memetim's voice is dripping with malice, each word a razor, cutting into the fragile thread of patience I have left. I feel Orcus hum in response, the scythe's blade vibrating with barely contained fury. I can almost hear the weapon whispering, urging me to let it loose, to end this once and for all.

"Over my dead body," I snarl, stepping in front of Layla, the protective instinct roaring to life inside me. Every fiber of my being is focused on her. She is the reason I fight, the reason I breathe. And if Memetim thinks she can take her from me, she's gravely mistaken.

Memetim's wicked smile widens, but there's no time for words now. Her blade is a blur of motion as she lunges, her speed surpassing anything I'd expected. The clash of steel rings out as Vassago intercepts her, their weapons colliding with a deafening crack that echoes through the chamber. The force of their impact sends a ripple through the air.

I'm already in motion, Orcus slicing through the air as I aim for Memetim's flank, but she's too fast. Too precise. Her strikes are like a storm—relentless, calculated, and devastating. I shift my weight, barely dodging a deadly blow aimed for my side.

Layla fights beside me, her movements graceful and lethal as she wields Drepane with deadly accuracy. But even she can't match Memetim's speed. Her strikes are expertly timed, the kind of calculated violence only someone like Memetim can muster. Blood splatters the stone floor, the sharp scent of iron filling the air, but it's not enough to throw off my focus.

I cannot—*will not*—let her fall.

But Memetim isn't just a warrior. She's an embodiment of destruction. She's learned to read us, to find our weaknesses, and exploit them. Her eyes flicker toward Layla, a look of satisfaction crossing her face as she moves with a predatory grace.

Layla's eyes widen for just a fraction of a second, and that's all Memetim needs.

With a feint that pulls me out of position, Memetim slips past my guard. Before I can react, her blade finds its mark.

The sound of steel sinking into flesh is sickening—a brutal, wet thud that reverberates through my chest. I freeze, unable to process it for an agonizing moment. Then the cry—her cry—pierces through the noise of battle, sharp and raw, a sound that will haunt me for the rest of my days.

My chest tightens. My world tilts.

Layla collapses, her body crumpling to the ground like a broken doll. The blood—*her blood*—pools beneath her, dark and unforgiving. Drepane slips from her grasp, his blade clattering to the floor with a hollow sound.

"No!" The word rips from my throat, primal, guttural. My limbs feel frozen in place, but instinct takes over. I launch myself toward her, every step driven by the desperate need to reach her, to *save her*.

But Memetim is faster, her wicked smile never fading as she steps in front of me, blocking my path.

"She was the weakest link," she sneers, circling like a predator savoring its kill. "It was only a matter of time."

The words are like daggers, each one twisting deeper. My chest tightens, and I can feel it—the bond between Layla and me is a faint whisper where it was once a roar, full of life and emotions. Now, there's nothing but *emptiness*.

No. No. No.

The emptiness presses in, suffocating me. The bond that had once been a steady pulse in my chest is gone, leaving behind only a hollow ache. My heart beats painfully in my chest, but it's not enough to quell the despair that threatens to consume me.

"Layla!" I roar; my voice raw, desperate. I try to push past Memetim, but she's unyielding, her blade flashing as it drives me back.

I can't feel her. She doesn't stir. Her body lies motionless, her face pale as the moon. The blood pools wider, soaking into the stone floor and creeping toward Drepane's edge.

I fight Memetim with everything I have, each swing of Orcus driven by fury, by the need to *reach her*. But I'm too late.

Before I can even get close, the air around Layla shifts. It's subtle at first, a ripple of darkness that folds inward. Her body—still and bloodied—begins to flicker, fading as though she's being pulled from this realm.

A low hum fills the air, vibrating through the ground, through my very bones.

"No!" I scream, throwing myself toward her, but my hands meet only the cold, empty ground. My fingers scrape against stone, desperately searching for something—*anything*—to pull her back.

But it's gone.

Her face is the last thing I see. Pale, serene—almost like she's slipping into a dream. And then, just as quickly, she vanishes into the void.

The chamber is silent. The battle rages on around me, but in this moment, the world has stopped. I stand there, my chest heaving, my heart shattering. I claw at the ground where she once lay, the blood-stained stone the only proof that she was ever here.

The bond is there but severed. And with it, a part of me no longer exists.

The pain is unbearable.

Orcus hums softly, a faint lament, but it does nothing to ease the emptiness that gnaws at my soul.

"Azrael."

Vassago's voice cuts through the fog of despair, sharp and clear. He's there, standing at myside, his expression grim. "Memetim and her army has disappeared."

I snap my head toward him, fury igniting in my chest. "I need to find Layla… and I *will* bring her back home."

He looks around, his gaze stopping on the bloodstained stone. "She's dead, Azrael! She's in the Empty." Vassago's voice drops lower, his eyes narrowing with concern. "No one has ever returned from it. We need to regroup."

I rise to my feet, my body trembling with exhaustion and rage. The chamber feels colder now, emptier—as if it knows what has been taken from me. My limbs are heavy, but I don't care.

"I'm not leaving her there," I growl, my voice low and dangerous. "I'll tear it apart, piece by piece, if I have to. I will bring her back."

The thought of the Empty chills me to my core, but the bond between Layla and me is still there, faint but unbroken. She's out there, waiting for me to find her. And I won't stop until I do.

Somewhere in the shadows, Memetim's laughter echoes—soft and cruel. A haunting promise of what's to come. But as I stare into the abyss where Layla vanished, I know one thing:

This war is far from over.

About the author

Peggy is a passionate author who thrives on crafting stories that delve into romance and thrillers, weaving tales that keep readers hooked until the very last page. Born on August 8, 1995, Peggy finds inspiration in life's twists and turns, as well as the works of literary icons like Penelope Douglas and Brynne Weaver. As a mother to four biological children and a loving mentor to many "adopted" kids, Peggy believes in the power of family and connection, themes that often resonate through her stories. When not writing, she enjoys exploring new creative avenues and diving into the thrill of a good book.

Pegngremlin.com

Made in the USA
Columbia, SC
29 April 2025